Ruthless

Ruby's Palace

Raw Justice

***

Cruel Secrets

Wicked Lies

Ugly Truth

Raising a Gangster

***

The Hunted

The Rules

The Choice

***

Deceit

Voice of Reason

DEDICATION

To my son-in-law

Royston Reeves

I am proud of you.

ACKNOWLEDGEMENTS

I would like to thank my editor, Robert Wood, who I am sure rolls his eyes every time he sees my habitual mistakes, but he painstakingly corrects them anyway. Thank you for great teamwork, for your patience, your perseverance and loyalty. And thank you for the extremely long hours of hard work you dedicate to making my books publishable. — Epworthediting.com —

I would like to acknowledge Deryl Easton's help with the research for this story; it has been invaluable. Also, for all her endless support and encouraging advice. *Thank you, my friend.*

Thank you, NotRights Book Club because you are all amazing. And to all the lovely readers, who have supported me over the years and spurred me on to write.

Outcast

By Kerry Barnes

Chapter One

Mitchell Swan at twenty-five years old was facing another few years behind bars. As he lay on the hard narrow bed in his cell, he felt his hands clammy with anticipation. Bernie Blackstone had been transferred to HMP Kingston in Portsmouth from Maidstone and was wanting a word with him. Mitchell knew that meant more than a gentlemanly conversation. There would be violence thrown into the mix. That was how it worked in the nick. Everyone had bravado, and a point to prove, but Mitchell just wanted to get on and serve his time. He could have asked to be moved or to make a report to the governor regarding the threats from Bernie, but he didn't bother. One day it would have to be dealt with, and if it wasn't today, it would be next week or next month. So it was best to face Bernie head-on and tell him his side of the story.

As he waited, he looked at the photos that he'd pinned to the wall. The large one was of his three boys aged one, two, and three. Standing behind them was their mother,

Gina, looking as though she was the main point of the photo, the boys merely an accessory.

His eyes switched towards the next photo, and his gaze remained there, staring at the only girl he had really loved – and who he would probably only ever love. The photo was taken in front of the Kingdom Hall. They were young in the picture, approximately fifteen, except for the guy standing to the right. He was much older. Mitchell rubbed his hip as a dark memory whipped through his mind. Staring at the photo, he wished he could have cut him out of it, but it would have meant that part of her would have been removed too. He smiled at her as if she were in the room. Her bright-blue eyes, the colour of forget-me-nots, were so alive and full of hope. Wherever she was, he hoped that she was safe and happy and that she forgave him.

The rustle outside the cell snapped him out of his thoughts and had him on his feet, with fists clenched into tight, white-knuckled balls. The door opened, and there filling up the whole door frame was Bernie. He was older than him, by twenty-three years. He had a name and a reputation, but he was also a member of Donald Brennan's, his father-in-law's, firm. And Bernie didn't come alone. He'd brought his sidekick, Malcolm, with him.

'There you are! You fucking sly little weasel! I bet ya didn't expect to see me, did ya, you fucking greedy wanker?'

Mitchell held his gaze but chose not to answer.

'Where's the money, Mitch?'

Mitchell just glared, not moving a muscle.

'Oh, it's like that, is it? Well, we'll soon see about that. Malcolm, duff this prick up. I want him talking.'

Mitchell watched as Bernie stepped aside.

In his place stood Malcolm, a stocky man, with popping biceps and pecs. His head was shiny bald, and it was hard to work out where his neck started and ended. He stepped inside and stood there like an immovable object. Without a single word of warning, he threw a left-handed punch. He was massively confident that Mitchell would be just like any other young lad inside. He'd automatically cover his face and double over to protect himself, affording Malcolm a clear shot of the lad's ribs, and Mitchell would go down. However, he was taken aback when Mitchell shifted aside with so much speed that he didn't see him move. He threw a right hook, but it only skimmed Mitchell. But what completely stunned him was the savage return blow. Mitchell was no weasel or wimp; he was clearly used to boxing. It unnerved Malcolm because he had sized up the kid and assumed that after one punch he would fall down like a sack of shit. Being a lump himself, he had won more fights than he'd lost. But he'd seriously underestimated the speed of Mitchell's reaction.

Mitchell glanced back at the man in the photo, the man he hated more than anyone, and something inside him snapped. He threw a fast punch that hit Malcolm so hard on the chin that it instantly floored him. As soon as Malcolm slid awkwardly between the two beds, Mitchell kicked the door shut. He jumped on top of the man, gripping his slippery bald head, and rammed it onto the floor. The crunch of the man's skull echoed as it hit the concrete. But Mitchell was still raging. The pent-up frustration from so many wrongdoings in his life had fuelled an anger that was now being aimed at the man on the floor. And the big bully, who attacked him for no reason whatsoever, was getting it. Again and again, Mitchell lifted the man's head by his ears and smashed it on the floor. A spray of blood shot from Malcolm's nose and covered his own face. Only then did Mitchell stop and look at the damage he'd caused. Malcolm's ear was ripped away from his head, and blood continued to pour from his nose.

Bernie was still outside. He hadn't been quick enough to keep the door open. Hearing the violent thuds, he panicked and began smashing and kicking the door for Mitchell to open up.

Mitchell was shaking, his knuckles throbbed, and his body was now covered in sweat. Taking deep breaths, he climbed off the lifeless man and paused to gain his sanity before he opened the door. Red-eyed, he glared at Bernie. 'Get your bulldog outta my cell.'

Bernie glanced down at the mess, and his eyes nearly popped out of his head. 'You fucking cunt!' he yelled, before attempting to throw a punch himself.

But Mitchell stepped back and dared Bernie with a sharp firm nod.

'Do it, Bernie, and believe me, you will end up worse than him, 'cos I won't stop. I will finish you off. Now, you either listen to my side of the story or you fuck off and stay away.'

Bernie was shocked. He'd only known Mitchell to be a reticent man, but seeing the result of Malcolm being battered, and so viciously, proved to be a useful lesson for him: never judge a book by its cover. He put his hands by his side and glanced back at Malcolm.

'Right, Mitch, we'll talk, and then you can tell me where the fucking money is.'

Mitchell shook his head. 'Nah, *I* will talk, and *you* will listen.'

Malcolm stirred and tried to get to his feet, but he was punch-drunk.

'All right, help me get him up and out of 'ere, then.'

Mitchell sighed. 'Bollocks. You unleashed your guard dog, now you can get him out of my cell. And tell him I want him back here later to mop the blood off me floor.'

Bernie wasn't listening. He wanted to help his long-term pal out of the cell and onto the landing, where the screws would take him to the hospital wing. Holding Malcolm as upright as he could, he supported him along the landing to the foot of the stairs. The screws were at the other end and not taking much notice until Bernie shouted for one of them to see to his mate, who he said had taken a tumble down the stairs, before he marched back to Mitchell's cell.

'So 'cos you brutalised me pal, you now think you're some kinda hard bastard, do ya?'

Mitchell shook his head. 'In case, Bernie, you haven't grasped the type of man I am, I will tell you. I was never a criminal, a villain, or a bank robber. I only ever threw punches in the ring, and I never fought on the street. So I couldn't give a monkey's uncle who's hard, or who's a name, a face, or a fucking cocksucking Joey. I'm just a bloke who ended up in 'ere because your mate, my father-in-law, grassed me up.'

Bernie was still standing when Mitchell sat on the bed.

There was silence as Bernie processed exactly what Mitchell was saying. He raised his eyebrow and sat down opposite. 'Okay, Mitch, man to man, no fucking nonsense, what the fuck do you mean when you said he grassed you up?'

'You tell me, Bernie, unless it was you.' He sighed. 'I dunno. Something tells me it wouldn't have been you, though.'

Bernie's eyes widened. 'Me a grass?' he replied, totally offended. 'Never!'

'Well, Bernie, between you, Donald, and Trevor, *one* of you grassed me up, 'cos why the hell would the Old Bill pull me in on a fucking armed robbery?'

Bernie stared for a while, and then curled his lip. 'Mitch, you drove the fucking van when the filth gave chase. When the cops blocked Trevor and me in the back, you did a runner, right?'

Mitchell was nodding in agreement with the facts.

'Well, you fucking prick, you may have got away, but they had your prints on the van. So none of us grassed. For fuck's sake, kid, you are a proper idiot, ain't ya?'

'Am I, Bernie?'

Bernie's eyes clouded over in confusion. It was the way Mitchell had said, 'Am I' that got him thinking but he still couldn't see what Mitchell was getting at.

'So if they lifted my prints from the van, how would they know it was me?'

Bernie stared, still lost.

'Bernie, I was never up for going on the job with you and Trevor. Never! When you and Trevor were in the back of the van, Donald held a gun to my head, *literally* held it to my head, and told me to drive to the job. He couldn't drive 'cos he was drunk, and so I had no fucking choice. He shoved the keys in my hand and opened the van door and pushed me inside. He handed me the boiler suit, and balaclava, and—'

Bernie held his hand up. 'Yeah, yeah, all right. So Donald forced you into it. But why would he grass on you? The filth would have no reason to think he was involved, so I don't believe they pulled him in. I was questioned for hours, and his name never came up.'

'Of course, they pulled him in, Bernie. Donald had his prints all over the fucking van.'

A deep frown etched across Bernie's forehead as confusion weaved its way through his brain.

'But, Bernie, it's bloody odd how *he* ain't serving time. And I'll tell you why. It's 'cos he grassed on me.'

'Nah, Mitch, you've lost me now. The filth had your prints, so they knew you were there anyway.'

Mitchell jumped up in frustration. 'You really don't get it, do ya? I had never been *inside* a police station before the robbery, so, therefore, I had no previous! So, Bernie, they never had my fucking prints in the first place to compare them to.'

Bernie's face dropped and his shoulders slumped partly from shock and partly because in a sense he had been duped by Donald Brennan as well. 'Shit!' he said, as he ran his fingers through his cropped hair.

'Fucking hell, Mitch, I thought you had a past. I never knew you were as clean as a whistle.'

Mitchell could see from the sadness that melted Bernie's face that the fight between them was over.

'The problem is, Mitch, you can't prove it was Donald though, can ya?'

Mitchell waved his hands. 'I don't give a fuck about that now. I'm serving eight years. I just wanna do me time, keep me nut down, and get on with it. I have plans for me future, so leave me alone.'

Bernie got up from the bed, feeling less of a man than when he arrived in the cell. He looked Mitchell over and instantly felt a tremendous amount of respect for him.

'And, Bernie, about that money—'

'Whatever you managed to get away with, Mitch, I think it is fair to say, now, it's rightly yours.'

Mitchell nodded. They understood each other, and there was no more to say on the matter.

***

Bernie returned to his own cell and felt guilty; it was a feeling that he'd never felt in his life. He'd been a doorman for the top clubs and had never thought anything of bouncing rowdy customers out on their ear. Robbing places and holding men at gunpoint never fazed him, and he certainly never lost any sleep over it. But Mitchell Swan had got to him. Not having kids of his own, he thought that if he'd been Mitchell's father, he would have protected the boy, but, by all accounts, Mitchell only had a mum. He should have stepped in years ago when Donald had first bullied the lad.

***

He thought back to when he had been the one who'd delivered Donald's message to Nobby at the gym for Mitchell.

He recalled the exact words. *If Mitchell Swan wants to keep his bollocks intact, then he'd better see me at the Red Lion on Saturday afternoon.* At the time, he assumed that this kid had taken liberties, by stealing something that belonged to

Donald or that Mitchell had bad-mouthed him in some way or other.

When Saturday arrived, they were all in the Red Lion having a drink. Donald, as always, had the table at the back reserved for him and his pals including Maxi Vent, Padlock Pete, Shay the Brick, and a few other numpties. The air was thick with smoke that lingered three feet from the ceiling, the floor was sticky, and the beer was flat. Cleo, the landlady, who was still trying to strap her tits inside her corset-style top, had just come down from the flat upstairs, followed by Donald. He remembered Donald smacking her arse as he moved past her and made his way to the table. He had his Crombie on over his suit, and his thick gold keeper ring on his little finger.

The pub was filled with pissheads and brown-nosers, all practically kissing Donald's feet. He worked for Donald, so he knew him well, but he was by no means one of Donald's gofers. They'd had a couple of post office robberies under their belts, and he knew Donald could have a ruck, back in his younger day. But he was getting older, and so he carried a gun or a knife and loved to frighten the living shit out of people. They found him reckless and either steered well clear or sucked up to him, buying him drinks.

He remembered the pub suddenly became quiet when Mitchell Swan walked in. He was tall, slim, and solid looking. He wore jeans and a black T-shirt, and his hair was fairly long. Bernie noticed the lad's expression; he was unfazed but not cocky. Mitchell scanned the room and headed for the table at the back where Donald was curling his finger for him to approach him.

Donald motioned to the hangers-on, and they got up and left. But Bernie remembered Donald calling him and Maxi over. It was evident that Donald wanted Mitchell to see the size of them and to take note that if Mitchell got lairy, then he would get a right good hiding.

Bernie stood by the table while Maxi stood on the other side.

Mitchell appraised them both and stared unflinchingly at Donald. 'You wanted to see me?'

Donald nodded and blew smoke in Mitchell's face. 'So, you've been seeing my daughter?'

Mitchell looked from Bernie to Maxi and then back to Donald. 'Who is your daughter?'

Donald leaped from his chair. 'Don't get fucking arrogant with me or I will do you serious bodily harm. You know full well who my daughter is.'

Mitchell shook his head. 'Sorry, but I don't know who she is. In fact, I don't know who you are, but you left a message, so here I am.'

Donald's eyes twitched, and his jaw clenched tighter. 'Get out the back. Me and you need to talk.'

Bernie opened the door that led from the main saloon bar to the pub garden. No one went out there because it was more like a scene from a David Attenborough jungle documentary.

He recalled Mitchell only looking anxious when he spotted the knife in Donald's hand.

'Remember me daughter now, do ya, ya cocky cunt?' growled Donald.

Tight-faced and white, Mitchell shook his head. 'No, I don't know who your daughter is.'

Donald lurched forward, holding the knife at Mitchell's throat. 'Gina. Her name's Gina.'

'Yeah, all right, yeah, I sort of know her,' Mitchell replied, in a flat and subdued tone.

Raging, Donald yelled, 'What do you mean, "sort of"? You know her more than just fucking *sort of*, 'cos she is now up the fucking duff with *your* baby. So now what are you gonna do?'

Donald dug the knife deep enough to nick Mitchell's neck. The blood trickled down to his collarbone but Mitchell didn't even flinch.

As Donald stepped back, and stood with his feet in line with his shoulders, he gestured with the knife, almost daring Mitchell to react.

Mitchell looked at the men surrounding him. 'How do I know it's mine?' he asked genuinely.

'You *what*! You dare ask a thing like that. My girl ain't no tart. She's a fucking good kid that you, boy, have knocked up. And I left her just a few hours ago breaking her little heart 'cos she thinks that you don't wanna know. She told me that she left a note at your muvver's house for you to get in touch.'

Mitchell frowned. 'Yeah, but she is always leaving notes. She keeps pestering me. We were together once, so she said. But I was drunk. She—'

'Shut it! Don't you give me that old chestnut,' screamed Donald, 'before you say something you will seriously regret. Let's get it straight. My girl has only ever been with you, and she doesn't lie to me. So you' — he pointed the knife at Mitchell — 'you need to do the right and honourable thing. Or do you wanna abandon your baby, leave my girl a single muvver? Well, boy, do ya?'

Mitchell was stunned, and it showed by the look on his face. His mouth opened, but nothing came out.

'Right now, I don't like to see my princess sobbing her heart out. So I suggest you man up, save up, and get a ring to stick on my girl's finger. She says she's in love with ya.' He looked Mitchell up and down. 'Gawd knows why. But, anyway, just so you know, I don't take too kindly to anyone hurting my girl. Do you hear me?' He poked a finger in Mitchell's face. 'You dipped ya wick, now take responsibility.'

Bernie watched as Donald cruelly ran the blade along Mitchell's chin, cutting him deep enough to leave a scar but not enough to kill him. 'Don't ever fuck with my family, Mitchell, or, see, your sweet ol' muvver? Well, let's just say you won't want to see her hurt, just like I don't wanna see my girl hurt.'

Donald walked away, leaving Mitchell clutching his chin and staring in disbelief.

Bernie wondered at the time if Donald's daughter did in fact know who the father was because she had a reputation. But no one would dare tell Donald about that, of course, for fear of losing a finger or a tongue.

When he returned to the bar and watched from the window, he noticed Mitchell walking away with a slight limp.

***

Now in his cell, Bernie realised that he had been mildly fascinated by Mitchell Swan all those years ago. Donald had managed to bully Mitchell easily back then because the younger man had yet to find his feet in life. But now? God help Donald Brennan when Mitchell was released from prison. There would be ructions.

Chapter Two

1983

Gina Swan added another tray of vol-au-vents to the glass-topped table that had been pushed against the wall to make room for the guests. Pleased with her table display, she greedily eyed the chicken drumsticks, the quiche, and the Scotch eggs, before she helped herself to the biggest prawn-filled puff pastry. With her mouth wide open, she shoved the lot in and wiped the Thousand Island dressing from her red lips, not realising she had smudged the lipstick right across her cheeks.

'Gina!' said Donald, in a disapproving tone. 'Do you have to, love?'

She spun around and caught the disgusted look on her father's face.

'Aw, leave off, Dad. For crying out loud, stop digging me out. If I want a vol-au-vent or ten, I will 'ave 'em.'

Sitting by the fireplace, dressed in a camel suit and a white shirt, with the necktie almost strangling him, Donald's appearance was, as always, top drawer. With a cigarette in one hand and an empty beer bottle in the other, he looked his daughter up and down. 'Don't it bother you that you're piling on the pounds, gal?'

Padlock Pete, a man in his mid-fifties, with a face full of pitted acne scars, shuffled uncomfortably and covered his snigger with a cough.

Gina shot him a look. 'And you can shut ya face, an' all.'

Donald stood up, and for a man of his age, he did it with sleek grace. 'Oi, Gina, watch ya mouth, gal. We're all 'ere to welcome your fella home, for your fucking sake, not ours.'

'He ain't me fella, Dad, he's me husband.'

Donald raised his brow and looked at the men in the room, who were all paying attention. 'Yep, he's your husband. I fucking know that.'

'And what's that supposed to mean?'

'Nothing. I'm getting a drink,' he spat, as he left the small dining room and stepped down into the kitchen. Aggressively, he ripped open the fridge door and mumbled under his breath, 'A big mistake, an' all.'

Gina ignored her father's sarcastic tone and turned her attention to fussing over the food. 'Anyway, I ain't fat. I'm fashionably curvy. No man wants a bag of bones, do they?'

Donald stared for a second at his daughter's chunky frame. Her long bleached hair was up and tied in such a way that she looked like she had a palm tree growing out of her head. Her bright-pink boiler suit, which was pulled in at the middle by an overwide belt, showed every lump and bump her arse had to offer. So much had changed. She used to be a pretty little thing, slim and naturally blonde-haired, with a sweet smile. But now she wore bright-red lipstick and applied orange foundation that covered her face and left a tide mark around her neck. His eyes followed her body down to her feet wedged in open back shoes, which showed her disgusting cracked heels.

Eight years ago, he felt proud when she joined him for a drink, and he often showed her off. Back then, he didn't mind treating her to a new rig-out or a fancy handbag and matching shoes. As much as he doted on her, he had to admit to himself that there was many a time that he wished she wouldn't swan into his local dressed like she thought she was still a size eight. The skintight dresses did her no favours whatsoever. And as for her boys, they were cheeky, if not rude. He loved them dearly and laughed off their behaviour, pretending that they were all a chip off the old block. However, there was many a time when inside he cringed. Jordan was the worst at humiliation, as if he got a kick out of acting so unsociably. Yet he was sick of telling Gina to reel her kids in; it did no good. She didn't have the time or the patience to discipline them, and as for himself, he neither had the energy nor the persistence to keep nagging her. He hoped that now their father was out of prison, he would pull the little buggers into line. Because, sure enough, Mitchell, the man of few words, would undoubtedly have a few more to say when he saw what cheeky little sods he had on his hands – if, of course, he cared enough.

His stomach churned; Mitchell would walk through that door at any moment. There could be grudges held, and Donald wouldn't wager which way it was going to go. He looked at the men and said, 'Leave us alone, lads. I need a word before Mitch arrives.'

The men all dressed in suits shuffled out of the dining room, past the living room, and assembled in the front garden as if they were waiting for a hearse to arrive.

Gina sat in the chair opposite to where her father had sat. 'What the fuck is the matter with you?'

Donald sat down again and swigged his beer. 'Gina, what's Mitch actually said? Ya know, about me?'

Gina rolled her eyes. 'Oh, not this again. I told ya, Dad, he never mentions your name.'

Donald stared for a moment. 'So you mean to tell me that when you went to visit him every other week, he said fuck all about me? And what about the boys? Did he ever say anything about them?'

Gina gave her father a look of spite. 'What do you mean?'

'Oh, come on, Gina, those kids in the sitting room look like an advert for the United Colors of Benetton.' He didn't flinch but continued to glare with his jaw tight.

Gina knew she shouldn't push him too far – not that he would hurt her. After all, she was his princess, and everyone knew it. However, her father was not the type of man to be rude to, even if you were family.

'Look, Dad, unlike you, my Mitch trusts me.'

Donald raised his eyebrow to an arched peak.

'I don't appreciate you accusing me of being unfaithful. If you must know, my boys could take after the Swan side of the family. And Mitch never knew who his ol' man was. He could have been Italian, Spanish, or Greek.'

'Or Jamaican,' said Donald, shaking his head.

'Little Jordan does not look fucking black at all! He may be darker than the others, but, as I said, he could quite easily 'ave taken after Mitch's farver, whoever the hell he was. And, anyway, my Mitch has never questioned it, so why the hell should you?'

Donald sighed and swirled his beer around in the bottle. He wanted to say, 'Of course he never questioned it because Mitch couldn't give two fucks about you, Gina.' But he kept his mouth shut and also kept the initial meeting he'd had with Mitchell Swan a secret, although, really, he should never have got involved in his daughter's business. It was only because she seemed at the time so broken-hearted; for when Mitchell had got her up the duff, he had wanted to walk away.

Before they could engage in any more conversation, they heard cheering at the front door.

Gina jumped up from her chair and clapped her hands together. 'That'll be my Mitch.'

Donald felt uneasy and hoped his men would soon return to the dining room, in case Mitchell used his homecoming as the day he would let rip.

As soon as Mitchell appeared in the doorway, Donald clumsily stepped forward with an outreached hand. His Adam's apple bobbed up and down, and he hoped that Mitchell wouldn't notice. The pause was too long, so Donald swiftly pulled his arm to the side and said, 'Right, well, welcome home, Mitch. Gina has laid out a good spread. I've brought some beers. No doubt, you'll be gagging to down a few.'

Clinging to Mitchell like a limpet, Gina flushed with excitement. 'Yeah, look, I cooked all your favourites, Mitch . . . Er, Dad, get me husband a beer.'

Donald didn't need to be asked twice; he hurried into the kitchen to take relief from the cold, intense eyes of his son-in-law.

Donald pulled a can from the fridge and watched as Padlock Pete, Shay the Brick, and a few other men in the firm greeted Mitchell, with handshakes and enthusiastic pats on the back. Yet something was brewing in Mitchell. Donald could almost taste the animosity in the air.

Mitchell, stone-faced, nodded and politely respected the handshakes, but his manner was cold, and, in fact, he didn't even speak.

Intrigued but wary, Donald glanced at Mitchell's frame and noted that although the man was tall and slim, underneath his jacket and that trademark T-shirt were ripped muscles. *So, had he kept the training up while serving his time?* he wondered. Privately, he thought he would have just sulked and let himself go – maybe even taken up drugs to pass the time away.

Donald pushed his shoulders back and returned to place a cold can in Mitchell's hand, hoping for at least a thank you, but, to his surprise, Mitchell held the can, looked it over, and said, 'I don't drink.'

'Aw, come on, Mitch. Have a pint with ya father-in-law, to welcome you home,' said Pete.

The room became quiet, and the tension grew, as Mitchell just shook his head.

Gina giggled. 'If me husband says he don't drink anymore then he don't drink anymore. Dad, fetch Mitch a lemonade.'

Donald, inwardly seething, nodded politely. 'Er . . . yeah, well, he's probably right. I should knock the booze on the head meself. Tone up me Derby, maybe.' However, inside he suspected that Mitchell was digging him out for being a drinker himself; after all, it was indirectly the reason that his son-in-law ended up in prison.

The men who were still squashed by the door, suddenly parted as three little boys bustled their way through. They stopped and looked up at their father.

'Say hello to ya dad then, boys,' said Gina, in her overly upbeat voice.

Jordan, the eldest at ten years old with large round dark-brown eyes, tilted his head and curled his lip. 'All right?' he said, in such a cocky voice for a young child.

Mitchell stared at all three, and slowly, he forced a smile, until his eyes met George, the middle boy with fairer hair, a slim nose, and blue eyes. Only then did his face light up.

Sonny, the youngest, was only eight and looked nothing more than curious as he peered up at the tall stranger, and like his brother Jordan, he too nastily curled his lip.

Without any hugs or any form of affection, Mitchell turned to Gina. 'Where is my mother?'

Gina glanced at her father. 'Well, I just thought. I mean . . .'

Donald stepped in, realising his daughter had no excuse for not inviting Diane over. 'I thought I would treat you to a slap-up meal. Just you and your dear ol' mum. She wouldn't want to be here with everyone. I'm sure she'd like you all to herself.' He grinned and his face flushed, now very pleased with himself.

Mitchell slammed the beer can, which had been thrust into his hand, down on the table. 'Oh, you did, did ya, Donald? Well, excuse me.' He waved his hands, gesturing for the guests to move out of the way.

'Mitch!' called Gina, as she ran after him and tried to pull him back into the room.

'Get off me,' he hissed, through gritted teeth, as he yanked his jacket clean out of her grasp.

Gina stopped dead in her tracks. As soon as Mitchell was through the front door, she spun on her heels and stormed back into the dining room, with a face like a wet weekend. 'I spent hours getting this place ready for his homecoming, an' all he wants is to see old drippy drawers Diane.' She glared at the three boys all helping themselves to the food and ran her hands across the back of their heads. 'And you three could have been more polite instead of standing there like the little gormless bastards you are. Now leave the fucking food and get up to your rooms.'

'Oi, Gina, leave off, gal. What did you fucking expect? The lads don't know him. Jordan was two when Mitch went away, George was a year old, and you were pregnant with Sonny. It's his fault they didn't go running into his arms. He didn't want them on prison visits, so don't you be so bloody hard on 'em.'

Gina began to blubber like a drama queen. 'Oh, look at all this.' She gestured to the table. 'And it was supposed to be such a good day, and it's ruined. Fucking ruined!' she screamed, stamping her foot.

'Aw, come on, love. Let's have none of that. He'll be back as soon as he's seen his muvver,' replied Donald, softening his tone, as he tried to put his arms around her.

Gina shot a spiteful look at the guests. 'Well, there's no need for you lot to hang around still.'

''Ere, hold on, gal. I've brought a shedload of fucking booze.'

Gina pushed her father away. 'Well, take it! And you can all fuck off back to your house, then, Dad, and have your own party.'

With her back to the door, Gina didn't see her mother Sylvia proudly holding a two-tier yellow butter icing cake, until she spun around to storm out of the room. It was too late: her anger-filled impatience stopped her brain from engaging, and her quick movements resulted in the cake flying backwards, smashing Sylvia in the face and coating her new outfit in heavily coloured icing.

Annoyed and embarrassed, Gina pushed her mother aside and stomped up the stairs, in floods of tears.

Donald was mortified; this homecoming for Mitchell was turning out to be a circus, and even worse, it was all happening in front of his pals.

'If she weren't my daughter, I would swing for her, the bloody cow,' spat Sylvia, as she wrestled with placing the remains of the cake on the table. Snatching a paper serviette, she tried to clean the icing from her face, while Donald clumsily attempted to help.

'Aw, get off, Donald. You're making it flaming well worse. And this cost a pretty penny, I can tell you that much,' she tutted, as she pulled the chiffon blouse away from her chest, while trying to see how much of the icing had stuck to her. Finally, she cleaned most of it off and then wiped her neck. 'So will you tell me what's going on?' she asked, as she watched everyone leaving with beer cans in their hands and under their arms.

'Party's over, Sylv. Mitch wants to see his muvver. Obviously, we aren't good enough for the prick.'

Sylvia had been married to Donald for thirty years and could only list a handful of times she had enjoyed being his wife. 'So where *is* Diane?' she asked, narrowing her eyes.

'Gina didn't invite her, and before you start, woman, I've already had it up to here with Gina for one day.'

Sylvia knew she couldn't push him too far, as he was likely to give her a backhander. Years of slaps and shoves had changed Sylvia. She wasn't weak and submissive; she just carefully picked her arguments with her husband and knew when to back off. She would have left him years ago, but she was too afraid of the consequences. Donald had a name for being a man who never made false promises. If he said, 'I will shoot you', then he would.

Sylvia had learned her lesson the day Donald insisted she stopped hanging around with her best friend, Lindsey. She ignored his wishes and was sure, since he was her husband, he wouldn't go that mad. She was right in the sense that he never bashed her up at the time, but he burned every one of her clothes, crushed all her make-up, and snapped the heels off all her shoes.

The only person who could have a go back at him was his daughter, the spoiled, shameless cow.

'Right then, I'll be off meself, Donald. I take it, you will be finishing the beers?'

'Hold up, Sylv. I think Gina will need help to clear this lot away. Why don't you stay and give her a hand?' He looked down at the cake on the carpet. 'The poor gal has worked her fingers to the bone preparing this lot.'

Sylvia stared at the food and shook her head. 'Don, see all those plates except the vol-au-vents? Well, I baked them, and cut the cheese and pineapple sticks, and made the cake, and—'

'Yeah, I get your point. And what?' he hissed, now ready for a fight.

'I don't want to get into a row with Gina. She's already smashed the cake in me face.'

'Reel your neck in, Sylv. That was an accident.'

'Whatever, Donald. The kiddies can help themselves, and any guests lingering can do the same. No point in me packing it all away.' She didn't wait for an answer. Instead, she turned to make her exit, but Donald viciously snatched the back of her hair.

'Get back 'ere! I'm fucking talking to you!' growled Donald, still wound up following Mitchell's abrupt departure.

Sylvia waited until he'd released his grip before she spun around. 'Leave off me, Don. I did my bit, and what thanks did I get for it? Nothing but a cake that took me all day yesterday to make, thrown literally back in my face.' She shut up the second she saw her husband's face twist into a nasty grimace. She knew that look and despised it.

'That was an accident. Can't you see the gal's upset? Now, clean this mess up.'

In a mad moment, Sylvia took leave of her senses. 'No, Don, I won't. I've had enough. I—'

She didn't get to finish. Donald lashed out and struck her around the head. Losing her balance, she tumbled onto the table, squashing the remainder of the cake.

As soon as Donald grabbed her throat to pull her up, Shay intervened, by gripping Donald's arm. 'Come on, Don, mate. That's enough.'

Don instantly dropped Sylvia. With one almighty backhander, he knocked Shay backwards into Padlock Pete. 'You ever stick your fucking great hooter in my family business again, and I'll blow your fucking legs off. Now, fuck off!'

Shay the Brick, the better looking of Donald's motley crew, knew when to back off. He gave Sylvia a look that said: 'I'm sorry.' He'd always had a soft spot for Donald's wife. She was a respectable woman who was as straight as they come. In her fifties, Sylvia was still very attractive. Her wavy red hair bounced as she walked, and her classy skirt and blouse accentuated her tidy-shaped body. Shay would have liked her for himself, but she was Donald's wife, and so she was definitely out of bounds, if, of course, he valued his life. He felt sick because he desperately wanted to help Sylvia, but if he squared up to the man, he knew he would get seriously bashed up or even murdered. Everyone knew about Donald's violent temper. It had followed him around like a looming shadow. But it was his unpredictable nature that made him reckless and feared. If Shay was being honest with himself, he wished he'd never been friends with the man.

Just as Donald was about to drag Sylvia around again by her hair, Gina burst through the door and glared at her parents. 'A right fucking show, yous two are. What's it gonna look like if my Mitch walks in here now, eh?'

Donald let go of Sylvia's hair and straightened his jacket. He shot a look at Shay and shook his head. 'And you, Shay, are a fucking wanker. I suppose you wanna get into me wife's knickers. Who the fuck do you think you are, eh?'

Shay wanted to shrink inside himself. He was wary of Donald because somewhere on his person was probably a knife, or, worse, a gun.

'Look, Don, mate, I didn't want you to kick off in here. It's your daughter's house . . .'

'That's right, Shay!' said Gina. 'Now, all of ya, fuck off home.' She shot her mother a spiteful look, totally unfazed that her father still had a clump of her hair in his hand. 'Jesus, you two fighting again? What if me boys saw ya, eh? It ain't a good example to set the kids.'

Shay wanted to laugh out loud. As if Gina was the pinnacle of motherhood. But he kept his mouth well and truly shut. He wanted no part of the unrest that was about to kick off, and kick off it did.

However, it wasn't Donald who launched an attack: it was Sylvia.

'Shut your big ugly fat mouth. I am sick of you, sick to death of you, you selfish, selfish cow!' she screamed at the top of her voice.

Donald had stepped back to grab his overcoat when he spun around to find his wife land a raw slap across Gina's face. He dropped the coat, and for a moment, he was shocked; he'd never in all their married life seen Sylvia slap their daughter or heard her shout that loudly before. What was more shocking, though, was when she turned to him and pointed her finger in *his* face.

'If you ever touch me again, Donald Brennan, I will fucking cut your heart out, the minute you fall asleep.'

The look on Sylvia's face was unrecognisable. She had clenched her jaw and narrowed her eyes while her face flushed crimson with anger. Suddenly, she turned to face the table and grabbed the long carving knife that was next to the cold meat. Clutching it tightly with her hands shaking, she yelled, 'I fucking mean it, Don. You ever touch me again . . .' She then turned to her daughter, who was stunned and could do nothing but clasp her red cheek. 'And you, Miss High and Mighty, you can look after your *own* kids. Don't you ever ask me for anything again.'

Unexpectedly, with her free hand, Sylvia picked up the broken top layer of the cake and smashed it into Gina's face. 'And you can take that, you bloody bitch. I should've drowned you at birth.'

With all the shouting and hollering, Jordan and his youngest brother ran into the dining room. Catching their grandmother launching the cake into their mother's face, they saw this as a perfect opportunity to start a food fight. Screeching with excitement, Jordan grabbed a handful of the bottom tier and threw it at his grandfather. For a little boy, his throw was powerful, and the cake hit Donald's new suit. Before Donald could stop the boys, they began throwing cake and vol-au-vents as if they were hurling hand grenades.

As soon as Gina realised what was going on, she attempted to grab her youngest while Donald chased after Jordan.

Sylvia, though, was through the hallway and out of the front door as fast as she could, followed by Shay.

The screams continued inside, with Gina incandescent with rage and Donald shouting at the boys.

As she marched along the road, Shay called after her. 'Wait! Sylv, I'll give you a lift home.'

With tears streaming down her face, she stopped dead and dropped the knife that she'd been clutching so tightly.

Shay caught her up and stood in front of her. 'Come with me, Sylv. You look shaken up, love.'

Seeing her stare with such an empty, resigned expression, he wanted to hug her. However, glancing back towards the house to see if Donald was in sight clearly demonstrated that he was not brave enough to handle the situation, and he knew it.

'Thanks, Shay, but I've got me own car. Anyway, you'd better not get involved. You know what he's like.'

'Are you gonna be all right?'

With her shoulders slumped followed by a long deep sigh, she replied, 'No choice, Shay. I'm used to it now. I married a bully, I made my bed, and now I must lie in it.'

'What will he do, though, Sylv?'

'I don't know, but he'll either leave me be or give me a good bashing.'

'Don't go back, then.'

'Shay, you're a sweet man. I've always liked you. I could never understand how you were friends with him, but the problem is, there is nowhere to run. He'll find me and kill me. Don't you think, love, I would've left years ago?'

Before Shay could say another word, Sylvia suddenly looked down to find a tiny hand slip into hers. It was George's. He gazed up and gave her a smile that was so gentle and kind that she felt her heart melt.

'Nan, can I come with you? I promise, I'll be good . . .' He frowned. 'Nan, don't cry.'

She wiped her eyes and smiled back. 'It's the wind making me eyes water, babe.'

'I'll come with you, Nan. I'll look after you. I can make a cup of tea now.'

Shay and Sylvia looked back at the house as the screaming and shouting continued.

'Please, Nan.'

Shay shook his head. 'What will Mitch come back to? Jesus.'

'If he has any sense, he won't come back,' replied Sylvia, before looking down at George. 'Except to take this one.' She squeezed George's hand.

Shay nodded; he knew exactly what she meant. 'You take care, Sylv, and if he does hurt ya, call the police.'

Jerking her head, she rapidly blinked.

'I know, it goes against the grain calling the Ol' Bill, but so does bashing your wife. Don't put up with it.'

He said no more, merely tapped her arm, and turned to leave.

She watched him walk away, and her eyes filled with more tears. *If only.* She had always liked Shay. And in her younger days, she'd hoped that instead of Donald, he would have asked her out. Even in his fifties, Shay was well groomed. Grey strands peppered his hair and made his crystal blue eyes stand out. He was the only one of Donald's pals who didn't have a beer belly, and at five feet eight, his body was in perfect proportion. She continued to watch, wishing him to turn back, grab her in his arms, and promise to whisk her away. Then again, she'd probably had the same thought ten times a day. She sighed and peered down at George.

'Come on, then. I tell you what, why don't me and you go for a burger and an ice cream?'

George beamed. 'Yes, please, Nan.'

Chapter Three

Diane responded to the knock at the front door with 'Who is it?'

Mitchell smiled to himself; his mother hadn't changed. 'It's a burly burglar who wants to pinch your diamonds.'

The door opened, and Mitchell gently leaned down and kissed his mother on the cheek before pulling out a cheap bunch of flowers from behind his back.

His mother's face was a picture. Her ruddy cheeks glowed, and her eyes gleamed.

'Mitchell, you daft so-and-so. Come in, come in, love.' She stepped aside for him to hurry inside, so she could have him to herself, away from the outside world. 'Oh, what a lovely surprise. I didn't expect . . . Oh, Mitchell, it's so good to see you. I'll put the kettle on and get these in some water.' She beamed and smelled the roses. 'Oh, my favourite.' Peering up, she frowned. 'Mitchell, you will stay for a minute or two, won't you?'

A good two feet taller than his mum, Mitchell placed an arm gently around her shoulders. 'Mum, I have all the time in the world.'

Mitchell wandered into the first room on the right, a small living room. It was just as it was the last time he'd paid his mother a visit. The small bay window held a few pot plants, framed by the jardinière net curtains. The small sofa and two armchairs faced the gas fire and the portable TV set was balanced on a table in the corner of the room.

'It won't be long,' Diane called from the kitchen.

Mitchell just smiled; he felt at home.

It was quiet except for the ticking from the clock. The Chinese-style rug under the coffee table, he'd bought for her from his first fight's winnings, was spotlessly clean, although now somewhat faded. Looking across at the mantelpiece, his eyes drifted fondly to the knick-knacks and the photos. The wonky pot he'd made in a pottery class at school held a few old biros, the model boat he'd built sat next to it, and the love heart stone he'd found on Hastings beach, as a child, was still there. He stared at the photo of the scruffy-looking lad with the monkey on his shoulder – a reminder of how much he'd changed. Those downcast eyes that looked so pitiful weren't who he was now. But it wasn't his mother's fault.

The photo said it all. His mother had saved her pennies from working in the factory to take him down to the coast in the school holidays. He remembered those times well. The smell of the sea air as they hopped out of the train at Margate Station. She would place a few coppers in his hands as his spending money. The brief trip around Dreamland Fairground was followed by a choice of candy floss or a toffee apple, and afterwards, they'd spend time on the beach. That day's outing would be the highlight of his school holidays.

'Here you go, Mitchell,' she said, as she handed him the cup and saucer with two chocolate biscuits on the side. 'Oh, Mitchell, I am so pleased to see you home, love.' She sat on the chair and pulled her soft cotton cardigan around her shoulders. 'I thought you would have gone to see Gina and the boys first.'

'I have, Mum, and now I am here to see you . . . Er . . .' He stumbled as he looked down at the floor.

'Mitchell, listen to me. I know you feel that you've disappointed me, but let's not talk about it, eh? I hold nothing against you, Son. You've served your time, and that's it. It's in the past.'

'I never said "sorry".'

She looked up and moved a wisp of fair hair away from her face. Her plump rosy cheeks beamed. 'No need, love, no need. Now then, tell me, how are the boys?'

With narrowed eyes, Mitchell tilted his head.

'What d'ya mean, Mum? Are you saying you haven't seen them?'

'Well, Son, you know how it is. I knew how much work you were as a lad, and Gina has three little ones to look after. She doesn't need me in the way.'

'Have you been to the house?'

Diane nodded. 'Yes, and it's hard for Gina. She's always up to her neck in everything, so I just said if she ever needs a babysitter, then call me, but the poor girl probably never goes out.'

Mitchell's eyes grew ever darker. 'And the money I gave you?'

'Oh, yes, I put it in an envelope and popped it through her letter box every Friday morning. Honestly, Mitchell, I never forgot a single week.'

'No, Mum, of course you'd never.'

'I just wished you'd let me visit you more often than just your birthday. I didn't mind going there, you know.'

Shaking his head, Mitchell reached for the cup. 'Mum, I didn't want you dragging yourself all the way to that shithole. Sorry, I didn't mean to swear.'

Listening to his mother was like enjoying a soft melodic tune, in contrast to Gina's high-pitched voice.

'Son, I would have visited you in a sewer, if it meant I could just see you. Still, never mind all that now. You're home, Son . . . They treated you all right though, didn't they?' she asked, hoping her nightmare-like dreams had been just that and her one and only child hadn't been picked on or bullied.

Mitchell sat back into the sofa and munched on the biscuit before he spoke. 'They didn't have chocolate ones like this inside, but apart from the lack of goodies, the food was okay. The screws, I mean officers, were very fair, and the inmates, well, it's not like school. We were all in the same boat, so it was fine, Mum, honestly.'

Diane realised then that her son wanted to keep his time in prison to himself. She admired him for that. There was no point in focusing on the past. This was a time for looking to what the future would bring.

'Oh, before I forget, those holdalls are still under the bed. Did you want to take them with you?'

Mitchell shook his head. 'No, Mum, not yet.'

She frowned. 'Are you not going back to the gym, Son? You always loved to work out, and Nobby's missed you. I still see him when I go to the post office.'

Right away, Mitchell realised that his sweet mother had never looked in the bags; it was so like her not to go snooping. Changing the subject, he casually asked, 'Have you seen Claire? Did she ever move back to the area?'

He watched as his mother's face melted into sadness. 'I am sorry, Son. I know you liked her a lot, and, yes, she did move back to the area . . . with her husband.'

Mitchell felt his stomach tighten, and a hot flush shot up the back of his neck. 'Who did she marry?'

Changing the subject, Diane replied, 'It's not important. Now then, I have some lovely steak in the fridge. Shall I cook you dinner? I've got a Black Forest gateau in the freezer.'

Mitchell shook his head and smiled. 'I'm not hungry, but how about I come back tomorrow, and we'll eat together then?' As he placed the empty cup back onto the coffee table, he noticed something missing. His eyes scanned the shelf, the mantelpiece, and the windowsill. A crumpled frown washed over his forehead. 'Mum, where's your Bible?'

Diane stood up. 'Let me take that from you, Mitchell. Would you like another cuppa?'

He peered up as he handed her the cup. 'Mum?'

'Aw, Mitchell, it's not in the house anymore.'

A sudden dark thought flashed through his mind. 'Oh no, Mum, you haven't been disfellowshipped because of me, have you?'

She lowered her head. 'No, not exactly, well . . . sort of, indirectly. It's complicated. But, Son, it was my decision to leave for good.'

Mitchell knew that one day his mother would be pushed out of the community. She would have been told that if he didn't come back into the congregation, then she would have to disown him, and he knew just how hard that was for his mum. He understood all the time she had contact with him, she would have to sit at the very back of the Kingdom Hall, like a fucking leper.

Chapter Four

Sylvia parked her car in the multistorey car park in the Walnuts Shopping Centre. Holding George's hand, she stepped into the piss-smelling lift and looked down at his sweet angelic face. 'How about me and you go to The Silver Lounge and have one of those tall glasses of hot chocolate with the squirty cream on the top and chocolate sprinkles?'

George beamed. 'And a burger, Nan. You did say a burger?'

'And a burger, babe.'

The Silver Lounge at the Walnuts Shopping Centre in Orpington was a café that Sylvia often went to after doing her shopping. She knew most people in Orpington, and being married to Donald, in some ways, it gave her respect. At times, she could laugh at the situation because as much as the locals respected her husband, the truth was they were probably too afraid to get on the wrong side of him. She, however, had no respect for him; she hated his bullying ways, and what was more, she hated what he'd turned their daughter into.

Guiding her grandson through the sixties red diner-style cushioned chairs, she made her way to the table that afforded a good view of the square. She liked to people-watch when she was bored. However, she didn't actually like people too much; as far as she was concerned, in her circle, in fact, in Donald's circle of mates, they were all fake.

'Right, little lad, so hot chocolate and a burger?'

George was shivering. 'Yes, please, Nan.'

She realised that after all the commotion back at her daughter's house, she had gone off with George and hadn't let anyone know. She sighed when she also realised he didn't have his coat on. The café was warm except for the draught as the door kept opening and closing.

'Georgie, shall we pop into the Centre and get you a jumper? You look frozen to death.'

'I'm all right, Nan. Don't worry.'

She smiled at his sweet words and wondered how her daughter could have produced such a clever and polite little boy. 'Okay, you sit there while I go and order.'

Sally-Ann smiled when she saw Sylvia approaching. 'Hello, Sylv. I'm surprised you're 'ere. I thought Mitchell was out today? Only Gina was telling me she was laying on a big do for him.'

Sylvia raised her eyebrow and shot Sally-Ann a glare.

Knowing that look, Sally-Ann realised she'd said too much. 'Sorry, Sylv. None of my business, eh?'

'Not really, Sally-Ann. Anyway, never mind. Can I have two burgers and two hot chocolates?'

Sally-Ann nodded. 'I'll bring them over, Sylv. All right?'

'Thanks, love.'

Sylvia and her grandson stared out of the window in silence. Sylvia watched the young group of teenagers dressed in their bright-coloured clothes in a fashion that almost mimicked the pop groups. Young lads with long hair, short at the sides, with pink shirts and baggy jeans. The women were wearing the Madonna look, with crosses dangling from their ears, the wild hair, and fingerless gloves; and then there were those women who dressed to impress the boss with their padded shoulders and bright-coloured hoop earrings. It was such a significant change from the sixties when she was out to impress. She still liked to keep herself smart, but she wasn't one for showing off, and so she wouldn't go out as if she'd just stepped out of a scene from *Dallas*.

'What are you looking at, George?' asked Sylvia, as she noticed her grandson staring at the small group of people in the centre of the square.

'Nan, why is that man standing there talking to everyone?'

Sylvia laughed. 'Oh, babe, he isn't talking to *everyone*, only a couple of winos.'

'What's he talking about? Can we go and listen?'

'No, George, he's just a Bible-basher.'

George screwed his face, totally confused. 'What's a Bible-basher?'

She tutted. 'Oh, they're Jehovah's Witnesses, babe.'

He screwed his face up again. 'What's a Joseph Witness?'

Shaking her head, with a half-smile, Sylvia replied, 'A pain in the arse. Anyway, enough of the questions. Look, here comes your burger.'

Sally-Ann placed the plates on the table along with the knives and forks wrapped in serviettes.

'There you go. Can I get you anything else?'

'Hot chocolate,' replied George.

'Cor, look at you,' said Sally-Ann, as the boy turned to Sylvia. 'You can see he's Mitchell's boy, eh?'

Sylvia raised her brow again and slowly twisted her head. 'And what's that supposed to mean?'

Sally-Ann instantly blushed. 'Oh, I mean . . . nothing, Sylvia. I was just saying . . .'

'Just fetch the drinks, love.'

Sally-Ann hurried away, feeling hot under the collar. She hadn't meant to insinuate that Gina's boy looking like his father was in some way a confirmation that he was Mitchell's son, but she could see how it looked. Rumours were going around that Gina's three boys all had different dads.

Sylvia stared at the burger and knew she just couldn't stomach it. Her mind was on the fight with her husband, and, instantly, she ran her hands over her hair to make sure it was smooth and not sticking up after Donald had almost ripped it out of her head. *Bullying bastard.*

Looking at her grandson as he continued to stare out of the window while devouring his burger, Sylvia felt a sick feeling in the pit of her stomach. Donald would no doubt see to it that she would regret holding the knife to his face in front of his pals, but more worrying, was how she would respond if he started on *her*. She'd never been so bold as to threaten him before, and holding that knife in her hand, she'd wanted to stab him. Actually, she had wanted to murder him. Something inside her today had snapped.

'Nan, can we go to the Centre and buy a jumper?'

Sylvia came out of her thoughts. 'Oh . . . What? I thought you weren't cold?'

With tomato sauce on his chin, his shiny blue eyes looked out to the little girl in the square.

Sylvia followed his eyeline. 'George, stop staring and answer me. Are you cold, babe?'

He continued to look at the girl. 'No, Nan, but she looks freezing.'

Gazing across to the square, Sylvia saw the child, who was dressed in a floral dress, a thin cardigan, but no woolly tights to cover her blue stick-thin legs. She tutted. 'Georgie, babe, if I fed, watered, and clothed every waif and stray, I wouldn't have a penny to buy you a burger. Now, wipe that sauce off your face.'

George held the burger with both hands and quickly finished the last of it before he grabbed a serviette and cleaned his mouth. His attention then turned to the hot chocolate. The squirty cream and the dark cocoa sprinkles had melted. After a careful sip, he savoured the taste and the warmth but then looked back at the girl who was hopping from leg to leg with her face down. 'Nan, would you like my hot chocolate?'

Sylvia was still mulling over what she should do next. 'What?' She looked at her own drink. 'No, George, you asked for it, now you drink it. I haven't even drunk mine.'

'Nan, can I give mine to that girl?'

'Oh, for Gawd's sake, you *will* keep on. Well, do what you want, before you pester the life out of me.'

'Are you gonna eat your burger?'

Sylvia rolled her eyes. 'No, go on. Take it.'

George didn't need to be told twice. He quickly wrapped her burger in a serviette, grabbed the tall glass of hot chocolate, and headed towards the counter where he asked the waitress to pour it into a takeaway cup.

Sylvia kept an eye on her grandson as he hurried over to the girl. She smiled to herself, thinking that when George finally grew up, he would be a charmer. She then watched as the two children stood awkwardly two feet away from each other. Both stared for a moment, before George, like a robot, held out the burger and hot chocolate. The little girl then shot a look at the man who was still addressing the square as if he had a big audience, before she took the offering and smiled. Sylvia noticed just how sweet she was, but at the same time, she also appeared very sad.

As George skipped back to the café, Sylvia clocked the man suddenly snatch the burger and hot chocolate from the girl's hands and toss them in the bin before he continued spouting off. Seeing the little girl standing there with her head low, almost as if she was ashamed, triggered something inside Sylvia. Whether it was the argument or fight that she'd had with her husband and daughter or the fact that George's good deed had been thrown back in his face, she wasn't sure. However, what she was damn sure of was that she wasn't going to have it.

'It's cold out there, Nan,' said George, as he climbed back onto his seat.

'You, babe, wait here,' demanded Sylvia, before she jumped up and marched out of the café, her jaw tense, jutted forward in a temper.

'Oi!' she said, as soon as she was a foot away from the Bible-basher.

The man stopped instantly, his dark eyes wide.

'My grandson, George, out of the goodness of his heart, gave that little girl his own hot drink, and you, ya spiteful bastard, threw it in the bin, and there you are talking about

God's will. You oughta be flaming well ashamed of yourself.' She then shot a glare at the young woman, who appeared just as forlorn as the little girl. 'And if you're her mother, then you oughta be ashamed as well. That kiddie looks frozen to death. I'm bloody sure that God wouldn't want *that*.'

The very pretty woman, who was wearing no make-up, and her fair hair hanging limply around her face, glanced at the man for some kind of direction. It dawned on Sylvia that the well-built spiteful-faced man called the shots as if he was the head sheep.

'My daughter is not allowed to take from strangers.'

'Strangers! Bloody *strangers*! He is a nine-year-old little boy who obviously saw that your daughter needed a hot drink. Christ! It's freezing. And as for not talking to strangers, I bet you don't know the people behind the doors that you all knock at, spouting your Jehovah shit.'

The two winos laughed and clapped as if they were watching a theatre show, which riled up Sylvia. 'Oh, stop it, you bloody idiots.' The two drunkards instantly stopped laughing. They knew who Sylvia was, or, more importantly, who her husband was, and they didn't want to get on the wrong side of her.

She turned back to face the dark eyes of the man, none too discreetly, looking him up and down. 'And understand this: if my nine-year-old grandson can see the child needs food and a coat to keep her warm, then, by Christ, the bloody social services will an' all. But you're all right though, eh? Dressed in a suit and a coat. So, a word of warning: if I see that little 'un cold like that again, I will be on the phone. So, take note, Mr Holier-than-Bloody-Thou.'

She said no more but spun around and stormed back to the café, where George was glued to the window.

'What did you say to that man, Nan? He didn't look very happy.'

'Oh nothing, darling. Only that I was very proud of you and that he should buy his little girl a coat. Anyway, come on, let's get you home, if you still have a home to go to.'

Sylvia was in such a daze that she forgot her grandson was in the back of the car. On autopilot, she drove towards Petts Wood instead of along Cray Valley Road. Once she reached Chislehurst Road, she put on her windscreen wipers. A gentle flurry of snow turned to water as it hit the screen. Christmas was just around the corner, a reminder of her past.

***

It had been the Christmas of 1954 when she'd met Donald at The Downham Tavern. She'd known who he was, but she'd never got into a conversation with him. He'd always been surrounded by his mates and girls, all wanting to suck up to him. He wasn't bad looking either, but it was more an air about him that made him attractive. That Christmas Eve, the Tavern was rocking. Everyone had come out to join the party. It was what everyone was talking about. She'd just managed to get a hairdresser's appointment and joined the row of women all under the dryers. She was eighteen years old, and her mother had allowed her to wear make-up, a drop of eyeliner, and a coating of mascara. She remembered her mother standing back and looking her up and down and saying, 'Well, you, my gal, will be turning heads tonight.'

And she wasn't wrong. With her hair cut into a perfect bob, short at the back and long at the front, she'd spent hours ensuring it was poker straight. She'd even fastened the long flicks to the sides of her face with Sellotape, until she was ready to leave. Dressed in a powder-blue pencil skirt and matching twinset, she slipped her feet into her pride and joy – her suede winkle-pickers. She'd saved all her money from working on her father's stall on Petticoat Lane selling wool. Oh, how at the time she wished she'd never gone that night – but she had.

With her girlfriend excited and full of giggles, they'd made their way through the crowds to the bar. A foot away was Donald and his gang. She noticed Shay, looking her way, and smiled back. He was so handsome back then, with jet-black hair and crystal blue eyes. She remembered drinking three glasses of Babycham followed by a gin and lemon, or, as her father would call it – mother's ruin. Unexpectedly, Donald pushed himself away from the bar and from the young woman who had her arm draped over his shoulder and turned to her. 'Well, look at you! Where have you been all my life?' he said, looking her up and down.

She recalled glancing behind her. *Surely, he wasn't talking to me?* she thought. He was Donald Brennan, a face, who could have any woman. Before she had the chance to say a word, he grabbed her hand and pulled her towards the dance floor. Looking the epitome of charm, he managed to make her feel as if she was the most beautiful woman in the world. She danced with him for three songs, and then she looked over his shoulder to see Shay. He couldn't have looked more hurt, to her eyes. Moments later, Shay left. The night continued, and as the drinks flowed, all bought by Donald, she was well on her way to being totally pissed.

For months, he treated her like a queen, sending her gifts, including expensive perfumes, and arriving for a date with a bunch of flowers. He even went as far as to arrive with two. One was obviously to sweeten her mother up. Then he'd worked on her father, sharing a few bevvies, and taking him to the racetrack and the dogs. By the time he was ready to pop the question, both her parents were ecstatic. They urged her to get wed as soon as possible.

What more could they have asked for? A wealthy young man, with respect and manners, who saw to it that the parents were treated well.

Shay was off the scene. She often looked out for him, but for months, all she saw was Donald and his other pals. The day she next saw Shay was the day she decided that Donald was the man for her. She'd been on the bus at the time travelling through Lewisham when she spotted Shay leaning against the railings with his arm around a girl. She assumed he was no longer free to pursue, so she accepted Donald's proposal and was married within a month.

By the following Christmas, Gina was born, a month early. A tiny bundle of skinny arms and legs. She fell in love there and then, and so did Donald. He must have wet the baby's head ten times – any excuse to go to the pub and celebrate. On Christmas Eve, she was home from the hospital and still very sore. The birth had been incredibly traumatic. Her heart sank as she walked through the door. Donald's friends, men and women, were in the living room, which at the time wasn't huge. They lived in Lewisham in a small three-bedroom semi. The music was loud, and the place was a mess.

'Welcome home!' they bellowed, in unison. But it was the last thing she needed. She couldn't host a party, not when she could barely stand. The baby was screaming because she wasn't getting enough milk, and having her a month early, nothing was a hundred per cent prepared. She recalled trying to smile and greet everyone, but it was far too much for her, and so she headed to the bedroom to get the baby settled and to take the weight off her feet as well.

Donald was pissed and annoyed that his wife wasn't the happy-go-lucky person he'd married. He burst into the room with a face like a smacked arse. 'What's your problem, Sylv? Everyone's downstairs to welcome you and the baby home, and you slink off up here. Me mates and their wives wanna see my daughter.'

It was those words that hit home – *his daughter*. Not their daughter but his. She hadn't argued but smiled instead and returned downstairs to all the oohs and aahs. She tried to be upbeat and pleasant, but she'd been in pain and felt drained. The doctor had told her to rest for at least three weeks; he'd given her iron tablets and said she needed to eat well and take her medication because she'd lost a lot of blood during her delivery. But Donald had dismissed the medical advice, stating that she was strong, and besides, what did women do out in the paddy field? They'd have a baby, strap them to their backs, and carry on working. She'd often wondered if that was true.

After an hour or so of the guests passing the baby around, the room suddenly appeared to cave in around her, and she hit the deck before she could save herself. She awoke back in the hospital having a blood transfusion and

Donald moaning that the episode had ruined his Christmas. She should have run then, taken the baby, and buggered off back to her mother's. But she didn't and she went home as soon as she'd got the all-clear to be discharged.

It was the way things were to be from then on. She was *his* wife, who had *his* daughter and lived in *his* house. What she wore, what she ate, what she drank, and who she mixed with were at his say-so.

***

As soon as she reached their house, she pulled into the drive and sighed. The large four-bedroom detached house was set back and nestled in between two large fir trees. The close was just off Chislehurst Road. By her standards, it was posh, but the money that paid for it was dirty. Donald wasn't the sleek businessman he'd led her to believe but a bank robber who could cleverly launder money. She stared up at the house and sighed again. If only she hadn't been so bloody naive. All the signs were there: the men sucking up to him, the cash he often flashed – he was a villain through and through. She shook her head and opened the driver's door and then cursed. 'Oh shit!' George had fallen asleep on the back seat. So much had been on her mind that she'd forgotten to drop him off at Gina's home.

Lifting his little body from the car, she grappled with the keys to open the front door. Once she was inside, she carried him into the lounge, placed him on the new pale-green velvet sofa, and hurried to the kitchen to turn the recently installed central heating up to its highest setting. Then she put the kettle on before she made her way back along the hallway to the phone on the wall. After dialling her daughter's number to let her know that George was with her, she tutted – the line was engaged. Nothing new there then. Gina was always on the blower to someone or other. The bills were paid by Donald, so her daughter didn't give a shit. Not that the little madam cared about much other than herself anyway.

Just as she returned to the kitchen to make a cup of tea, George appeared. His fair hair stuck up like a cockatoo, and his rosy cheeks glowed. 'Nan,' he said, in a sleepy voice, 'can I stay with you tonight, please?'

Sylvia leaned against the kitchen units looking her grandson over. 'Well, once your bleedin' mother gets off the phone, I'll be able to ask her.'

'She won't say no.'

Sylvia smiled; he was right. Gina's kids were either with a neighbour or with her.

A screeching of brakes outside the house told her that Donald had returned, and she knew there would be ructions.

Little George, with his sweet innocent face, smiled. 'I bet that's Grandad.'

However, Sylvia was more concerned that if Donald was pissed and decided to kick off, George would witness something nasty. 'George, darling, do your nan a huge favour.'

George beamed. 'Yeah.'

'You stay here in the kitchen and keep quiet, babe.'

With her heart now pounding, she could hear Donald struggling to open the front door, which meant only one thing: he was drunk.

'Please, babe, promise me you'll stay in here.'

George frowned when he saw the worry lines on his grandmother's face. 'I promise, Nan.'

'Good boy.'

Sylvia looked at the entrances to the kitchen, one via the hallway and the other via the lounge. The units stretched along half the wall and then carried on into a recess. 'Hide in there, babe.'

George knew this was serious. Even though he was a young lad, he was aware that he must do as he was told.

As Sylvia walked into the lounge, she peered back and felt relieved that George was out of sight. She wished she'd taken him home because she knew deep down that Donald with a drink inside him would kick off.

Suddenly, the front door flew open and banged against the wall. She could hear Donald growling and mumbling under his breath. Her blood surged around her body as fear gripped her. She shot her eyes to the back door and thought perhaps it might be best to make a run for it and grab George on the way.

It was too late; Donald was in the room. His eyes were hooded and mean, his face white and spiteful looking. She could see he'd had a skinful, just by the way he swayed and glared with an evil glint. One eye wandered while the other remained transfixed. And Sylvia knew that meant he'd had more than seven pints. It was her cue to get out of the room as quickly as possible. Yet, as if a happy cloud had descended upon him, his expression changed. The corners of his plump bottom lip lifted, pushing his cheeks up to his eyes.

'Come 'ere, babe. All is forgiven. Let's forget we even had a barney, eh? What d'ya say?'

Am I seeing things? thought Sylvia. But the more she inspected his expression, the more she was confused. Still, she wasn't going to look a gift horse in the mouth, and so, quickly, she gave him a nervous fake smile. 'Yeah, oh, go on, then, love. No harm done.' She wondered if in his pissed state he would recognise that she was acting overly accommodating. She didn't have a choice, though. Her grandson was in the kitchen, and she didn't want to row in front of him, not when she knew damn well the argument could quickly become violent.

Still very wary, she couldn't take her eyes off her husband as he slowly approached. It wasn't until he was an inch away from her face that she saw his smile instantly change to a twisted, psychopathic smirk. She knew then that she had to get away from his clutches, or he would beat her. But as she spun around to leave, he snatched the hair at the back of her head.

Sylvia let out a squeal.

Donald hissed into her ear, 'You should never 'ave threatened me, you bitch!'

Totally and utterly terrified, she couldn't move. She thought that if she kept quiet and didn't struggle, he may just carry on hissing and spitting, releasing his rage. But she was wrong.

With his hand gripping her head, he pulled his arm back, and just like bowling a cricket ball, he launched her head so fast that her face smashed into the corner of the thick smoked-glass table top. No sooner than he'd realised how much force was behind that blow, he knew he'd gone too far. For a second, he couldn't open his eyes. The sound was disgusting. It wasn't like a knock or a crack, but a squelch followed by a thud as Sylvia's body collapsed onto the floor.

Taking a deep breath, he opened his eyes to find the most hideous sight before him. And he had been in enough fights to know what a battered victim looked like. But this was on a whole other level of gruesome.

His breathing quickened as he placed his hands over his mouth. He shook his head, hoping it was a dream, and that his wife of thirty years or so was just knocked out and the blood covering her face was merely from a scrap. But no amount of wishing could change the fact that the whole of her eye socket was open, the eye was out, and her pretty face was now a ghoulish and hideous mess. Shocked by the sight and the fact that he'd done that to her, his wife, the woman he was supposed to love, it left him powerless to move. His brain just couldn't comprehend it. The blood still poured from her eyeless socket and pooled around her face, coating her hair and the rug. He was too drunk to see her chest gently rising and falling and naturally assumed that from the state of her she was dead. With his mouth filling with water, he rushed to the bathroom to throw up. On all fours with his head down the pan, he heaved and heaved, until there was nothing left in his stomach to bring up. Then he leaned against the cold tiles and gasped for air. Smashing his head back in anger, he cried, 'Jesus fucking

Christ, why, why did you have to wind me up? Why couldn't you 'ave just . . . ?' He smashed his head again until his ears began to ring. Then, suddenly, he thought he heard a sound coming from somewhere inside the house. *Was it the bang of a door?* he thought. Another wave of sickness coiled around his stomach, and he heaved one last time.

Slowly, while taking deep long breaths, he pulled himself up from the floor and gingerly walked back along the hallway into the lounge. He faltered as soon as his eyes rested on his wife. Holding his hands to his mouth, he crept closer. The sight was sickening but very sobering all the same. With a sudden clear head, he realised he had to find a way out of the predicament and with the sense not to mess things up.

As he looked around the room, it suddenly hit him. He would make it look like an accident. The new rug they had bought to go with the modern sofa would be perfect.

He looked at the thick shag pile and then back at Sylvia. He had to gauge it just right. Once the idea was firmly planted in his head, he got to work. Removing her right shoe, he then placed it on its side by the end of the rug closest to her. He now needed to push the rug from the other end to make it look as though she'd tripped, lost her footing, and landed head first onto the table. Luckily for him, the rug wasn't stiff, so he managed to wrinkle it up with ease.

He stood back and looked at the arrangement. If he had walked in and seen the sight as it was now, the sequence of events would have been precisely what he would have assumed. Somehow, his mind wasn't fuzzy anymore; he was stone-cold sober. He now had to act as if he'd come home and found her like this. Another idea sprang to mind, and he hurried from the lounge, snatched his car keys from the hallway cabinet, and silently opened the front door. Looking around, he noticed that the close was quiet. Once he'd closed the door behind him, he removed his front door key, threw it in the dirt, and began banging on the front door. Calling through the letter box, he said, 'Sylvia, I've lost my keys again. Let me in, love.'

After a few more bangs and shouts, he then walked across his garden to his next-door neighbour's property, Denise Galluzzo – the lawyer.

He knocked and stepped back. After a short moment, she opened the door, dressed in a blue business suit. She always looked impeccably dressed. Her long dark hair, sleek without even a kink, shone like satin. With her arms crossed, she was silent, with just a tilt of her head as if to say 'What do you want?'

Her stance and the way she spoke always had Donald feeling on edge. She was beautiful as well as classy, and obviously she came from a well-to-do family or had probably studied at Cambridge University.

'Sorry to bother you, but I've left my keys indoors, and me missus is in, but . . . er, she ain't opening the door.' He pointed to Sylvia's car in the driveway. 'I drew up a little while ago. I've been knocking, but . . . well, now I'm a bit concerned, like.'

Denise raised her well-defined brow. 'And what would you like *me* to do?'

Donald could tell from her tone that she was obviously being sarcastic.

'Do you have a crowbar or a hammer?'

Denise looked him up and down. 'Do I look like I would have a crowbar?' she spat at him. Then a beady eye shot across the drive to Donald's car. 'I would have thought you would have one in the boot of your B-M-W.' She drew out the letters, with all the sarcasm she could muster.

With Donald's patience now wearing very thin, he said, 'Look, love, I'm asking you because I don't have a tool I can use to break into my own home. Me wife's not answering the bloody door, and I am worried. 'Cos, look, it's snowing. Her car's in the drive. She wouldn't walk anywhere in this poxy weather, and, like I said, she ain't answering the door. Can you help me or not?'

'What if she's simply taking a bath?'

'Shower, love, she always takes a shower. Every night at ten o'clock before she goes to bed. It's six o'clock, and I've been knocking for longer than it ever takes for her to be in the shower. So you can see why I'm concerned. Please help, or I'll go to the other neighbour. I am worried, love, that she may have had a fall. She said earlier that she felt a little dizzy.'

'Wait there.'

Donald felt his heart pummelling, but he had to hold it together.

Denise returned moments later with a crowbar in her hand. Surprisingly, she didn't hand it to Donald but marched across the snow-covered lawn to his drive. 'Knock again, just in case.'

Donald let her take the lead and did as he was told. But he knew that as soon as she clapped eyes on the horrific sight, he would have to put on a first-class act.

She stepped back away from the door and handed him the crowbar.

Like a pro, he had the door swinging off its hinges and stepped forward, calling his wife's name.

The heat from the inside hit Denise first; it was overly warm.

'Sylvia!' Donald called up the stairs again, before turning to his neighbour and frowning.

She nodded for him to walk on. He knew then that he would have to walk into the lounge and prepare himself for an almighty gasp. He hesitated first, thinking how to react, then, discreetly, he sucked in a deep breath before taking strides into the lounge.

'Oh, Jesus Christ!' he bellowed, as he hurried over to Sylvia. For a moment, his dishonesty took a back seat. Stunned to see that she seemed to be lying at a different angle, his true instincts took over, and he walked over the crumpled rug, pretending almost to trip himself. He even managed to kick her loose shoe out of the way, all the while knowing that his neighbour was right behind him.

'My God!' yelled Denise.

Donald was now on his knees beside his wife. He had her head in his hands. 'Quick, please call an ambulance.'

But Denise was dumbstruck. She couldn't take her eyes away from the horrendous state of Sylvia's face. The blood was thick and black, a pool of which surrounded her head. But also, there was some on Sylvia's hands. A million thoughts tumbled through her brain. What if her neighbour had been murdered and the culprit was still in the house? Could the accusing finger be pointed her way? Her prints were now in the room, and she had rowed with Sylvia only two days ago, over the fir tree that needed to be taken down.

'Please help me. Please, Mrs Galluzzo. Call an ambulance.'

Denise snapped out of her trance and hurried to the phone in the hallway, where she dialled 999, gave the details, and hurried back to Donald. 'Is she breathing?'

Donald was rocking his wife in his arms. 'Oh, I don't know,' he cried.

Denise got down on her knees and carefully held Sylvia's wrist, feeling for a pulse. Her own heart was racing, and so it was hard to tell. But when she felt how cold the woman was, and looked at her chest, she could tell that Sylvia wasn't breathing. To be sure, she placed her two fingers on the woman's neck – there was nothing.

Determined to mess up the scene, Donald picked up his wife and carried her limp body to the sofa and laid her down.

'Oh shit, I don't think we should . . .'

Donald glared at Denise. 'What?'

Looking back at the pain on Donald's face, she decided this wasn't her place to tell him what to do; after all, what she'd just seen was so shocking and would no doubt give her nightmares for years to come.

'That poxy rug, I knew we should have stuck it down. If she tripped once, she tripped ten times.'

Denise looked at the crumpled rug, then at the loose shoe, and finally, the corner of the glass table. A wave of nausea enveloped her, and she took a few deep breaths. In silence, they waited for the ambulance, a sobbing Donald still holding his wife while Denise stood rooted to the spot.

Chapter Five

In terror, George ran through the open field that ran alongside St Paul's Wood Hill. He tried to remember his way home. His grandmother had walked with him a few times. She'd always said that she liked a brisk walk now and then. Luckily for him, he vaguely remembered the way.

The snow was heavy and bit at his face. His thin long-sleeved top was not warm enough to fight off the elements. But his raging heart and the adrenaline furiously surging through his body kept him warm enough to continue. No one was around. The field was eerily quiet, and so he ran as fast as he could until he reached Hoblingwell Park and then on to Cotmandene Crescent. He knew the way now. He continued on, down Broomwood Road and over the bridge to St Paul's Cray. His lungs burned, and his legs felt like mush, but he knew in his mind he had to get home and somehow pretend he'd been there all along. He couldn't get the vision of his grandfather's angry expression, as he'd smashed his Nan's face into that table, out of his head. Tears blinded him as he ran on towards St Mary Cray.

Once he reached his street and slowed down, he bent over with his hands on his knees and gasped for air. There, just ahead, he could see his brothers in the front garden trying to make snowballs.

Jordan was about to pound Sonny with a handful of snow when he looked up.

'Where have you been? Muvver's been looking for ya.'

George was bewildered.

Jordan was laughing as he shoved the snow into Sonny's face and bent down to scoop up more for another go.

With legs like jelly, George slowly walked to the front door, only to have a snowball smacked into the back of his head.

'Tell Muvver you're here and then help me make a snowman, George.'

Silently, George crept inside. His throat burned from the cold and his ears ached. All he really wanted to do was to go to bed and hope it was all just a dream. His mum wasn't in the living room, so he wandered into the dining room. Some of the party food was still on the table, some on the floor. But remnants of the cake had stuck to the wall above the fireplace. There on the chair at the end of the table, with her head resting on her arm, was his mum.

Beside her was an empty bottle of wine and a wine glass turned on its side.

'M-Mum,' he stammered.

Slowly, she lifted her head, and George knew she was drunk.

'Tell the others to come in and shut that fucking front door. All of ya, get your 'jamas on and get to bed.'

She slumped her head back down and moaned.

George didn't bother to do as he was told. He was also reluctant to tell Jordan or Sonny what had happened at their Nan's house; they would never have listened anyway. Instead, he dragged his tired legs up the stairs, kicked his wet shoes off, climbed onto the bottom bunk, pulled the blankets over his head, and cried.

It was an hour later, after all the boys were in bed asleep, when the scream came. At first, George thought he was dreaming, or perhaps it was a fox, but then he heard those words of pain. 'No! No! No!'

Jordan was the first up from his bed, followed by Sonny. George was still trying to push other images from his mind. He didn't quite grasp that his mother had been told the news that her mother was dead. He followed his two brothers as far as the landing but was too afraid to go downstairs.

Jordan and Sonny ran into the dining room. 'What's the matter?' asked Jordan, standing a couple of feet away from his mum, as if her scream would become contagious.

Gina tried to catch her breath as she stared at her three boys. The shocking news should have snapped her out of her drunken stupor, but because of the copious amounts of wine she'd consumed, she couldn't think straight.

'I need your farver!' she wailed. 'Where's Mitch? I need him here.'

'Muvver, what's happened? Why are you crying?'

'Oh my God, it's awful, but I need your farver here now,' she said, ignoring Jordan's plea for an answer.

'Muvver, what's going on? Why were you screaming?' he asked again, knowing that his mother didn't scream like that for attention.

Slowly, she stopped crying and wiped her eyes. But once she saw the black mascara on her hands, she got up from her chair and stared in the mirror and tried to wipe the make-up away. 'Get me a baby wipe, Jordan, please, there's a love,' she said, as she snivelled.

Jordan ran from the room, up the stairs to the bathroom, and returned with the packet. ''Ere, Muvver.'

She snatched it and started cleaning her face while sniffling. 'Take your bruvver back upstairs to bed, there's a good boy.'

'But, Muvver, what's going on?'

'For Christ's sake, do as you're bloody told,' she yelled, impatiently.

Jordan huffed, barged past his mother, and bolted to his room, followed, as always, by Sonny.

George sat on the top step of the stairs, not wanting to face his mother but equally disinclined to go back to bed. Then he saw the front door open and his father stroll in.

Mitchell gazed up and tilted his head to the side. 'It's late, Son. Why aren't you in bed?'

George felt a warm feeling and wondered if it was because of his father's words or his actual tone. He nodded his head in the direction of the dining room and watched as his father walked in.

***

'Oh, Mitch, Mitch, I am so glad you're home. It's me mum. She's dead,' sobbed Gina, not having seen the look of anger on her husband's face.

Mitchell stared at his wife in disbelief. He'd planned to have firm words with her over his mother's treatment while he was in the nick. 'What?' he said, as he also clocked the state of the room. It certainly wasn't like this when he left. There were remnants of cake everywhere, some of it trodden into the carpet and some still on the walls.

Gina was expecting him to run to her and offer a dramatic embrace, but he didn't. He stopped in his tracks and just gawped.

'She's dead, Mitch. Dad just called me. He found her dead. Oh my God, what am I gonna do, Mitch?' she said, as she put her hands to her face and cried.

Mitchell stepped forward and put his arms around her to offer her a compassionate hug. He could hear the children coming down the stairs. So everything he'd planned to talk to her about had now been swept away in a heartbeat. However, he didn't expect Gina to scream over his shoulders at the boys. And almost burst his eardrums in the process. 'I fucking told you two to go to bed!'

It was hard to take in. His mother-in-law, for whom he actually had the utmost respect and had pitied at the same time, was dead. Hearing the boys hurtle back up the stairs, and the sobbing from his wife stop, he pulled away. He assumed he and Gina would sit down and she would explain what had happened to their grandmother before the little boys fell into a nightmare dream. It was a huge deal for any youngster to hear. And he wanted to know more himself. As far as he knew, Sylvia was as fit as a fiddle. 'Sit down and tell me what happened.'

Gina wasn't happy. She assumed that her husband would be holding her, stroking her hair, and telling her everything would be okay; instead, he had a questioning look on his face.

'I don't know, but I can't get my head around it. She was here one minute, then Dad called me to say she'd died. It was something about her tripping over the rug and smashing her face on the table. He's with the police now. Mitch, what am I gonna do? My mum's gone, Mitch. She's gone.'

So many thoughts swirled around Mitchell's brain. The dining room was a mess, Sylvia was dead – and all in the space of a few hours. And his wife's reaction to their children was puzzling: it was cold if not harsh.

'Well, shouldn't we sit the boys down and explain what happened first? She is their grandmother. This will hurt them too,' he said, as he looked over his shoulder.

'They're young. They'll get over it. And they weren't that close to her anyway. It's me that won't get over it,' she cried.

'I'm sorry, Gina, really I am. I do think we need to tell the boys, though.'

'And what about me, eh? She was my mum.' Gina then gave a pout and then huffed. 'I think I need a drink, Mitch.'

He frowned. 'You sound like you've already had a good drink. Why don't you get cleaned up and have a lie-down? It must have been a right shock. You don't know how she died, then?'

'It was a shock, and all I know is what me dad told me.'

She gave him a sorrowful smile. 'And what about you, Mitch?'

'I'm going to tell the boys that their grandmother is now in heaven.'

Gina felt a tight sensation in her chest but refused to admit to herself that at that point she was jealous of her own boys. It seemed Mitchell was more determined to see to their needs over and above her own. Although she did know that she needed to sober up, the thought of her mother dead wasn't truly resonating with her, and she knew it.

'Mitch, shouldn't we wait to hear from me dad first? He may need picking up from the police station and he'll want to come back here to his family. He must be devastated to have been the one who found Mum dead.'

Mitchell inclined his head and looked his wife up and down. 'I think you should get cleaned up and perhaps drink a strong coffee before you make any decisions.'

'What's that supposed to mean, Mitch?'

'Well, I don't want to argue, but you look a mess and stink of wine. So just go and take a shower and then have a strong coffee or take a shower and then go to bed for a while.'

Gina gave Mitchell a glance of annoyance before she left the room and stomped up the stairs like a spoiled child. She stripped off and stood under the shower. Less than five minutes later, she was out and wrapped in a towel. The shower had partially sobered her but not enough for her to stay awake. Three bottles of wine had ripped the energy right out of her. She headed for their bedroom to get dressed into her silk wrap where she sat on the bed to massage body lotion into her cracked heels. But when she felt the soft cushioning beneath her, she lay down and instantly began to snore.

Mitchell heard her and rolled his eyes, but he wasn't concerned with his wife's feelings this minute; he was more concerned with the little boys. Quietly, he climbed the stairs and popped his head inside their bedroom. He was very surprised to find them asleep. At least they looked to be. But just as he was about to leave, he spotted George flick open one eye. Curling his finger, he beckoned George towards him.

George looked at his two brothers who were sound asleep. He slipped from out of the covers and crept over to his father, who took his hand, and together, they walked down the stairs to the dining room.

'Are you okay, George? You look peaky, Son.'

George slowly nodded as his eyes flicked around. He studied his father's face.

Mitchell wondered if between the phone calls and Gina's loud mouth the boys had heard what had happened because George certainly appeared grief-stricken. 'Did Mummy say that Nanny Sylvia is up in heaven?'

George remained silent as he gazed into his father's blue eyes.

'Were you close to Nanny Sylvia?'

George's eyes suddenly welled up, and two huge tears plummeted down his cheeks. Before he had a chance to wipe them away, his father, who really was more of a stranger to him, suddenly put his arms around him and pulled him close, whispering that everything would be okay.

George wasn't used to being hugged; in fact, the only person who really showed any affection was his Nanny Sylvia, and that wasn't all the time. Now she was gone, he was scared. If his grandfather guessed that he'd been in the house, then perhaps he would do the same to him as he'd done to her. He hugged his father tightly because he knew the only person who would protect him was this man with the blue eyes and the slight limp – Mitchell Swan.

'Hey, Son, listen. Everything will be okay.'

'Will it, Dad? Will it?'

Mitchell knew there was more to the question because he sensed that George was almost begging him to promise everything would be all right.

***

By 7.00 a.m., Gina was up and shuffling her way into the bathroom. As she stared into the mirror, all her memories from yesterday came flooding back. Suddenly, her heart beat faster, and a wave of sickness washed over her. 'Christ!' she said aloud, when she remembered her father's phone conversation informing her that her mother was dead. She shook her head and went over it again. Surely, it was a mad dream? Then she remembered her husband had returned. Rushing from the bathroom and down the stairs, she found him in the kitchen sipping a cup of coffee. He looked even more handsome than when she'd first met him, and suddenly she became very self-conscious of how she looked right now.

'I see you have sobered up, Gina,' he said, in a slow cold voice.

'What? Yes, but Jesus, Mitch, what did you expect? I had some awful news. Me muvver's dead.'

She tried to put on the tears but had to sit down on one of the kitchen chairs first.

'You might want to phone your dad to find out exactly what went on, since you were nine sheets to the bloody wind yesterday.'

Gina took a few deep breaths, pushed her fringe out of her eyes, and walked back towards the hallway where the landline phone hung on the wall. She cleared her throat, dialled the number to her parents' home, and waited. There was no answer except the sound of the answerphone kicking in. 'Dad, it's me, Gina. Call me when you get home, please.'

After returning to the kitchen, she put the kettle on to make herself a cup of coffee.

Mitchell stepped aside.

'He's not in, Mitch, so all I can do is wait and find out what happened. I feel so upset,' she whined, longing for some form of affection. However, she knew deep down that he only married her because it was the right thing to do. In fact, their short married life had comprised of a few quick loveless shags, if he'd had a drink. And it was always initiated by her. She knew it wasn't making love – far from it, in fact. She'd felt the anger in every stroke; it was just lucky that she liked it rough.

The only thing she could never understand was why Mitchell had such high morals when he was so against religion. Still, he was her husband, and a very handsome one at that. She wanted to be the apple of his eye, not the result of his duty.

After two big gulps of coffee, she went back up to the bathroom to get herself made up in the hope he would find her attractive. All the heartache she was feeling for losing her mum would be mitigated for a short while at least if Mitchell would carry her to bed and take her mind off the situation. She loved sex, and now her husband was home, she expected to have it at least once a day with him. *A girl has needs*, she thought, *and should not go without*. Suddenly, as she looked at her face again in the mirror, she could see in some ways she actually looked like her mother. Her eyes filled up again. She may not have been close to her mother, but she'd always loved her and would miss her for not being around to help out with the boys or to pop to the hairdresser's with her.

She jumped when the phone rang in the hallway. Hurrying downstairs to answer it, she hoped it was her father.

Mitchell stood in the doorway of the dining room with his coffee cup still in his hand, feeling as though he was a visitor.

Why hadn't he answered the phone? This was supposed to be his home too, she thought, glancing his way again before lifting the receiver. 'Hello?'

'Gina, it's me, ya farver. I'm coming over to yours. Are you okay, love?'

The sentimental tone in his voice had her bursting into tears. 'Oh, Dad, what happened? I can't get my head around it.'

'Listen, my gal, I'll be by in a minute. You just wait until I get there,' he replied.

'Okay, Dad. I'll put the kettle on.'

'So, your dad is on his way over, then?' Mitchell said, as she replaced the receiver.

Gina nodded. 'At least he can tell us what happened, eh?'

Mitchell raised an eyebrow. 'Was he there when it happened?'

'I can't remember exactly what he said, but I don't think so. Oh, I dunno. Anyway, why are you looking at me like that?'

'Like what, Gina?'

'I dunno. All kinda suspicious like. I mean, you wouldn't dare think that me dad had hurt me mum, would you?'

Mitchell scoffed because he knew that it wasn't a genuine question but a statement – and it sounded like a threat.

'What is it with you and me dad, Mitch? Anyone would think you hated him.'

'Hmmm, would they now? Well, then, they would be bloody right, Gina. Just because he is your father and' – he cleared his throat – 'my father-in-law, doesn't mean I have to like him, and we both know why, don't we?'

'For Christ's sake, are you ever gonna forgive him for being drunk that night? Mitch, he didn't realise he had drunk so much. It wasn't as if he'd done it deliberately.'

Mitchell glared and curled his lip. 'Your father held a fucking gun to my head and made me get in that van because he was too fucking pissed to drive himself. He was a bully, Gina, and nothing else. I served time – all because that stupid, stupid man got drunk.'

'Eh, come on, Mitch. That's my farver you're talking about.'

'Yeah, Gina, you're fucking right there. It's your father I *am* talking about and stop with "the big I am" act. Your father did have a reputation years ago, throwing his weight around, but he can't hurt me no more. I've served a lump of time over him and I learned a lot, including how to treat people. And let me tell you, respect is earned. You may be the daughter of a one-time dangerous hardman, but he's old now, Gina, fucking old. So, stop living in his shadow.'

Gina listened with her mouth open. Mitchell was so cold. He didn't shout or scream; he just stood there as cool as a cucumber and spouted his sermon.

'I dunno how you can talk to me this way, Mitch. I'm the muvver of your three boys, and I've just learned that me own muvver's dead.' The quiver in her voice was deliberate.

Mitchell rolled his eyes. 'Look, I'm sorry, and I *am* sorry for you losing your mum, but please don't expect me to be all over your dad, because I won't be. In fact, I think it's best that I'm not here when he comes by.'

Gina suddenly grabbed his arm. 'Mitch, don't do this. You're my husband, and he's my dad, and this is a time when we both need you.'

Mitchell narrowed his eyes and stared to see if Gina was being genuine or not. He could never really work her out or trust her. He decided to give in and took a seat at the table.

'Thank you, Mitch. Families need to pull together at a time like this.'

Mitchell looked up at his wife and wanted to tear into her again because she'd never considered his mother when he had to go to prison. Gina had more or less cast her out. However, he would keep quiet and do the honourable thing for his sons, more than anything else.

Gina left the room to get herself dressed.

Mitchell remained seated, drinking the dregs of his coffee, and was surprised to see Jordan standing in the doorway staring at him. Mitchell smiled. 'Hello, Son, come in and I'll fix you some breakfast. What do you normally have?'

Jordan looked his father over. 'I normally have cake,' he said, with a smirk.

Mitchell would have laughed at the cheek of the lad, but today he wasn't in the mood. 'Cereal it is, then,' he replied, as he pushed himself up off the chair.

'Nah, I said cake,' said Jordan, firmly standing his ground.

Mitchell turned around. 'Excuse me, Jordan, but I said you can have cereal. I may not have been around for a while, but I'm your father. I'm not the enemy.'

Before another word was said, Jordan heard the key turn in the lock and hurried to greet his grandfather; he knew it was him because only he had a key outside their immediate family.

Mitchell stepped into the hall to see Jordan jump up and hug the man.

'Grandad, Grandad, did you go to the police station? Did they arrest you?'

Mitchell then realised that Jordan had been earwigging, and so he was surprised that he wasn't in floods of tears like George had been. He assumed that Jordan perhaps hadn't fully understood the graveness of the situation.

Donald appeared tired and creased around the edges. He looked up after ruffling Jordan's hair. 'Hello, Mitch. Cor, terrible state of affairs. I bet you didn't expect to come home to this, did ya, mate?'

Mitchell inclined his head. 'Er, no, of course not.' He didn't really know what else to say.

'Is Gina in the kitchen or upstairs? I bet she's beside herself.'

Mitchell bit his bottom lip. 'Well, she's taking it very well, considering.'

'Considering what?' snapped Donald.

'Considering Sylvia was her mother.'

'Oh, yeah, sorry. It's been a very long night. Any beers in the fridge?'

Mitchell shrugged his shoulders. 'I wouldn't know.'

The icy air was sensed not only by Donald but by Jordan, who swiftly sidled up to his grandfather. 'I'll get you one, Grandad.'

'Good lad,' said Donald, as he patted his grandson's backside.

Following Jordan into the dining room that led into the kitchen, Donald walked over to the armchair that he always sat in and rubbed his hands in front of the fire.

Mitchell watched how Donald quite naturally made himself at home.

Jordan returned with a beer and a bottle of Pepsi for himself.

'Oi, you can't have Pepsi at this hour of the morning. It'll rot your teeth,' said Mitchell, as he attempted to take the bottle from his son.

'Aw, leave him, Mitch. A Pepsi in the morning won't make a lot of difference.'

Mitchell gritted his teeth when he saw his eldest son grin at him.

Sonny must have heard the front door bang. He came tearing down the stairs with his thick dark mane sticking up in all directions. His grandfather was like a magnet as Sonny flew at him and made himself at home on his lap.

Any other father would probably have felt a tad jealous, but Mitchell didn't. He was honest with himself – the little boys knew no different; however, the old man, who held the boys' attention, was to blame for him not having been part of their lives.

Mitchell heard heavy footsteps as Gina made her way down the stairs. The instant she was in the room, Donald jumped out of the armchair and put his arms out to hug her. 'Oh, my babe, she's gone. It was fucking awful to find her like that. They dragged me in for questioning, but they had nothing on me to say that I killed her.'

Mitchell narrowed his eyes. He found that sentence so odd.

'How did she die?'

For a moment, Donald let go of Gina and threw Mitchell a cold glare. 'She tripped over the rug and hit her head on the table.'

Mitchell watched as the old man turned his face away and pulled Gina and the two boys into a tight embrace. *Where was George?* he wondered, before he left the room and headed upstairs to the boys' bedroom.

He paused in the doorway and saw George slowly peel back the blanket and peek at him.

'Your grandfather's downstairs. Did you want to go down?'

George suddenly pulled the blanket back over his head.

Mitchell stepped inside, kneeled by the bed, and pulled the cover away from George's face. 'What's up, buddy?'

With his eyes wide and afraid, George silently shook his head.

'Come on, Son. It's time to get up. I think your mum and your grandad will want to talk to you all,' he said, trying to coax the youngster out of his bed.

George, however, appeared so worried that Mitchell had the urge to hug him. But, instead, he held out his hand. 'Come on, George. You can come with me.'

Hesitantly, George climbed out of the bunk bed, gripped his father's hand, and walked downstairs with him.

There was a pregnant pause as soon as Mitchell and George entered the room.

'There you are, George. Come and give your grandad a hug.'

When those words left Donald's mouth, George stood frozen to the spot – where he literally wet himself.

Jordan spotted what had happened first and rudely pointed. 'Pissy knickers George.' He laughed. 'George has wet himself. George has wet himself,' he sang, until his father told him to shut up.

Gina looked at the wet puddle on the rug and felt a wave of disgust. 'Why you dirty, dirty little boy. Why didn't you use the toilet? Now look at me new rug. Fucking ruined. Now, get back up the stairs and get cleaned up, you rotten little bastard.'

Mitchell was dumbfounded and concerned.

George let go of his father's hand and fled from the room.

Mitchell didn't stop him but glared at his wife. '*Seriously*, was that even *necessary?*'

But it wasn't Gina who answered. It was Donald.

'Come on, Mitch, the boys are strong-willed little lads, and Gina has to keep them in check, or they will run amok.'

Mitchell bit his lip again, but inside, he was on fire. 'I'll go and make sure George is okay. Has he ever done this before?'

Gina shook her head. 'No, but I ain't having it, Mitch, pissing all over the floor.'

Mitchell left the room and hurried to find his son, who was standing in the bathroom and shaking all over. Turning him around, he saw George's face almost grey and his eyes like saucers. 'What's the matter, Son? Tell me, are you sick?'

George shook his head.

'Get cleaned up and come back downstairs.'

Shaking his head again, George edged backwards towards the toilet.

'Hey, come on, George. What is it? You're trembling, Son.'

But George couldn't speak; he was absolutely terrified.

'I tell you what. You get changed and I'll take you to see my mum. How about that? I bet she even has ice cream.'

Mitchell clocked his son's shoulders relax, albeit only a fraction. 'Would you like that?'

George nodded.

'Okay.' Mitchell finally knew he was getting somewhere, and he also knew that to find answers he would have to get him away from this house. 'Right, shall I invite Jordan and Sonny?' he asked, trying to get to the bottom of his son's fear.

George shrugged his shoulders.

'What about Mummy?'

Again, George shrugged his shoulders.

'What about your grandad?'

That was it: the fear behind those eyes suddenly reared its head, and Mitchell knew then that for some reason George was terrified of his grandfather.

'I tell you what, George, how about just me and you go, and I can show you where I used to box, and, perhaps, we can get some chocolate on the way?'

George smiled and nodded.

Chapter Six

Diane was stunned to find her son and grandson at the door. 'Mitchell, is everything okay, love?'

Mitchell shook his head. 'No. Gina's mum had an accident yesterday. She tripped, apparently, and fell onto the table hitting her head.' He mouthed the words, 'She died.'

'Oh my gosh,' gasped Diane. 'Quick, come inside.' She peered down at George and gave her grandson a sympathetic smile. 'How about I get you something nice to eat, and a hot chocolate. It's still bitterly cold outside.'

Mitchell guided George into the living room while his mother hurried to the kitchen to fix up a hot drink.

'You are safe here, George,' said Mitchell, as he ushered his son to the sofa.

With watery eyes, George peered up and smiled.

'You can talk to me. I'm your dad. Okay?'

George nodded but he still looked wary.

'What are you scared of? Is it your grandfather?' asked Mitchell, careful to keep his tone gentle.

He suspected it was, because at the mention of his grandfather, the little boy recoiled, and his eyes grew wider.

Just as he thought he might get somewhere, Diane walked into the room with a big tray of hot drinks and goodies.

She placed them on the coffee table and sat in her chair. 'Ah, dear George, it must have been an awful shock, my little sweetheart.'

George cast his eyes down to the floor.

Diane looked over at Mitchell and mouthed the words, 'What's going on?'

'Er, I'm not sure yet, but can George stay with you for a while? I have things to take care of, and I think George would like it here,' he replied, as he looked at his son.

'Of course, he can stay here. Would you like that, lovey?'

George instantly nodded.

'I bet Gina is in a terrible state. You get back. I should think she'll have a hundred and one things going through her head right now.'

Mitchell drank the hot drink, while chewing over a very sickening thought. He had to be sure of his theory, so before he left, he kneeled down in front of his son and whispered, 'Did you see your grandfather do something terrible, George?'

George's head jolted as if he'd suffered an electric shock. He was pale with worry.

'It's okay. Listen, I know you don't know me very well, but, no matter, I love you, Son, and I'm going to protect you, and . . .' He looked at his mother. 'And Nanny Diane will too, won't you?'

Diane got up from her chair, sat beside her grandson, and placed her arm around his shoulders. She attempted to sound upbeat. 'It'll be nice spending time together. I've got games, and I'm a dab hand at cards.'

She guessed that Mitchell knew what George was worried about, and she also realised that this wasn't the time or place to ask questions. She'd leave that to her son.

Mitchell had to know what George had seen back at Sylvia's, before he left his mother's house. 'Your grandad hurt your nan, didn't he?' he said, slowly and gently.

Suddenly, George got up, flung his arms around his father's neck, and sobbed uncontrollably. His whole body shook as the heartbreaking cries left the back of his throat.

Mitchell held his son close until the sobs died down.

Diane grabbed a few tissues from the velvet-covered tissue box. 'There you go, George. Have a good blow,' she said, as she wiped her own tears away first. It was shocking to think that her grandson had witnessed something so terrible, and she was biting her lip to stop herself from asking the questions.

'George, I need to go back and talk to Mummy. You wait here with Nanny Diane, and I'll be back. Now, you have to be a very brave and big boy for me.'

George nodded, but his expression told Mitchell he was still afraid.

'It's okay. Your grandfather won't come anywhere near you. I am your dad, and I make the decisions.'

George nodded again.

'Good. Now, you may have to speak to a policeman. How do you feel about that?'

'No!' snapped George.

'It's okay, but why not?'

'I'm not a grass.'

Mitchell's expression turned pale; he was surprised that his son would even understand a term like that. But then he realised that while he was away, his sons were being dragged up not only by their mother but by Donald too.

After George had calmed down and was happily watching cartoons and drinking hot chocolate, Mitchell pulled his mother into the kitchen out of earshot. 'Mum, I think Donald murdered Sylvia. It was something he said when he came back from the police station. And that little lad in the living room wet himself this morning when he saw his grandad. I won't push him for the gory details. Let him get used to the idea that he is safe here.'

Diane used the tea towel to wipe her eyes. 'Oh, Mitchell, this is so awful. Do you really believe that Donald would hurt, I mean kill, his own wife?'

Mitchell nodded. 'Yeah, Mum, I do. He's a bully.'

'Okay, Son, well, you'd best be careful as well then, but don't you worry about George. I will make him feel at home.'

Mitchell kissed his mum's cheek and left the house to return to his own. The snow had now turned to grey slush, and his shoes were not the best footwear to have in these conditions. However, luckily, the buses were still running, and he managed to hop on to one. After a few stops, he was at the end of his road. He trudged along the pavement feeling the horrible squelch beneath his feet and took a few deep breaths to clear his head. He had an inkling that there was more to Sylvia's so-called accident than Donald was letting on. He knew his wife didn't have a clue, and he could bet all his stolen money that she would never believe it. She acted as if the sun shone out of her father's backside.

As soon as he approached his front door, he braced himself before marching in.

Donald was still seated in the armchair by the fireplace in the dining room. His head was at an angle, and his mouth was open, catching flies.

When Mitchell looked in the kitchen, all he could see at first was Gina's backside. She was bending over putting something in the oven.

He paused and listened for sounds of his children's whereabouts, but, upstairs, it was deathly quiet. He crept into the kitchen and waited until Gina closed the oven door before saying anything, just in case she jumped and burned herself, or him, for that matter.

As she closed the door and placed the tea towel on the side, she nearly jumped out of her skin when she saw her husband. 'Oh, for fuck's sake, what are you doing creeping about like that?'

Mitchell sighed. 'Where are both the boys?'

'Oh, they're with Frances, up the road. I told her what's happened, and she said she would have the kids for me.' She looked behind Mitchell. 'Where's George?'

Mitchell didn't answer her. Instead, he flicked his head, indicating that she should follow him into the living room. Out of curiosity, she did as he asked. Mitchell closed the door behind them and took a deep breath but paused because he didn't know how to broach the subject.

With her hands on her hips, Gina inclined her head. 'What's up, Mitch? Come on, spit it out.'

For a moment, Mitchell saw a very genuine expression on his wife's face. And for once, she wasn't drenched in make-up or even chewing gum.

'Gina, I've taken George to my mum's.'

She nodded. 'Yeah, I know, and?'

'He saw something, Gina. Something a little boy should never have seen.'

Gina instantly straightened up, and her face flushed red. 'Er, so what was he supposed to have seen? 'Cos that lad has a lively imagination, and when Garfield came over, it was only to fix the light in the bedroom – nothing more, I swear it.'

Mitchell stepped back and glared at his wife. He held her gaze and watched her cheeks turn an even deeper crimson. 'That's *not* what he witnessed.'

'Oh, right, so what's he talking about?'

Mitchell looked at the door. 'When I left the party to go to my mum's, where was George?'

Gina crinkled up her forehead. 'I dunno. He was playing with the other two, I suspect. Why?'

'Are you sure he wasn't with your mum?'

Gina tutted loudly. 'I can't play games here, Mitch. Why are you asking me all these questions?'

'Okay, well, I reckon your father killed your mother and George saw it.'

'What!' shrieked Gina, as she threw her hands to her mouth.

'Listen,' he said, as he grabbed both of her arms. 'Your dad was always arguing with your mum, and he said something really fucking odd.'

Gina shook herself free. '*What?* What did he say, then?'

'Well, when he came in, he said, if you remember, "They have nothing on me to say that I killed her."'

Gina looked at Mitchell as if he were nuts. 'And? So? Please don't tell me you would have my dad found guilty on a fucking statement like that. Oh, come on, Mitch. I know you dislike him, but really?'

He grabbed her arm again. 'George saw what happened, I am sure of that. He fucking pissed himself when he saw your dad. He's absolutely terrified of him.'

Gina waved her hand. 'Oh, for God's sake, you believe the dramatics of a nine-year-old? Seriously? Mitch, you've been away all these years, and you have no idea what George is all about. He's a big tart, full of drama. I bet he turns out to be gay.'

Mitchell ground his back teeth. 'And whose fault is that, eh? That I didn't see my kids?' He pointed to the wall. 'Oh, yeah, that fucking waster in there.'

Gina was livid; all she'd wanted was a lovely homecoming and her husband by her side treating her like her father had. However, it hadn't worked out that way. He'd come home and fucked off to his mother's and was now accusing her dear ol' dad of murdering her mother. As if losing her mother wasn't bad enough. 'Mitch, please.' She threw her hands in the air. 'Please would you just stop this. Go and get George and bring him home before he comes back spouting Duteromomomnomie or whatever the fuck it is.'

'No way, Gina! George is staying with my mum until I get to the fucking bottom of it, because if our little boy witnessed your father killing your mother, then . . .'

'Oh, shut up, you moron. Of course my dad never hurt my mum, and when I get my hands on George, he will feel my fucking boot up his arse, saying such terrible things like that. I swear to God, the kid ain't right in the head.'

Mitchell felt his stomach twist as he held back from strangling the life out of the woman. Every nerve in his body was alive and all because he had a sudden sense that his little boy would be bullied. Gina's words were sharp and indignant, and yet George was only a young lad. 'Well, right in the head or not, he is fucking terrified, and I wanna know why.'

Gina tried to stop him from confronting her father, but Mitchell pushed her aside with a mighty shove.

'Mitch, stop! What are you doing?' Her voice sounded almost hysterical.

By the time Mitchell walked into the dining room, Donald was awake and on his feet. 'What the hell's going on?' he asked, as he wiped the dribble from his cheek.

'My son is afraid of you. He bloody wet himself, and you, Donald Brennan, are gonna tell me why!'

Donald straightened up and looked at his daughter, who merely shrugged her shoulders.

'Mitch, what the hell is all this really about? I mean, we put on a do for your homecoming, and you've been like a bear with a sore head. So, spit it out. What's your problem?'

'Did you murder Sylvia?'

Donald glared. 'You *what*? Don't be so fucking soft. Of course, I never. And how could you accuse me? She was my wife. I loved that woman, you saucy bastard.'

'Well, George seems to think you did.'

Donald, looking the worse for wear, put on a fake laugh. 'That lad lives in fairyland.' He shook his head. 'Aw, for Gawd's sake, Mitch, you don't believe him, do you? I mean, he wasn't even there—'

'When you killed her, you mean. That's right, ain't it?'

'Don't be stupid. He wasn't there when I found her!' He lowered his tone. 'Look, he's only just outta nappies. He has a wild imagination. How could he have seen anything when he was here and I wasn't? He's saying it for attention. Probably the middle child syndrome.'

Mitchell shook his head. 'I was hoping you would be honest with me, but it looks like you ain't.'

Seeing Mitchell turn to leave, Donald called out, 'Oi, where are you going? What are you gonna do, Mitch?'

Mitchell stopped in his tracks and turned to face the anxious-looking Donald. 'Why are you so concerned, Donald? If you never killed her, then you've nothing to worry about, eh?'

Gina grabbed Mitchell's arm. 'Don't tell me you are calling the police, are ya?'

He shook her off. 'I'm going to talk to my son. No one' – he looked piercingly at Donald – 'I mean no one, frightens my boy, not the way you have. 'Cos if he's lying about seeing you hurt his grandmother, then why is he so afraid of you, enough for him to piss himself?'

Donald sighed and ran his hands through his hair. 'I dunno. All I know is he's a bit of a girl at times.'

Mitchell sensed Donald was worried; in fact, he almost seemed defeated.

'Please, Mitch, just bring George back here, and we can sort all this out as a family.'

Mitchell looked at Gina right between the eyes. 'As if we've ever really been a family.'

He slammed the door shut before either Gina or her father could answer.

Chapter Seven

By nine o'clock that evening, the police knocked at Diane's door.

Mitchell smiled at his son. 'It will be okay, I promise. I am going to be right here with you.'

Diane escorted Detective Marshall and Detective Winter into the living room, where she offered them each a seat and a cup of tea.

Marshall gave her a generous smile as he accepted the offer. He was a big man with a full ruddy face and a rough straggly beard and a stocky build, unlike Winter, who was as thin as a rake with a thick mop of jet-black hair. He was much younger than his colleague and was dressed in a suit that was a lot smarter.

Winter was very particular when he was offered a drink. 'No milk, one sugar, please,' he said, with a cheeky wink.

Mitchell assumed the older detective would be the one who would do most of the talking, but, surprisingly, it was Winter who dived right in.

'So, George, my name is Steven Winter. Now you are not in any trouble at all. In fact, George, I think you are going to help us a lot. Is that okay?'

George looked up at his father for assurance, then back at the detective, and finally nodded.

'So, George, would you like to tell me about your day yesterday?' Winter said, with a beaming smile.

Marshall glanced at Mitchell Swan, who was sitting next to his son, clearly a devoted father. Yet, he knew Mitchell; he remembered the questioning in the station over the heist. He was cold and unflinching back then. He wondered if the time Mitchell had served inside had in any way changed the man. The fact was that right now, Mitchell wasn't a suspect, and neither was Donald Brennan, although he would love to see that man behind bars. He'd tried to nick him for a dozen crimes in the past, but Donald always seemed to have an alibi. He was eager to hear what this little lad had to say.

George was obviously baffled as to where to begin, so Winter prompted him. 'So you were at home with your mum and your brothers, then. Is that right?'

George nodded. 'I was watching the telly in the living room and Mum was making food for me dad's party.'

'And where was your grandfather?'

'He was helping me mum, I think. Then my Nanny Sylvia and my grandad had an argument, and my nan left the house and took me to the café in Orpington, and then—'

Marshall was scribbling notes, and he held his hand up for the youngster to stop. 'Er, do you know the name of the café, George?'

George looked at the ceiling and then nodded. 'The Silver Lounge. We had hot chocolate and burgers.'

Winter leaned forward on his chair. 'George, do you know what time that was?'

'No, but it was after me dad left the house and after Nan argued with Grandad.'

Diane came into the room with a tray and placed it on the coffee table. She was quiet, not wanting to interrupt, but she took the red cup and handed it to Marshall and indicated that the blue cup was for Winter.

'George, do you remember if anyone spoke to you at The Silver Lounge and would possibly remember you there?'

George nodded. 'The lady that gave us the burgers and the hot chocolate, she spoke to Nan, and she said I looked like me dad.'

Winter and Marshall looked at each other with a smile.

'After the hot chocolate and the burger, where did you go, George?'

George's face turned white, and he pushed himself further back into the sofa. Right away, both detectives could see the boy was getting anxious, perhaps reliving something.

'It's okay, it's only us. You're safe here,' said Marshall, in a soft tone.

George looked at all the eyes in the room, before he said, 'I went back to Nan's house with Nan, but when she heard Grandad coming in, she told me to hide in the kitchen. I did, and then . . . And then . . .' He stopped, suddenly covering his eyes and pulling his knees up under his chin.

Winter, however, wanted to know more. He had to know more. 'George, did you see your grandfather push your grandmother?'

George was breathing fast, but he managed to nod before Mitchell grabbed him, pulled him onto his lap, and held him tight. George looked at the two detectives and nodded.

'Okay, George, you have been so helpful. Thank you very, very much.'

George still had his face covered and was silent, but they could all see him trembling.

Once the two detectives finished their tea, they thanked Diane. Marshall turned to Mitchell. 'We'll follow this up, and if it's okay, we'll come back.' He glanced at George who was obviously traumatised. 'And, hopefully, have another little chat with your son, when he feels ready. Thanks again.'

Mitchell smiled. 'Yes, of course, detective.'

After the detectives left, Diane put the phone receiver back on the hook. The phone had been ringing all the time Mitchell was there, and, in the end, she'd just removed it.

'How about I cook us up some nice egg and chips, and I do believe I may have a few hot dogs. What do you say, George?'

George removed his hands from his face and tried to smile, but the tears were trickling down his cheeks.

'That's settled, then. Hot dogs and chips.'

Mitchell smiled. He remembered his mum being so sweet to him when he was hurting. She'd always loved to feed him, and, really, if he didn't have such a fast metabolism, he would probably have ended up weighing twenty-five stone.

They'd hardly finished their meal when they heard a loud, aggressive bang at the front door.

Diane began to get up, but Mitchell stopped her. 'I'll go.'

Looking at the fear on her grandson's face, Diane tried to take his mind off his problems. 'I think we should make some fairy cakes. What d'ya say, George?'

But George was far too anxious to hear who was at the door to pay any attention to his grandmother.

He didn't have to wait long.

'What the hell is going on, Mitch? I've had to get a cab over here. Your muvver has taken the phone off the hook. Me dad's in a right two and eight, and I wanna know what the bloody hell you are doing here. You and my little boy should be at our house. I've just lost me mum, Mitch. Don't you have any compassion?'

Diane stayed put and hoped that Mitchell would send Gina back home. But it was apparent that Mitchell didn't have a chance to do anything.

Within a few seconds, Gina had barged past him and made her way into the dining room. 'There you are! Get ya shoes on, George. You're coming home with me, right this minute. All this bleedin' nonsense about your grandfarver.'

George paled yet again, but, this time, Diane stepped in. 'Sorry about your mother, Gina. It must have been a terrible shock. Why don't you leave George with me, so he's not under your feet?'

'What!' she shrieked, as she glanced at Diane. 'No, I won't leave him with you, and, Diane, I don't think it's right that you are encouraging them to stay. Mitch is my husband, and George is my son. They should both be at home, especially since I'm now grieving, in case you haven't bleedin' noticed. Christ, Diane, didn't you teach your son any respect?'

'Oi, now, that's enough, Gina! Why don't you sit down calmly. I can explain what's going on.'

Gina was not in the mood for her husband to be so bloody judicious. She pulled her oversized fur coat from her shoulders and dropped her bag on the floor before pulling a chair out and sitting down.

Diane looked at her daughter-in-law and felt guilty for her own thoughts. She'd noticed the beads of sweat around the girl's hairline and her top lip and the thick coating of foundation along with the layer upon layer of mascara. She hardly looked the picture of a grieving daughter. And if she was being honest with herself, she disliked the girl immensely. All the while Mitchell was in prison, she'd tried to be a part of her grandsons' lives, but it was always met with a snub or impatience, until Gina had practically said 'Don't call me, I'll call you.' She knew what was really going on, and although it was none of her business, she felt Mitchell had the right to know. She had planned to tell him of his wife's suspected infidelities when the time was right.

'George, do you want to go upstairs? In my old room, there are a few of my old toys still there,' said Mitchell, encouragingly.

George leaped from his chair and ran from the room; he hadn't even acknowledged his mother.

'So, what the hell's going on?'

'The police have—'

'You *what*? You've called the filth, have ya?' she spat, as she glared at Mitchell and then at his mother. 'Seriously?'

Diane felt very nervous about Gina because she spoke with such venom.

'Gina, George saw your father do something bad, and just so you know, he *was* with your mum. She took him to The Silver Lounge where they had food, and then she took him home, so George witnessed exactly what happened. He saw how your mother died.'

'So come on then, Mitch, how *did* my muvver die?' Gina asked. She almost choked on her words and a genuine tear filled her eye.

'Gina, I know it's difficult because I know how much you love your dad, but George saw him, love. He ain't lying. Your dad hurt your mum. George went back to your mum's house with her, and she told him to hide in the kitchen before your dad came in.'

Gina allowed a tear to plummet down her cheeks. 'I don't believe him, Mitch. I know me own dad, and he wouldn't have done that. But George does tell lies.'

Mitchell gave her a sympathetic smile. 'I know it's hard to take in, but it's true.'

His almost even-handed tone irritated Gina and made her jump up from her chair. 'Oh, shut up. This is fucking ridiculous.' She shot a spiteful look at Diane. 'And don't you go all high and fucking mighty on me, rolling your eyes 'cos I swore.'

'Gina, if what we're saying is right, then the police will know soon enough. They're probably on their way now to The Silver Lounge, and if neither your mum nor George was there, then . . . well, I'll hold my hands up and apologise. To you and to your dad,' said Mitchell.

The realisation hit Gina like a ton of bricks. If George had gone to the café with her mother, then obviously Mitchell would believe George. All she could do was huff. 'Very well. Now then, call him down. I'm taking him home.'

Mitchell instantly jumped up. 'No, he can stay here. I don't want him upset.'

Gina glared at Diane and then back at Mitchell. 'And you think he is better off here than with his own muvver, do ya?'

'Oh no, it's not like that—'

'Oh, shut the fuck up. No one's asking you!' snapped Gina, before she shot another evil glare at her husband. 'Mitch, call George down. I'm taking him home. I don't want my son around a selfish, uncompassionate grass and a Bible-bashing idiot.'

'Gina, I think you'd better leave. There's no need to talk to my mum like that. She has done you no harm. She's only trying to help.'

'Fucking sticking her beak in, you mean.' Mumbling under her breath, she began to collect her belongings to leave.

'Gina, love, please don't go off like this. I can see you're very upset. Why don't you have a cup of tea and wait for a taxi. It's freezing out there, and you and Mitchell have a lot to talk about.'

Diane's sheer calm composure and reasonability had Gina now raging. As she left the room, she said over her shoulder, 'Stick ya tea up your fucking arse. And as for you, Mitchell Swan, I thought you were more man than that, listening to a nine-year-old and calling the filth. I thought spending time inside, you would have known that you just don't grass.'

As Gina stormed to the front door and stepped outside, she was followed by Diane and Mitchell. Something in what his wife had just said had raised Mitchell's usually controlled temper to a point where he wanted to hit Gina, but, instead, he bit his lip and breathed in deeply through his nostrils.

'Go home, Gina, before I forget I *am* a man.'

Looking him up and down, Gina laughed. 'I thought you were made of better stuff, Mitch. I guess I was wrong. You're nuffin but a weasel, a copper's rent boy, you stinking grass. Just you wait till my—'

Before she'd even had the chance to finish, Diane came from behind Mitchell, and, totally out of character, she pushed Gina away from the doorstep. 'Go home, Gina!' she yelled, before slamming the door shut.

Mitchell was gobsmacked. He'd never witnessed his mother losing her temper. 'Sorry, Mum. This trouble should never have come to your door.'

White-faced, Diane shook her head. 'No, Son, it's not just my door, it's yours too. Now, then, let's talk about what's to be done next.'

Before they left the hallway, Gina banged and kicked the front door.

Mitchell had had enough. He flung the door open and glared. 'Go home, Gina. There's nothing more to say except this: your father, your fucking precious dad, *is* an informant, mark my words. And if you really wanna go there, then carry on pushing your luck, and you'll get more than you bargained for. So shut your mouth about me. I wanna know why my little boy is terrified of your ol' man. And know this: a real man or woman would do whatever it takes to protect their kid. Now turn around and fuck off home.'

Gina's bag slid off her shoulder, and she stood there defeated. He was right: she should be protecting her son. And she knew in her heart that if it had been Jordan or Sonny, then she would have been concerned and backed them to the hilt. However, it was George, the child that

127

she'd never been able to bond with. The middle son, who was the complete opposite of her other two. She should have felt guilty over her lack of love for George, but she hadn't and knew she never would. She wasn't cruel insomuch that he never went without. He had food in his belly and clothes on his back. But there was something very different about George: they were just not on the same wavelength. She could laugh with Jordan; he was cheeky and funny, and she admired him. Sonny was a mini Jordan, her baby, who for all his cute smiles and brazen ways, she could forgive him anything. They were like her own father, but George was different. He was the fair child, the aloof one, always quiet and deep in thought, much like Mitchell. Perhaps she would have turned against her father and questioned him over her mother's death if indeed it had been Jordan or Sonny pointing the finger. But she wouldn't defend George over her father, and now she'd made it crystal clear to her husband, she wasn't going to go back on it now.

Chapter Eight

Eden sat on the end of her bed looking down at her bony knees just visible below her cotton dress. At least the room was warm; her mother had crept in and closed the window before hurrying downstairs again. The Bible remained on her lap. She was almost eleven and found the words so hard to understand. Bible lessons were supposed to make it easier, but the words still whirled around, jumbling into one another.

'Eden, come down now. Your tea is ready!' hollered her father, from downstairs.

She could sense the irateness through his tone. He was always angry and showed it in the way he spat his words out through gritted teeth.

She didn't want to make him angry again, so she hurriedly hopped off her bed. But she'd forgotten about the Bible nestled on her lap. The bang as it hit the wooden floor made her gasp and shake all over. The Bible's spine had torn away from the front cover. If her father saw that she had damaged the Holy Book, she would be in so much trouble. Quickly, she picked it up and slid it under her pillow, before hurrying downstairs.

They lived in a modest three-bedroom semi-detached house, with minimal furniture. The kitchen was old-fashioned but very clean. The living room merely had a green fabric three-piece suite, a Formica coffee table, and a bookshelf. There was no television or stereo system.

She hurried into the dining room that was just as sparse with only a table, six chairs, and a wall cabinet. Smiling as sweetly as she could, she took her seat at the table against the window. Her father sat to her right and her mother to her left. They said grace before her mother silently passed her father the bowl of mashed potato.

Claire, her mother, was a delicate-looking woman with soft dainty features. She sat up dead straight, almost like the chair itself. To Eden, her mother was beautiful with her golden hair pulled back into a neat ponytail and her eyes the colour of forget-me-nots. She'd never seen her mother wearing make-up or fashionable clothes – just plain dresses and flat shoes. However, it was their way. Like her mother, she would dress the same because she wanted to be part of The New World Order, come the day of Armageddon.

'What was that bang?' asked Gabriel, her father.

Keeping her head tilted down, Eden peered through her eyelashes, too afraid to tell a lie for fear of the balls of fire and being excluded from God's Earthly Paradise and yet equally anxious of what her father may do.

'Well, speak up, Eden.'

'I . . . er, I mean, I, er . . . I got up from the bed when you called me for tea, and the Bible fell onto the floor.'

Gabriel slammed his cutlery down by his plate. 'You would never have dropped the Bible if it was in your hands – as it should have been!'

Eden felt her throat tighten. *If he was this angry over her dropping the book, what would he do if he discovered she had damaged it?* she thought.

'Go to your room now and fetch your Bible. I want to see it.'

'Aw, Gabe, leave it, darling. It's teatime. Let's just eat our meal.'

'Be quiet, woman!' he yelled.

Eden stared at her father for a moment. With his dark brown eyes, framed by neatly trimmed brows, his hair so precisely cut, and his shirt so perfectly pressed, she wondered if there was anything regarding his appearance that was imperfect.

He was an elder, a well-respected member of the Kingdom Hall. He'd thrust this position down her throat so many times that she would never forget it. She couldn't ever be seen to do anything wrong because it would reflect poorly on him. The thought of the consequences if she did was sometimes worse than the idea of living in hell for all eternity.

Getting up from her chair, she felt her body go hot. It wasn't a new feeling; she'd often felt it when she was about to receive a punishment.

'Hurry along, child. I don't have all day.'

The tears welled up, but she knew if she cried, he would get more irritated. By the time she reached her bedroom, she'd heard fists banging on the table and two voices arguing below. She knew her mother was defending her but wished she wouldn't do that. If her mother got a backlash because of it, then she would add guilt to her feelings of despair.

After removing the Bible from under her pillow, she gazed, hoping that she'd been wrong and the book was intact, but it was worse than she'd imagined. Holding it tightly as if by some miracle it could be glued back together, she hurried down the stairs, hoping to stop the argument taking place between her parents.

Standing a foot away from her father, she held out the Bible.

At first glance, he didn't notice the damage, but not satisfied, he snatched it from her hand and inspected it. It was so apparent to anyone: the cover was ruined.

Eden heard the gasp from her mother and knew then that defacement of the Bible was bad – very bad.

'Aw, come on, Gabe. It was obviously an accident,' her mother pleaded.

'Shut up, woman. Eden has destroyed the Bible, and you cannot get more disrespectful to Jehovah than that! And you can think yourself lucky that you're with child or you would be reprimanded for trying to stick up for the little devil.'

'Please, Gabe, she's a little girl. She wouldn't deliberately destroy the Bible.'

Eden saw the panic on her mother's face and wondered what could be so bad that her mother looked so alarmed.

'Leave the room, Claire, this instant!'

'No, Gabe, I won't leave the room!' she yelled, as she tried to get in between her husband and daughter.

From nowhere, Gabriel's hand sharply slapped Claire's face, hard enough to propel her backwards. As she hit the table, she tumbled awkwardly to the floor, but the sound of the crash made him furious.

'I warned you, Claire. Don't ever interrupt me when I am teaching this child to be a good person. You want her to have a place in God's Paradise, don't you?' he spat.

Claire pulled her hands to her mouth, her eyes wide, as she nodded in submission.

Eden looked at her mother and then at the cruel eyes of her father. 'It was an accident, Father. I promise. I didn't mean it. I—'

A sharp slap to her right cheek shut her up instantly.

'You keep quiet and hold out your hands.'

Assuming he was going to smack her, she did as he asked but held them out, palms facing up.

'Turn them over and clench your fists.'

Eden frowned but didn't question it.

'Now, you keep them there. I will show you that you'll not deface the Good Book again.' With that, he snatched the Bible, gripping it with both hands, and lifted it above his head. With an almighty force, he bashed Eden's knuckle, almost taking the skin down to the bone.

The pain shot up her hand and along her arm. She felt her insides prick with the stabbing of a thousand needles. Automatically, she screamed.

'Shut up and hold that hand still,' he bellowed.

'No!' yelled Claire, as she tried to intervene. But she wasn't quick enough.

He thwacked Eden's other knuckle, but this time, he'd held her wrist himself. The result was horrific. The skin peeled away, and the back of her hand instantly turned blue.

Eden didn't scream this time. She just hopped about clutching her hands, trying to take in deep breaths.

Claire grabbed her daughter, scooped her up, and ran upstairs to the bathroom. Placing the child on the toilet seat, she tried to unclasp Eden's hands so that she could see the damage that Gabriel had inflicted. She gasped and stared at the mess. 'Oh, my darling.'

Eden leaned back against the cistern, the blood draining from her face, and for a moment, she lost consciousness.

Claire carried her daughter's thin limp body to the bedroom and laid her on the bed, before hurrying to fill a bowl of warm water and then fetch some clean cloths to wipe the blood away.

As she passed Gabriel in the dining room, she sneered his way. 'Eden is unconscious. I will have to take her to the hospital. She needs stitches.' She was firmer in her tone than she'd ever been before and expected a backlash from him.

However, for some reason, he didn't scream at her. He merely replied in a cold voice, 'No, she won't. Just clean her up. There are bandages in the box under the sink and Dettol too.'

Finding some unopened cloths and the bandages, and filling a clean bowl with warm water, Claire hurried back upstairs. Her mind was in turmoil. Of course, she believed God had his reasons for everything, but when God tests the love you have for your husband, then doubt momentarily weaves its way in.

Eden was now conscious and whimpering when Claire kneeled beside her bed. She peered at the left hand; it was bruised and the skin was grazed. Then she gently took Eden's right hand and wanted to throw up. The blue bruise had spread and covered her daughter's entire hand. The deep gash had blood all over the sheet and was clotting. Knowing that Gabriel would never let her take Eden to the hospital, she had to patch this up soon or else the wound may never heal, and Eden could suffer from a nasty infection. Gently, she dabbed the warm water over the wound.

Claire felt a lump in her throat when she saw her daughter turn to face the wall and a tear trickle onto the pillow. Eden didn't even wince. The pain she'd suffered must have been so immense that having Dettol dabbed over her wounds was nothing in comparison.

'I am so sorry, my little garden of Eden.'

Turning her head to face her mother – her eyes filled with tears – she whispered, 'Can I go to God's kingdom now? Will he let me in?'

All Claire could do was nod and stroke her little girl's thin fair hair and wipe the beads of sweat away from her forehead. She couldn't speak. How could she ever say anything that would make this situation any better?

Chapter Nine

It was mid-morning and Mitchell was sitting at the dining room table playing Trump cards with George. The last two days had been a matter of keeping George occupied to stop him from having a complete meltdown. It was enough to tell him that whatever his son had witnessed was horrific; no doubt in the future, he would need psychotherapy treatment. Yet George couldn't say precisely what he'd witnessed because he would shake and go very white. Hence, Mitchell had stopped asking and instead he had tried to make George feel as safe and comfortable as he could possibly be. He was surprised that George hadn't asked for his mum, because, in reality, he knew George saw him more or less as a stranger, but they had bonded, nevertheless.

The doorbell rang, and Diane called out, 'I'll get it. You two stay where you are.' She wiped her wet hands on the tea towel and hurried along the hallway. She could see two shadows through the mottled glass, and slowly, she opened the door. Right away, she recognised Detective Winter and stepped aside.

'Hello, come in, come in,' she said, as soon as she saw the rain pelting down. 'That will do us good. Hopefully, it will wash that grey slush away.'

Winter wiped his feet, glanced over his shoulder, and looked back at Mrs Swan. 'Yes, so gloomy out there.'

Detective Marshall followed his colleague inside. 'Good morning,' he said, as he removed his tweed trilby.

Diane blushed and gestured that they should go into the living room. 'Would you like a hot drink?' she asked, with a warm, beaming smile on her face.

Marshall nodded. 'Yes, please. Anything going would be good, with two sugars.'

Diane glanced at Winter. 'The same as before, detective?'

Winter was surprised by her memory. 'That would be great, Mrs Swan.'

Mitchell heard his mother and the detectives and told George to remain at the table while he slipped through the adjoining door to greet the two men.

'So, we have an update,' said Winter, as he sat down, on the sofa, hoping that Mitchell would do likewise.

Marshall unbuttoned his coat and sat down, and then Mitchell took his seat in the armchair opposite.

'We followed up on your son's story—'

'Story?' interrupted Mitchell.

'Well, we can't call it a statement as such. It was nothing formal, and, of course, we have to take into account the boy's age, but, anyway, we followed everything up. The waitress at The Silver Lounge remembered serving Mrs Brennan and George at 2.30 p.m. and recalls them both leaving together. We saw George with his grandmother on nearby CCTV. So the waitress's statement confirmed that your son was with his grandmother at least an hour before her death. A neighbour of Mr and Mrs Brennan's wrote a statement to confirm that Mr Brennan was at the house at 3.30 p.m. the same afternoon.' He paused and gauged Mitchell's expression.

'You don't look surprised, Mr Swan.'

'Why would I be? That little boy in there' – he pointed to next door – 'is seriously troubled. He wet himself as soon as he laid eyes on his grandfather. Now, that isn't a kid being dramatic. He won't speak about what actually happened, not in detail. He still clams up.' He paused and raised his eyebrow. 'Tell me, detective, how did she die? I mean what were her actual injuries?'

Winter looked at his colleague and back at Mitchell and sighed. 'I shouldn't be divulging this, but she died through a brain haemorrhage. Her eye was pushed to the back of her head with such extreme force that it fractured her skull. So, initially, Mr Brennan's account for what he found would actually fit the injuries.' He paused and bit his bottom lip just at the point when Diane entered with a tray of hot drinks and biscuits.

She laid the tray on the coffee table and pointed to the blue cup. That's your one, Detective Winter, and that one' – she pointed to the other extra-large mug – 'is yours, Detective Marshall.'

They both thanked her before she left the room to keep George company.

'You were going to say?' prompted Mitchell.

'Hmm, well, the thing is, the coroner found bruising at the back of her head as if her hair had been pulled out. And a tuft of hair was missing. Anyway, Mr Swan, we just want you to know that Mr Brennan has been brought back to the station for questioning. We are waiting on a full coroner's report before we charge him.'

'So, I take it, then, that my son will be needed again at some point?'

Winter shook his head. 'No. It won't be necessary. He is very young, that's a fact, but the information he gave us was useful to the extent that we will be treating this as a murder inquiry. So, all we need to complete the formalities is a statement from you, regarding who was at the house when you came home, and anything you can remember before you left.'

Mitchell tilted his head to the side. 'You have more evidence, don't you?'

Winter bit his lip again. 'Yes, we do. A man came forward and gave a statement regarding a fight at the house after you had left and before Mrs Brennan had left. So, we have a motive at least.'

'Can I ask, Detective, why you are telling me this? I would have thought that you wouldn't inform a family member of anything unless they're called as a witness.'

Winter smirked. ''Cos, Mr Swan, I think considering the past and you serving time, you would like to hear that the man will get his comeuppance. After all, he grassed you up.'

'So, it's true, then.'

Winter nodded. 'I don't believe I'm telling you anything new, am I, Mr Swan?'

Mitchell sighed. 'He wasn't in court to give evidence against me, so I could never prove it. But of course, I knew it was him.'

'You're not planning on revenge are you, Mr Swan?'

'No way. I'm home now and I've three boys to take care of.'

'You didn't hear it from me. Anyway, we have wanted that man behind bars for a long time. I'm all for anyone trying their luck, but that man has done some nasty things to innocent people. People who are not just in his circle but innocent bystanders, if you get my drift.'

Mitchell nodded. He was bowled over by the detective's candidness. He obviously wasn't the skinny nerdy jobsworth he initially looked like. This copper was a no messing, straight-up kind of man, who didn't suffer fools gladly.

Mitchell toyed with the idea of asking who the person was who had given a statement against Donald. In the end, he decided that perhaps it wasn't worth it.

* * *

Five minutes after the detectives had left, there was a loud banging sound at the door. Diane stayed with George while Mitchell answered it. It was obvious it was Gina, by the way she was venting her anger with the door knocker.

Mitchell glared at his wife. 'Really, Gina, do you have to practically smash the door down?'

Dismissing him, she barged her way into the hallway. 'Mitch, what the hell's going on? Me dad's down the cop shop. You're here with my son. And I'm at home on me own, with me muvver not even fucking cold.'

'Keep your voice down, will you! George is in the dining room. He doesn't need the drama.'

'Drama, fucking *drama*, Mitch? You and George have turned this into a fucking drama. My dear ol' mum tripped and hit her head, and that was that, which was bloody bad enough, but now . . .'

She stopped and forced a snivel. 'Now you have practically moved into your muvver's, and George is making up all kinds of stupid stories!'

Before Mitchell could calm her down, she spun around. 'Where's ya muvver?' she bellowed.

Just as she was about to go charging through the house, Diane appeared in the hallway. 'I'm here, Gina.'

Gina's hazel eyes snapped with fury as she looked Diane up and down. 'I suppose this is all your doing, eh? You've got your son back in your holier-than-thou clutches, and for a bonus, you've got me boy as well. I bet it was you putting

144

that fucking nonsense into his head. You're brainwashing him, like all you Bible-bashers do.'

Grabbing Gina by her shoulders, Mitchell looked her in the eyes. 'Now, you listen to me, and you listen good, right?'

Gina was breathing hard and fast in a temper.

'My mum had nothing to do with all this. I brought George here because he was terrified, and, yes, Gina, I mean terrified of your father. So, until we get to the bottom of this, I want George to stay here. And for your information, Gina, your father isn't down the nick because of anything George said. He is down there because someone else grassed him up for the fucking bully he is.'

Gina's eyes searched her husband's face for any sign of compassion, but it was blank. 'He may be a lot of things, but a murderer he ain't. So now are you coming home so we can be a family, who, like other normal families, should be supporting each other at a time like this?'

Mitchell couldn't argue with his wife's loyalty to her father. To be fair to her, Gina would naturally be livid that anyone would dare accuse him of murder. She worshipped the bastard.

So he lowered his voice to take the sting out of what he was about to say. 'Gina, it's hard for you to think that your father may have committed such a terrible crime, but the police wouldn't be questioning him if your mother's death was an accident.'

'Gina, love, why don't you stay and have a hot drink? Perhaps we can talk this through,' said Diane.

'You *what*? Keep your fucking nose out. This conversation is between me and my husband.'

'Gina, you are in my mum's house.'

'Well, I wouldn't be if you were at home with your wife and children, like you're supposed to be. To think, Mitchell Swan, I waited all those years for you, and now you're out, you go running back to mummy.'

Diane left the hallway and returned to the dining room to find George at the table with his hands over his ears.

'I don't owe you anything, Gina,' Mitchell said, now angry to see his mother so upset. 'Your father put me behind bars to save himself, so if you want to be angry, be angry at him for it all.'

'It wasn't like that, Mitch, and you fucking know it.'

Mitchell's patience was wearing very thin now and the back of his neck was getting hot. But he'd learned to control his temper in the gym. 'Your father held a gun to my head, and when the robbery went fucking bandy, and he was questioned, he grassed on us all. That's the truth of it.'

'That's *not* what happened, Mitch.'

'Oh no, Gina? Well, let me tell you something. The police never had a print from me before this because I was never in any trouble with the law. So the only connection to that robbery was your father, and he was the only one who didn't do time. I know your father grassed on me, and I bet, deep down, you know it too.'

Suddenly, Gina dropped her bag and gave Mitchell a hard slap around the face. 'You bastard, you're doing this deliberately to have my dad locked up out of revenge. Was it you, then, who killed me muvver to set me dad up for her murder?'

'What! Don't be bloody ridiculous.'

Gina stood with her hands on her hips and raised her brow. 'Well, you disappeared all afternoon and evening, so where the fuck were you?'

Insulted and not in the mood to argue over a stupid theory, Mitchell grabbed Gina's arm. 'Go home and take your idiotic notions with you.'

She shook him off. 'Mitch, I warn you now, if you aren't home by the end of this morning, then it's over between us. Me and my kids will have nuffin to do with you. I will make sure of that.'

Pushing him away from her, she reached down, scooped up her bag, and pulled the front door open. 'And one more thing, Mitchell Swan. If you go against me and my family, you'll be sorry.'

With a smirk and a shake of his head, Mitchell slammed the door in her face.

She banged on the door. 'I mean it, Mitch!'

As soon as he turned around to head back to the dining room, he stopped dead in his tracks to find George standing there.

'Dad, can we stay with Grandma Diane, please?'

Sensing his son was pleading, Mitchell nodded.

***

Kirsten Tibble, Gina's long-time friend, tried to stop Jordan and Sonny from making a mess of her new carpet. She was about to give them their last warning, when, to her horror, Jordan stared her straight in the eyes and dropped his cup of chocolate milkshake. The contents covered a large area of her new deep, thick cream pile that was less than a week old. *That's it*, she thought. She'd had quite enough. She'd tried to be tolerant – to be forgiving to the kids – not least because she assumed they were grieving over the death of their grandmother.

'Jordan, you fucking sod!' she screamed, just as Gina was walking up the garden path.

With that, Sonny copied his brother, by pouring his drink over the carpet. 'Why, you fucking horrible little boy,' yelled Kirsten, just before the knock at the door. 'Wait there and do not bloody move.'

No sooner had she opened the door than Gina came marching in. 'Oh, is that right then, Kirsten? I could hear you as far as the *front gate*! My kids are fucking horrible, are they?' Storming into the living room to make sure her children were okay, she was entirely oblivious of the mess they had made.

'Gina, they have just thrown chocolate milkshake all over me new carpet. Look!'

Gina was a big woman, but Kirsten was even bigger, and louder. The whole street was wary of her. She wasn't quiet; even the pavement thundered when she walked along it. However, Gina wasn't bothered by Kirsten's size or reputation. She was so livid with Mitchell right now that all she could think to do was to get her kids home and sit down with a massive tub of ice cream for comfort.

'Come on, boys. You ain't staying where you ain't wanted.'

Unlike Gina, Kirsten wasn't caked in make-up. She was plain-looking, with red hair pulled away from her face in a ponytail. She wore baggy trousers and a loose top and was probably a size twenty-four on a good day.

'Now hold up a fucking minute, Gina. You ain't going to walk out of here and leave that mess your boys have left. I saved up a whole year for a new carpet.' She shoved Gina in the back. 'Go and see what they've done, will ya?'

Gina stepped back into the living room and could now see the mess. 'Kirst, I've had a fucking terrible day. Mitch is at his muvver's with George. As you know, I've told you me ol' man's down the cop shop, and, Kirsten, me dear ol' mum is fucking dead. You don't honestly think that right now I am worried about your carpet, do you?'

Kirsten stepped forward. 'Unless you wanna add a trip to the fucking hospital to your list of woes, I suggest you clean that up and teach your little bastards some respect. And, Gina, I'll be honest with you. Right now, I ain't surprised that Mitch is staying away. And another thing: we all know your ol' man battered your dear ol' mum, Gawd rest her. So, you wanna wake up, girl, and smell the coffee.'

Gina stood with her mouth open. She'd never expected her mate to turn on her like that over a stained carpet. But the angry look on Kirsten's face told her that she'd better try to get the stain out. Instantly, her temper was raised. She shot a look at her two boys, who were giggling as if this was all a game. She bit her lip to stop herself from screaming at them and then turned away before she slapped them both.

But Kirsten wasn't finished and huffed loudly. 'Christ, if they were my boys, they would get such a bloody hiding. You mark my words, Gina. If you don't pull them into line now, you'll have two unruly men on your hands.'

Gina stared at her friend and then looked at the grinning faces of her kids. She was about to retaliate, but Kirsten beat her to it.

'I swear to God, if you don't, I will remind you of this day. Now, the cleaning stuff is under the sink. I'm off to me muvver's for a cup of tea, and I hope, Gina, that you get those stains out.' She then glared at the two boys. 'And you two need to help your muvver.'

As soon as Kirsten left the house, slamming the door behind her, Gina dropped her shoulders and allowed tears to plummet down her face. She wasn't crying for her mother or her father but for herself. She would be alone with her children with no real income if her dad went to prison, and if Mitchell decided to call it a day.

'Muvver, can we go out to play?' asked Jordan.

Her son's words snapped her out of her self-pitying moment. 'Yeah.' It was all she could say before she headed for Kirsten's kitchen to fill a bucket with warm water.

Fortunately for her, the new carpet had been coated in some protective chemical, so the chocolate milkshake washed off easily. She poured the dirty water away, grabbed her bag, and closed the front door behind her. Her own home was practically opposite Kirsten's, just three doors along. She glanced up and down the street looking for her boys, but they were nowhere in sight.

The cold ripped through her sweatshirt, and she pulled her coat around her. The jerky movement caused her to slip on the ice and take a tumble and land on her backside. For a moment, Gina was stunned and fell again, trying to get to her feet.

Brenda Garnet, the middle-aged woman who lived across the road, laughed loudly enough for Gina to hear.

'Oh, fuck off,' spat Gina, angrily.

'Sorry, Gina. Are you all right, love?' She was surprised because although Gina had a foul mouth on her at times, they both liked a laugh, and she knew her neighbour would typically have laughed at herself, but not today, it seemed.

'Nah, I ain't all right. Me muvver's dead, me farver's down the nick, and me husband's . . .' She stopped, covered her hands over her face, and burst into tears.

Mrs Garnet, or Brenda to her friends, hurried over and helped Gina to her feet. 'Oh my God, Gina. I'm so sorry, love. Come into mine for a cuppa.' Really, she wanted to hear all the gossip. She was bored of being stuck inside due to the snow and her bad back. She wished her time away, longing for the summer so that she could lean on her front gate and chat to the neighbours, putting the world to rights.

Gina allowed the woman to help her up, and she snivelled all the way to Brenda's house, grateful that she could at least have someone to talk to.

Inside, it was set out in the same way as her own house. The first room on the left was the living room and the next room on the left was the dining room, although Brenda had her dining room open-plan with the kitchen. To the right was the stairs going up to the three bedrooms. Her son Riley saw to it that his mother never went without, so she had all the mod cons and the stylish archway that opened up into the dining room.

Gina followed Brenda and sat down at the table while Brenda put the kettle on.

'Fucking terrible news, Gina, about your mum. How did she die? She wasn't ill, was she? I mean, I saw her a few days ago in that expensive blue coat and fur-lined boots. She looked a picture of health.'

Gina was like a gaping fish trying to answer the questions, but, in the end, she waited until Brenda drew breath.

'It was an accident. Me muvver tripped over a rug and hit her head on the table.'

'What? At her house, or yours, or where exactly?'

Gina screwed her nose up. 'Brenda, what is it with you? Have you become a detective now?'

Brenda had her back to Gina filling the teapot. 'Darling, it's no use getting a half-cocked story, 'cos ya know what it's like around here, babe. Gossip is rife. And if I don't know all the facts, then I can't put people right when they start coming out with their versions. And you know me, babe. I like to stop the gossip in its tracks. How many sugars?'

'Oh, er . . . three.'

'See, babe, that's where you are going wrong. Three sugars! No wonder you're putting on the pounds. And sugar ain't cheap. Anyway, you were saying your mum died at, where did you say?'

'Oh yeah, at her house.'

Brenda turned around with two mugs and a giant teapot. She put them on the table and sank heavily onto her seat.

'Must have been an awful shock for you to find her like that.'

Gina stared at the rounded middle-aged woman with dyed ginger hair and lipstick that had bled into the wrinkles around her mouth. 'I didn't, Brenda, me dad did, and now . . .' Her eyes began to well up again, and she had to pause to stop the crack in her voice. 'And now, they have him down the cop shop accusing him of killing her. Christ!' She shook her head and wiped her tears. 'As if me dad would do that? He fucking loved me mum.'

Brenda raised her eyebrows, knowing full well that Donald had never loved Sylvia once. He had been shagging half of Orpington. However, Brenda could see that Gina was in a right old state and decided not to push it.

'There, there, babe. You let it all out, and I'll fetch some more sugar for ya tea.'

Gina took a sip and noticed the plate of chocolate digestives on the table. She realised just then that she hadn't eaten all day. Taking one and nibbling it, she watched Brenda place the bowl of sugar on the table.

Changing the subject, Brenda said, 'I see a new family have moved in down the road. He's a fucking ugly fella and a lot older than the missus. Pretty an' all, she is. I would have said she was with him for his money, but then I saw their furniture as the removal men were carrying it through. He ain't rich, that's for sure.'

Gina took another biscuit and sighed. 'I'd better go and find me boys, before they get up to no good. You know what they're like. They're a proper handful, but I can't blame them. While my Mitch was inside, I had to bring 'em up on me own. It's gonna be even harder now, with me mum not around.' That thought had her turning on the waterworks again.

'Gina, now you listen to me. You have three beautiful boys. That's something you should be grateful for. I mean, I lost two boys and a girl before I had my Riley.'

There wasn't much that Gina could say in consolation to that. 'How is Riley? I haven't seen him for a while.'

Instantly, Brenda jumped on it. 'He's just fine, thank you, and seeing a charming girl, pretty as . . .' She looked Gina over. 'Slim and clever too. I think she comes from a well-to-do family.'

Gina knew that that information was aimed at her. She assumed then that Brenda had got wind that she and Riley had been sleeping together a year back.

'Ah, that's nice.' It was all she could say.

'Yeah, anyway, so where's Mitchell? I thought you had a party for his homecoming?' Of course she knew all about the homecoming because the shouting and hollering coming from the house could be heard in her own back garden.

'He's at his mum's.' She sighed again. 'I dunno, Brenda, it's like he came home with no intention of staying with me. I have no idea why. I visited him all those years he was inside, and now, it's like I'm a piece of shit at the bottom of his shoe. And as for his muvver sticking her oar in.' Once Gina was on her high horse, she let her mouth run. 'Ya know she's got my little George there, converting him into a Christian or something? I swear, she's like a cult leader. My Mitch is different. He was all right in the nick, but now, he's gone all weird. He took my George and claims that George is terrified of me farver. I mean, what a load of bollocks. My George loves me dad. I do believe it's all her fault, though – his muvver.'

Brenda was listening, totally intrigued by it all. She kept her mouth firmly shut to let Gina spill the beans, in between mouthfuls of biscuits.

'So, anyway, I said to Mitch, "Either you come home, or you can fuck off." I mean, really, with all what's happened, you would have thought he would be there at home to support me and the boys. But, oh no, he's at his

157

muvver's. Well, they can all fuck off. I can do this on me own. I've got me mates . . .'

'Yeah, 'course you have, babe. And you can always call on me for a chat.'

Gina nodded and wiped a dry eye. 'And my boys will need a grandma, and . . .'

'Whoa, girl, no one never said nuffin about me being a grandma. Not to your little buggers, that's for sure. I do cups of tea and lend an ear. I even offer a shoulder to cry on, but I don't do babysitting.'

Gina saw the change in tune and decided to go home. 'I'd best be off. The boys will want their tea, no doubt.'

Brenda watched Gina walk down the path from her front porch. She thought about everything that Gina had told her and mulled it all over in her mind. She had always said that one day, sooner or later, the past would catch up with you and bite you on the arse when you least expected it. If she was being honest, she would have told Gina that her father was a no-good, loudmouthed bully. He probably bashed his wife every Friday and shagged a new tart every Saturday. But she wasn't cruel enough to add insult to injury by spouting off *that* as well. Her gut instinct told her that the day would come when cocky Donald Brennan would get locked up, and to her mind, even if he didn't kill his wife, he had probably killed someone or seriously injured many others. So perhaps he had got his comeuppance.

She knew Donald for what he was. He had even tried it on with her, a good few years ago. But that was when she was a size ten, had naturally red hair, and an hourglass figure, like Marilyn Monroe.

As for Mitchell and Diane Swan, she'd not known too much about them except for the fact that come rain or shine, that woman was there as regular as clockwork posting a letter through Gina's letter box. She assumed it was money.

What was it that he saw in Gina? she wondered. Mitchell, in her eyes, was a very handsome young man. And everyone in the street knew that the only boy in Gina's pack who could possibly be Mitchell's was George, the sweet one who often played on his own. The other two were like little monsters: loud, brash, and nasty with it. But it wasn't just their ways: it was their dark eyes and hair; they looked nothing like Mitchell's or Gina's complexions. And, naturally, the idea that Jordan and Sonny weren't Mitchell's was at the back of everyone's minds because Gina was a slut; she always had been and always would be.

Brenda wasn't blind or stupid. She knew that when her lad had come out of the Army, Gina had given him a homecoming present. And for a few nights back then he was going back for seconds, thirds, and fourths. So she was only too thankful that Gina hadn't called today to say she was knocked up again. Brenda had warned Riley that Mitchell was no small fry; he could handle himself, if the rumours from the boxing club were correct.

* * *

Gina almost lost her balance again – this time on her own front doorstep – but she managed to grab the door knocker and steady herself before ramming the key in the lock. Pushing the door wide open, she hurried inside, hoping to find that Mitchell had had a change of heart and was there ready to make a proper go of their marriage. It had got off to a lousy start, admittedly, but everything was in a terrible state; nothing was normal, not by a long chalk. She felt a tear trickle down her cheek when she realised that the house was empty. As she was about to search the freezer for supper, she heard her two boys run through the hallway.

'Muvver! Muvver! Guess what! Me and Sonny have found a bike. Come and have a look!'

Gina closed the freezer door and glared at her two sons; their faces were full of life and excitement. *It shouldn't be that way*, she thought. They had just lost their nan, and here they were, hopping up and down over a sodding bike.

'Where did ya find it?'

'Just down the street by a skip. Muvver, I reckon someone's lobbed it out.'

Gina opened the freezer door again. 'Did you want chicken nuggets for tea?'

'Muuuuvver, can we have the bike?'

'I don't care, right now, Jordan.' She pulled the packet of nuggets from the freezer and slapped it down on the worktop before searching for the chips.

'So, we can, then, Muvver?' asked Jordan, totally oblivious to his mother's downtrodden expression.

'I fucking said I don't care. Now, do what you have to do, Jordan, and be back here in fifteen minutes for ya tea.'

Jordan and Sonny still didn't recognise their mother's change in tone. They hurried back out of the house and down the street to where the bike was propped up against the lamp post, alongside a skip belonging to Mr Cole, the father of Vance and Warren.

Jordan glanced around before he placed his hands on the handlebars to push the bike away from the skip, but he stopped dead when he heard Warren call out, 'Oi.'

Jordan, still gripping the handlebars, turned to face his arch-enemy Warren, who was eleven years old, a year older than himself.

'Don't you dare touch my bike.'

Jordan laughed. 'It ain't yours anymore. You threw it out, and now it's mine.'

'I didn't throw it out,' said the stocky blond lad with faded freckles and a harelip.

'Yeah, you did. I pulled it out of the skip!'

Unexpectedly, Warren was pulled back inside as Mr Cole stepped forward. 'Jordan Swan, get your thieving hands off that bike and fuck off home.'

Jordan stared at the tall tired-looking man and held his gaze for longer than any ten-year-old should.

'Let go of that bike, Jordan, or I'll have you arrested an' all, like ya grandfarver.'

Those words sent Jordan from calm to manic in a split second. 'Don't you say anything about me grandfarver, 'cos when he gets out, he'll be around here giving you a proper five-knuckle sandwich.' Jordan threw the bike away from himself and held up his fists. 'Go and get your boys. Go on, and I'll fucking show ya! Go on, get 'em. We'll have a fight.'

Mr Cole looked Jordan up and down. 'Go home, Jordan. Just go home.'

'Scared, are ya, Mr Cole? Scared I might bash 'em up?'

'Jordan, don't push ya luck, boy. I'll be 'aving words with ya farver.'

Jordan suddenly lowered his fists and tilted his head to the side. He was confused as to why Mr Cole would be having a word with his father. He didn't even really know his dad and vice versa. 'You do that, Mr Cole, if you know where he is.'

An exaggerated deep laugh left Mr Cole's mouth. 'Cor blimey, boy, so your ol' man's been back five minutes and he's took off already, has he? Well, I ain't surprised. Your farver is a respectable man, unlike your grandfarver, and I bet he took one look at you and him' – he nodded to Sonny – 'and ran like the clappers.'

Just as Jordan was about to give Mr Cole another mouthful, Mrs Cole appeared at the door whispering something. Suddenly, Mr Cole's demeanour changed. His face softened. 'Look, er, Jordan, I am sorry, lad. I knew your grandfarver was down the station. But I didn't know why. I'm very sorry about ya grandmuvver. Sylvia was a lovely woman. Anyway, son, you get off home. It's too cold to be out.'

Jordan kicked the bike and stormed off, so annoyed that he was arriving back at his house with no bike. He'd asked his mother for one for the last couple of years, but she would always come home with a new coat, or dress, or endless pairs of shoes, rather than a bike for him. He was even more annoyed when he walked into the kitchen to find the chicken nuggets still in the bag on the side . . . and his mother sitting by the fire in the dining room with a bottle of wine in one hand and a glass in the other.

'Where's dinner, Mum?' asked Sonny, who was always starving.

'If you want something to eat then do yaself a sandwich. I ain't cooking tonight.'

Sonny didn't need telling twice; he hurried to the kitchen and made four tomato sauce sandwiches.

Jordan was fuming. 'Why can't you be like other muvvers who bake fairy cakes and who would buy their sons bikes for their birthdays?'

Gina looked up from her glass. 'If I was like other muvvers, that smart remark of yours would have been wiped off ya face with a backhander. Now go and make yaself a sandwich, run the bath, and get ready for bed.'

'No, I ain't going to bed.'

'Cor, Jordan Swan, if your farver were 'ere right now, he'd—'

'Well, he ain't 'ere, Muvver. He's never been 'ere. I don't even know him, and why has he made George tell the police that me grandad killed me nan?'

Gina was open-mouthed. She'd not realised that her sons knew what had been going on. 'Who told you *that*?' she demanded.

'I heard *you*, Muvver, on the phone, and when Grandad was here talking about it.'

Gina lowered her eyes. 'Yeah, well, Jordan, I have no idea why your bruvver has said such terrible things about your grandfarver. Or why your dad doesn't want to come back or why that Diane has stuck her wooden spoon in.'

'So it's all George's fault that me grandad will go to prison, is it?'

Gina was only half listening. Her mind was on her husband, and what it was that had turned him off her. 'Er, yes, Jordan. Er, please, love, just get yaselves off to bed, will ya?'

'Did Grandad hurt Nan, though?' asked Jordan, his face now forlorn.

Gina took a large gulp of her wine and shook her head. 'No, Jordan, of course he never. I think the police want to make sure your grandad goes to prison because they don't like him. Now then, if you want, you can go into the living room and watch a film. Just get your 'jamas on first.'

Gina knew her son was tough and lacked a lot of emotion, except anger. He was good at anger, so she decided to let him grieve in his own way and in his own time.

Sonny offered her a sandwich, holding the soggy contents between his grubby fingers.

She smiled and shook her head. 'No, you eat it all, my baby boy.'

He returned a cheeky smile and left the room to follow his brother. He always followed Jordan.

Chapter Ten

Gabriel stared at the damaged Bible and then back at Claire. 'You need to stop mollycoddling her. She's almost eleven years old, not three. I don't see the other children in Bible practice struggling with the words.'

'Gabe, I think she may be dyslexic.'

'Hush, woman, that is just a newfangled term the teachers are spouting off now to excuse them for not teaching a child to read and write.' He paused and sighed. 'This is what we are surrounded by – rules and laws that are not written by God. The fact is, Claire, Eden is lazy when it comes to her Bible reading, and to destroy the Bible is the Devil's work.'

'But, Gabe—'

'Hush your mouth, woman. If you make excuses for her, then you are as bad, if not worse.'

'Her hands are still weeping and swollen. They will ask her about it at school.'

Slamming his fists down hard on the table, Gabriel jumped up. 'She is to stay off school and learn Jehovah's work. She doesn't need school, only to learn to read and write. She will not be going on to college or searching for some fancy career. She has The Truth to preach. She hasn't the time for school, or their ignorant ways. So taking time off, won't matter.' He slammed his hands down on the table and then ran his fingers through his hair in frustration. 'You just don't understand,' he huffed. 'And I am not really surprised, but, anyway, the less Eden spends at school away from the sons of Satan, the better. Now, stop nagging me about her.'

'But I am *worried*. It's been twenty-four hours, and she is very poorly. She's shaking. And her little hands are so—'

'Enough, Claire. Maybe she will learn before she ever thinks to damage the Good Book again. Now, I'm going up to our bedroom to study.'

'Gabe!' Claire raised her voice. 'She's sick. I don't know what's wrong, but she needs a doctor.'

Gabriel glared and curled his top lip. 'Are you undermining me?'

She shook her head and rose to her feet. 'Gabe, please listen to me. She could be dying.'

A twisted grin lifted the corners of Gabriel's mouth as his eyes darkened. 'Don't you ever undermine me again.' A quick slap across her cheek was enough to make Claire gasp and clutch her face.

As soon as Gabriel was out of the room, Claire searched one of the unpacked boxes for a painkiller. Carefully, she opened the lids of the cardboard boxes marked 'Bathroom'. Most of the contents were for him – his soaps and his deodorants. But the last box contained tablets. The problem was they weren't antibiotics, only anti-inflammatories. She hurried up to Eden's bedroom and stopped at the foot of her bed. Her little girl was so white and she was clearly shivering, even though there were beads of sweat on her forehead. She crept closer and felt her neck. The child was burning up. Quickly, she helped Eden to sit up and gave her the tablets.

With heavy, sad eyes, Eden looked at her mother and then tried to smile. But because she had so little energy, she could hardly lift her cheeks. Slowly, she put the tablets on her tongue and took the glass of water offered to her. She swallowed the pills, but with great difficulty. Her throat was so sore, and her head felt as if it was in a vice and being tightened.

'It hurts, Mummy,' she whispered, as she rested her head back onto the pillow.

'Your hands, my darling?'

She nodded. 'And my head and my throat and everywhere. If I die, tonight, Mummy, will I go to Jehovah's Earthly Paradise, or will he say no?'

Claire pulled her daughter close to her and hugged her tight. 'You are not going to die, not tonight, and if you do, Jehovah will welcome you with open arms.'

She listened to her daughter's wheezy breathing and felt the heat coming off her. She knew then that Eden either had tonsillitis or worse. She needed antibiotics, and there were some, but they were in their bedroom in a box labelled 'Claire's Bits'. How could she get them without Gabriel asking questions? She had no choice. She was fully aware that her husband didn't like any medication of any kind; he believed that only God could make you better.

As soon as she entered their bedroom and picked up her labelled box, she noticed the tape had been removed.

Gabriel was sitting up on the bed reading and making notes. He peered at her and grinned. 'I have removed your *special box*.'

'What?' she questioned, while glaring back at him.

'I told you, woman, that I will not be overruled in my own house. I am an elder, and as my wife, you should learn to respect that, and if I say I do not want any medication under my roof, then you must trust that I have good enough reason. Now, leave that box and come to bed.'

She felt her stomach as he patted the bed and loosened his tie.

'I must see to Eden,' she said, before turning to leave.

'I said, come to bed! You are my wife, and you must do as I say. Now come to bed.'

With her left eye twitching and her hands shaking, she continued to leave the room and ignored him.

However, that proved to be a huge mistake. In a fast movement, he leaped from the bed, grabbed her hands, and dragged her back. She didn't scream or fight; there was simply no point. She would end up with more bruises, and she had her unborn baby to think about.

All she could do was relax and allow his large fat fingers to paw her body. She'd tried so hard to love him, but she couldn't and probably never would. She'd married him to honour her parents' wishes.

As an elder, he was well respected in the community. He was so high up in the congregation now, that no matter what he did, he was never wrong. In her heart, though, she didn't believe it. She had no choice but to suffer for her sins, and that meant abiding by Gabriel's rules. His thirst for sex was insatiable, and in the first year, after Eden was born, he had made her bend over at least four times a day. He would tell her not to wear underwear unless she was going out. 'A husband has needs, and it is a wife's place to satisfy them,' he said.

However, intercourse tonight was not going to be quick. She knew that look, the dark, malevolent eyes, and the way he licked his lips. He nodded for her to strip while he took his clothes off. She knew then that this was going to be a long night. And she so desperately wanted to get back to her daughter, but she had a duty to perform.

He nodded again, and she began dancing naked in front of him, followed by a foot massage. She hated his feet, the crooked toes, and the thick skin. She had no choice but to massage his whole body – every crease and wrinkle. Holding back the vomit idling at the back of her throat, she thought that if she placed her lips around his manhood, then he would come quickly, and it would be over. She was wrong. He slapped her face to stop her and pushed her off the bed.

'Get up and bend over. I don't want to see your face tonight. You can imagine it's him instead. You would like that, wouldn't you, whore!'

She did as he said and positioned herself. She was ready for the pain, which, no matter how much she cried, he didn't care about. But her daughter's need was such that she wanted this over with. The pain and shock almost had her collapse to her knees as he thrust his penis into her anus. He plunged it so hard, she was lifted off the bed. Pushing her face into the quilt, he viciously pummelled her. She struggled to breathe and tried to move her head to the side to catch at least enough air so as not to suffocate. When eventually it was over, he pulled away and left the room. She slumped on the bed gasping and struggling to fill her lungs, but as soon as she could breathe, she felt the pain. 'Oh, why, oh, why?' she cried to herself.

Slipping back into her modest clothes, Claire hurried to her daughter's bedroom, gutted that she was empty-handed. She had to think of some way to help her child. She could clearly see that Eden was burning up, and she had to do something, or her only child may die. She tried to rationalise what she was about to do. If God turned her away from his kingdom for disobeying her husband, then she thought it wouldn't be Eden's fault. None of what would happen would be, unless, of course, she needed a blood transfusion, and then that would be a whole different issue.

Scooping Eden in her arms inside the blanket, Claire hurried down the stairs. Sliding her feet into her backless slippers, she quietly closed the front door behind her, before rushing along the path and up the road. She hoped to be able to find a phone box to call for an ambulance. She had no money and no one else to call. Her parents had died years ago, and the only family was the community. But her husband was the head of it all.

As she hurried away aimlessly, she didn't feel her feet getting wet or cold; she was so desperate to find a phone box.

* * *

Brenda Garnet was in her dressing gown and her hair in curlers when she opened the front door to let the cat out. She shivered and wondered if perhaps her pet would be better staying in. As she looked down the road, she was surprised to see that the street lamps were all working; the vandals hadn't attacked them as they had in most other parts of the neighbourhood.

As her eyes focused, she could see a woman carrying a child. She looked to be struggling. Instinctively, Brenda called out, 'Are you all right, love? Can I help?'

Claire stopped and turned to face the direction of the voice. Her arms were aching from carrying Eden's dead weight, and her lungs stung from the bitter cold. She felt useless, tired, and weak. 'Oh, please, could you . . . ?' She didn't finish.

Brenda hurried down her path and tried to take the child from Claire. 'Quick, you go inside, love. I'll carry the kiddie.'

Once the woman took Eden from her, and effectively seized control, Claire realised just how burdened and exhausted she felt. Nervously, she followed and watched as the neighbour laid Eden on the sofa, pulled a blanket from the armchair, and gently placed it over the top of her daughter.

'Thank you, but I need to get to a phone box to call for an ambulance. I'm not sure what's wrong with my daughter. I er . . .' She paused, trying to hold back the tears that no doubt would tumble like Niagara Falls. 'I need to—'

'You need to sit down. I can call an ambulance from me own phone. Now then, I used to be a nurse, well, for a year. That was until I got pregnant. Anyway, what's wrong with the little kiddie?'

'I, er . . . I don't know. She has a sore throat, a headache, and she's burning up.'

Brenda glanced at the bandaged hands. 'And what's she done there?'

Claire's eyes widened. She would have to lie. 'My daughter fell over.'

Brenda kneeled down beside the little girl. She felt her forehead and then lifted the blanket and the child's nightdress.

'What are you doing?' asked Claire, as she observed carefully.

'I just want to make sure she ain't got a rash, like meningitis, but she seems okay. Does it hurt her to look at the light? Does she have a stiff neck?'

Claire shook her head. 'No, I don't think so.'

'Sweetheart, can you open your mouth for me?'

Eden slowly opened her eyes to face an older woman with kindness on her face. She opened her mouth for the woman to see.

'Good girl. Can you open a little wider?'

Eden did as she was told.

'Oh, you poor thing. You have tonsillitis.' She felt the child's forehead. 'And a high temperature. I think I can help.'

Claire was so desperate to get her daughter better that she didn't question the kind lady anymore; she just let her take over. Sitting on the comfortable chair, she watched as Eden was helped into an upright position and handed some tablets to take.

Brenda went into the kitchen and shortly returned with a glass of cold blackcurrant juice and a mug of tea.

Offering Eden the juice, she said, 'There, sweetheart, that should ease those tablets down. Now then, I'll be forgetting me manners. I'm Brenda Garnet. Everyone calls me Brenda or Bren, and you must be our new neighbours.'

Claire nodded as she gratefully sipped the hot tea. 'I'm Claire, and my daughter is Eden. We moved in a few days ago. Is Eden going to be okay?' She checked on her daughter, who finished her drink, yawned, and drifted off to sleep.

Brenda looked the woman over. 'I've given her paracetamol and some antibiotics. There are enough for a complete course, so she must take them three times a day.'

'Oh, thank you so much. Are you sure you don't mind?'

Brenda saw Claire's delicate features and softness in her eyes. Her heart unexpectedly went out to her. 'Of course, I don't mind. Oh shit, I forgot to ask. Is she allergic to penicillin?'

Claire shrugged her shoulders. 'She's never had it.'

'Well, we will soon see if she is.'

There was a silent, almost awkward, pause before Brenda broached the subject. 'Er, what about your husband? Is he not at home, then?'

Again, Claire had to lie, and she knew that God wouldn't take kindly to that. 'Yes, he is working late.' That wasn't a complete lie.

'So where have you come from?'

'Scotland. I used to live in Orpington once, over the other side of the main road, but we moved back because of his work.'

'And what does he do?' asked Brenda, wanting to know the ins and outs of a duck's arse.

'Er . . . Well, he's an elder at the Kingdom Hall . . .'

'Oh . . . I see. So he's, I mean, you're one of those Jehovah's Witnesses, then?'

Claire looked up and nodded. It was the first time she felt awkward admitting her faith.

Brenda looked at the child. 'Look, love, I know you have your certain ways and beliefs, and whatnots, but as far as I'm concerned, children come first, so if this little girl needs hospital treatment, then she should have it. I don't believe that God would be against that.'

'Oh no!' said Claire, quickly jumping in. 'No, I was trying to get to a phone to call for an ambulance. Of course, I would get my daughter medical attention, but I was fortunate to have met you.' She blushed.

Brenda warmed to the young woman. As she peered down at Claire's sopping wet slippers, she said, 'I'll get a pair of socks for you. We can't have you coming down with the lurgy an' all. Now then, you drink that tea before it gets cold, and we can then work out what we're gonna do.'

'Well, I really should get her back home.'

Brenda raised her eyebrows, in concern. 'I think it's better if this little one stays here in the warm on the sofa or up in my son's room. There's a double bed. You can both sleep there. I have central heating, and the temperature is always kept constant. So you'll not get cold. I have a spare nightie.' Brenda didn't give Claire the chance to reply before she was by the doorway, flicking her head for Claire to follow.

However, fear took hold and stopped Claire in her tracks. 'I'm sorry, I can't stay. I have to get back home.'

'But, love, it's cold. Eden is sick and—'

'I know, but you don't understand. I really appreciate what you have done, and I am so grateful for the tablets, but I have to take her home.'

Brenda could tell by the panic in Claire's voice, and the desperation in her eyes, that the reason for not staying was far more worrying than she cared to imagine. 'Okay, my sweetheart. Let's get the little 'un wrapped up warm. You put my wellies on. You look to be my size,' she said, peering down at Claire's feet. 'And I have a warm coat, too small for me. It'll do you a turn, though.'

Claire smiled awkwardly. She wasn't used to accepting help from anyone outside her congregation.

Eden stirred and opened her eyes. She sat upright, her eyes heavy. 'Mummy, where are we?' she whispered.

Brenda then noticed how pale the little girl was. 'Are you feeling any better?' she asked, hoping the paracetamol was beginning to kick in.

Eden nodded. 'Yes, thank you.' She tried to smile.

Once Claire had slipped her feet into the wellies and gratefully put her arms in the warm coat, she scooped her daughter up.

Brenda added another blanket around the girl's shoulders. 'You don't have to go, ya know, love.'

All Claire could say was, 'I do.' But it was the look of anguish on her face that said so much more.

Brenda popped the tablets into Claire's coat pocket. 'And don't forget: every three hours, watch she doesn't have a reaction, although I think she's okay. But if she gets worse, take her to the doctor's.'

Claire nodded, and tried to wave as she hurried down the garden path. The cold wind had dropped. There was still a trace of bitterness in the air, but it wasn't burning her face or lungs like it was before. Her main concern was that Gabriel didn't take their disappearance out on Eden. It wasn't her fault at all; she couldn't help being ill.

The front door was pulled open as Claire tried to fiddle with the lock, her hands still shaking from carrying her daughter.

'Where have you been?' demanded Gabriel, as he glared with so much anger in his eyes.

Claire ignored him and pushed past, taking her daughter up to her bedroom. She felt her husband on her heels as she climbed the stairs, his angry breath hot on her neck.

'I want answers, Claire!' he hissed.

Still she continued, to Eden's bedroom, until she managed to lay her child on the bed. He stood in the doorway, but Claire, in a moment of confidence, closed the door in his face. However, to her horror, he opened it and barged in.

'Gabe, I am getting Eden undressed. Please wait outside, and we can talk then.'

'How dare you tell me what to do. I want to know where you have been with Eden?'

Claire felt her daughter's head and was pleased that she was cooling down. She then straightened the blanket and laid it neatly over her.

Just as she was about to get up from tending to Eden, Gabriel snatched her by her hair and pulled her to her feet. 'Do not ignore me, wife.'

'Gabe, she is very sick. I went to get her help.'

Before she could explain more, from nowhere, a hand slapped her hard across the cheek and then another struck her other cheek, knocking her sideways. She tried to gain some stability, but Gabriel punched her so hard in the chest that she flew backwards, hit the cabinet, and slumped to the floor gasping for breath.

Although still dazed, Eden managed to pull herself upright and slide off the bed to stand between her mother and father. She stared at her father's rancorous expression. His hair, which was usually combed back, had fallen forwards, and his eyes were red with rage.

'Get to your bed, Eden. You are obviously not ill. You liar, child. You evil little liar!'

Instantly, Claire found that she had got her faculties back. 'Leave her alone, Gabe, please. Look, I am so sorry I went against your wishes. Punish me, but she isn't to blame. She is poorly. I swear to you.'

Seeing the marks he had left on Claire's face, he realised that it wouldn't look good in the Kingdom Hall. There would be questions. He took a deep breath and stormed from the room, snarling, 'It's lucky that you are with child or you would feel my punishment. You whore!'

Eden waited until he was gone before she flung her arms around her mother. 'I'm sorry, Mummy. I'm so sorry.'

Claire helped her daughter back into her bed and left, closing the door behind her. She knew she herself, though, would suffer in other ways.

Chapter Eleven

6 months later

The courtroom was packed to the rafters. The press were in their element. Donald Brennan, a well-known villain, was in court for the murder of his wife. The headlines were sensational, with each paper claiming an exclusive scoop and all putting their own spin on events in court.

Outside the reporters flashed their cameras as Gina, in her bright floral blouse and skintight black trousers, marched up the stairs to the court. Padlock Pete was by her side. Her father had insisted that his friend should look after her, since he'd heard that Mitchell had filed for divorce.

She'd been warned that reporters would be there, so she'd plastered on her make-up, given her lips an extra layer of Max Factor Marilyn Ruby Red, and added two lots of false lashes.

Although she'd given her statement, the prosecution decided not to use her because she would be a hostile witness and so make their case against her father more difficult. And the defence were not at all keen to involve her either: they felt her loose tongue could jeopardise their case. However, everyone knew that a guilty verdict was highly likely because the evidence against him was overwhelming. It was just a case of proving murder over manslaughter.

Gina managed to hold her head up high in the public gallery. She received a few sharp looks from spectators and press alike. They wanted to gauge her emotional state. After all, her father had allegedly killed her mother in the most gruesome way. They got what they wanted: she sat there with a look that could strip wallpaper.

As Shay entered the witness box, Gina glared, daring him to glance her way. She would give him what-for, no question. It didn't take long to get a reaction from her. As soon as he said that her father had got into a fight at Mitchell's homecoming, she couldn't hold her tongue any longer and jumped up from her seat. 'You were after me muvver for yaself, you fucking liar, Shay.'

Gasps from the jury and a few from the gallery should have been enough to prevent her from saying more.

But then the judge called out that she would be in contempt of court if she spoke out again.

Gina, however, was still fuming; she simply didn't care. 'Oh, fucking choke on ya cucumber sandwich. You want me ol' man behind bars anyway. That fucking Shay is lying, but you ain't listening. So fuck you!'

Pete tried to shut her up by pulling her back down into her seat. 'Leave off, Gina.'

The judge banged the gavel numerous times. 'Get her out of my courtroom, this instant!'

A security guard tried to pull her up from her seat, but she smacked him over the head with her bright-red handbag. 'Get ya fucking dirty, pervy hands off me right now. I can walk out on me own.'

The security official let her go and stepped aside for her to make her own way out.

She glanced back. 'It's a fucking kangaroo court anyway.'

Pete was close behind, shaking his head and mumbling apologies.

The guard prodded her in the back, and growled in her ear, 'If you don't get a move on, the judge will have you locked up.'

'All right, mate, she's going,' said Pete, knowing that Gina could quite easily turn around and lamp the guard one, and he really didn't want to be left babysitting Gina's boys, that was for sure.

Gina stormed from the court, past the security, through the main doors, and on to the pavement. Fumbling in her bag for a cigarette, she sparked it up and took a few deep pulls, ignoring the flashing cameras.

Pete grabbed her elbow. 'Come on, Gina, let's get away from here.'

She pushed his hand away. 'Did you fucking hear that no-good wanker Shay? He was singing like a canary. I tell ya what, Pete, if I ever get me hands on him, I will cave his head in. My farver would never have killed me muvver, just 'cos they had a row. I mean, who don't row? Every marriage has its ups and downs.'

She looked at Pete for approval, but he didn't nod. Instead, he just shook his head. 'Gina, has it never crossed your mind that ya father *did* kill ya mother?'

'What?' she spat.

'Well, has it not crossed ya mind? I mean, you've practically disowned your son, 'cos he said he saw it. Shay saw them rowing, and I have to be honest, babe. Don did say to me that he would give her what-for when she left the party.'

Gina stubbed her cigarette out and pushed Pete away from her. 'You wanna watch what you're saying, Pete. I mean, I don't think me dad will be too pleased with you.'

He waved his hand. 'Look, love, I ain't said anything to anyone except you. You're like a niece to me, and I don't wanna see you ruin your life over this. Mitchell is your husband, and I'll tell you this for nuffin, he's a very good man. You wanna try to work things out with him. And what about little George?'

With a look of spite and a deep huff, Gina turned and said, 'He ain't no fucking son of mine. That Diane has brainwashed him, and as for Mitch, he ain't no man. He's abandoned us! So, he can have George and his muvver and stay the fuck away from me.'

'What do you mean he's abandoned you? Doesn't he see the other two boys or give you money?'

'Well, yeah, all right, he gives me money – not a lot mind you – but my boys won't have nuffin to do with him. My Jordan told him the other day to fuck off.'

'Aw, Gina, you haven't turned them against him, have ya? Because trust me, girl, they will need a father in their lives once they become teenagers. And, Gina, George is only a little lad. He needs his mum, so you should maybe go and see him.'

'Oh, is that right, eh, Pete? Well, he should have thought about that before he told lies and had me dad locked up for a crime I know he didn't commit. And besides all that, Pete, I *can* bring up my kids without a man in my life, actually. And as for George, he would rather live with Mitch anyway.'

With slumped shoulders, Pete gave up arguing with her. She was her father's daughter, all right. She was stubborn and selfish. He realised then that Gina had no feelings for the child. He'd noticed it before. Clearly, there was a clash of personalities because George's quiet nature and sweeter ways were galling to her. It was obvious she loved the other two, always laughing at their antics, even though at times he knew they drove her up the wall. She had been so lucky having a mother who was always on hand to help her and a father who would always put his hand in his pocket for her and the boys. However, she was such a spoilt and selfish woman at times, he wondered why she'd wanted any children in the first place.

'I'm gonna get off home, Gina. This trial will go on for days. Why don't you come with me, love, and come back tomorrow?'

Gina huffed like a teenager. 'I ain't got much choice. The judge will lock me up if I go back in there today.'

As soon as they reached Gina's house, Brenda came hurrying down the street. She was dragging Jordan by his arm, with Sonny running to keep up. 'Gina, I won't be keeping an eye on your two kids again!' She stopped dead, almost throwing Jordan towards his mother. 'Go on, Jordan, tell ya muvver what you've gone and done!'

'Aw, get off me, you ol' bag.'

'Ol' bag!' echoed Sonny.

'Jordan!' shouted Pete. 'Have some respect for your elders.'

'And you can fuck off, an' all,' spat Jordan.

Gina suddenly lunged forward and grabbed Jordan by his T-shirt. 'Of all days, Jordan, you have to pick today to be a git. I've been up that court worried to death that ya grandfarver's gonna go away, and you have to cause more problems. Both of ya get inside. You're grounded.'

She was on the point of following them, when Brenda shrieked, 'Don't you even care what that brat's done?'

Gina sighed heavily and turned to face Brenda. 'Me dad's up in court. Me husband's fucked off. Me middle lad's been brainwashed by his Bible-bashing grandmuvver. I nearly got done for contempt. Now you're asking me if I wanna know what he's done. Well, no, Brenda, I don't. Right now, I couldn't give a flying shit.'

'Ya know what, Gina, you all belong in prison, the whole fucking lot of ya. And mark my words, Gina. In a few years, you'll be visiting that little shit, as well as your father.'

Pete was about to follow Gina inside the house, but he was stopped dead in his tracks when the door was slammed shut in his face. He sighed and then headed back along the garden path. It was a blessing in disguise really because that was his cue never to go knocking on that door ever again.

If Donald got done for Sylvia's murder, then he would be away for a long time, and given his age, he probably wouldn't see the light of day, and if he did, he would be too old to throw his weight about. A soft cool breeze touched his face, and at that moment, he felt a sense of freedom. It was then that he realised he'd lived in fear of Donald Brennan, pretending to be pals and laughing at the man's jokes, but did he really like the man? No.

He glanced across at Mrs Garnet, who was visibly shaken, with tears running down her cheeks. Hurrying over, he placed an arm around her shoulders. 'Let me walk you back, darling. Tell me, what did that little brat do?'

Brenda wiped a tear and sniffed back the emotion; in the main, she was a tough woman. 'Well, probably nuffin to most people, but I love my little cat. I've had her for years, and that . . . that bastard kid of Gina's tried to kill her by shoving her into my washing machine. Luckily for me, the machine is on the blink and takes a few seconds before it fills up, and it allows me to open it at any time. But if I hadn't caught him, he would have killed that cat, and she is so trusting, she wouldn't have fought him to get away. By

Christ, I wished she'd left a big scratch down his face. Mind you, I bet that wouldn't have taught him a lesson. He's not right, that one.'

'Nope, Mrs Garnet, he certainly ain't.'

'And before that, the pair of them upset the little girl from down the road. They ripped her magazines and threw flea darts in her hair, and then, I dunno what Jordan did, but the little kiddie screamed. I can't babysit them two anymore. They're a nightmare. They're enough to drive anyone to drink.'

Once she was inside, Pete waved goodbye and walked away from the street and from Donald Brennan's daughter for good.

***

Gina was in the kitchen putting the kettle on and buttering slices of bread, while her two sons sat quietly at the table. Sonny stared at his brother's face and tried to copy the conniving smirk. He knew they would be in trouble if their mother actually listened to Mrs Garnet, but he could see that Jordan wasn't bothered at all.

As his mother placed a large plateful of sandwiches on the table, along with her cup of tea and two plastic beakers of juice, Sonny felt his stomach turn over. He wondered if he could lie like he knew his brother would if she asked them about what they had been up to today. For unlike Jordan, Sonny was now cringing at the thought of what his brother had done to that little girl. At the time, though, he'd thought it was funny throwing flea darts at the girl's hair. But it wasn't so amusing when she didn't react and carried on walking with about ten darts hanging from her locks. Jordan wanted to get a reaction from her because that was Jordan all over. He loved to watch his victims get riled up. However, the little girl continued on with her head down staring at the pavement while clutching an armful of magazines. In an instant, Jordan had leaped over the wall and snatched the magazines and laughed. 'Bible-basher, Bible-basher,' he called her.

Sonny knew the little girl was frightened; he could see the terror in her big round eyes, but all she could do was watch in fear as Jordan ripped the pamphlets up, threw them in the air, and danced around while he laughed his head off. The little girl tried to run away from Jordan. But he grabbed her arm and pushed her to the wall, pinning her there. It was only when she screamed that Jordan let her go. But then Mrs Garnet rushed out of the front door in a flash and held Jordan by the scruff of his neck before he could get away. Sonny recalled looking at his brother's face while Mrs Garnet gripped him tightly and watched him sneer at the little girl in a way that said he wasn't done. She was cute, but her eyes were wide and afraid, and her bony arm had a red bruise from Jordan's grip.

They all sat in silence and ate their sandwiches. Jordan never said a word; he just stared at his mother's sad and possibly disappointed expression. Once they had finished their food, he reached across the table and touched their mother's arm. 'I'll take care of us, Muvver. You've got me and Sonny. George can live with Mitchell. We will be all right, just you watch. We'll have plenty of money, and no one will upset you again, I promise you.'

Gina looked up and realised that her sons were growing up. It wouldn't be long before Jordan would be a teenager. And he was right: she didn't need Mitchell, and George would just be a nuisance getting under her feet.

***

An hour earlier

Eden was beside herself with worry. She was supposed to deliver a few of the new *Watchtower* magazines to her Aunt Rachael, her father's sister. Now, all she was left with was a bag of shredded paper. She could do nothing except allow Mrs Garnet to put them in the bin. She hurried to her aunt's with fear in her lungs and nothing in her hands.

Rachael, at forty-two, was a year younger than Gabriel and was sour-faced and bossy. No one ever interrupted her when she spoke and no one dared question anything she said.

As Eden stood on the doorstep, her knees began to wobble.

When Rachael opened the door, she glared at Eden with contempt. 'Where are the magazines, Eden? You were supposed to bring them to me earlier!' she spat, as she glared at the child's empty hands.

'Well, I, er, this boy, he took them from me, and he threw flea darts in my hair.'

'*Boy!*' shrieked Rachael, as her small eyes narrowed even more.

'Yes. He took the magazines, tore them up, and threw them everywhere. I—'

'You let some *boy* take all the magazines?'

Eden felt her throat tighten and the tears began to well up, but she tried to blink them away. 'I couldn't stop him, Auntie Rachael.'

Rachael, a big woman, dressed in a long floral summer dress and black plimsolls, almost took up the complete door frame. She was taller than her brother; in fact, she was probably the tallest person in the congregation. Glaring at Eden in anger, her left eye began to twitch, and her lip curled.

'Well, get off home and tell your father that you were cavorting with some young lad who threw God's Word away. Let's see what he has to make of that, shall we? Because, young lady, you should have been minding your own business and not getting involved with those outside the congregation.'

'Well, Auntie Rachael, it wasn't like that. I didn't speak with him. He just—'

'Just get off home and tell your father what happened. He will have to come himself, if you can't be trusted to run a simple errand.'

Eden didn't argue. She hurried away before she copped a smack from her aunt, who was quite spiteful at times. Before her aunt closed the door, Eden heard her mumble something under her breath, like 'bastard child'.

Knowing how cross her father would be, she took her time going home, thinking of how she could explain what had happened. She couldn't lie because she would go to Hell, but if she told the truth, he wouldn't believe her, and she would, no doubt, get smacked hard or made to sit in a cold bath until he thought she'd learned her lesson. She detested that punishment; she hated how he would sit on the chair and watch her shivering. In her mind, she knew it was the worst form of reprimand because he never did it when her mother was at home.

Worrying about her punishment, she was in a daze as she entered the kitchen. But she snapped out of it when she heard moaning and groaning coming from upstairs. She assumed that her father was hurting her mother, as he'd done so many times in the past. However, this time, she felt the need to intervene because the deep guttural moans sounded more like a cry for help. Then she heard her father saying, 'It will be all right. Just breathe.' She slowly climbed the stairs, confused by her father's words. What was going on? Her mother was in pain and crying and her father was trying to comfort her.

As soon as she reached her parents' bedroom, she gasped at the sight of her mother lying on the bed with her legs apart. She was propped up but straining and sweating. *The baby was coming, but surely it couldn't hurt like that?* thought Eden. It was supposed to be a good thing. They were all looking forward to the new baby, especially herself. But this wasn't right, seeing her mother's face so twisted in agony. Her hairline dripping with sweat made Eden want to run to her and try in some ways to help, but she was also scared. She wasn't sure if it was the fear of the unknown or the terror on her mother's face and the pain in her eyes.

Her mother screamed again and fell back onto the pillow.

At that point, her father noticed her out of the corner of his eye. 'Quick! Run and fetch your Aunt Rachael, now!' he yelled.

Eden was fearful for her mother and instantly spoke without thinking. 'Shall I call for the doctor or an ambulance?'

'No!' he screamed, as he hurried towards Eden, grabbing her shoulders. 'You do as I say right now. Go and fetch Rachael!'

Eden took one last look at her mother's red and sweaty face and ran like the wind to her aunt's. It was getting dark, and usually she would never go out alone, but this evening was a different matter. Gasping for breath, she banged on her aunt's door.

'What on earth!' shouted Rachael, as she pulled the door open.

'Mummy's . . . Mummy's—'

'Spit it out.'

'Mummy's having the baby, and Daddy said to fetch you right away.'

Rachael flicked her plain brown slippers off her feet, slipped into a pair of low-heeled sandals, and removed her apron, before snatching the house keys from the hall table.

She pushed Eden along the garden path in front of her. 'Hurry, child.'

As soon as they were out of the garden, Rachael passed Eden and took long strides, half skipping and half running. Eden thought she looked like a giant with her square shoulders and long solid legs, and she found it impossible to keep up. Passing the house with the broken gate, she noticed two boys at the window. They were the very same ones who had ripped apart her magazines and thrown flea darts in her hair. Now they were sticking their tongues out and pulling faces. Eden put her head down and didn't look back.

By the time her aunt had reached the end of the road, Eden had had to run at full speed to catch her up. She didn't like her aunt, although she would never voice her thoughts. Aunt Rachael had a know-it-all look about her, and she wore a vinegar sneer as if everyone was beneath her, except her brother. She seemed to take direction from him.

As soon as they entered through the back door, Rachael ran up the stairs without even removing her sandals.

Eden anxiously hurried behind. But the house was quiet. She assumed then that her father had called for an ambulance and her mother was on her way to the hospital. However, when she stepped inside her parents' bedroom, she knew that something very serious had occurred. Her mother was now lying down. Her face wasn't red and sweaty but pale and sickly. Then Eden saw all the blood on the sheets. There was so much that there was even a pool of it by the foot of the bed, along with a pair of scissors.

Pushing past her aunt, Eden ran to her mother's bedside but only to be pulled back by her blouse.

'Leave the room this instant,' screeched Rachael, as she spun Eden around, ejected her from the room, and slammed the door behind her.

Eden leaned against the door, desperate to hear her mother's voice. But all she heard was the sound of a baby whimpering. *So the baby was born, but why all the blood?* she wondered. *And why wasn't it like at the pictures with her mother sitting up in the bed holding the new baby?*

She strained hard to hear what was being said. All she could make out was her father saying, 'It was too late to call anyone. I had to intervene. Now it is up to Jehovah. He will do what is necessary.'

'She has lost a lot of blood, Gabe. Should we not call a doctor, or a midwife, or get her to hospital?'

'Hush, Rachael! You know as well as I do that they will give her a blood transfusion and Claire would not want that.'

'And the baby?'

'She is perfect. I've cut the cord and wrapped her in a sheet.'

Eden noticed how his voice softened when he spoke of the baby. *So she had a sister.*

There was silence from the bedroom, and Eden felt anxious for her mother. She thought about fetching the neighbour who helped her when she was sick. But going against her father's wishes would, without question, lead to severe punishment. However, if she went without asking, then she wasn't exactly going against anything. Thinking about her mother again, she hurried down the stairs and went out through the back door.

The dark skies would have made her uneasy, but not this evening. She ran back along the road and stopped at the foot of Mrs Garnet's path. Her lights were off, and her cat was on the doorstep. She hesitated, but the picture of her mother's white face shot through her mind, and it gave her the gumption to knock.

Brenda wasn't long in opening the door, and as soon as she clapped eyes on Eden, she hurried her inside. 'What's the matter, Eden? Is everything okay?'

'No, my mum's just had a baby, and there's blood everywhere, and . . .'

Brenda glanced up and down the road. 'Where is your mum now, sweetheart?'

'In her bed in our house, but she's—'

Brenda didn't let her finish. 'Who's with her?'

'Oh, my dad and Auntie Rachael, but my mum's not well, and there's so much blood.'

Eden saw the woman's eyes soften as she gave her a compassionate smile.

'Eden, sometimes when mummies have babies, there is a bit of blood, but that's okay. Has Mummy had the baby?'

'Yes, yes, but she is sick. I know she is, and there's so much blood, and Daddy won't take her to the hospital even though Auntie Rachael said maybe he should.'

Eden searched Mrs Garnet's face hoping that she would take her seriously.

'Why won't your daddy take your mummy to the hospital?'

'I don't know, but please, please help.'

Brenda could see the desperation on the child's face. As much as she wouldn't interfere in a couple's business, she still felt she had a duty as an ex-nurse to help if she could.

***

But by the time Brenda reached Eden's house, it was too late.

Eden had dragged her in and up the stairs, with Brenda feeling awkward and uncomfortable that she had arrived unannounced and unprepared.

As Eden pushed the bedroom door open, both she and Brenda took a couple of seconds to take it all in. Eden couldn't believe what she was seeing.

By the window stood her father holding the new baby wrapped in a blanket. He was swaying and humming a lullaby, and on the bed lay her mother. The lower part of her nightdress was soaked in blood, but she was white, like a wax figure. Aunt Rachael stood biting her nails while staring at the lifeless body.

Brenda didn't bother to introduce herself. She rushed to the bedside and gripped Claire's wrist, feeling for a pulse while her eyes took in the amount of blood on the bed and on the floor. She recognised then that Claire had bled to death. A sudden anger surged through her. She was aware now they were Jehovah's Witnesses; she knew they allowed this to happen; and yet they weren't doctors or nurses. The poor woman may not have needed a blood transfusion, just a method to stop the bleeding. She glared at the husband holding the baby and noticed him smile as he rocked the newborn. It sickened her.

'Is my mum going to be okay?'

Brenda looked at the man and then at the tall woman. It was their place to tell the child her mother had died, surely, but they ignored her.

'Eden, would you go downstairs and put the kettle on? There's a good girl.'

Eden frowned but did as she was asked. The moment the child was out of the room, Brenda launched into one.

'That poor woman is dead. You do bleeding well know she's dead, don't ya?'

The lack of response had Brenda seething. 'Right, well, there is nothing I can do here except to call the police and make a statement. You should've called an ambulance . . . You should've—'

'Rachael, see this woman out, will you?' said the man, as he peered down and sneered at Brenda.

'Oh, I will go all right, but I will speak to the police.'

She noticed the tall woman, Rachael, shuffle nervously before holding out her arm, indicating that she should leave.

'You will go to prison for this,' said Brenda. It was her last-ditch attempt to piss off the man.

'No, I won't, because it was her wish to have the baby at home. Now, please leave, or I'll call the police myself and have you arrested for trespassing.'

'I *am* leaving. And you call yaself religious. You should be locked up, allowing a beautiful woman like that to die. Shame on you.'

'Get out!' bellowed Gabriel.

Brenda noticed how dark and spiteful the man's eyes were and decided to leave the house of horrors.

Eden was in the kitchen and didn't see Brenda leave through the front door. All she saw was a hand that seemed to come from nowhere and slap her cheek so hard that she toppled over.

'You ever go against the family again, Eden, and you will find yourself in very deep trouble. Now then, your mother is with Jehovah now, and you have a duty to help care for your sister, so no more running off to that 'evil woman! Do you hear me?' growled Rachael.

Eden regained her balance and lowered her eyes. She dared not touch her cheek, although it felt like she'd been stung by a thousand wasps. And she wouldn't allow the tears, which were waiting there, to fall or even to whimper in sorrow. She knew, though, that she would carry around that lump in her throat and pain in her heart for ever.

Chapter Twelve

1991

Eight years on

Gina stood admiring her new stonewashed shorts and pink crop top. She'd lost a total of three pounds, and in her mind, she was now slim. Her permed curly hair and new make-up gave her a sense of confidence – not that she lacked much of it now. But she felt it was time that she spruced herself up, went after a decent fella, and stopped these one-night stands. It may have satisfied her sexual needs at the time. But the next day, she was often plagued with a feeling that she couldn't always understand; it felt dirty, but, still, she was good at brushing her feelings aside.

The boys were off making a few quid, and she was getting ready to visit her father. He wasn't looking himself of late, and so she thought she would take him in the new tracksuit and trainers that Jordan had got for him.

The cab beeped outside, and Gina collected her handbag, checking that she had the VO and the plastic bag with the new sportswear. *That should put a smile on her dad's face, especially if he knew it was from Jordan*, she thought, as she skipped down the path to the waiting cab.

The queue going into HMP Maidstone stretched up the road. All the visitors were getting annoyed because the sun was beating down, and there was nowhere to escape the rays. Gina fanned her face for fear of her make-up melting. She carried extra to reapply if need be. There were so many men who she believed were looking her way. And, of course, she didn't want to show her father up.

However, really, he would have much preferred her to dress more modestly, especially after he heard one of the inmates from the last visit say, 'Fucking hell, someone should tell her you can't wear Daisy Dukes when you have an arse like Daisy the Cow.' Donald had ignored the comment, pretending he hadn't heard it because, really, he should have stuck up for his daughter and floored the geezer for being so rude. But he was tired and getting on, and the last thing he wanted was to get rucking and either end up in hospital or down the block.

As soon as the queue began to shrink, Gina found herself at the gate with one of the younger officers. He was stopping the visitors going through until the first lot had been searched and stamped. Gina smiled and winked, and when the young man laughed, she assumed he was flirting back. 'I bet you're roasting in that uniform, ain't ya, mate?'

The young man ignored her and looked ahead as if she wasn't even there. Instantly, Gina was offended. 'Oh, fuck ya, then, you rude prick.'

'Carry on, and I'll deny you your visit.'

Gina would have given him a mouthful, but she had to see her father; he seemed anxious when she had spoken to him on the phone.

Once she was through the search area, where she handed in the new clobber, she was escorted to the visiting room. She paused before she spotted her father already seated. Giving an exaggerated wiggle, she walked over to him. It was simply because she'd clocked Davey Rees, a well-known villain, who was a little younger than her own father; he was loaded and due out soon.

Donald shot her a fierce look and nodded for her to sit down. 'For fuck's sake, girl, stop eyeing up the men in 'ere. It's embarrassing.'

'I can't help it if they want to gawp at me.'

Donald rolled his eyes and waited for her to sit down before he leaned forward. 'Now listen to me, Gina, and listen good, right?'

Gina felt the urgency and instantly focused on her father's face rather than on the other men in the visiting room.

'What's going on, Dad?'

Donald shot his eyes to the left, then to the right, and whispered, 'I am gonna get either stabbed up or worse, if your boy don't return what don't belong to him.'

Gina sat up straight, searching his face for any indication of this news being a joke. 'What are you talking about?'

He looked about him again before he spoke. 'Jordan, by all accounts, is becoming a bit of a handful—'

'Oh, for fuck's sake, he's only a lad. He don't bring trouble to my door.'

Donald clenched his jaw and narrowed his eyes. 'Shut it, Gina, just . . .' He lowered his voice. 'Just listen, right, and please, girl, take this seriously. This is no joke and no game. I could be stabbed in me bed, if your boy don't do as he's told.'

'What's he meant to have taken, then?'

'A fucking collection of very expensive watches.'

Screwing her face up, Gina shook her head. 'Aw, come on, Dad. He may be a bit of a bugger, but he wouldn't rob a shop. He's only eighteen years old.'

'I never said he robbed a jeweller's. He fucking burgled a house.'

'And why is my Jordan being accused?'

Donald's face flushed red, and he ran his hand through his thinning hair while he gritted his teeth. 'It was him, Gina. He didn't do it alone, and his pal has a big mouth. So every single one of those watches has to be returned, or I will get it, and once they've done me in, they will come after him.'

'Who did he steal the watches from?'

'Bernie Blackstone.'

Gina frowned. 'But Bernie is . . . well, he's like me own uncle.'

Lowering his head, Donald sighed. 'No, Gina, he ain't. We fell out years ago, after the job with your Mitchell.'

'He ain't my Mitchell, Dad, and we both know that. In case you forgot, Mitch lives his life with George, not me or my other two. He broke my heart, and so did George, but they can both fuck themselves. I don't need them. I've got my two boys.'

She leaned back on her chair, pulled a packet of cigarettes from her clutch bag, and offered her father one. He shook his head.

'I gave up.'

'That's good, Dad.'

'No, I gave up 'cos you didn't send me in the money I asked ya to. Anyway, fuck all that. It's good for me health, but, see, Jordan, he certainly *ain't* good for me health, the little fucker.'

'All right, but, Dad, why did you fall out with Bernie?'

'Long story and it don't matter now anyway.'

'Dad, tell me. I wanna know.'

'It's all over the fucking robbery.'

'Go on.'

'Bernie and Trevor were in the back of the van with the holdalls. Your Mitch was in the front driving the van. During the trial, it came out that there was a hundred grand short. Bernie reckons that Mitch had a couple of holdalls upfront with him, and he threw them out the window when they were getting away.'

'What? A hundred grand? Why, the tight fucking bastard. That should have been for my kids and me. I'm gonna go and have it out with him and—'

'Reel ya neck in, Gina. You will not do anything, right?'

She lit up a cigarette and took a deep drag. 'The sly bastard, eh? But why has Bernie got the arse ache with you?'

'He wanted a cut of that hundred grand, but when he met up at Portsmouth Prison with Mitch, Mitch told him that I grassed him up. And for some reason, he saw fit to believe him over me.'

Gina took another deep drag, her hands now shaking. 'But how could you have grassed, Dad? You weren't even there. You were drunk, so Mitch drove the van, and that was that.'

Donald looked nervously around. 'Gina, the filth pulled me in because my prints were on the van and the key ring.'

Gina shook her head. 'But why would Bernie think you grassed up Mitch? He was caught red-handed with Trevor in the back of the van, wasn't he?'

'Yes,' said Donald, running his hands through his hair again. 'Mitch got away, 'cos he was fast and could outrun the police, but Bernie and Trevor were trapped inside the back of the van.'

'Oh, for Christ's sake, Dad. It's obvious then that either Bernie or Trevor grassed to get a lesser sentence, so why are they threatening you?'

Suddenly, Donald snatched a cigarette and lit the end until it glowed bright red, sucking on it to fill his lungs. 'Trevor went a bit senile, so he didn't really say much. However, Bernie said he'd served his time, and although he couldn't prove I grassed up Mitch, he wanted to part company with me. He wouldn't go after Mitch for the money because he felt the boy had suffered a serious injustice.' He lowered his tone and mumbled, 'A load of bollocks, that is. But, anyway, Jordan stealing his property means the gloves are off. And, Gina, you have to understand, my reputation in this place is diminishing. First George's accusation and now this bit of bother with Jordan.'

'Dad, leave Jordan to me. I'll make sure he gives the watches back.' She stared into space, still thinking about the hundred grand, that by rights should have been half hers.

'Good girl. I knew I could count on you.'

'I'll take them back to Bernie along with a piece of my mind, the old bastard.'

'Shut it, Gina. For fuck's sake, you'll get me done in. And there's another thing, babe, which you really won't wanna hear.'

Gina raised her brow.

'Jordan is, er . . . well, a bit pushy with the girls.'

Gina stubbed out her cigarette and curled her lip. 'He may be a git, Dad, but hurt a girl? Leave off. I tell ya, my Jordan is a handsome lad. I have girls queuing up for him.'

'Just 'ave a word, is all I'm saying, love.'

Gina left that afternoon feeling uncomfortable. Her father had always been shown respect, wherever they went, but today had been different. On her previous visits, the inmates from other wings would pat him on the back or nod to acknowledge him. And they would always smile or wink at her, but not today. Today, they looked away.

The journey home was long and tiresome. She fidgeted in the back of the cab going over everything her father had told her. As soon as the cab drew up outside her house, she pulled her purse from her bag and then paused. 'Er, change of plan. Take us to the boxing club down the Cray, would you?'

The cab driver turned around to face her. 'That closed down a few years ago.'

'What?'

'Yeah, love, there's a new one in Bromley, if you fancy the sport.'

'Oh, ha fucking ha. No, I want to see the owner.'

'Nobby? Yeah, he has moved the business to Bromley.'

'Take us there, will ya?'

The cab driver didn't answer. He swivelled back and pulled away.

As soon as they reached the corner of the road, she spotted Jordan with a few lads all smoking a joint. She tutted and focused instead on the talk she would have with Nobby because if anyone would know about Mitchell, it was his old trainer.

The cab drew up opposite the new club, allowing Gina to get a clear picture of the size of the place, but what hit her hard was the signage – 'The Swan Gym'.

Slapping a note into the driver's hand, she stomped across the road, as fury built up with every step. *So that's what he's spent the money on*, she thought, as she drank in the sheer size and newness of the place.

Just as she was about to pull the door off its hinges, she stepped aside to allow a tall blond-haired lad out first.

He was tanned and had a gym bag over his shoulder. His white T-shirt showed his toned chest. He smiled, and his face lit up. 'Excuse me,' he said, as he held the door open for her.

Then it hit them both. 'Er . . . Mum?' said George, tilting his head to the side.

Gina stared at her son, having not recognised him immediately. She was so used to Jordan and Sonny with their dark hair and dark eyes, so seeing an almost blond-haired lad with pale blue eyes and a soft, fresh look somewhat knocked her off balance. '*George?*'

'Mum, it's lovely to see ya. Do you wanna come in? I'll get you a nice cold drink,' he said, with excitement.

At first, Gina was gobsmacked. She had spent years being angry with her middle child, convincing herself that she hated him. But seeing him all grown up, with such a kind and open face, she was speechless, and despite her crass character, she also felt awkward. There was something about him that made her want to put on a modest dress and wipe all her make-up off.

'Please say you will stay, even for a few minutes?'

Gina then realised that George had assumed she was there to see him, her son. As if all her common ways were knocked out of her, she nodded and then smiled sweetly.

'Come in. We have a canteen area, where we can grab a coffee or cold drink. Or would you like to go somewhere nicer, say in The Glades?'

Gina couldn't believe how grown up George was. His words were articulate. He still had a south-east accent, but his tone was soft and his movements sharp.

Wanting to have a nose about to see what Mitchell owned, she said, 'The canteen is fine.'

George held the door open until she was inside, and then he walked with her, showing off the gym. 'Over that side behind the partition is the boxing ring. We've just had a new one put in. And this area, as you can see, has the treadmills and weights. We want to get a few more machines installed but upstairs, so it's a bit more private for the ladies. And over there is the canteen or drinks room, and that's the changing area with showers.'

Gina couldn't believe how big and modern the place was. It was so different from the gym in the Cray. This wasn't just a boxing club; this was a moneymaking business. And it was busy with people coming and going and nodding at George as they passed. They were dressed in shorts and T-shirts, some even sporting what she now saw was the Swan logo. Gina felt as if she'd just walked onto a movie set. It was a world so different from her own. But then reality kicked in, and her annoyance began bubbling.

The gym was obviously bringing in a lot of money, and Gina was in no doubt that Mitchell had kept the hundred grand and then invested it on this keep-fit empire. As her eyes flicked around, she saw the Swan logo on drinks bottles, towels, and even the crash mats.

The canteen area consisted of four round tables, a number of chairs, two vending machines, and a tea/coffee making area. It was bright and clean.

'What would you like to drink?'

'Oh, er, coffee's fine,' she said, but, really, seeing all of this, she could have done with a brandy.

Plonking her bag next to her chair, she eased herself down, and continued to look around and take it all in while George made the drink. He sat opposite her and placed her coffee on the table while he drank from a bottle with the Swan logo on.

'I was hoping that one day you would come and see me.'

She smiled again sweetly, unsure how to answer that. Yet something was telling her to keep George onside, for now at least.

'I thought it was about time, really. You know, to put our differences aside, and . . .'

'Oh . . .' He paused, not really knowing how to respond.

'I wanted to see how you were doing, ya know, just to catch up.'

With her back to the door, she didn't hear Nobby standing there.

'A bit late for that, eh, Gina?'

She turned her head to see the short stocky balding man edge around the table and stand by the coffee machine.

'What are you really doing here, Gina? I mean, the boy's done fine without you.'

'Nobby, please leave it. She's me mum,' said George.

'Ya mum, eh? Where was she when you nearly died having your appendix out, and when you got run over, and—'

Suddenly, George jumped up. 'Stop it, Nobby, please. Come on, me mum wasn't to know. So leave it, please. I just want some time alone with her.'

Nobby sighed, patted George's back, and began to leave. But before he did, he leaned into Gina's ear and whispered, 'You don't deserve that boy.'

She wanted to tell him to fuck off but decided to keep her mouth shut.

'Sorry about that, Mum. Nobby's very protective. He's been like a grandfath—' He stopped, having realised what he was about to say, and sat down again.

But Gina felt a pang of jealousy. It should have been *her* father who George looked up to, not the balding midget called Nobby.

'Maybe I should go.'

George reached across and grabbed her hand. 'No, Mum, please don't go yet. You haven't even told me about Jordan and Sonny and yourself. I mean, how have you been? Are you working? And me brothers. How are they?'

Gina inwardly smiled. Her middle child was desperate to be part of her life again, but it was evident he was doing all right without his family.

'Yeah, I am okay. I still live in the same house. I can't afford to move. Ya grandad's house got repossessed, so we couldn't stay there. Jordan left school, and he's finding it hard to get a job. Ya know what it's like.'

She didn't mention that Sonny had got himself expelled and was just hanging about with Jordan, trying to earn a bob or two. 'Anyway, tell me about you, George. What's life been like for you, babe?'

'I've missed you, Mum. And I've missed me brothers.'

But that wasn't what she wanted to hear. She wanted to know about the business and the money.

'So, it looks like you've built an empire, and ya dad's done well.' She chuckled. 'Even got ya name on everything.' She held up the coffee cup with 'SWAN' printed on the side.

She noticed how George blushed and then smiled.

'Oh, that's my idea. I have a sideline of bottled water and other bits and pieces.'

Gina's eyes widened. '*You?*'

George nodded enthusiastically. 'Yeah, I'm going to study business and hopefully grow this into a chain of gyms and sports equipment. I might even have a range of health products.'

How in the hell did I give birth to this one? she thought. He was so different from his brothers.

The Swan logo was obviously a great earner. *Yet, George wasn't the only Swan, was he?* she mused. He could get his two brothers involved and help them out, and between the three of them, they could earn a fortune.

'You've done well, and you're only seventeen. I am so proud of you. Just you wait till I tell ya bruvvers. They'll be up here in a flash to see you. They are full of ideas, and Jordan has a head for business. He could help you no end,' she said, excitedly, now believing her own babbling.

George was nodding politely, but as much as he would love to have his brothers by his side, their reputation preceded them. He had kept his nose clean, and instead of running with the wrong crowd, he'd spent his spare time in the gym. He preferred adult company and keeping fit. He was too young to be a trainer, yet he helped the young lads box, and he was liked by everyone because he was kind and patient.

Just as Gina was putting a plan together to bring Jordan and Sonny to the gym, she noticed George look beyond her, and his eyes slightly widened.

She turned her head to see Mitchell.

Mitchell gave his wife a sardonic stare. *She wouldn't be here unless she was after something*, he thought.

After Donald was sentenced to a lengthy spell in prison, Mitchell's life changed enormously. He didn't have any further dealings with the woman, not after he'd got full custody of George.

He decided he and George would move away – to a new flat in Bromley. He wanted to distance himself from Orpington and the Crays to give George a fresh start. Initially, the only time he returned to Gina's was to post the child maintenance through the door and go to the gym. But then, once he went into partnership with Nobby and moved the business to newer and larger premises, he posted a monthly cheque instead. There was no reason ever to go back. As for his mother, she moved to a place on the coast, when George was old enough not to need babysitting.

Gina watched Mitchell walk up to her with his arms folded over his now broad chest. He was bigger, and his hair was shorter and greyer. However, even the years hadn't aged him at all; in fact, he seemed younger and fresher with a summer tan. Her heart beat so fast, she could feel the quickening pulse in her neck. It was the same feeling she'd had the day she'd first laid eyes on him outside the gym in St Mary Cray. She'd loved his sultry expression. Standing next to George, she could see that her son was his double except he had a sunny face.

'What are you doing here, Gina?'

'Dad, she came to see me. We're just having a drink.'

Mitchell placed his hand on George's shoulder. 'No, Son, she is here for something else. She came here to see me. Didn't ya, Gina?'

His slow and harsh words actually made her feel a little uneasy. His toned body and confident stature had her feeling insignificant. But only for a moment. Because as she glanced around the place once more, the flash surroundings made her think she was owed. However, she wasn't going to show herself up, not today, not in front of Mitchell.

'No, Mitch. I've been thinking about George a lot lately. I always think about him, and I just wanted to see that he was okay.'

'Well, now you have, you can do one.'

'Dad, please, don't.'

Mitchell remained silent and glared at Gina.

Without shouting or swearing back, she collected her bag, stood up, winked at George, and turned to leave.

'We can catch up another day, babe. I'll let Jordan and Sonny know that you asked after them.'

George was about to get up and run after his mum, but Mitchell held him down. 'No, Son, wait here, please. She is up to something, and as much as that may hurt you to hear that, believe me, that woman is a heartless bitch. Nobby told me she was here and what was said, so let me tell you, boy. I did call her when you were in the hospital. I called her twice, in fact. So trust me when I say she is after something, and it ain't rekindling a relationship with you.'

George felt his heart sink. As much as he was happier living with his father, he had longed for his mother to have at least sent him a birthday card or invite him over for dinner once in a while. He wasn't stupid; he always knew that he was different from his brothers, and, sadly, he was well aware that he wasn't her favourite son. She loved his brothers but not him. He waited until she was out of sight before he got up with a resigned look. 'She wasn't here for me, then, Dad?'

Mitchell gave his son a compassionate smile and shook his head. 'No, Son, she never has been. She probably got wind that we have a flourishing business and came to see it for herself.'

'Well, maybe, she'll be proud of me now.'

Again, Mitchell offered a gentle smile. 'No, George, she'll be thinking of ways to get out of you what she can. Just be careful, lad, that's all. Tell her nothing.'

Chapter Thirteen

Sunday was a day of rest for Eden, insofar as she could sit in the Kingdom Hall and drift off in her own little world. She knew in her heart that dreaming of a different life, like the ones the girls in her class had shared, was a sin. However, she could at least admire their bright clothes, their baggy striped jeans, and coloured belts, and even the short miniskirts and high shoes – not that she would ever be allowed to wear such stuff. She accepted that she would be required to do some form of job – perhaps some cleaning part-time in order to use her time wisely, so her father said, by knocking on doors and spreading The Truth.

Seated next to her was her sister Beatrice or Beatie as their father called her. She was eight years old with long butterscotch-blonde hair. Her pretty floral summer dress reached her knees, and covering her arms was a hand-knitted cardigan, a gift from Aunt Rachael. She was the favourite, but Eden loved her too, even though Beatie could act spoiled at times. Anything that ever went wrong in the house, Beatie was always blameless.

Eden knew that Beatie was afraid of the punishments because she'd watched her being beaten, whipped, stripped naked, and left in a cold bath for hours.

However, something lately had changed. Her father was acting differently towards her. He was allowing her to stay up later and sit with him and massage his feet or his back. He told her it was a good thing that she was making her father relax, enabling him to concentrate on The Truth and to keep his congregation safe from evil influences. She felt uneasy every time he asked her to touch him, but it was better than an ice bath.

Eden looked at her little sister, who was swinging her legs under the chair and gazing in admiration as their father spoke. He held the Bible in his hand and paced the floor, filling the room with his deep voice.

It would have been the ideal time to dream of the future and allow her mind to drift away from her father's preaching to the converted and focus instead on her favourite thought that had constantly swirled around her head. She wanted to go to college or take up an apprenticeship in the hairdresser's.

But not today; not ever again would she dream of career opportunities. Because last Sunday after the meeting at the Kingdom Hall, she had made the brave move to ask her father if she could enrol once she left school. However, the second she mentioned it to him, he hissed in her face and

called her 'a selfish girl'. She was to spread the word of The
Truth and to take care of Beatie, or she would never get to
live in God's kingdom after Armageddon.

She recalled vividly what happened that night when
Beatie had gone to bed.

***

He told her to go to the bathroom. Dreading it, she shook
all over. The cold, the humiliation, and his eyes staring at
her. She was older and had grown breasts and pubic hair,
and she even had regular periods. It was embarrassing; she
wasn't a little girl, and this wasn't bath time – this was
torture.

He stood at the top of the stairs after closing Beatie's
bedroom door. 'Go on, get in the bathroom.'

'Please, Father, I am sorry. I will be good. I'll spread
The Truth. I'll do extra chores, but please . . .'

'Get in the bathroom and take all of your clothes off.'

'But, Father, I am eighteen years old. I am not a child.'
No sooner had she got the words out of her mouth than he
launched himself at her. Dragging her by her hair, he took
her into the bathroom and locked the door. She hated the
bathroom, the chair in the corner, the coldness of the white
wall tiles, and the lino floor covering.

'Please, Father, I beg you.'

He wasn't looking at her face or hearing her words. He slapped her cheek so hard, she toppled, and that's when he threw himself on top of her and tried to pull her dress over her head. But the zip was fastened up to her neck. As much as he tugged and pulled, all it did was tear into her skin and strangle her. She felt as if he was going to rip her head off her shoulders. As he fought to get her dress off, her knees bashed the bath side. Trying so hard to stop him hurting her anymore, she whispered, 'Okay, I'll take it off. Please stop.'

As he removed his grip on the dress, she fell to the floor, breathless. She gasped a few times, and then bruised and battered, she stood up and unzipped the dress and let it fall to the floor. After removing her underwear, she stepped into the bath that he'd already filled with cold water. That was when he took his place on the chair and smirked.

She knew what he was looking at; it was her nipples that were erect from the ice-cold water. Then she noticed something beside the chair. Her heart beat fast, and in her mind, she prayed, *please, God, no.*

For a while, she lay there, trembling, with her eyes closed. She knew her lips would be blue, the shivering would turn into relentless shaking, and then she'd feel sharp pins stabbing her, until, finally, her body would go numb from the cold and the sense of death would worm its way into her bones. It was always at this point that her father would leave the room as if he always knew when she'd had enough.

But, she recalled, that night was different. He didn't wait until she was feeling death calling; in fact, he didn't leave the room for her to get out. Instead, he demanded that she stand up. She did, and then he made her get out. As she tried to cover her breasts and her private area, he laughed and got up from his chair. 'Come here!' he growled.

She stared at the object in his hand and knew the punishment had just begun.

'Bend over that chair.'

She didn't argue or even try to run because she had nowhere to go. She bent over, closed her eyes, and hoped it would be over soon. The first swipe of the cane hurt like hell, and she jolted upright, but he pushed her back down. She heard the cane whooshing through the air and then the thud as it hit the tops of her legs. She was desperate to scream, but she held it in, along with the vomit that wanted to force its way out. Taking a deep breath in through her nose, she waited for the next strike but there was a pause. He was playing with her mind. The last stroke, when it came, was brutal. The cane lashed across her buttocks, sending a rattling echo of pain along her spine up to her neck. She let out a muffled cry, still desperate to hold it in so that her sister wouldn't hear her. One further stroke, and she knew she would have buckled under the pain. He knew it as well. He left, slamming the bathroom door behind him.

Her backside felt as though it was on fire, burning and stinging like nothing earthly. She wondered then if suffering the torrent of fireballs outside God's Paradise would be worse than this.

Staying motionless, she allowed the fire under her skin to cool down while she paced her breathing to calm her mind. Tears stung her cheeks as she recalled those whooshing sounds and the thuds.

***

Even now, after a week, Eden found it very painful to sit for long periods, especially on a hard chair.

Relieved that the meeting in the Kingdom Hall was over, Eden watched as the congregation slowly made their way out of the door, each member acknowledging Gabriel's public talk and praising him. Beatie skipped over and clutched his hand, and he responded reassuringly. Eden could never recall him being like that with her.

Rachael stood by her side and smiled broadly as two of the elders' wives came to join them. Jennette, a woman in her late fifties, who always wore a fixed grin showing her protruding teeth, looked Eden up and down. 'Gabe has done so well bringing you up by himself. And I must say you are a credit to him, and little Beatrice, likewise. Such a fine man, he is.'

Eden smiled, nodded, and glanced over at her father. He was staring, but as soon as he caught her eye and noticed she was with the gossips in the congregation, he hurried over and nodded politely, before steering her away.

'You have work to do, Eden. Don't stand there idly chatting. The window has been left open in the small room, and it appears that someone has poked litter through. There's a broom in the broom cupboard.'

Eden didn't need to be asked twice; she was happy to be out of his sight. She carried the broom and dustpan and brush and made her way to 'the small room', as it was aptly named. He was right: there was a lot of rubbish strewn everywhere. As she swept the empty drink cans and crisp packets into the middle of the room, a woman's voice startled her; it was her Aunt Rachael.

'Why has your father sent you here?'

Eden turned to face her. 'To tidy the room. The window was left open. There was rubbish everywhere.'

Rachael raised her brow sharply. 'Really?'

Eden was confused. 'Yes, why, Auntie Rachael?'

'I find it strange that he wants you removed from our company. Is everything all right, Eden? Because you do know you can always come to me if you have a problem. You know, I promised your mother that I would take care of you.'

Eden felt her bottom lip quiver at just the mere mention of her mother's name. She wanted to tell someone what had been going on in the house. The cold baths, the whippings, the uneasy feelings she had about her father, and recently, being touched by him.

Rachael stared, waiting for an answer, but Eden faltered for a moment until her instincts kicked in.

'Everything is fine, I think. My dad just wanted me to make sure the room was tidy.'

With a scowl, Rachael gave her niece a sharp nod and walked away.

Wiping a tear from her cheek, Eden tried to imagine her mother asking Rachael to look after her. *Surely, Rachael would be the last person she would ask?* she thought. She sniffed back another tear when she heard laughing and chatting outside the room. Recognising the voices, she took a few deep breaths and attempted a smile, before her three friends, Chloe, Caleb, and Mark entered the room.

'Your dad said you were in here cleaning up. Mum is having Bible study at ours on Tuesday, and she said that afterwards we can have some music on, but only until ten o'clock. It will just be us and Mum. What do you say, Eden?' said Chloe, with her huge round innocent-looking eyes. She was also very attractive, with dark skin and jet-black hair, like her father's.

'Er, yeah, sure.'

Mark clapped in excitement. 'Great!' He was Chloe's not so exotic brother, who was sweet and kind with a generous smile, a mop of copper-coloured hair, and a mass of freckles. At eighteen, Mark was still very boyish looking and the image of his very pale-skinned mother.

Caleb, the most handsome lad in the congregation, was nineteen. Muscular and manly, he was already taken. Chloe and Caleb were to be married as soon as Caleb's flat had been decorated.

Eden noticed how Mark stared at her. He often did, and the second she caught him, he would smile, and she'd smile back, but the expression today was different. It was as if he wanted to talk to her. She wasn't in the mood, though, and sensed that the elders were instigating something.

Her Aunt Rachael had suggested to her that she should spend more time with Mark, but as much as she liked him, she wasn't interested in anything romantic and certainly not marriage just yet. But she knew that even if she did have romantic feelings for anyone, they would have to be like-minded, meaning a member of the Jehovah's Witnesses. She was happy to have friends in the congregation, and she enjoyed their company, but she knew no different. None of the children was allowed to have friends outside The Truth. They weren't to celebrate birthdays or even Christmas. In fact, Eden had never in her life tasted birthday cake because it was regarded as a sin.

Her family community was all based within the congregation. They had strict beliefs, and she dared not stray from them, or the punishment would be worse than a whipping.

Chloe put her arm around Eden's shoulders. 'Hey, are you okay? You look as if you have been crying.'

Eden smiled. 'I'm fine, thank you, Chloe.'

Chloe flicked her long dark hair over her shoulders. 'You can always talk to me, you know.'

Eden nodded but was surprised when Chloe suddenly hugged her. 'Never suffer anything alone.'

Those kind words made Eden feel as if she could confide in Chloe. They had been friends for years. Chloe's grandfather was a senior elder from another Kingdom Hall, and often her father and Chloe's grandfather would get together over a bottle of brandy. They were almost the same age, and while they discussed The Word or The Truth, Chloe and Eden would play board games.

Being such good friends, Chloe, Mark, and Celeb helped Eden to clear the rubbish, but although she was grateful for their help, she really didn't want to rush and have to spend time alone with her father.

Once they had finished, Eden had no choice but to wander towards the back of the hall. Her father was talking to the last of the stragglers. Beatie was still holding her father's hand but hopping and tugging, willing him to end the conversation.

As soon as she saw her sister, she released her grip and hurried over to Eden. 'So are you going to marry Mark?' She giggled.

Eden winced. 'What?'

Beatie giggled again. 'Mark's mum said you might get married.'

Annoyed, Eden gently pushed Beatie in the back. 'Run along. Aunt Rachael will be waiting for you, and you know she doesn't like to be kept waiting.'

'Aw, do I have to go?'

'Yes, you do,' replied Eden, in a rather harsh tone. Her nerves were on edge because she knew she would be going home with her father alone this afternoon, and she hated the thought of it.

As Eden walked towards her father's car, she caught sight of Chloe again and they locked eyes. At that moment, she wished she could feel just a quarter of the happiness that Chloe felt. Her smile was real, her eyes shone with delight, and she was always ready to laugh at the simplest things. Eden smiled and waved before getting into the rear of her father's Ford Escort.

'No!' he shouted. 'Get in the front with me.'

Eden did as he demanded, and as he pulled away, she stared out of the side window, taking in snippets of how other people lived – the 'others' who would never be chosen, come the day of Armageddon. Two girls were strolling along the road together, both in short skirts and wearing a ton of make-up. They were probably thirteen. Although she was much older, she had never worn cosmetics, short skirts, or even a genuine smile. She'd never dared to laugh along with the sinful jokes in the classroom, and she'd never fought back when she'd been bullied at school. In fact, sitting here in her father's car, she felt as if all the joy had been sucked out of her very existence. Her life was shrouded in a culture of fear. And then there was the possible idea that often invaded her thoughts — *what if The Truth wasn't actually the truth?* It only lasted a few seconds before guilt took its place. And yet when her father spouted those words in the Kingdom Hall in front of everyone: 'And only Jehovah can judge us, not the outsiders, the worldly people, who live under Satan's rule', his eyes would always rest on her.

She just hoped that this day of Armageddon would come soon, so that she could live, as her belief promised, in fields of flowers, where she could pet the animals and feel the love on an Earth made new — in paradise. It would be the opposite of what her life was like right now.

The car stopped, and Gabriel got out and collected his briefcase from the rear seat. Eden stayed for a moment.

'Come on, love. Let's get inside and have some lunch.'

His expression was different; his face seemed flushed and cheery. It wasn't right; and it wasn't him. But she did as she was told, only to find his arm around her shoulders. She stiffened but continued on inside.

The kitchen clock sounded very loud. But it wasn't the clock; it was her heart or her pulse she could feel.

Gabriel placed his briefcase on the table and began removing his jacket and then his shirt.

Eden instantly looked away and was about the leave the room when he stopped her. 'You leave when I say you can leave. Now, you will do as you are told.'

She froze to the spot, her breathing heavy, but her blood raced around her body, rhythmically pounding in her temples. She felt sick.

He poured himself a glass of water and drank it while making a gulping sound; it was followed by a sharp intake of breath before he placed the glass on the draining board.

'Come with me upstairs, Eden.'

She wasn't sure what was worse, the sharpness of his angry tongue or the sudden sickly way he asked her to go upstairs with him. *A chamaeleon at its best*, she thought. A sudden clutch of her arm told her she had no choice. She had to follow him. He was strong: she knew that from the time he'd tried to rip her dress off.

As soon as they reached the landing, he stopped and turned to her with a wet-lipped smile, followed by an arched brow, and then his eyes stared down at the open collar of her blouse.

Eden felt a thousand wasps swarm around her stomach and an invisible hand tighten her throat. Panicked, she turned to leave, but, from nowhere, his hand grabbed her.

'No, Eden. You dare run off. Go into my bedroom. You have work to do.'

With shaky hands, she held her palms up. 'What work?'

He dismissed her question and shoved her in the direction of his room. She'd not been inside since the terrible day when she saw her mother lying there dead on the bed and the blood dripping onto the floor. Holding her breath, she remembered the scissors, and a feeling of dread ripped through her. She knew she must do as she was told or something very sinister may come her way.

His words rang in her ears again. 'Only Jehovah can judge.'

There was no one to help her, no one who would believe her. All she could do was hope that he didn't cause her too much pain and humiliation.

'I want you to massage my shoulders, Eden, like your mother used to. She was your age when we were married. She was very good at serving her husband. She was a good wife, and you, dear Eden, will be a good daughter. Now, take away the tension in my shoulders, and I will guide you from there.'

With trembling hands, Eden kneeled on the bed behind her father and began to massage his shoulders. The feel of his clammy skin made her nauseous. As she followed his demands to move her hands lower down his back, she could hear him moaning in pleasure. Unexpectedly, he spun around and grabbed both her wrists. He was so fast that Eden gasped.

'Don't you move,' he said, as he pushed her down on the bed.

The darkness that seemed to have crept into his eyes and the tightness of his face made her feel terror. He was like a demon possessed. She was afraid of demons. She'd been threatened on a daily basis that they would come for her if she was a bad girl. Was her father one of them now? He stared intensely at her while he removed his trousers and his pants. She'd never seen a man's penis before, not in the flesh, and not so huge. Rigid with fear, she knew in her heart what was about to happen. She didn't fight him off when he slid his hand up under her skirt and snatched her underwear away from her. She didn't fight when he ripped the front of her blouse open to expose her breasts. Yet when he forced her legs apart and thrust his penis inside, the pain shot through her like a red-hot poker and caused every muscle inside to tense up. For a moment, she thought he was going to remove himself. But he didn't. He forced his penis into her again and again. The pain was immense, so much so, that she couldn't bear it. She screamed and tried to scramble away, grabbing at the quilt in a desperate act to escape. Unsuccessfully, she turned on him, writhing and wriggling to break free. Clawing at his neck, she desperately tried to push him off, but he gripped both her wrists again and pinned her down while he continued moaning, groaning, and pummelling her, until, finally, he let out a pleasurable cry and his body slumped onto hers. She could feel his beating heart and his sweat on her chest. She could smell his body odour, and it sickened her. Then she felt the soreness down below and realised that it wasn't a sense of feeling dirty or humiliation that plagued her: it was anger. The fear she'd built up for months dreading he would do this to her had now gone. She'd worried so much when she saw him undressing her with his lecherous eyes, but now he had committed that dark act. She was no longer a virgin. He'd taken what she'd held dear. He had taken what didn't belong to him. That trepidation was no longer there; it was over.

Once he caught his breath, he jumped up from the bed and looked down at the blood. He wiped his mouth and sneered. 'Get the bedclothes cleaned.'

Eden was stunned. *Was that all he could say?* She sat up, put her underwear back on, pulled her skirt down over her knees, and got up from the bed. Her muscles in her legs hurt and shook when she stood up, and then as she peered down, she saw the blood. It wasn't as much as her mother's, but it was there on the bed and for a different reason. Quietly, she crept from his room and into her own, where she changed into a pair of trousers and a long-sleeved T-shirt.

She heard him flush the chain and leave the bathroom and hoped and prayed he wouldn't come to her room for more. She really couldn't stand it. She couldn't live a life like this, but even the idea of taking her own life was a sin. She wished her mother had never gone to the neighbour's that day to get help for her. If she had died naturally, then she would have stood a chance of going to paradise when Jehovah resurrected the believers of The Truth.

'I said clean up the bedclothes, Eden!'

She ignored him. *Besides, what more could he do now?* she thought.

Allowing the tears to trickle down her cheeks, she stood staring out of her bedroom window at the houses opposite, wondering what their lives were really like. Deep in a self-preserving trance, she didn't hear her father bound into her room until she was pushed across the bed. Her trousers and knickers were pulled down and the cane tore at her bare skin. She didn't scream or yell; she just lay there submissively and waited for him to stop. He was tired by the time he'd finished, and she was red raw with three-inch welts striped across her backside.

'When I say clean the bedclothes, I mean clean the bedclothes,' he spat, before he marched from her room.

Like a robot, she got up, got dressed, and made her way to her father's room to do as he ordered. She bit down hard on her lip and tasted the blood in her mouth as a terrifying thought came to mind. *Would he do this to Beatrice once she reached her age?* The idea made her stomach lurch. As she was about to grab the bedclothes, she saw the blood again and thought once more of her mother, her sweet, kind mother, who had truly loved her. She would never feel that love until she left this earth and was chosen to join paradise in God's kingdom.

Chapter Fourteen

Gina placed a pizza in the oven and poured herself a glass of wine. It was Sunday evening, and neither Jordan nor Sonny had shown their faces since Friday. She wasn't bothered; they often went off and stayed away if there was somewhere more exciting to be. More often than not, they would go up to the gypsy site to drink and wheel and deal. They were out of her hair, so she didn't mind.

Kicking off her shoes, she put her feet up on the pouffe and savoured the crisp, cold glass of Blue Nun.

Jordan came crashing through the door, laughing and out of breath, followed shortly by Sonny.

'See, Bro, I told ya I would beat you in a race.'

'Jesus, where were you racing? Through a pig farm? You both stink to high heaven. Go and get showered, and, Jordan, I wanna word. It's important.'

Jordan was at least five feet nine inches tall, and if he'd grown a beard, he would have looked like a man. It was only his clean-shaven chin that gave him a youthful appearance. His cocky expression and confident stature also added to his maturity. Sonny was much the same, only an inch shorter.

'What's so important, Muvver?' asked Jordan, as he made his way out of the living room and into the hall.

'I'll tell you when you smell like Lux or Lynx, not pig shit.'

She sat back and enjoyed her glass of wine, the first of the evening. She could hear her two lads laughing and play-fighting, and her thoughts returned to George. How different he was. She sighed. At least with Jordan and Sonny she could have a laugh and be herself. George had got to her; he was a polite and gentle-looking boy – even sophisticated. Yet he had money, and so did Mitchell, which, by rights, should be half hers.

Jordan returned after a few minutes with his hair dripping and his T-shirt wet in parts.

'Couldn't you even dry yourself off, before getting dressed?'

'Shut up nagging, Muvver. Now, what did you wanna talk to me about?'

Removing her legs from the pouffe, she sat up straight and placed her glass on the side table. 'I've been to see your grandfarver, and he tells me that you have some valuable watches.' She paused and waited for an answer.

Jordan chuckled. 'And what if I have?'

Gina lost her temper at Jordan's smart-arsed remark. 'Oi, don't you get so bleedin' clever with me, Son. Tell me! Do you have a load of valuable watches?'

He could tell she was annoyed, and when she got angry, she was a bit of a handful. In fact, she could easily throw whatever was in her hand at the time at him. 'Why, Muvver?'

'You have to give them back, like, tonight.'

Jordan laughed again. 'I never said I had any, and if I did, I wouldn't give 'em back, not if they were valuable.'

Gina jumped up and raised her hand. 'You, my son, will fucking give them back or else your grandfarver will get hurt.'

The cocky expression on Jordan's face changed. 'Hold up, Muvver. Keep ya hair on.'

'For once, boy, do as you're told!' she yelled and lowered her hand.

'You'd better tell me who's threatened to hurt me grandfarver, and I will fuck 'em up good and proper.'

'Shut it, Jordan. Now then, hand them back, and no one gets hurt. Do you hear me?'

Jordan glared in defiance. 'I ain't taking nuffin back, and I swear to God, I will cripple anyone who lays a finger on me grandpops. On my life, I will.'

Gina shook her head and sighed. 'And I swear to God, Jordan, I am losing my fucking patience. Take the watches back or I swear I will drop you like a sack of shit. Son or not, you ain't putting your grandfarver's life on the line through your fucking pride or greed.'

Jordan said no more and left the room. He bolted up the stairs only to return a minute later with Sonny on his heels and a vicious expression on his face. 'I'll take 'em back, but how do you know I won't get me head caved in? And I wanna know who's grassed and who's threatening to harm me grandpops.' He stood holding a rolled-up piece of velvet material.

Gina assumed it contained the watches.

'Ya grandfarver told me that you were to take the watches back to where they came from, and no one would be hurt. But if they aren't returned, then he'll get knifed, and you will too.'

Jordan stared with a hateful look on his face. 'And who's grassed?'

Gina waved her hand. 'I dunno. One of your drippy mates, no doubt.'

Jordan flicked his head for Sonny to follow him, and they were both gone before Gina could settle herself back in the chair. She watched them out of the window and wondered why Sonny was looking behind him and all around as if he was uneasy. It wasn't like her youngest boy to come across like that. He was just like Jordan. They even walked the same, with their hands in their pockets and with a cocky swagger as if they had a stiff leg. She picked up her glass of wine and was about the take a swig when she smelled the pizza and hurried to turn the oven off before the cheese turned black.

***

Jordan was raging and stormed ahead towards the travellers' site. He'd really trusted his mate when they'd burgled Bernie's house. It had been his own idea and his plan. His mate Rocco came along because he was a dab hand at picking locks.

Jordan knew Bernie as one of his grandfather's cronies and played what he thought was a blinder. Bernie was minted. He may have served a large lump of bird, but he had a few decent robberies under his belt. Jordan had clocked his routine and waited until Bernie had gone for his Sunday lunchtime pint before he broke in. He wasn't greedy, as he saw it; he only nicked the watches. He could have taken the other jewels, but he resisted the temptation, and now the old codger wanted everything back. But Jordan's rage was aimed at the lad who snitched. His pal Rocco from the travellers' site was now his enemy. The bastard had taken his share of the watches as well, and now he'd had the cheek to grass him up.

Sonny grabbed Jordan's arm to pull his brother back. 'Jordan, what are you gonna do?'

'Fuck Rocco up good and proper, the slimy, no-good piece of shit.'

'But, Jordan, there's just me and you. He'll have his bruvvers and cousins, and, fuck me, half the site behind him.'

Jordan stopped and turned to face his brother. 'Well, I ain't gonna let that bastard get away with it.'

Sonny grabbed his brother's wrist. 'Don't go charging in, Jordan. We need to think about it, or they will just smash the living daylights outta me and you.'

Jordan unexpectedly chuckled. 'Sonny, seriously, Bro, you don't think I would let anyone touch a hair on your head, do ya?'

Sonny kept his hands in his pockets and looked down. He knew Jordan meant it, but, even so, Jordan couldn't take on the whole gypsy site. 'Jordan, Mum only has two sons now. She can't lose us an' all.'

'Don't be so dramatic, for fuck's sake. And George ain't fucking dead. He just lives with Mitchell, that's all. Fucking little liar, he is.' Pulling a packet of cigarettes from his pocket, he sparked up one, and took a deep drag on it.

'Don't you ever miss him or think about him, Jordan?'

'What? No, I don't. If it wasn't for him, me grandad would be at home in his lovely house, and our mum wouldn't be traipsing up to the nick every other week, so, no, I don't miss the fucking wanker.'

'All right, Jordan, but can we hold off going up to the site until we have a plan?'

'Okay, okay. You're beginning to sound like George, whining like a girl.'

Sonny sighed with relief and took the fag from Jordan to have a pull.

As they both leaned against a wall, Jordan spotted the blonde Bible-basher. She was heading his way. He'd seen her plenty of times over the years, but after the magazine incident, he'd never really got to talk to her. He found her a little odd, insomuch that she wore plain dresses and old-fashioned flat shoes. She often walked timidly with her head down. However, he was secretly attracted to her because she was different. Even without any make-up on, she was a looker. She had pretty blue eyes and her hair was long and wavy but shone every shade of gold. She rarely glanced his way, and if she did happen to catch his eye, she'd instantly look away.

Jordan watched as she approached him. Just as she was about to walk past, he pushed himself away from the wall and stepped to her side. He could see straight away she tried to walk faster. 'Hey, sweetheart, don't you wanna say hello? We are kinda neighbours, ain't we?'

She ignored him and continued on.

'Oi, that's a bit rude,' he said, as he hurried to catch her up. 'Darling, I only wanted to say hello. Me name's Jordan. What's yours?'

She didn't answer. Looking downwards, she picked up her pace.

Gently, he grabbed her arm. 'Hey, slow down. I'm not a monster, ya know. Why won't you say hello?'

He felt her arm go rigid. But she didn't pull away; it was as if she was terrified. He let go of her then. 'Sorry, darlin', I ain't gonna hurt ya. What's ya name?'

She looked up then at his face and shyly whispered, 'It's Eden.'

'Well, ain't that a beautiful name. It's just perfect for a beautiful girl. Look, Eden, I know it was years ago, but I'm sorry for throwing the flea darts in your hair and ripping your booklets, but I was just a kid back then, a bit naughty, like. I'm grown up now. Flea darts ain't me thing.'

'It's okay,' she said, still looking at him, but then she reverted to looking at the pavement again.

'So where are you off to, Eden?'

'I have to collect my sister from my aunt's, who lives just up the road.'

'Do you fancy going out some time? Maybe for a burger in the High Street or the cinema to catch a movie?'

He watched as she looked up again at him, and her whole face turned pink. He'd never seen a girl embarrassed before, and he'd never actually asked anyone to go for a burger with him either. His way of dating was to share a bottle of booze at the park or in some gypsy's caravan before getting his end away. Eden was different; he assumed she was a virgin, which made her his next conquest. He wanted her, and he would have her.

'Oh, that's kind of you, Jordan, but I can't.'

He laughed. 'There's no such word as "can't". 'Course you can. I'll pay, so you don't have to put your hand in your pocket.'

'I'm sorry, Jordan. I really can't.'

She turned to walk away, but before she could, Jordan wrapped his arms around her and kissed her on the cheek. 'I won't give up,' he said, as he let her go.

Totally shocked, Eden stood frozen for that moment, until a high-pitched sound came from up the road.

'What on earth is going on?'

Jordan was enjoying the sweet smell of Eden and was angry that some ugly tall bitch was sticking her nose in. 'Mind your own business, woman.'

Rachael ignored him; she marched down the hill towards them, dragging a young girl with her. 'You are late, Eden. I have had to bring Beatrice myself, and I can see very clearly *why* you are late.'

'Oi, Missus, she ain't done nuffin. I only asked her her bloody name.'

He stood defiantly as the woman turned to face him. 'Get away from her, you son of Satan. She will be disfellowshipped for this.'

Jordan had no idea what the woman was on about. 'Oh, fuck off, woman. She ain't done nuffin. It was me. I wanted to get to know her.' He huffed loudly. 'You fucking Bible-bashers are all the same. Ya think you're better than me, but look what you've gone and done now. See, the girl's about to cry, and I fucking never did that. But you did, you nasty bitch.'

Rachael snatched Eden's arm and dragged her away, hissing something in her ear.

All Jordan could do was watch.

'You're best off away from that lot, Jordan. They're all a bunch of oddballs.'

Jordan nodded and looked away. 'Let's go and pay ol' Bernie a visit.'

'What? Seriously, Jordan? Only, I'm not sure. Can't we just leave the watches on the doorstep, knock on the door, and do the off?'

'For fuck's sake, Sonny, man up. I wanna face ol' Bernie and tell him he should be more careful. He just needs to know I ain't no chicken, and then he might even think twice about threatening to hurt our grandad.'

Sonny swallowed hard; he didn't like the plan at all. In fact, he hadn't been too happy that Jordan and that twat Rocco had even planned to rob Bernie in the first place. He had suggested to his brother's friend that they should keep the watches for a long time before trying to sell them in case someone became nosey, but, obviously, the suggestion had fallen on Rocco's deaf ears.

By the time they reached Petts Wood, the sky was heavy with black clouds, and there was a slight chill in the air. But Sonny was sweating under his T-shirt, trying to keep up with Jordan's long strides.

They stopped directly outside Bernie's house, and Jordan looked up and down the road. It was dark enough not to be seen by curtain-twitchers, and the front garden was heavily hidden by the tall trees and thick hedges.

Suddenly, Jordan snatched Sonny's top and dragged him between two prominent bushes. 'Shush, Sonny. I don't want anyone to see or hear us. Got it?'

Sonny narrowed his eyes. 'Okay, but—'

'Shut up and follow me.'

As Jordan stealthily crept along the inside of the front garden, Sonny followed. Bernie's car was parked in the drive that ran along the side of the house. The front porch light was on, but there were no other lights showing. Jordan looked around before he hurried along past Bernie's car into the back garden.

The patio was only lit by small garden lights that were placed between the block paving and the lawn. The outside lights that lit up the full extent of the garden were off. Along the back wall of the house were two sets of French doors and the back door that led straight into the kitchen.

Jordan crept towards the French doors and carefully peered in.

Bernie was sitting in his armchair and smoking a cigar. The chair was facing the opposite end of the lounge to a big television set. Beside him was a side table and on it was a decanter containing some sort of liquor or other and a cut-glass tumbler. He was watching an old black-and-white movie, but he had his back to Jordan, so he was unaware of the lad's presence.

As Jordan turned to Sonny, he gave him a dirty grin. He was about to open the back door when Sonny grasped his shoulder. 'What are you gonna do?'

'Give him back his watches,' he whispered, as he tapped the rolled-up parcel that was tucked inside his tracksuit top. 'Listen, you just wait here, all right? You don't need to come in. I'll only be five minutes.'

Sonny nodded but shivered. He didn't like the look on Jordan's face; still, he didn't really want to get into trouble himself.

Once Jordan turned the handle on the back door, he heard a creak, and then Bernie shouted out, 'Who the fuck is there?' His voice was deep, and for an old man – as far as Jordan was concerned – he sounded menacing.

Jordan put the watches on the kitchen counter and pulled a knife from a knife holder that was next to the cooker. Before he had a chance to attack Bernie in the lounge, the man himself appeared. Standing well over six feet tall, with broad shoulders, a square jaw, and a boxer's corrugated nose, Bernie looked the hard doorman he once was.

'So, it's you, Jordan Swan. You should have knocked, you sly little bastard.' He looked Jordan over. 'But you're here now, and with me watches, I hope, for your sake.'

Holding the knife behind his back, Jordan nodded towards the rolled-up velvet cloth.

'I thought better of you. I would've thought your grandfarver would've taught you some fucking manners. Nicking off your own kind, ain't the done thing. I served time with your ol' man, Mitchell. Now, I can tell, you ain't raised by him, 'cos he's a right decent, straight-up geezer. I hear you're becoming a bit of a nuisance.'

Jordan glared with a smirk, almost mocking Bernie.

'Don't you come it with me, boy, with your wannabe hardman act.' Bernie shook his head and grinned. 'You ain't hard at all, boy. I've heard that you're 'aving it with the pikeys up the site, and a whisper in my ear told me that you're a wrong 'un. And you forced yaself on a young girl from Orpington, didn't ya?'

Jordan's eyes suddenly widened. 'No, I never.' He gripped the knife tightly and protruded his bottom jaw.

Bernie clenched his fists. 'Oh, yeah, you fucking did, 'cos I have eyes and ears all over this manor, and your behaviour has caught my attention. The girl you helped yaself to—' Bernie stopped and glared at Jordan, who was shaking his head. 'Don't deny it, boy!' His voice became raised, and the deep serious tone stopped Jordan in his tracks.

'You interfered with the daughter of a very good friend of mine. She was fifteen, and in my books, Jordan, that's too fucking young. And to make matters worse, the poor cow is too terrified to go to the cop shop. I fucking despise lads like you. You have the looks but not the respect. So be warned. You will pay one way or another for that girl's cherry. Now, you'd better have made sure that every single one of my watches is in that makeshift bag or I'll break one of your fingers for every watch missing.'

Jordan was getting wound up with every breath he took; he gripped the knife so tightly in his hand that his knuckles went white. 'They ain't all there, 'cos Rocco still has half.'

'Nah, he don't. He tried to pawn one locally, the silly billy. I know what comes and goes. Like I said, I know this manor, and when I told the pawnbroker that my watches had been stolen, he showed me one that was pawned the very next day. Now I had to laugh 'cos I thought how fucking stupid that kid was, and then, when I paid him a visit, he wanted to row. He even got his older bruvver to 'elp him.' He paused and then laughed. 'They are both at Queen Mary's hospital now. I think they're having their jaws wired up. Anyway, back to you, Jordan. You did me wrong, boy. I—'

Before he could finish, Jordan was flaring his nostrils and planning where he was going to plunge the knife. Just as he lunged forward, Bernie stepped aside, out of the way of the blade. With his huge fists curled tightly in a ball, he ruthlessly slammed a punch into Jordan's face. The impact was so hard that it sent Jordan into a surreal feeling of slow motion. Tasting the coppery blood in his mouth, he buckled to his knees and dropped the knife. Reeling from the blow, he could hear a high-pitched ringing resonance in his ears and then the sound of a deep voice before he was back to some kind of reality. Instantly, he went into survival mode and tried desperately to scramble to his feet while reaching for the knife. A sudden blow hit him on the other side of his head. This time he felt a crunching, cracking sensation that echoed and vibrated around his skull. The second punch had broken his jaw. With a final blow, he was out cold, face down on the kitchen floor.

Bernie bent down, grabbed the knife with one hand, and with the other, he lifted Jordan's head up by his hair and ran the freshly sharpened blade down his right cheek. He watched as the skin and muscle flapped open. The blood ran like tar down Jordan's face and neck. Bernie dropped him and stood there, waiting for the boy to come round. He'd known Jordan had the knife. He had seen it in the reflection from the glazed back door. As he continued to wait, he saw something move outside. Quickly grabbing the knife before stepping over Jordan, he went out to face whoever was there.

Once he realised it was the younger brother, he yelled, 'Don't bother running. You'd better make arrangements to get your bruvver to the hospital. He needs a few stitches.'

Sonny turned around and stared, totally shocked by the size of the man. Jordan had only told him that Bernie was an old man, but he'd never said that he was the size of an All Black rugby player. And he was too young to remember the man himself.

'Well, don't just stand there looking gormless, boy. Get your bruvver outta my kitchen before he makes any more mess.' He stepped back, knowing that the younger lad was too wary of getting too close to him. 'Don't you even think about coming to my pad again. And you tell your bruvver – if he ain't already brain-dead – that he took fucking liberties, and if he ever returns, he'll be leaving in a black sack.'

Sonny's eyes were like saucers. Then, when he looked at the state of his brother, he realised that this wasn't a ruck with a few scallies: this was the work of a real gangster. He had the massive arms, the shovel-like hands, the deep voice, and the scarred face. Those were the marks of a man who didn't get to where he was by being nice. Weak-kneed, Sonny skirted around Bernie and stopped short of his brother, who struggled to get to his feet.

The blood that covered the white floor tiles had turned everything into a makeshift ice rink and impossible for his brother to stand up. Sonny could tell that Jordan's vision was obviously impaired because his eyes were so swollen from the clumps he'd received that he could barely open them. And the slice down his cheek was horrendous.

Sonny took in all the graphic details as he contemplated what to do first – either attempt to hold his brother's face together or to try and hold him up.

'Oh, for Christ's sake!' bellowed Bernie, as he barged past the two lads and pulled a tea towel from the drawer. He pushed it against Jordan's face. 'Get him outside, before he damages me kitchen.'

Sonny was trying to hold Jordan up but found himself slipping and sliding in the blood.

Then, from nowhere, Bernie grabbed Jordan by the shoulders, lifted him up off the floor, and placed him outside.

Seeing the blood now seeping through the tea towel and through Jordan's fingers, Sonny knew he had to do something quickly.

'Look Mr, er, please, I know we did you wrong, but I ain't got any money on me, and he needs the hospital. Please can you drive us? I swear, I won't call the police or nuffin.'

'Not my problem. He's just like your sly old grandfarver, another fucking wrong 'un. And I was fond of your grandmuvver. A real diamond, she was. Now, take your dirty scummy bruvver and fuck off. And you wanna hope you don't get tarred with the same stinking brush.'

Sonny was struggling to hold his brother up.

Jordan, with the towel held to his face and an arm around his brother, mumbled under his breath, 'Cunt.'

'Get him outta my sight before I swallow you both up like a fucking earthquake!'

'Shut up, Jordan,' hissed Sonny. 'Let's get out of here before we end up in a black sack.'

***

It was a serious feat to get to the hospital. Jordan's legs were off-balance, and every time he swayed and clutched Sonny's body to realign himself, he could feel his brother straining to stand up straight enough to hold them both upright. They had managed to get halfway down Midfield Way when a copper's car pulled over. Under normal circumstances, both boys would have scarpered. Sonny was struggling, and Jordan didn't know if he was Jordan Swan or an ugly duckling. The injuries to his head and face had really knocked him into next week.

Two officers leaped from the car and helped Jordan onto the pavement.

Sonny was relieved that they were taking over.

The first officer, an older man in his late forties, of medium build and with a well-trimmed beard, pulled out his notebook and asked Sonny for his details. 'What's your name and address?'

Sonny answered the questions truthfully until he was asked what had happened to Jordan. That was when he faltered. He thought of Bernie, and that enraged look on the man's face, and he didn't fancy his chances if he grassed. So he told them that they were attacked by a group of youths and Jordan came off worse.

The police called for an ambulance and Sonny was allowed to travel with his brother to the hospital. It was in the ambulance that he got to see the true extent of the damage to Jordan's face. All he could think of was how fortunate Jordan was not to lose his eye. The wound was deep and would need stitches, but the swelling around his eyes and jaw looked more of a concern.

While a team of nurses saw to Jordan's injuries, Sonny sat in the waiting room. It was two o'clock in the morning, and he guessed his mother would be worried. He watched a few people come and go, mainly elderly folk who had taken a tumble. But other than that, it was quiet in the section he was in. He looked at his bloody hands and his bloodstained shirt and wondered why he was in this predicament. He loved Jordan and wanted to be like him since everyone seemed to have respect for him. He had the birds and the mates. He could fight as well, even against older lads, and he had a name for himself among the travellers. Being Jordan's brother, he was offered the same respect. He wondered if his life would have been any different if he had lived with Mitchell instead. One of his friends had told him that George was probably as tall as Jordan and doing all right for himself; he was part-owner of a gym. He wasn't sure if he believed that bit of the gossip because, surely, if Mitchell owned a gym, then he would have given them all a share. He had, after all, always kept up the monthly maintenance payments and given them a bit extra come birthdays and Christmas. He sighed and felt his eyes become heavy; it had been a long evening, and his mind was all over the place. Just as he dozed off, the doctor appeared.

'Are you Mr Swan's brother?' he asked, coldly.

Sonny jumped up and nodded.

'You may as well go home because we will be keeping him in under observation. He may have concussion. We've stitched his cheek, and he is on a drip at the moment, so go home, get some rest, and you can come by later on today, after two o'clock. By then, he may be okay to go home.'

'Will he be all right, doctor? Only those lumps on the side of the head. I mean, he's not brain-dead, is he?'

The doctor wanted to laugh, but he kept a straight face. 'No, not brain-damaged, but he may have some swelling of the brain, which will go down, given rest. He was obviously struck with a weapon, so, again, he needs rest and care, and then he should be okay.'

He left, leaving Sonny stunned.

Sonny knew the only weapons used to bash Jordan were the man's fists and the knife to cut his face. He was thankful that he himself hadn't suffered a punch from Bernie. Leaving the hospital, he walked home, planning how he would break the news to his mother.

Chapter Fifteen

Five hours earlier

Eden looked back at Jordan, only to see him still looking her way.

Then Rachael pushed her hard to move along. She growled in her ear, 'You are a dirty whore, Eden. You should never have let a man touch you. And if you think Jehovah will let you into his kingdom, then you are very much mistaken.'

'Please, please, believe me. I never let him touch me. I wasn't embracing him. He just hugged me. I wasn't . . .' She stopped to catch her breath and wipe her eyes. 'Please, it wasn't what you think.'

Rachael cackled like a witch on cocaine. 'You think I am foolish and gullible to believe that, young lady!' Prodding Eden hard in the back, she snarled again, 'Just you wait, and we will see what your father has to say about it.'

When Eden heard the word 'father', her breathing intensified, her nostrils flared, and a hot sensation enveloped her. From nowhere, she stopped dead in her tracks. Her muscles tightened and every nerve in her body was electric.

'You have no idea, Auntie Rachael. My *father*, is the one who touches me. He has helped himself to me, my own *father*!' The second the words left her mouth, she instantly regretted saying them.

Rachael's eyes were huge, and her face became white with spite as her hand gave Eden the hardest slap she could.

Eden gripped her mouth and felt the inside of her cheek bleeding.

'You evil child. How dare you. You are not good enough to even live under that man's roof. You're like your mother. She was a whore, in case you didn't know. My brother took her in and protected her reputation. He could have married any girl, but no, out of the goodness of his heart, he married your mother, and you now dare to say such disgusting things about him.'

Eden put her hands by her side and clenched her fists. Normally, she was a thoroughly submissive girl, but the one thing she wouldn't put up with was for anyone to say unkind stuff about her mother. Her mother had been no whore; she had been good and kind. A tear rolled down her cheek. 'You told me I could come to you, talk to you. You said you promised my mum you would look out for me. But you won't, will you?'

'I would have looked out for you, Eden, but this accusation is evil, cruel, and a lie. And you will be punished severely for this, just you see.'

It was dark, but they were standing under a street lamp, and Eden could see every wrinkle, mole, and black hair on her aunt's face.

'I'm not lying, and oh, yes, Auntie Rachael, I know I will be punished severely. I am always punished, and I don't even know what for, half the time, what with the cold baths—'

'A cold bath? Is that all? Think yourself lucky,' spat Rachael.

Eden was adamant now she must fight her case. She had to be believed. She so desperately wanted someone to be on her side, but she knew now, at least, that her aunt would never ever believe her over Gabriel.

'He beats me.'

Rachael shook her head. 'Shut up, Eden, before you spout more lies and end up regretting them.'

Eden would have just gone home with her head down and her mouth shut, but when Beatie laughed and said,

'Liar, Eden, liar', it was all she could take. Lifting her skirt, she turned to the side and pulled down her knickers, so that her aunt and Beatie could see the black bruises that covered her backside and the tops of her legs.

Rachael glanced around, to see if anyone was about. 'Straighten yourself this instant, Eden. You dirty slut, showing your naked body in the street, in full view of everyone.'

Eden was stunned. 'Didn't you see the marks?'

'All I saw, Eden, was you undressing in the street. I knew you were trouble. From a very young child, you always had that look of strife waiting to happen.'

Eden looked at her sister. 'Beatie, please tell Auntie Rachael what Father does to me. Please!' she cried, in desperation.

But Beatrice just shook her head.

'Daddy is a wonderful man, a good man.'

Eden glanced back at her aunt and knew then that she was alone, and she would have no help when she faced the wolf. He was the man who so many respected and looked up to, and yet she knew what he did was wrong. He was a wolf in sheep's clothing.

It took her aunt an intense tug of her dress to force her inside the house. She believed at that point her father would kill her. He wouldn't just leave her in the cold bath. Oh no, he would drown her.

As they stood in the kitchen, Gabriel got up from his chair and studied the expression on Rachael's face. He noticed that she looked furious, but he also clocked that she was gripping Eden's dress. His initial thought was that Eden had let her mouth run away with her. Yet he noticed how she was breathing fast and shaking. He relaxed his shoulders as he stood up from the table. 'What's going on?' he asked, with his hands on his hips and his head tilted to the side.

Eden hated it when he narrowed his eyes and licked his lips as if he was excited about a potential drama, or, worse, the punishment he was about to inflict. She knew she wasn't stupid; she'd known for some time that her father liked to punish her, although, again, she realised she was far too young and insufficiently worldly-wise enough to understand why.

Rachael let go of Eden and pushed her further inside the kitchen. 'Your daughter was cavorting with a reprobate in the street. She needs to be spoken to.'

Gabriel turned white with rage, and Eden could see his lips tighten.

'And what exactly was she doing, Rachael?'

'She was embracing a young man while he was kissing her.'

'What? No, that's *not* what happened,' insisted Eden.

'Did that lad not have his arms around you?' spouted Rachael.

'Well, er . . . yes, but it wasn't like that. I didn't—'

'Enough, Eden. Be quiet!' roared Gabriel, before lowering his tone to speak to Beatrice. 'And what did you see?'

Beatrice looked at Eden and smiled. For a moment, Eden thought her sister would be on her side. She got that very wrong.

'She was hugging that boy, and he was kissing her.'

'I see.' He glanced at Rachael. 'Out of the mouths of babes.'

As Eden stared at the lino, with its parquet style design, she heard her father unbuckling his belt. She looked up to see him standing there clutching the wide brown leather strap.

'Take Beatie up to her room,' he said, while he partially wound the belt around his hand.

'I think Beatie should see what happens, in case she has any ideas of becoming a whore herself,' said Rachael, now pleased with herself.

'No, Rachael, because Beatie is a good girl. She would never ever do that, would you, my darling?'

Rachael knew when not to argue and swiftly gripped Beatrice's hand to take her out of sight, but her niece dug her heels in. 'No, Auntie Rachael. I want to watch.'

Gabriel heard her and said firmly, 'No, Beatie, I want you to sleep well tonight.'

Those words indicated very clearly that Eden was in for the beating of her life. She looked her father in the eyes and felt her gut twist as fear engulfed her. As she witnessed his mouth crease into a smirk, the blood drained from her face. He was getting immense pleasure from watching her squirm. With a tormenting grin, he curled his finger, beckoning her to come to him.

Plunged into complete panic, Eden suddenly turned and ran for the back door. Clawing at the door handle to turn the slippery knob, she ripped a fingernail clean off the nail bed, but she didn't feel the pain. Escaping was her only thought, and if she didn't make it out of the house, he would almost certainly kill her. The door was open, but she felt her dress being snatched. Terror gave her another surge of adrenaline to fight on. She yanked the hem of her dress out of his hand and ran down the garden path and along the street. Sensing him almost upon her, she tore on, running for her life until the only sound was her own heavy breathing. The footsteps behind her had stopped. He had given up. She looked down the road, and he was nowhere in sight. Gasping for breath, she felt her bowels moving and vomit was ready to shoot up out of her mouth. She fought to hold it down. She had to carry on, in case he used his car to track her down. Just as she calmed her breathing ready for the next sprint, she saw headlights, and her instant reaction was to throw herself over the wall of a garden. It was the right decision but the wrong place: she landed in a pile of compost, which reeked. Just as she stood up, a dog barked and the lights came on in the house. It was followed by a woman bellowing, 'Who's there?'

Eden stayed silent and waited until the woman returned into her home and the road outside was quiet. Brushing the eggshells and potato peelings off the back of her dress, she climbed back over the wall and took the next side street, knowing that she had to make a plan.

The only person she could think of who would help her was Chloe. She would tell Chloe's mother, and hopefully, if they were as kind as everyone said, she could perhaps live with them. Chloe's mother had always been so nice and motherly to her over the years, especially since the death of her mother.

They would understand, they would believe her — she repeatedly told herself — as she walked with a fast pace towards their house. Every time she saw headlights, she hid as much as she could behind lamp posts or in gardens. By the time she reached Chloe's house, she was shivering and shaking relentlessly. It wasn't for the cold that had crept into her bones but the abject terror. A gentle tap and the hallway light was immediately turned on, and a soft orange glow had her sigh with relief because she'd finally reached the house of safety. She hoped.

Monica, Chloe's mother, was wearing a quilted dressing gown when she answered the door. But her face, which always wore a gentle smile, seemed sterner. Eden assumed it was because she was knocking at the door uninvited, *but this was an emergency*.

'You had better come in, Eden.'

Eden stepped inside but suddenly felt uneasy. She realised that Monica was expecting her.

'Go on through. Gareth is in the kitchen.'

'Is Chloe in?' asked Eden, confused.

'Eden, go on through into the kitchen. We need to have a talk.'

The penny dropped, and Eden knew that her father had been in contact already. He would have guessed that she would go to her best friend's. She wanted to kick herself, but as she turned to face Monica, she thought she saw a glimmer of hope.

With a sympathetic smile, Monica offered her a seat at the table opposite Gareth.

'Let me make you a drink. Orange or lemon, Eden?'

'I don't mind, thank you.'

Gareth was wearing a beige suit and white shirt. His hair was beginning to thin out at the top, but he was, nonetheless, a handsome man. Eden had always liked him simply because he had an open, friendly face with big crystal blue eyes set against a Mediterranean complexion.

'Eden, your father has called. He sounded very upset. He said he thought you may come here, and he has asked us if we could talk with you.' He paused and fiddled with a serviette. 'Look, we know you were seen with a boy, embracing him. And we are also aware that you took your clothes off in the street. It's a sin, you know. A cherished sin.'

Eden listened to Gareth's softly-spoken words and then turned to Monica, who had placed the juice on the table and taken a seat next to her. Both seemed to be empathetic, without saying too much at all.

Eden bit her nails and stared at the table.

'It's okay, Eden. You can talk to us. We can help you, but you must be honest, and, of course, repentant,' said Gareth.

Eden looked up, and for a moment, she wished that they were her parents. Their home was warm and cosy; the light-coloured walls, the carpet, and the soft lamps in the corners of the living room made it homely. The house was more significant than her own home. The kitchen-diner was open-plan and led straight into the living room. Dominating the space was an imposing fireplace, and when the fire was lit, it brought the room alive. But Eden loved the potpourri that smelled so sweet, and the dried flowers dyed in pastel colours, which were simply layers of prettiness.

She flicked her eyes to Monica, who nodded. 'Yes, Eden, you can talk to us. I was friends with your mum, as you well know. She would want you to be honest and open with us, so that we can help you.' She grabbed Eden's hand. 'We only want the best for you, Eden.'

Those words had Eden breaking down. She covered her eyes and felt the sobs building up in her chest as she battled a tide of emotion that was sweeping into a tsunami. Her shoulders shuddered up and down as she cried her endless pent-up tears.

Monica put her arms around Eden and held her while the girl choked on her sobs. As they slowly subsided, Eden pulled away and wiped her face, using a tissue that Gareth handed her.

'Good girl, that's it, you tell me in your own words, sweetheart, exactly what has been going on.'

'It's my dad. He has . . .' Her bottom lip quivered as she fought to say the words that stuck in her throat.

Unexpectedly, Gareth got up from his chair. 'Go upstairs, Monica. I need to have this conversation in private.'

Monica glared at Gareth, but before she could leave her seat, Eden found her voice again.

'He raped me!' There, she'd said it, and now they would protect her from him, surely?

'*What?*'

'He raped me, Monica.'

'Stop, Eden, stop this,' said Gareth. 'I have spoken with your father, and he warned me that you would deflect the current situation with the boy. Apparently, you tried it with your aunt by stripping off in the street.'

'No, no, please, please. You have to believe me—'

'Eden, please stop. Do not say another word, or you will find yourself in very deep trouble, and you know how Jehovah judges liars.'

'But . . .' She glanced at Monica for some sign that she would listen, only to find that Monica had her eyes firmly fixed on the kitchen table, her right hand over her mouth, shaking her head.

'He did, he did!' she yelled, now more afraid not of the punishment but of the fact that they didn't believe her. They didn't know her at all because she would never make this up, ever.

Monica looked up and patted Eden's arm. 'Eden, please, darling, you must stop this ridiculous accusation, for your own sake. Your father is an elder, a well-respected elder of our Kingdom Hall. You must see that this deflection of The Truth is an act of evil.'

Monica's sympathetic, soft-toned voice cemented the fact in Eden's mind that Chloe's parents would not believe her. She knew her father was a convincing man; she'd seen him talk publicly every week. The congregation loved him: they hung on to his every word; they shook his hand; and they praised him at the end of every Sunday meeting. It was so ridiculous that Gareth and Monica should believe her. She stopped and stared into nothing. Her life as she knew it was over. She had no one else she could trust and nowhere else to go. She would have to live as her father's whipping boy and hope that Jehovah at least would see fit to accept her into his kingdom on the day of The New World Order.

Gareth and Monica left the room, but Eden could hear them talking outside. She listened to their words.

'She will bring The Truth into question if she continues with this accusation. I am calling a meeting tomorrow at the Kingdom Hall. I will ask Gabriel for his permission, and I will call in Brothers William and Clarence and have this whole mess cleared up. In the meantime, Eden can stay at her aunt's. I don't want her anywhere near Chloe or Mark. From now on, we must encourage Mark to look for another suitable wife within The Truth. She is not to bring her Satan ways to our own kids. I will take her to her aunt's myself, but I'm going to call Gabe now and let him know what's going on. He must be so worried. And how awful, Monica. To think all he has done for the child, even bringing her up as his own.'

Eden replayed those words: 'as his own'. *What did they mean?* she wondered. Was he saying that Gabriel wasn't her real father? Surely, her mother would have told her if she'd been married before. She strained to hear what Monica was saying.

'I know, Gareth. I do feel sorry for him and for him being all alone bringing up two girls. You would think that Eden would hold the family together, not tear it apart.'

Eden allowed another tear to trickle down her face, and, at that moment, she hoped that what they said was right and that he wasn't her biological father. She wiped the tear away and huffed to herself. She switched off, knowing that they were on Gabriel's side. It was all for nothing. She should just have taken the belting and got on with it. Now she was causing all this upset, she feared that Jehovah would look down unfavourably on her.

Gareth drove Eden to Rachael's where she was greeted as if she was loved. But after Gareth drove away and out of sight, and the fake sympathetic smiles and overenthusiastic wave were dispensed with, she counted down from ten for her aunt to let rip. Four, three, two, one.

Right on cue, the words hit like a thunderbolt. 'So you think you're clever, do you, trying to deflect the blame on to your father? How disgusting are you? But I must say, I am not remotely surprised. You take after your mother, all right.'

Eden wanted to stand up for her mother, but she was too afraid to answer back in case her aunt, who was a big woman, took a belt to her. The bruising on her backside was still black and blue, and even attempting to sit down was like hell on earth.

'You can stay in the spare room. Go on, Eden. Go up there now and just keep out of my way, or I may well end up repenting with all I have for the sin of murder.'

Eden kept her head down and hurried up the stairs and into the small front bedroom with the pokey window. She sat gingerly on the hard lumpy bed and could smell the musky odour. She sneezed and opened a window to let some fresh air in. For late summer, it was bleak outside and dark, except for the glow of the street lamps. She stared off into the night for hours, just wondering and dreaming, until she saw a boy walking down the street. He had his hands in his pockets, but as he got closer, she could see it was the lad whom she had met earlier. He was one of the two boys who lived up the road. The nearer he got, the more she could see, and as he approached the house, she spotted the blood on his shirt and his face. Unexpectedly, he looked up, and for no other reason than perhaps awkwardness, she waved. He stopped and waved back before walking on. For a moment, she didn't feel alone. She wished she could decipher what the feeling was, but whatever it was, it was like a lifeline to the outside world of all the sinners, the sons of Satan.

Chapter Sixteen

It wasn't visiting time yet, but that didn't stop Gina. With yesterday's make-up on, a fake bun tied in her hair, and her backside squashed into a pair of shorts, she clomped along in her high heels, much to the embarrassment of Sonny.

He wished she wouldn't wear those crop tops. They showed her jelly belly, and, really, they should, in his opinion, only be worn by teenagers with a toned and tanned midriff, not a muffin top. He never went out with her, not even to go shopping because secretly he was ashamed of her. She flirted with any man she ever laid eyes on, and today, he guessed she would be no different.

The minute they bowled on to the ward, a nurse jumped up from her station holding her hand up to stop them.

But Gina totally ignored the nurse and began eyeing all the patients to find her son. No young slip of a nurse would stop her.

'Sorry, Madam. Madam!'

Sonny tapped his mum's arm. 'The nurse is talking to you, Mum.'

Gina turned to face the panic-stricken woman. 'Where is Jordan Swan? He's my son.'

'Uh, sorry, but visiting is not until two. If you would like to come back then——' She stopped when she saw Jordan's mother wave her hands dismissively.

'Which bed is he in?' asked Gina, looking around. Then her eyes landed on the lad who was sitting upright in the bed at the far end of the room. 'Never mind!'

She marched on towards Jordan, leaving the nurse red-faced and flummoxed.

The nurse wasn't in the mood for a fight, so she decided to leave the woman and the accompanying teenager to it.

'Oh my God!' screeched Gina, her hands now thrown to her face.

Sonny stared at his brother's stitched cheek, and although it resembled a fat man's belly in a tight shirt, it actually looked better than it did a few hours ago.

'Hello, Muvver. Did you bring me some grapes?'

Gina leaned over and tried to hug her son without actually hurting him. She knew she could be heavy-handed at times.

'All right, Muvver. Sit down, will ya. Don't make a show.'

Gina plonked herself into the soft padded chair, which had a hole in the plastic, and it made a farting sound. It prompted her to announce to the occupants of the ward that it wasn't her farting but the chair.

Sonny rolled his eyes and looked at his brother, who was shaking his head.

'Muvver, go home, will ya? I'll be out tonight. There's no need for you even to be here. I've just taken a bashing, that's all.'

Gina stared at the damage to her son's face. 'I've a good mind to pay Bernie a visit, the nasty fucking bastard.'

Jordan glanced at Sonny, who shrugged his shoulders, intimating that he had no choice but to tell their mother.

'Muvver, leave well alone, will ya? Bernie will get it, don't you worry about that. So keep ya hooter out of it.'

Gina stared off into space while chewing her fake thumbnail, which eventually came off, and she spat it out onto the floor. 'I am going to pay your farver a visit. I'll let him know what's happened. He might have a word or even pay you a bit of dough to get plastic surgery or go on holiday, or, well, I dunno . . . I mean, he has all that money from the fucking great gym he's bought. And it's not just a bog-standard one, but it's got a canteen, loads of equipment, a . . .' She gasped for breath. 'And George even has his own named range of sports stuff. He has "Swan" written on everything. I tell ya, those two are raking it in, and I think yous deserve a chunk of it. Besides, you're both his boys an' all.'

Jordan sat up straight. 'Muvver, does me farver know anything about me?'

She shook her head. 'Why do you ask?'

''Cos I have an idea.' He glanced around and leaned towards his mother to tell her of his plan. She nodded as he whispered, and then, once he'd finished, she clapped her hands fast with excitement. 'You, Jordan Swan, are a genius. See, George, he may be bright, but you, my boy, are one step ahead of everyone.'

***

George opened up the side doors of the gym and guided the truck backwards. Once the driver slammed on the brakes, George opened the back door and beamed when he saw the boxes. He couldn't wait until they were all unloaded; he had to see the contents right away.

Mitchell came bounding over. 'So this is them, right?'

George used his penknife to cut the tape and open the box. He pulled out a tall plastic drinks container and held it up. 'Yeah. Perfect, Dad. What do you reckon?'

Mitchell took the bottle and turned it around in his hand. 'It has a good grip on it, the logo print is high quality, and the flip lid with the mouthpiece like a straw is a brilliant idea. How many have you ordered?'

George grinned. 'I saw the sample two weeks ago, so I knew they would work well. I have ordered two thousand.'

Mitchell saw the excitement in his son's eyes, and it warmed his heart. 'So, do you think two thousand people will turn up to the rave?'

George winked. 'Dad, I've got the best DJ, you've got the farm, and the news is out, so Saturday night, I will be quids in. Now then, we need to get these babies filled up and packed up again.'

Mitchell laughed. 'You are lucky that we ain't on a water meter. Won't they be expecting spring water or something?'

'Dad, seriously, they pop ecstasy, speed, whatever, and dance for like five hours. They need fluids, and they know the risks, if they don't drink.'

Mitchell raised his brows. 'As long as you, my boy, don't start popping pills.'

'I ain't that daft, Dad. Trust me. If those stupid kids wanna pop ecstasy and dance all night, burning up inside, I can't stop them. But what I *can* do is make sure that they drink plenty of water and make a bundle for meself.'

Mitchell smiled knowingly. George was smart and had a keen eye for business. Also important, he was clued-up when it came to keeping his mouth shut.

Still admiring one of the bottles, Mitchell didn't see Bernie walk through the back door until he heard the man's deep gravel voice.

'All right, Mitch?'

Mitchell looked up and nodded. 'Yeah, good as gold, Bernie. Have a butcher's at me boy's latest invention.'

Bernie took the plastic drinks bottle and fiddled with the straw that was attached to the lid. He smiled and nodded. 'Reminds me of a baby's juice contraption, but it looks trendy, and that's what the teenagers like these days.'

Laughing, George said, 'They love 'em, Bernie.' He removed the bottle from Bernie's hand, ready to pack everything away.

'Is everything all right, Bernie?' asked Mitchell, in a lowered voice, as he stepped closer.

Bernie nodded a few times, assuring Mitchell that their business was fine.

But Mitchell could tell that something was troubling Bernie. His eyes shifted around, and for some reason, he appeared awkward.

'Can we have a word? I've got something I need to tell ya, mate.'

Mitchell led Bernie to the office upstairs above the gym. 'Come in, Bernie. Do you fancy a drink? Brandy?'

Bernie shook his head and took a seat opposite Mitchell in the small but comfortable office.

'So, I have come to do the manly thing and let you know that I beat up your boy Jordan.'

Mitchell clasped his hands in front of him and leaned back on his chair. 'I take it, Bernie, you had your reasons?'

Bernie nodded and rubbed his hand over his bristly chin. 'He stole from me, Mitch. Now, he did bring me watches back, and so, in all fairness, I would probably have just given him a right telling off.' He stretched his neck. 'But when he crept through me back door, I do believe, Mitch, he was gonna stab me. I saw him in the reflection of the glass holding a knife behind his back. So, anyway, I gave him a couple of fists, and I took the knife, and cut his face . . .' He held his hands up. 'I know, maybe, I went a bit too far with the slice, but, Mitch, that lad is a right nasty bastard.' He stopped and waited to see a reaction.

Mitchell stared for a moment, taking in what Bernie had said. Considering the fact that Jordan was his son, he should have, by rights, as a father, gone nuts, but instead, he sighed. 'I've heard as much myself, Bernie.'

Bernie jumped on the fact that they were on the same page. 'He's helped himself to me mate's little girl, and I've heard that it ain't the first time. The boy has no respect.' He held his hands up again. 'And I know, Mitch, it's not your doing, 'cos look at George. He's a right decent kid. And we both know while you were serving out your time, ol' Brennan was dragging those boys up. They take after him, Mitch. He's a wrong 'un, and so is that Jordan. Anyways, I just thought I should let you know.' He paused and waited to ensure that Mitchell was genuine in his reaction. 'Are we still good for business, Mitch?'

Mitchell nodded. 'Yeah, of course. Look, to be honest, I wouldn't even know Jordan if I bumped into him.'

Bernie laughed and shook his head. 'Well, he's a cocky sod, with a nasty sneer and a scar now. I think he favours himself as Danny Zuko from *Grease*.'

As they left the office to go downstairs, Bernie turned to Mitchell. 'I may be way off, Mitch, but are you sure that Jordan *is* your son? I mean, you're fair-haired, and I've known Gina all her life. She was a bonny little blonde-haired baby, but she's not so bonny now, but, well, you know what I'm saying, don't ya?'

Mitchell smiled and then shrugged his shoulders. 'I slept with her, and you know the story, so he could be mine, but who knows? I can at least say that I kept up the maintenance and the offer to be in their lives, but Gina didn't want any of it, except the money, of course. The boy has never called at my door and never even been to see George. Really, I don't see him as my son. I mean, how could I?'

Bernie smiled sympathetically and tapped Mitchell's arm before he left. 'So on the business side of things, I've got the imported ecstasy pills arriving Friday. Me chemist geezer has tested the goods and they ain't mixed with any nasty shit. Have you told George the reason why you are gonna be at the rave yourself?'

Mitchell shook his head. 'No, he's a good lad. He doesn't ask too many questions, plus he is so enthusiastic about his own business – the drinks bottles, the healthy lifestyle – that he has no interest in what I do. But me boy's not silly either. So if he does have an inkling, he keeps it to himself.'

***

Two hours later, when George and Mitchell were sparring in the ring, Gina showed up. George was stunned to see her again and so soon.

Mitchell pulled his pads off and gave Gina a nod, along with a knowing grin.

Gina felt a little self-aware, even though this time she'd dressed more modestly in a pair of jeans and a longer T-shirt, although it was still low-cut. She had big boobs and always found it a waste if half of them weren't oozing over the top of her outfit. She'd applied waterproof mascara in preparation for putting on the waterworks without ending up looking like a panda.

George chuckled and held up his gloved hands. 'Oh, give me a few minutes, Mum, and I'll have a quick shower and lose these.'

Gina smiled and nodded, but Mitchell knew full well that she was here to see him.

As soon as George was out of sight, Gina put on her best performance. She forced tears to well up, and her hands shook as she covered her mouth.

'What's the matter, Gina?'

'Oh, Mitch,' she cried, 'you know me. I would never come here unless one of our boys was in trouble.'

Mitchell climbed down from the ring, grabbed a towel from the ropes, and wiped his face. 'Go on.'

'It's our Jordan. He's gone and got himself into a spot of trouble. The poor little beggar is in the hospital with concussion and a terrible knife wound down his face. His eyes, well, you wouldn't recognise him, Mitch . . .' She snivelled, took a deep breath, and held her hand up as if she needed a moment.

He guided her to the canteen area and offered her a seat. 'Coffee?'

She sniffed back the fake tears and nodded. 'He is in Queen Mary's Hospital, Mitch. It was lucky they didn't kill him. The doctor said it was touch and go.'

'So what happened?' asked Mitchell, as he placed a cup under her nose and sat opposite.

'Well.' She stopped and took a deep breath. 'He's only a lad, and you know how it is. He was just trying to make a few quid. Anyway, he got caught up in the wrong crowd and bought some stuff on tick in bulk to sell on, but as soon as he took the goods, he got as far as Cray Station, and he was jumped by a gang. They beat him bad and took the lot. The problem is, Mitch' – she paused as she took a deep breath for effect – 'these men who gave him the goods now want their money, and if you saw the state of him, you would know they mean business.' She stopped and tried to gauge Mitchell's reaction, but he was poker-faced.

'You should go and visit him, Mitch. I think it would make a world of difference.'

'So let me get this straight. Jordan took a large parcel on credit. I am guessing it was drugs, and he was going to make his own bit of money on it by selling it in smaller lumps. So once he got all the money together, he was going to pay the men back?'

'Yes, yes, I didn't like to say drugs, but you know what it's like.'

'And so then he was beaten up, and these other men took the drugs from him, and now he owes the original dealers the money?'

Gina sighed heavily. 'Yeah, that's about it, Mitch, but ya see, I don't have the money, and I know that if he can't pay it back, they will kill him.'

Mitchell chewed his bottom lip. 'How much does he owe?'

He could see the sudden relief and satisfaction on Gina's face. Her eyes were now bone dry, and a vast smiled adorned her lips.

'I knew you would help, Mitch, and our Jordan will be so relieved. He's terrified that they are gonna come and shoot him.'

'How much, Gina?'

'Oh, yeah, er, ten grand.'

Mitchell coughed, placed his cup down on the table, folded his arms, and smiled. 'Bloody hell, that's a lot of dough. Tell him to come and see me in a few days.'

'Yeah, yeah, Mitch, no worries. Shall I come back the day after tomorrow?'

'Not you, Gina. Send Jordan, when he has recovered, and Sonny.'

'Sonny?'

'Well, yeah, it's not safe for Jordan to walk around alone, not after previously getting robbed, now is it?'

'Oh, no, okay, thank you, Mitch. I knew I could count on you to help our son.'

Gina was up and out of her chair by the time George came into the room.

'Aw, you're not off, are you, Mum?' he asked, before shooting his father a nasty glare.

'Sorry, George, the thing is, your brother is in the hospital, and I have to get back to him.'

'Oh, no, is he okay? Is it serious? Shall I come with you?'

She shook her head and hurried past George. 'Sorry, George. He can't have visitors, but he'll be okay soon enough. Sorry, I can't stop.' And with that, she was gone.

'What did you say to her, Dad?'

'George, sit down. We need to talk.'

George sat down reluctantly. 'She is still me mum, and I do want to get to know her again, and me brothers.'

'Okay, George, you *can* get to know them. They will be here soon enough, with their hands out to collect ten grand.'

'*What?*'

'Your brother Jordan and your mother have concocted a story to get money out of me, and that shows ya that she never knew me at all. If Jordan or Sonny wanted a few bob, I would have helped them.'

'But, Dad.'

Mitchell was angry, and his eyes were stormy. George knew that look and didn't push him too far.

As Mitchell told George Bernie's side of the story, and then Gina's, George's face dropped. He had been blindsided by his own mother. His shoulders sagged wearily as he silently left the canteen. Yet he still wanted to believe that his mum had feelings for him, and although she had concocted a story, he suspected she may genuinely be down on her luck. So, he would have liked to have heard her version of events.

Chapter Seventeen

Rachael's shrill voice rang like spears through Eden's head.

'Come downstairs and make sure you are presentable. None of your shenanigans, do you hear me, Eden?'

'The whole street can hear you, Auntie Rachael,' mumbled Eden, under her breath.

Having only had an hour's light sleep, Eden felt sluggish. She straightened her crumpled dress and used the old brush that sat on the bedside table to remove a few knots and to smooth down her hair. Staring out of the window for a brief moment, realisation hit her. The internal judicial committee meeting would determine her fate. Although she'd heard of people being disfellowshipped, she didn't know of anyone from her congregation who had been. The faces were all regulars. There were a couple who sat at the back of the Kingdom Hall, who no one really spoke to. But, other than what she'd gleaned, she didn't really know what it meant to actually go through the grilling process. She bit her lip, and a cold shiver ran through her. *It would be so embarrassing to have to tell the elders what her father had been doing to her.* But she decided it was the right and truthful thing to do.

Hopefully, it would put a stop to him ever hurting her again, or her sister. However, she knew that he loved Beatie so much more. She'd never seen him even chastise her.

Rachael was in her starched Harris tweed suit, with her nose in the air. She could have looked quite feminine if she'd added a scarf or a pair of lady's shoes instead of tan leather brogues. She looked like a school headmistress, except she wasn't one. She made dress alterations and took in ironing for a living. Like most of the congregation, she had a low-paid and part-time job so that she could go knocking to spread God's Word.

'Right, young lady, we are going by cab. Your father will be there, but he will not be allowed in the meeting.'

Eden nodded but didn't smile. She was relieved that he wouldn't be present.

'You will be asked about the boy, and you must answer truthfully.'

'But what about Dad?'

Rachael glared with eyes that could have fired spears. 'He will be in the main hall but not in the small room.'

'I mean, what will happen to him when I tell them what he did?'

Rachael's chest heaved up and down and her cheeks flushed crimson. 'Stop this nonsense now, Eden. You will never ever go to God's Paradise if you continue to lie. The elders have been called to conduct the meeting regarding the boy. Your dear father has nothing to do with it. So, you shut up with your stupid unfounded notions, and I mean, Eden, no talking out of turn!'

Eden's tears spilled over and ran down her cheeks. She didn't bother to wipe them away. She knew then that she would be walking into a lion's den. No one would be by her side, not even her aunt to hold her hand. After climbing into the back of the cab, she winced as she sat on the seat belt. Her backside and the tops of her legs were still very sore. She suddenly relived that whipping and knew that it would never stop unless she told someone. She had to tell the elders and hope that one of them would believe her. At that moment, she wondered if she loved her father and tried to remember any good times she'd had with him, but trying to recall any pleasant memories was like grabbing at a smoke ring. She concluded that, actually, she didn't like him at all – never had, in fact. If it hadn't been for Beatrice and the way he doted on *her*, she probably would never have known that he could be any different.

As the cab drew into the car park of the Kingdom Hall, Eden spotted her father and Gareth with three other men. They were older than her father, maybe in their sixties and seventies. One of the elders was very large, with a huge belly and thin white hair combed back. He wore a brown over-ironed suit that shone at the creases. An ancient-looking elder, who was grey and round-shouldered, wore a black fitted suit. Then Eden's attention was drawn to a third man. Everything about him was dark: his skin, his eyes, and his suit. His hair was greasy, but his brown shoes, in contrast, shone like burnished copper.

They all glanced her way and waited, in their important attire, each holding an official-looking briefcase.

She held her breath as her father walked towards her cab. He opened the door for her to get out and gently placed what to the others would have looked like a loving arm around her shoulders. Leaning in with a smiling face, he whispered, 'Do not mention my name. They will never believe you anyway, daughter of Satan.'

Glancing back to the cab, she saw Aunt Rachael, still seated in the front with an evil grin smacked across her witchlike face. Looking forward, Eden saw the three men nod politely and make way for her father to guide her to the small room, the room that she'd cleaned and polished. It was still clean because she'd shut the window so that no vandals could get in.

The bang was loud as the door was closed behind them. The fat man introduced himself as Brother Paul Whitlock. He then introduced the dark elder as Brother Clarence West and the older elder as Brother William Shaffer. They sat in a row behind two tables that had been moved together. It was evident that the room had been altered; in fact, it was set up as a court. She sat down on the chair opposite and waited until the elders had their notes and Bible on the table.

Their hands were clasped together as if in prayer.

It was Brother West who was eager to get started. He smiled, showing his short teeth and large red gums. 'So you are eighteen and menstruating, then?'

Eden searched the other two men's faces to see if they were offended or found that question or statement a little rude and personal. She was met with a nod, encouraging her to answer.

'Yes.'

'And as a young woman, you will naturally have wants and desires, but we call that Satan's work.'

Eden stared, waiting for the question.

'Well, do you have desires?' his voice was harsh, with an aggressive undertone.

'No,' replied Eden, honestly.

'No, Brother West!' he corrected her, with a smart look on his face.

'Sorry. No, Brother West.'

'Aw, come on, Eden. We already know that you do have desires. You have been seen in public with a boy your age embracing each other, and you know unless he is a Jehovah's Witness, it is a sin.'

She shook her head. 'No, it wasn't like that.'

'Where did he touch you?' asked Brother West, licking his lips eagerly.

'Nowhere,' she replied, flatly.

'You are not a child, Eden. Where did he touch you? Was it your breasts, your lips? Where?' demanded Brother West.

'Nowhere. He just hugged me. I never . . .'

'Stop!' screeched Brother Shaffer. 'You are only to answer the questions we put to you. We need to establish if you are telling the truth and if you are repentant for your sins. If you do not tell the truth and repent, then Jehovah has told us that you will not enter his Paradise, The New World Order.'

Eden felt her bottom lip quiver. This was so unnerving. What did they really want from her? And the questions seemed so personal. It was obvious that these elders wanted her to admit to something that she hadn't done.

'Where did he touch you, Eden? Between your legs, your buttocks?' continued Brother West, with his cruel eyes, eager to hear some sordid account.

Eden shook her head. 'I've already told you. Nowhere.'

'Did you like him touching you? Did you touch him? Did you feel his penis?' the elder continued.

Feeling her heart beating outside her chest, Eden struggled to answer, since her mouth was almost glued shut with fear.

'Answer me. Did you touch his penis?' grilled Brother West.

She shook her head and allowed a tear to trickle down her face before she wiped it away.

'A tear, eh? Is that guilt, Eden? Did Brother West mention a truth? Did you touch the boy's penis?' questioned Brother Shaffer.

'No!' she managed to blurt out.

'You are very defensive, Eden. Thou doth protest too much.' Brother Shaffer paused and allowed Eden to wipe another tear before he lowered his tone. 'It's okay, Eden. We understand. We just want to get to the truth, and to be completely sure that you are repentant of your sins.'

Humiliation was turning to anger. And with every breath, Eden was fighting to keep her mouth shut. It was all wrong. While these three old men glared at her, making all these disgusting accusations, what they should be doing was interviewing her father, the only one in the Kingdom Hall who had been repulsive to her.

'God has given you his spiritual food, and you were present last week when the words from *The Watchtower* were discussed. Did you not listen, Eden? The cherished sin was the main topic, and you were at the Kingdom Hall on Sunday, were you not?'

She nodded frantically, but her throat was closing up. Each man leaned forward, their eyes judging her, showing the importance of their superior rank in the community. She was beneath them – a subservient – and they expected her to be submissive and agree to their version of events. But she desperately wanted to fight her corner.

Brother West, though, was like a dog with a bone. And when he saw the beginnings of what he thought was an embarrassed flush, he gave a ridiculing grin, before he said, 'So, let's start from the beginning. You allowed this boy to touch your breasts and fondle you between your legs and——'

Something inside her snapped, and she looked up with the glare of a wild animal. 'Yes, he did, he did. He bent me over a chair and whipped me. He made me massage him, and then he pulled my legs apart, and he raped me. He raped me!' She suddenly lowered her chin, covered her face with her hands trembling, and cried.

All three men sat back as if they had been walloped.

Eden took a few deep breaths and removed her hands. She looked at each man in turn. 'But it wasn't the *lad*. It was my *father*! He raped me! He beat me! He fondled my breasts, he touched me between my legs, *and* he put his penis inside me!' She stopped to catch her breath as her heart continued to beat so fast her throat felt as though it was being strangled.

'Enough! Enough!' bellowed Brother Whitlock, who was now red from the neck up.

Brother West took up the baton again. 'We were warned that you would avert this accusation. Eden, I truly believed that today you would be truthful and ask Jehovah to forgive your sins and repent, but it seems to me that you have not. Don't you want to join Jehovah's New Order, or would you rather die at Armageddon where the birds will peck the flesh from your carcass?' He shook his head in disappointment and sauntered from behind the table and stood a few inches from her, deliberately invading her personal space. With his hands on his broad hips, he huffed. 'Gabriel is a good man, an elder in a respected position. There is, as you know, Eden, the "Two-Witness Rule". Two members of our congregation saw you with that young man, and they, as you know, were your Aunt Rachael and your own dear sister. And yet, Eden, you claim it was your father who did these hideous things to you.' He shook his head. 'You do know that Jehovah hates a liar. As elders, we are here to guard The Truth and to keep our congregation clean by not having a baptised sister who is a bad influence corrupting the members.' He stopped and looked her up and down as if she were shit on the bottom of his shoe. 'You can never spread the word of God. And you will need to beg forgiveness from your father for the cruel and evil words you have just spoken. You must wait here, Eden, while we pray and speak with God.'

Eden felt the heaviness of her own body. Her heart still pounded as each elder left the room. They didn't believe her, and now she would go back to her father's house knowing that everyone would hate her. She would be the girl who brought the work of their congregation into question, and they would never have that.

She listened, but all she heard were echoed mumblings coming from the Kingdom Hall. She looked at the two scars that ran across her knuckles and wondered if she would die come the day of Armageddon. Or would Jehovah see that she was truthful and allow her to escape the ball of fire and terror of his wrath?

It was an hour or so later when the elders returned to the room. She followed them with her eyes as they took their places. Brother West wouldn't look at her, but Brother Whitlock did. He was the only one who spoke from then on; the other two merely looked away as if she was Satan himself.

'We have prayed, and through God's Holy Spirit, we sadly have to disfellowship you.' He paused and waited for Eden to speak.

However, she had nothing to say; she knew all she could do was to listen.

'You understand that you must not have contact with anyone in the congregation. If you come to the Kingdom Hall, you must sit alone at the back and must not speak with anyone. Do you understand?'

Eden nodded. She'd not been believed, and if the experienced elders didn't believe her, then who in this world would? Tears plummeted down her cheeks; they were not for being disfellowshipped but for being left feeling so bereft and alone.

'Under the humane circumstances rule, you will be allowed to live in your father's house but you are not to talk about or even refer to religion. Your father has kindly offered to have you under his roof and put food on the table for you.' He stopped and sighed. 'You are a fortunate young lady, Eden, because you are not a child anymore. You could have found yourself homeless. So when your father . . . well, when Gabriel takes you home, you must show him you are grateful for his kindness.'

Those words – *grateful for his kindness* – echoed around her head. She knew deep down what that meant. But she didn't understand why Brother Whitlock faltered before referring to her father as 'Gabriel'. She assumed it was down to the disfellowship laws.

'Do you have any questions?' asked Brother Whitlock.

'No, I understand.'

With that, the elders rose and vacated the room, leaving Eden alone with her thoughts.

She listened to more muffled sounds from outside and knew then that she must go and face her father and her aunt and suffer the brutality that he would almost certainly inflict upon her. With graceful movements, she got up from her chair and walked out of the room that led directly into the Kingdom Hall. Without even acknowledging anyone, she marched out of the main door. Feeling their eyes boring into her back, she continued along the path that divided the car park. It was warmer outside, and she felt the heat on her shoulders, warming up her body that was iced to the bone. If improved her mood. But not for long.

Her Aunt Rachael stopped her by spitefully digging her talons into her shoulder.

'And where do you think you are going to, miss?'

Eden turned slowly and glared belligerently. 'Away, *Auntie Rachael*. I have been disfellowshipped, much to your pleasure, no doubt.'

'Why, you, rude, impudent child!'

'No, Auntie Rachael, the elders have deemed me a young lady and made it clear that I am *not* a child.'

Rachael glared in disbelief at the confidence in the girl. 'And why on earth would you think that I would get pleasure from that?'

'Because, *Auntie Rachael*, you always smiled when I felt pain, and when I cried, and when I longed for a comforting arm around my shoulders. When you knew *that man* was going to beat me, I saw your grin of satisfaction. I—'

A sharp slap around the face stopped Eden from continuing. She didn't touch the cheek, even though it stung like a bee; she merely glared and smiled back. 'You can't hurt me anymore and neither can he, Gabriel. I mustn't call him "Father" anymore. Not that I've ever wanted to.'

Raising an enquiring eyebrow, Rachael looked at Eden's eyes, from one to the other. 'They told you that you were not his real daughter, did they?'

Eden smiled. 'No, Auntie Rachael, but *you* just did.'

For the first time, Eden actually got a sense of pleasure from someone else's displeasure. She watched her aunt flush bright red and place her gloved hand to her mouth and then cover the other hand as if she was about to stop herself from speaking again. She enjoyed the look of uncertainty on her aunt's face, instead of those piercing looks that always had her trembling. But it was as if something inside her had changed. It was a sense of freedom, an uplifting awareness of her shackles being removed. From behind her, she could hear Gabriel's voice calling her; it was sweet on the surface. But she knew that tone was put on for the public; the undercurrent was violent aggression like the bubbling volcano ready to erupt.

Spinning around to face him, she saw the tightness in his skin. His jaw locked to one side and his eyes were wild with venom.

'Get in my car,' he growled deeply under his breath so that she could hear but the men behind him couldn't. He glanced at his sister and nodded for her to usher Eden into the car.

Waving goodbye to the elders and thanking them, Gabriel got into the driver's seat and glared again at Eden.

Rachael dug her clawlike fingers into Eden's arm so harshly that Eden squealed.

'Get in the car, or you will be in so much more trouble,' hissed Rachael, violently.

Eden looked at Gabriel's piercing eyes and felt her knees almost clanging together. Her bowels were moving, but, worse, she felt sick. She got in and shuffled over, as far away from her aunt as she could, and then pushed herself against the corner of the back seat. As they drove away, she looked back to find the elders talking and laughing. *Had they not seen the struggle?* She concluded that if they had, they didn't care. However, when she looked forward, she caught Gabriel staring at her in the rear-view mirror. An evil smile parted his lips and pure hatred burned in his eyes.

The journey home was painful. Eden felt acid burn a hole in her stomach. She knew this was the precursor to what would happen once she was alone with him. Sitting ramrod straight, Eden jumped when he stopped the car outside her aunt's. She had assumed that Aunt Rachael would be accompanying them home. What with enduring these events and the fear of the inevitable consequences, it had totally escaped her mind that her sister was missing. *Where was she?*

A sudden feeling of relief came over her. One of the sisters from the congregation would be at the house babysitting, so she would be safe for the present. But that tiny hope was dashed the minute he opened her door and gripped her arms, whispering, 'It's just you, me, and the punishment.'

Feeling as though she was about to go to the gallows, her legs buckled. 'Please,' she whispered. 'Please, Gabriel, forgive me.'

He didn't listen, didn't even respond to her calling him by his name. With an almighty shove, he pushed her through the back door and into the kitchen. Locking the door behind him, he kept his eyes on her while he walked to the door that led to the rest of the house and slammed it shut. Cruelly, he slowly slid his belt from his trousers and wound it around his hand. 'Bend over that chair,' he shouted.

Eden swallowed hard and took two steps towards the chair. It was the one that her mother always sat on. The chair that always remained empty. Not even Beatie sat on it.

She'd always wanted to be graceful and serene like her sweet mother but where had that really got her? Glaring at the empty seat, she noticed the dust that had accumulated on the PVC cover. Before she'd even had a chance to do as he ordered, she heard the whistling sound as the leather belt split the air and landed hard across her back. The shock shot up her spine, blurred her vision, and sucked the air out of her lungs.

Whether it was the empty chair, or the undeserved beatings, or the probing elders with their disgusting accusations, something snapped inside her. She gripped the back of the chair, and, in one fluid movement, lifted it up off the floor and spun it around, catching Gabriel in the ribs, as he held the belt ready to lash her again.

She watched him gasp and double over, clutching his side, but it was short-lived, as he straightened up and pulled the belt back. She was still grasping the back of the chair and tried to smash it into him again, but the belt caught her first, across her face. She thought it had broken her nose, but she dared not give up, or he would murder her. Screaming like a wild animal, she charged at him with the chair legs aimed at his chest. He staggered back against the wall. With every bit of anger designed to fuel all the strength she could muster, she rammed the chair into him again, and the second she saw the look of horror on his face, she pulled it away and watched him slump to the floor. Repeatedly, she struck him with the chair, hitting him about the head.

However, the next time she swung the chair, he managed to grab the legs and wrestled her with them until he broke her grip. Throwing the chair to the side of him, he got up and lunged forward, ripping at her hair and pulling her to the floor. Climbing on top of her, he savagely punched and punched until his fists were covered with blood and he could no longer see her white skin or the blueness of her eyes. Out of breath, he stopped and clambered off.

Eden felt the blood trickle down the back of her throat and the numbing sensation as her eyes, lips, and cheeks began to swell. She tried to focus, to see what he was going to do next, but one eye wouldn't open, and the other was flicking around like an old black-and-white movie. He had his back to her at the sink. She could at least hear the water running. Slowly, she turned to her side and coughed to stop herself from choking. Gingerly, with every part of her body shaking, she managed to get to her knees and then to her feet. The blood ran down her chin, and like a stream finding the nooks and crannies, it trickled down her neck and pooled at the lace collar of her summer dress. The sound of the running water was muffled, her vision was blurred, and her jaw wouldn't move.

Her body swayed as she tried to get her balance and be at one with her surroundings, and then she heard him say, 'You had a place here. You could have stayed under my roof, but not now, you dirty slut. Get out! And know this, Eden: if you dare try to go to the police, they will not believe you. Not over me, they won't. I am a respected man of the community, and you, Eden, are nothing but a whore, like your mother was.'

Although she could see his outline, the actual detail was blurred and the sound was very muted. Bright daylight shone into the dimly lit kitchen from the back door as he unlocked and opened it, and she knew then he was letting her go. Feeling sick as the intense pain hit her, she nevertheless managed to get out of the house and along the garden path. What she would do once she was away from this house of horrors was another story. One thing she did know was that she needed the hospital. Her mouth needed stitches because she could feel it filling with blood, and when she swallowed, it made her feel sick.

Chapter Eighteen

Although Kirsten was as hard as nails, underneath her sour face and massive build she had a soft side to her, but she only saved it for the right people. Brenda, on the other side of the street, was suffering from dementia, and Riley had asked Kirsten if she would make sure that his mother had her lunch. He told her he would pay her for her inconvenience. Kirsten would have done it for free because two doors along lived her own mother, for whom she made lunch every day, so another light lunch to make was no skin off her nose, and she liked to help if she could.

With a plate of cheese sandwiches covered in cling film in one hand, Kirsten closed her front door with the other. She put her keys in her bag and walked down her garden path. She would have carried on, but gripping her stone wall, there was a young woman who was dressed in an old-fashioned summer dress that was covered in claret. Instantly, Kirsten placed the plate on the stone pillar and held the young girl up. She was clearly ready to collapse.

'Dear Gawd,' she said, as she looked around, hoping that whoever had done this to the young woman wasn't still about. 'Let me get you inside, darling. You need to go to the hospital, pet,' she said, as she took a closer look at the girl's battered face.

Supporting the injured girl's arm, Kirsten guided the youngster into her living room. 'There, love, sit down, and I'll get you cleaned up and call an ambulance. Give me a minute.'

A creature of habit, Kirsten had a routine that she had to stick to or it would cause her undue anxiety. She hurried to Brenda's, shoved the cheese sandwiches on a plate in her kitchen, and then sprinted to her mother's and did the same. 'Can't stop, Mum. I'll see you later,' she called out, as she closed her mother's door behind her.

The girl was in the same position on the sofa when Kirsten returned. Wincing at the girl's injuries, she headed for the kitchen to fill a bowl with warm water and a drop of Dettol. She had a first aid kit and inside was a lint cloth. Her kitchen was like a clinic: it was so clean in appearance and everything was white. She liked to keep a tidy house and prided herself on it.

After pulling a footstool close to the sofa, Kirsten filled the cloth with the warm water containing Dettol. She began by gently dabbing the blood from the girl's face. 'Ah, love, what the 'ell happened? I bet a geezer did this to you, eh? Fucking men! What's your name, sweetheart?'

'Eden,' the girl whispered, through blood dribbling from her lips.

'Eden, shall I call the police?'

Instantly, Eden gripped Kirsten's wrist and tried to shake her head.

'Okay, darling, okay. I won't, but we need to get you to hospital. You might have a broken jaw and your lip may need a stitch, and . . .' She paused and sighed. 'You need to get seen to, love.'

Kirsten's concentration on Eden's injuries was interrupted by a series of sudden hard knocks at the front door. Both Eden and Kirsten froze for a moment. Eden thought it was Gabriel, and Kirsten assumed it was the girl's fella, if, of course, she had one, and he was responsible for the injuries.

'Kirst, it's me. Open up.'

Kirsten sighed and got up. 'Sorry, babe. It's my gobby neighbour.'

As she opened the front door, Gina bowled in. 'Kirst, I need a favour. I'll pay ya, but I can't get a cab, and I need to pick my Jordan up from the hospital. They are letting him out but what with the state of him, he can't get a bus. You ain't doing nuffin, are ya?'

'Well, Gina, as it happens, I am.'

Gina didn't take the hint but carried on through and into the living room.

'Fucking 'ell,' she said, the minute she clapped eyes on Eden.

'Gina, I can't help ya today. I've got stuff to do.'

Gina was just staring at Eden. 'Who did that? Ya boyfriend? I'd fuck him off, if I were you.'

She turned to face Kirsten. 'I wouldn't ask, Kirst, but I really do need a lift.'

Kirsten gritted her teeth. 'Have you no fucking compassion, Gina? Can't ya see I'm helping Eden here. Look at the poor girl.'

Gina glanced back. 'Yeah, I can see the fuck up fairy's paid her a visit. So, why don't we take her to the hospital and kill two birds with one stone?'

Kirsten rolled her eyes. 'You don't give up, do ya, Gina?'

Gina kissed Kirsten on the cheek. 'Come on, girl. You know you love me, really, and looking at . . . What's her name again?'

'It's Eden, Gina.'

'Well, looking at her boat, she needs a few stitches, and you ain't exactly Nurse Florencegale.'

'Florence Nightingale.'

'Whatever,' replied Gina, eager to get going.

Gina was about to continue to rabbit on, but Kirsten held her hand up to shut her up. 'Eden, would you like me to take you to the hospital? I think me mate's right. You might need some stitches.'

Eden nodded and allowed Kirsten to help her up off the sofa.

***

Eden held her head in her hands all the way to the hospital. Every bump in the road was like a hammer to her head. And this Gina woman's voice was like a parrot's squawk.

'Mitch is gonna give my Jordan a few grand and about time, really. Did you know that they own a bleedin' great gym in Bromley? They even have the Swan logo on everything. I tell ya, Kirsten, that middle lad of mine is clever and handsome, and he loves his mum.'

'His mum? Who's that, then?' asked Kirsten, with half her concentration on the road.

'Me, you silly prat!'

'Aw, sorry, Gina. I thought you meant he had a stepmum or something.'

'Nah, he wanted to take me to dinner and everything.'

Kirsten raised her eyebrows, which was commonplace when it came to Gina's stories. She knew from experience that they were seriously exaggerated at best; otherwise, they were out-and-out lies.

As soon as they reached the main car park at Queen Mary's Hospital, Gina was out of the car. 'Kirsten, I'll meet you back here as soon as Jordan is discharged.' She didn't wait for an answer but hurried off in a dress that was so tight it restricted her stride, and to gather any speed, she had to exaggerate her wiggle.

Kirsten was glad of the break from her friend's shrill voice and all the bullshit stories. She opened the rear passenger door and helped Eden out. 'There, babe, I'll walk you to the A & E. They will take over. Is there anyone you want me to call?'

Eden's one visible eye opened wide as she shook her head.

'Are you gonna be all right?' asked Kirsten, now genuinely concerned for the girl.

Eden nodded and walked in through the double doors with Kirsten holding her arm. She guided Eden to a chair in the waiting room and walked over to the reception area to book her in, although the only information she had was the girl's first name. Before Kirsten left, she removed a five-pound note from her purse and shoved it between Eden's fingers. 'If you get in trouble, you know where I live.'

Eden couldn't smile; it was simply too painful. But she nodded and squeezed Kirsten's hand to say 'thank you'.

Eden watched as the large woman with red hair put into a tight ponytail walked away.

She was alone again. The pain was now unbearable, and the future looked very frightening. She was now in the world of the worldly people who were evil, so her community told her. She closed her eyes to rest from the brilliant light, and within a minute, a voice asked if she was Eden. When she opened them, she was faced with a man in a white top and blue trousers. She thought he was a doctor – never considered that he was a nurse. However, she'd not been inside a hospital before in her life. Jehovah's Witnesses tended to stay away if they could help it.

'Hi, Eden, I'm Nurse Pitman, but you can call me Kevin.'

The first thing Eden noticed about him was his friendly round hazel eyes; then, she saw his beaming smile.

'Can you walk okay, Eden?'

She nodded and rose from the seat. Right away, he took her arm and walked her slowly to a cubicle where he shut the curtains behind them. 'Now then, sweetie. You pop yourself up on the bed there. I'll help you. We don't want you falling off and adding a bruised bum to your woes.'

If he only knew, she thought, ruefully.

His feminine and kind voice immediately put Eden at ease and seemed so at odds with what she'd been brought up to believe. Gay men were referred to as worldly sinners, the work of the Devil. *But Kevin wasn't evil, he was kind*, she decided. Once she was settled, he began wiping the blood from her face and checking her injuries. He was gentle and considerate, and he seemed to know exactly where on her face it hurt.

'Can you speak?'

Eden didn't want to; she was terrified that someone would contact Gabriel, and he would come here and take her back to that house for more beatings. She shook her head.

Kevin smiled. 'It's okay, sweetie. You don't need to, but I want the doctor to check you over. Before we do that, I am going to give you something to stop the pain. How about that?' he said, as he ran his soft fingers across her brow. 'No one will hurt you here. Do you understand?'

Eden nodded, fervently hoping he was right.

***

After the doctor had checked her over, he made the decision to keep her in overnight. It was Kevin who had suggested she should, for her own protection, if nothing else. The medical staff put two stitches inside her mouth and two in her lip. They also gave her medication to help bring down the swelling and morphine for the pain and to help her sleep. Fortunately, her nose wasn't broken and neither was her jaw, although they were severely bruised. But in a week or so, she was told that she would make a full recovery.

Kevin wasn't only a nurse; he was also a volunteer for the homeless, and he worked for the Orpington Baptist Church. It was his day off, but he wouldn't enjoy it unless he knew that Eden was safe. It wasn't what she'd said but rather what she hadn't said. He could see so much pain in her eyes and the fear, and he knew how that felt. He had been thrown out at sixteen as soon as his parents knew he was gay. He assumed this wasn't a boyfriend thing or the girl would have called her parents or a friend. He sensed this was done by someone closer to home, and possibly a relative – a male relative, almost certainly.

After breakfast, which Eden had taken ages to eat, Kevin arrived – this time in jeans and a T-shirt, with a newspaper and a few leaflets under his arm.

Eden tried to smile, but she was still sore, although much of the swelling had gone down.

Before dragging a chair closer to the bed, Kevin pulled the curtains around for privacy.

'I don't know your circumstances, and I am not here to pry either, sweetie, but I thought if you needed help, a place to stay, maybe, then I have some information that may help you. I work at the Baptist Church in Orpington, you see. They have people who come in and help the homeless, abused women, um . . .' He stopped and tried to see if any of what he was saying resonated with her.

'Thank you, Kevin. You are so kind,' she said, quietly.

She took the leaflet and stared at the word 'homeless'. She *was* homeless; she was alone with nowhere to go. She knew no one outside of her community, and she was told she must never talk to them.

Kevin saw the desolation in her eyes as she stared at the pamphlet.

'They are discharging you in a minute. I can drive you to the church, if you would like me to.'

Eden felt a cold shiver run up her spine and could hear Gabriel's words: 'The church is for sinners, for the evil worldly people. You must never ever enter their door.' She smiled again at Kevin. 'Yes, please, Kevin, if you really don't mind.'

'I don't mind, Eden, and if you want to talk, I am all ears. And I have an obligation to keep what you say to myself. But, either way, my intention is to make sure you are okay. If you don't have a place to live, then those people' – he nodded at the pamphlet – 'they can help.'

Eden hadn't realised that people outside her congregation would ever be kind and helpful. She assumed that she would be on the streets begging for food.

***

Jordan, Sonny, and Gina waited until the cab pulled away before they stepped off the pavement.

'Fuck me, I never knew me ol' man owned this gym. I've passed it a few times on the bus. Why didn't he tell us? Does he think we ain't good enough, eh?'

Gina grabbed his shoulder. 'Now, my boy, you listen 'ere, right? Don't go in all mouth, 'cos he'll more than likely throw you out. Be nice and friendly, and remember, Jordan, this was your idea, so get on your fucking drama queen shoes and think of the ten grand.'

Sonny stepped back and scrutinised the tidy-looking gym. He wondered what his father looked like, and George, for that matter. They hadn't seen him in years. His name was mud in their house, and they referred to him as 'the grass'. Even on the prison visits with their grandad, he always asked how 'the grass' was doing, and, of course, no one knew because George wasn't part of their life anymore. Suddenly, Sonny's heartbeat quickened; he was entering the world of his father and brother. A surge of excitement was suddenly dampened, though, when he heard his mother say, 'And remember, boys, if it wasn't for those two, your grandfarver would be free.'

Sonny did love his grandfather and missed him terribly but visiting him inside the prison wasn't a pastime he relished. He would have been a hundred per cent in on gaining a reputation like his brother, Jordan, if he hadn't been shown the consequences.

Jordan was the first through the door. He was still bruised, and his scar was covered by a neatly taped piece of wadding.

Gina eagerly followed her son – she couldn't wait to get her hands on all that money.

Trailing behind them, Sonny admired everything in sight.

Mitchell had sent George on an errand after school, so he knew the boy wouldn't be about, and he could have it out with Jordan. He was checking one of the treadmills when he spotted Gina and the two boys walk in. He stopped what he was doing and strolled across to them.

Jordan's usually cocky demeanour seemed to deflate. He was in entirely alien territory. His father was a big man, strong and muscly looking, with a glare of scrutiny in his eyes.

'I think we had better talk in my office.'

Gina smiled sweetly and nodded. 'Yes, of course. We don't want every Tom, Dick, and Harry knowing our business.'

They climbed the stairs in single file, and Mitchell held the door open for the three of them to enter his office. There were already three chairs facing the desk, and they all took their seats while he took his. He stared at them all in turn. He wanted to laugh when he recalled Bernie's description of Jordan, especially since the boy was wearing a black leather jacket on such a warm day. Jordan's calculated grin instantly riled him up. He glanced at Sonny and was surprised that the lad seemed to have a softer appearance, more gentle, and his smile was childlike and not sinister.

'So, me muvver tells me that you are gonna pay me the ten grand to pay off the dealer,' said Jordan, as he sat back in his chair with his calf bouncing on the knee of his other leg.

'Well, I did sort of say that you would help our boy out, Mitch.'

'Gina, I never said I would help him out. I told you to tell Jordan to come and see me. It was you who assumed I would give him the ten grand. I was going to offer him some good advice.'

'You what!' barked Jordan.

Mitchell could see right away that Jordan took after his mother. It was the same look of disdain and the familiar angry snarl.

'But, Mitch, you said to come back and . . .' She paused, trying to think what his exact words were.

'Jordan, whose idea was it to say that you were robbed of the drugs and now the dealers want to kill you, and for ten grand?'

Jordan sat up straight and stared at Mitchell as if he were an equal. 'Dunno what you're on about?'

'Oh, I think you do. It's the oldest trick in the book. You think that by coming to me with your face black and blue would mean that I would believe your story.'

'It's true, Mitch. Look at the state of your boy. He has had his face beaten to a pulp. God knows what they would do next—'

'Shut it, Gina. You came here to scam me. And you, Jordan. Be upfront. You're a so-called hardman, so tell the truth. You thought you could scam me and use your injuries somehow as proof that you were being honest.'

'Like I said, I dunno what you're on about,' said Jordan.

'Nah? Well let me tell ya, you are like your grandfather, a scammer and a wrong 'un. Your reputation ain't good, mate, and if you are going to be a burglar, then make sure you don't nick off your own kind. You knew Bernie.'

Suddenly, Sonny's eyes were wide, and he sat up straight, looking at his brother and mother. He could tell that Jordan wasn't bothered what his father thought of him, but his mother had turned scarlet.

'So, about that ten grand, Gina? You didn't think that I would just hand over that amount of money on your pathetic story, did ya?'

Gina jumped up from her chair. 'Well, you *should* hand over the money. These two have just as much right as the other boy—' She stopped when she saw Mitchell look behind them.

His eyes widened.

Before Mitchell could move, George was in the room, beaming with excitement.

'Mum, I didn't know you were here, and Jordan.' He glanced at his elder brother and gasped at the state of him. He then looked at Sonny. 'Sonny,' he nodded politely, in acknowledgement.

But then Jordan jumped up from his chair and looked George up and down. 'Grass!' he yelled, as he stepped closer, almost nose to nose with George.

'Wait! Hang on. I thought, maybe, we could, ya know, kinda get to know each other again. I was a kid at the time, Jordan.'

'Yeah, well, you had our grandfarver locked up, and you get to have the good life. You have all this, and we, me and Sonny, have fuck all.'

George stepped back; his cheeks reddened, and he cast his eyes down.

Mitchell glared at Gina. 'See, you brought the boys up to hate their brother, and now look at what you've done. I hope you're happy with yaself.'

'Shut your mouth, Mitchell. No one speaks to me muvver like that,' spat Jordan, still glaring hatefully at George.

Mitchell tutted loudly. 'Gina, you'd best leave and take him with you.'

'Oh, don't you worry, you wanker. I *am* fucking leaving. And you' – Jordan said, looking at his younger brother – 'ya weasel, you wanna watch ya back, you fucking grass.' He moved fast, daring George.

Mitchell pulled George back and stood in front of Jordan. 'You, Jordan, are your grandfather's double. I bet Donald is proud of you.'

'Come on, boys, let's leave them to it, the tight-fisted bastard.'

Jordan shoved the chair away and followed his mother out of the room.

But Sonny waited a moment; he looked at George and gave him a sympathetic smile before gently touching his hand.

As soon as they left the building, George took to the punchbag and spent fifteen minutes releasing his pent-up anger and the hurt.

Chapter Nineteen

Eden had no expectations as she followed Mrs Riven, the hostel manager, along the overgrown garden path to the main door. It was graffitied with '*Shannon woz 'ere and hated every fucking minute*' scrawled across it. And things didn't get any better when she heard a woman shouting from inside and using choice words. Eden's stomach did a backflip.

'Take no notice, Eden. The girls can sometimes get a little frustrated. The house isn't huge, but the rooms are equipped enough for a short stay until we find you more appropriate accommodation.'

With Eden still finding it difficult to move her painful jaw, she smiled instead.

Mrs Riven opened the main door with a key attached to a huge bunch. Once she and Eden were inside, the smell of sour milk, urine, and marijuana hit them.

A girl was leaning against a door frame to one of the rooms on the ground floor and shouting to someone. She had on just her pyjama bottoms and a vest top. Holding a large joint in her right hand, she had a cup of something or other in her left. She glanced at Eden, looked her up and down, and grinned. 'Cor, would you look at the state of yer. Someone did a right fecking job on yer. I hope you fecking stabbed the bastard,' she said, with a thick Northern Irish accent.

The sheer harsh tones and swearing made Eden recoil slightly. The girl was milky white with black hair and ocean-blue eyes. She looked rough, with sores around her mouth and a front tooth missing. Eden noticed the tattoos on her arms, and she suddenly felt so out of place.

'Hey, I'll not bite, yer know. My name's Kathleen, and you can call me Kat.'

Eden smiled and tried to say 'Eden'. But her voice was a mere croak.

Kathleen looked at Mrs Riven. 'What did she say?'

'Her name's Eden. Now then, Kathleen, you know you're not to smoke that stuff in the house, and you make sure you leave Eden alone. Do you understand?'

Kathleen straightened herself. 'All right, Mrs Riven. I'll not be the one Eden needs to be worried about. That's for sure.'

Shaking her head, Mrs Riven guided Eden up the stairs. But she didn't get far; two women, who Kathleen had been shouting at, suddenly appeared.

One had a carrier bag in her hand. She threw it over the banister. 'There, Kat. Take your stupid suit. It was fucking stained, anyway. As if Randy could go to court wearing that piece of shite.'

Mrs Riven yelled for the girls to move out of the way.

The loud one wasn't a slim girl like Kathleen. She was much older and chunkier, with hundreds of thin scars, which started at her wrists and continued all the way up her arms. The younger one looked meeker and nervous. She had straggly thin hair and love bites all up her neck. Both stomped back up the stairs, not bothering to reply.

It was a relief when Mrs Riven opened the door furthest along the landing and said to Eden, 'This is your room.'

Eden stared at the bed against the wall and could visualise the bedbugs hopping up and down. The carpet was frayed around the edges and threadbare in places. The light shone in from the one Victorian sash window, which was curtainless.

'Here are the keys. One is for the main door and this one is for your room. You have your own bathroom. Well, it's a toilet and shower just through there.' She pointed to the battered door. 'And you share the kitchen downstairs. I would suggest that you keep your food in your room and invest in a small fridge, if you can. Someone from one of the local charities will pop in maybe tomorrow with a few bits to keep you going. Oh, and Mrs Mortimer will bring all the forms you need to sign on and claim housing and other benefits. Okay?'

Eden turned to face the small sharp-nosed woman, who had cropped hair and thick black-rimmed glasses. 'Thank you so much. It's so kind of you to help me,' she managed to mumble.

Mrs Riven blushed slightly. She wasn't used to girls being so polite. Eden was clearly different: she was grateful and accepted everything that was offered without quibbling.

'I'm sorry, Eden. I wish I could offer you a more . . . Well—'

'This is just fine,' interrupted Eden.

As soon as Eden was alone, she closed her door and had a good look around. The bed was old and stained, but it would be fine. The bathroom needed a good scrub, but the toilet flushed, and the shower dribbled out lukewarm water, so at least she could keep herself clean.

Sitting on the edge of her bed, she uncurled her hand from the pharmacy bag that she'd gripped so tightly. If she swallowed the complete contents, she could probably end it all. If Jehovah didn't see fit to take her into his heavenly kingdom, well, then, she deserved not to be there.

As she emptied the tablets into her hand, she almost jumped out of her skin and spilled them onto the bed. Someone was banging on the door. She assumed Mrs Riven had forgotten something, but as she opened the door, she found Kathleen standing there, still in her pyjama bottoms.

She looked past Eden and spotted the drugs on the bed. 'Oh, yeah? So what were you doing?'

Eden glanced over her shoulder and turned crimson.

Kathleen shoved Eden aside and scooped up the tablets and then read the label on the bottle. 'Fecking Jesus, Joseph, and Mary, you do know these will earn yer a fecking fortune, don't yer?'

Eden had no idea what Kathleen was talking about.

'I'll tell you what. I'll give yer five pounds for them, right this minute.'

Eden was stunned but also in pain. She pointed to her swollen jaw.

Kathleen smiled. 'Eden, that's nothing. I have paracetamol. You don't need fecking morphine. If yer jaw was hanging off, then, yeah, but not for a bruise when you can earn a fiver. Jesus, why did they send yer out with all that shite?' She glanced around the empty room. 'I know, little Eden, that you're running from something bad, and you need money and clothes and a fecking blanket.' She threw her hands in the air and slapped them on her hips. 'They didn't even give you a clean sheet for yer bed.'

Eden was completely mesmerised by the way Kathleen spoke and how she treated her as if she were a child. Yet Kathleen was probably not much older than herself.

'I tell yer what, Eden, you have no clue, do yer?'

Eden felt a sudden wave of emotion. The tears in her eyes welled up and her nose tingled.

'Hey, listen to me. Crying won't help. Now then, first things first. You need some clothes and some food.'

'I have no money,' Eden managed to whisper, forgetting about the five pounds that Kirsten had given her.

'No, and you won't need any. We do the rounds at five.'

Eden tilted her head to the side.

'Never mind. I'll call for yer at half past four. You can come with me.'

Kathleen noticed how Eden appeared so lost and confused.

'Oh, okay, listen, but don't tell the other girls, okay?'

Eden nodded.

'The baker's closes at five. The council pays the baker to leave the leftover bread so the duck man can feed the birds in Priory Gardens. He's always late, so I get me week's worth of bread and cakes. I'm not greedy, mind.'

Eden smiled but then she felt her lip sting as it tugged on the stitch.

'Why do you want to help me?' asked Eden.

'Why?' Kathleen paused and sighed. 'I'll be honest with yer. I want the tablets. I sometimes find it hard to sleep, so if I'm coming down from drugs, they help me.'

'Here, take them,' said Eden, as she picked up each tablet from the bed and closed Kathleen's hand around them, before she even had a chance to think straight.

Kathleen stared directly into Eden's eyes. 'You can't be like this, Eden. Yer are alone in this nasty, cruel world. You need to survive, and being nice will kill yer.'

Unexpectedly, Kathleen popped the tablets back into the bottle, slipped them into the pocket of her pyjama bottoms, and left without a word.

Eden sat back down on the bed and felt hot tears sting her bruised cheeks. *That was a quick lesson in trust*, she thought. Now she was not only alone, cold, and in pain, but she was hungry too. And the one person who could have ended this miserable existence of hers had just left the room.

For ten minutes, Eden stared into nothing while the tears streamed down her face. The next knock at the door made Eden want to swear, but she remained quiet and hoped whoever it was would go away.

'Eden, it's me, Kat. I've got yer some stuff. Would yer open up?'

Eden quickly hopped off the bed, wiping away the tears, before she pulled opened the door to see Kathleen holding two black sacks.

'Right, listen, don't tell the others, but the room next to mine downstairs is empty. The girl there went back to her bastard of a husband and left everything behind. So, here's a clean sheet, some clothes, and a kettle — for a Pot Noodle — oh, and a quilt.' She stopped and glared at Eden's face. 'Why, whatever is the matter?' She put her arms out and hugged Eden.

For the first time since her mother had died, Eden felt the warmth of the embrace.

For a while, Kathleen hugged her. 'Now then, I'll not ask you what happened to yer. But know this. You can come to me and tell me, if yer want to.'

Eden nodded and let out a chuckle. 'Thanks for that, Kat.'

'Oh, right,' replied Kathleen quickly, now feeling embarrassed. 'I'll leave yer to look through the bits. Sling out what you don't want, and here's a box of paracetamol. Yer really don't want to be hooked on the morphine.'

***

Once Kathleen closed the door behind her, Eden felt a slither of excitement. She tipped the contents of the black sacks onto the bed, and right away, she spotted a pair of jeans. She had never in her life been allowed a pair of jeans. She hoped they would fit. They weren't exactly perfect, but they were comfortable. The tops were a size bigger than she was, but they smelled clean and would do the trick.

Underneath a sweatshirt, Eden found a pair of trainers. They were scuffed, but, luckily for her, they did fit. It was a strange feeling wearing modern clothes. Quickly, she folded them neatly at the foot of her bed, placed the sheet over the mattress, and then the quilt – with its Poirot clown duvet cover still on it – over the top. As she screwed her own bloodstained summer dress into a ball ready for the bin, she felt a five-pound note in the pocket. She smiled. Having money on her was a pleasant surprise. She then recalled where it had come from – Kirsten.

After filling the kettle with water from the sink, she switched it on to check it worked. It was a relief to see it boiling. All she needed now was a Pot Noodle. She sat waiting for Kathleen to return, hoping to get some bread or a cake. She was so hungry now that her stomach was creating an anthem of its own. With the five pounds that Kirsten had given her, she could buy a Pot Noodle, some tea, and milk.

Half past four came and went, and Eden felt deflated. She decided to knock at Kathleen's door. She tapped gently at first and then more loudly, but there was no answer. Turning the handle, she was surprised: the door opened. It was gloomy inside with the burnt orange curtains closed. But there on the bed, with her legs dangling down, was Kathleen. She was dribbling from the corner of her mouth.

'Kat,' whispered Eden, as she stepped closer.

There was no response. She tried whispering again but it made no difference. Then she resorted to tapping her, but it was evident that Kathleen was out of it – completely gone.

Eden decided she would go it alone. She wanted to help her new-found friend, but as soon as she stepped outside her door and gingerly closed it behind her, she bumped into the big woman from earlier. She put her in mind of a man. Her physique was square, her jaw was angular, and even her freckled face was muscly. Her hair was cut close to her head, and as she blinked, Eden could see the woman's pale eyes were laced with white eyelashes.

'Did she nick any meds off ya?'

Eden shook her head. 'I gave her my morphine tablets. I guess she needed them more than me.'

'Fucking Irish user, that bitch.'

Eden's eyes were again drawn to the scars up the woman's arms.

Rolling her sleeves down, the woman stepped back. 'Be careful in here. They're all after something. What did she promise ya?'

Eden shrugged her shoulders. 'She didn't, but she gave me a quilt, a clean sheet, and a few clothes and other stuff.'

'Yeah, she probably nicked most of those from outside the charity shop. She always does.' She smiled compassionately. 'Look, me name's Dela. And yours?'

'Eden.'

Dela raised her brow and smiled. 'Pretty name for a pretty girl. So you and Kat are even, then. That's good, 'cos, Eden, you don't wanna be owing anyone in here. Everyone's on the scrounge.'

Unexpectedly, Eden's stomach rumbled.

'You're hungry, eh?'

Eden nodded. 'I'll go to the shops in a minute. And thank you, Dela.'

Dela nodded and walked away.

Leaving the hostel, it was just a ten-minute walk to the High Street, and Eden knew precisely where to go. The baker's shop was in the small parade at the bottom of the High Street, close to Priory Gardens. Her mother used to take her there to feed the ducks. She hurried along, trying not to look anyone in the face, hoping that no one from the Kingdom Hall would recognise her. She assumed she looked different in her new rig-out.

To her dismay, she could see the shutters were coming down, and the shop workers were busy making their way to the bus stops.

Eden ran as fast as she could. Even though the pressure on her face was causing her a lot of pain, she had to get some food. The baker's shop was shut, and the lights were off. Scooting around to the back entrance, she spotted clear plastic bags filled with bread of all types. There were bags upon bags of loaves and big crusty rolls. They smelled heavenly. And there were also mouth-watering doughnuts, cream slices, and fancy tarts still in the square white cake boxes. She knew she couldn't carry them all, but by putting all the cakes into one package and holding the tied ends of all the bread bags, she managed to skip away with enough for herself, Dela, and Kathleen. As she hurried along the road, she felt a wave of excitement. This was the first time in her life that she was doing something naughty, but it felt exhilarating.

A group of teenagers, who were gathered by the roundabout, called after her to join them. She didn't stop. Her arms were heavy, and her face was throbbing. Yet her mind was suddenly full of dreams. She was free. Free to map out her future. Free to make her own choices in life.

As she approached the hostel, she could see an ambulance outside. The excitement of being free dissolved and dread took its place. As soon as she was inside the main building, she noticed a paramedic at the door of Kathleen's room. She stopped at the foot of the stairs. She wanted to know what was going on but was also afraid. The paramedic then stepped away from the door. He was radioing through to someone. Then she heard those words: 'The patient is deceased.'

Eden was unable to move. Her hands shook, and her heart raced. Then she saw Dela walk out of Kathleen's room.

The second she spotted Eden, she hurried over and urged her up the stairs. Eden didn't resist; she allowed Dela to push her along. Once they were inside Eden's room, Dela closed the door. 'Listen, Eden, Kat's dead. She overdosed on a load of pills. No doubt they were yours that you gave her, weren't they?'

Eden felt the blood drain from her face as she nodded.

'Eden, the police will be here soon, and there'll be questions. You just tell them that she must've nicked them, 'cos the bottle inside her room has your name on it.'

The bags of bread slipped through Eden's fingers. She placed the boxes on the bed and clutched her head. 'Oh no, I should never have let her. I mean, I had no idea she was, well, suicidal.'

Dela placed her arms around Eden and hugged her. 'You weren't to know, Eden. It's not your fault.'

'Oh, Dela, what shall I do? I have murdered Kathleen.'

Dela checked to make sure the door was closed. 'Shush . . . You never killed her, you idiot. She killed herself, and it wasn't just your morphine she downed. There were a few other tablets in her room. You would never have stopped her. She was determined to end it.'

'But—'

'No buts, Eden. She was so broken that no one could fix her.'

Sitting down on the bed, Eden cupped her face in her hands and cried.

***

After leaving Eden to herself for half an hour or so, Dela decided it was best to take her to her own room, to keep her company for the moment. It was apparent that Eden was nothing like them. It was just the way she talked and even looked. She was so sweet and yet incredibly naive. Dela thought about her own little girl who was in care. She was blonde with blue eyes and a sweet smile – just like Eden.

As they scooted past Kathleen's door and escaped the hive of activity, Eden stopped. She had to look in. However, what she then saw could not be unseen. Kathleen lay dead on the bed. She didn't seem at all peaceful, even though she was out of her misery. Her face was grey, brown rings circled her eyes, and vomit caked her blue lips and transparent cheeks. Her eyes were open and staring into space. The picture in her mind suddenly flicked to her mother lying dead on her blood-soaked bed.

Dela plucked Eden from her nightmare by pushing her away and into her room. She shut the door and locked it right away. 'Make yaself at home, Eden. I'll put the kettle on.'

The room was very different from her own. Dela had a single bed with large cushions that made it seem more like a sofa. Against one wall was a cabinet with a kettle and packets and tins of food. Beside it was a fridge. A wardrobe and a small cabinet were set against another wall. And along the furthest wall, there was a round table with four chairs – above which hung a massive picture of George Clooney.

Eden's eyes rested on a basket beside the bed. She could see it was filled with baby clothes and teddies. However, she kept her thoughts to herself. Everyone here had a story, and she knew, like herself, that the women probably wanted to keep their secrets to themselves too.

Eden sat at the table, still shaking. 'Thank you, Dela.'

Dela had her back to Eden. She had grabbed the bread and cakes from Eden's bed and was now buttering a couple of the rolls. She had some cheese in the fridge, and so after making two mugs of tea and filling the rolls, she placed them on the table.

'I don't know if I can eat now.'

Dela, with a mouth full of cheese roll, raised her eyebrows and nodded to the food.

Eden tore a bit of bread and gently popped it into her mouth. She was careful not to split the stitches. The taste of the fresh roll infused her taste buds, and within a few minutes, she'd devoured two rolls, a doughnut, and had drunk a whole mug of tea. Right away, she felt better.

The feeling was short-lived, though, when a policeman knocked on Dela's door.

Dela told Eden to stay put as she opened the door and allowed the officer into her room.

A handsome man in his thirties, he was stocky and muscular, but he had a gentle smile. 'I'm Sergeant Morley. Are you Eden?'

'No,' Dela replied, but she signalled to Eden to talk to the policeman.

'Eden, did you give Kathleen Lanigan your prescribed medication?'

Before Eden could answer, Dela jumped in. 'No, she never. Eden went out to get some shopping and forgot to lock her door. Kathleen must have helped herself. She did know that Eden was on painkillers. I mean' – she stopped and pointed to Eden's face – 'the girl's just been beaten up and can't really speak. The geezer fucked her jaw up.'

The young officer held his hand up for Dela to stop talking. 'Is that correct, Eden?'

Feeling herself blush, Eden tentatively nodded.

'Are you sure about that, Eden?'

'Yes,' she managed to whisper.

Morley glanced back at Dela, who stood with her arms crossed.

'As much as I liked Kat, she was a bit of a tea leaf, Gawd rest her soul.'

The officer nodded. 'Was she under a psychiatrist, do you know?'

Dela nodded. 'She's been in and out of rehab more times than I've had hot dinners. She'd attempted suicide before and ended up on the nut nut wing for two months.'

Morley nodded, thanked them for their help, and left, closing the door behind him.

'I thought they were going to arrest me.'

'Well, so did I, and if you had told the truth, then, believe you me, they would've done. But Kat does have a record for this, and she's served time for thieving. Listen to me, Eden. I have just lied for you, so don't you dare go back and tell the truth 'cos I have to be a pillar of society. I have to show the courts that I'm a good person, so I can get me baby girl back.'

The look of sudden desperation in Dela's eyes forced Eden to nod. 'Of course, Dela. Don't worry.'

Eden reckoned that everything she'd done since leaving the Kingdom Hall was probably sinful; and it was enough for Jehovah to let her die, come the day of Armageddon.

Chapter Twenty

George loaded the last of the boxes into the back of the van and jumped in the front with Nobby. Bernie and Maxi walked on ahead to Mitchell's new Audi. By the time they reached the field, the music was already booming. It was dark, but George could see thousands of luminous glow-in-the-dark rings. The ravers wore them around their necks. Whistles were blown to the beat of the music, and droves of people were dancing, dressed in every bright colour under the sun.

Nobby shook his head. 'Fucking mental, if you ask me. I dunno why your father gets involved. I mean, this is a young man's game.'

George laughed. 'Nobby, Dad ain't involved. He only organised the farmland. It's me who organised the rest.'

Nobby grumbled under his breath, 'Yeah, and you're too young.' But Nobby knew that Mitchell was more involved than he'd let on, although he couldn't tell George about that. He wanted George just to stick to the health side of the event. Little did George know that Bernie, Maxi, and a guy called Jensen Jack were all involved in serious illegal business with his father.

Mitchell didn't leave prison without gaining some knowledge of the outside underworld. He'd kept the gym all above board for his son, but, of course, that had cost him more money than he'd saved from the heist. The office at the gym was perfect for doing business, though. No one would ever suspect a thing.

Nobby drove the van across the field and parked by an enormous DJ set-up. As they opened the back doors, hordes of people made their way over. It was Nobby's first rave, and he'd never experienced anything like it. The power of the music not only sent every one of his nerves on edge, but the boom-boom sound made his false teeth rattle. DJ Spiderman was yelling 'jump, jump', and the ravers were making a racket.

But the second the sweaty punters were there with their money, Nobby got to work handing out the bottled water. He clocked Mitchell, who was across the field with four youngsters surrounding him. Each girl wore a red T-shirt and a bowler hat with money belts around their waists. He sussed that they were the runners. He saw the customers approaching them and swapping the ecstasy pills for a tenner. Then he switched direction and spotted George, who was taking fivers for the bottles and grinning like the Cheshire Cat, proud of the fact that this was his baby. Yet he knew that just a small pouch of a hundred Es, as they were referred to, would make thousands of pounds for Mitchell's firm.

George was too busy selling the bottles to take too much notice of what his father was really doing.

Maxi, a massive lump of a man, was there as a bouncer, along with the giant and ex-boxer Jensen. Each man had their own team to make sure that the rave wasn't hijacked by another mob.

Mitchell had initially set up and paid for the rave. He was the promoter and had used a private radio station to advertise the venue, which really was just a large field with access to electric through enormous generators. However, this was a big deal, and the punters were loving it. Any wannabe dealers attempting to muscle in would get a right good larruping and would be sent on their way with a clear message not to mess with him.

It was Bernie who had sourced the ecstasy tablets. He'd had them tested, making sure they were not made from any dangerous additives. The runners were given strict instructions that if any punter looked younger than eighteen, they wouldn't get served. And Mitchell underlined this. He was crystal clear when he also warned the runners that if they did serve the under 18s, they would get a hiding and told to fuck off with no wages.

After an hour, George sat on the empty box at the back of the van, while Nobby unloaded more of the bottles. George gazed around and watched the crowd dancing and hopping about, all in their own mad world. He knew then that he never wanted to be a part of that scene. He'd much prefer to be kicking a football or sparring in the ring.

In the crowd was a lad who was not dancing. He was watching and observing. He didn't buy the drugs or the bottled water. He wasn't dressed in bright baggy trousers or wearing a luminous ring; instead, he had chosen to wear a black jacket and a white T-shirt. His eyes were fixed on George, hating the boy with every fibre of his being. He glared with spite as George counted a bundle of money. It should have been *his* money. He held the bottle with the Swan logo on it, which he'd snatched off some twat who was off his nut, and stared at the name – his name.

Shooting a look to his left, he clocked Bernie; automatically, he fingered the scar down his cheek. With his other hand, he felt for the knife hidden in his jacket pocket. His eyes rested on Mitchell, and he tightened his grip on the blade. This whole set-up should have been run by his grandfather, not Mitchell – and certainly not supergrass George. With his grandad inside, Bernie and Mitchell had taken the right piss. He had been led to believe that Bernie used to be one of his grandfather's sidekicks or henchmen, not in any way in his grandfather's league – and the same could be said for Maxi Vent. He had been another one of the old firm. Now it looked as if Mitchell was in charge while his dear ol' grandpops rotted in prison. He flared his nostrils, as the situation was eating him up inside.

Just as he was about to head over to Mitchell, a young woman, with a pretty face and a black bowler hat on her head, nudged him. 'You look like you could do with feeling the vibe. I've got some good Es, a tenner a pop.'

Jordan's eyes darted to the money belt. In one quick movement, he unsnapped the clasp on the belt and released it. Managing to catch it before it hit the ground, he turned to walk away.

'Oi, no, wait! That ain't yours!' she shouted, in desperation.

His hand stung from being scratched by the girl's long nails as she tried to take back the belt. It instantly angered him. He stopped, turned around, and punched her hard in the face.

The crowd were too busy to notice the girl with blood all over her face swaying from left to right. She was desperate to focus on where the man with her belt had gone. However, her eyes were blurred with tears, and her nose hurt like hell. As she weaved in and out trying to find him, she was grabbed by Bernie.

He pulled her away from the masses to a quieter area. Bernie had spotted that not only was she not wearing her hat but her belt was missing. Then he noticed her bloody nose. 'Who the fuck hurt ya?' he grilled.

She was trying to stop her nose from bleeding while crying at the same time. She'd been so desperate to earn a few quid, since she was on her last fiver and she owed money to her pimp, that the injury was nothing but an inconvenience.

'I'm sorry. He just unclipped me belt before I could stop him, and then, as I clawed his hand with me nails, he walloped me one. Oh my God, I'm so sorry.' The fear of the repercussions were weighing heavily on her.

'Never mind that. What did the cunt look like?'

She wiped the last of the blood from her nose using a tissue that Bernie shoved in her face. 'He was quite dark-skinned, had a black leather jacket, white top, and a big scar down his cheek.'

Bernie blinked and then frowned. 'Which cheek? His left or right?'

'His right.'

'Okay, well, you'd best fuck off home, now. You ain't no good to me in that state.'

'I am sorry. I guess I ain't gonna get paid, then?' she asked, as it seemed her last hope of freeing herself from the pimp was now an unreachable dream.

'You what? You're fucking lucky I ain't demanding the money off *you*. Now then, if I do find out that you were part of a scam, ya see that nose of yours? Well, it will be kicked clean off your face and be having its own funeral.'

The girl swayed again but nodded politely. She was about to walk away when he pulled her back. 'Hold up, kid. 'Ere, take this,' he said, as he pushed a fifty-pound note into her hand.

'Cor blimey. Fanks, Bernie. Fanks so much. You don't know what this means to me.'

'Go on. Fuck off, before I change me mind.' He knew she was in trouble. She'd worked three raves, and each time she'd turned up, she had a bruise or a dirty great love bite on her neck. She wasn't a junkie either. She was just a girl in a bit of trouble with a pimp working her for what he could. Still, he wouldn't get involved; it wasn't his business.

Bernie had to break the news to Maxi and Mitchell that a lad had not only run off with their money and some pills, but the thief also fitted the description of Mitchell's son Jordan.

Mitchell looked around. 'Are you sure?'

'No, but the lad has darkish skin, he was wearing a leather jacket, and he had a scar down his face.'

Maxi chuckled. 'Well, he's robbed the wrong money belt because that girl had just handed me her takings so far. She only had a few pills on her.'

'Cor, she was so frightened that I'd lose it with her. I sent her home, poor cow. That little bastard did a right number on her. There was blood everywhere.'

Mitchell shook his head. 'I would love to know if it was Jordan.'

Bernie nodded. 'Well, if he has a scratch on his hand, then it was him. She said she clawed him trying to get the belt back. I tell ya, he's a loose cannon and a bit wobbly in the nut.'

'Right, call in the runners, get them paid, and we'll do the off. George has sold out of bottles. And Nobby is ready for bed. No doubt the Ol' Bill will be sniffing around soon enough.'

They all looked over to see both George and Nobby in the back of the van just staring at the ravers.

***

It was past one o'clock in the morning when Miranda, who everyone called Randy, arrived at the hostel. Her nose was still throbbing, but the second she slid her key in the lock, he was there, appearing from behind the lamp post. Her heart plummeted. She knew he would demand sex and then

361

take her fifty-pound note. But she didn't owe him fifty pounds. He'd told her that if she paid him twenty pounds, then she was free to work for anyone she liked.

His arm banged against the main entrance, stopping her from going in. He had that soapy look, and she clocked the dark rings around his eyes. He'd been on the cocaine, and she hated him for that alone. She stared into his eyes; in her mind, she was stabbing him over and over.

'Come with me, Randy. You are gonna pay off some of ya debt. I've got two men that need seeing to.' He grinned and licked his lips.

She didn't move but continued to stare at him. His dirty jeans, his manky, greasy black hair, and his stubble told her he was losing it. If he wasn't always smoking, drinking, and snorting, he might have been half-decent looking.

Mehmet was a pimp. Three years ago, he was a well-respected one with half a dozen women working for him. But he had become lazy. Now he only had Randy, the tiny and weakest girl, working for him. He'd picked her up off the streets when she was fourteen and got her working at fifteen. He would ply her with drugs, but little did he know that she didn't need them anymore: she was clean.

'No, Mehmet, please. I will pay you the twenty quid, and then we're done.'

Viciously, he grabbed her around the throat. 'We're done when I say we're done. Do you understand me?' He spat in her face.

She struggled to try to release his grip but it tightened, and then she could hardly breathe. In a panic, she clawed and scratched his hands, but she didn't have the breath to scream. Slowly, she felt her body become weak as she buckled. Black dots filled her eyes. Suddenly, he let her go and jumped back. She coughed and spluttered and tried to get to her feet.

Mehmet was glaring behind her. Randy followed his eyeline to see the new girl just standing there looking on. Weirdly, she was holding his stare.

Gasping for breath and still spluttering, Randy stumbled over to the girl and stood behind her. She wondered if perhaps he knew her.

Mehmet grinned. 'I'll be back, Randy, and you now owe me fifty quid. Every day that you don't pay, it goes up.'

With the new girl by her side, she bravely said, 'Fifty quid and the debt will be paid? Is that right, Mehmet?'

'Yeah.' He laughed and then snorted through his nose. 'But you won't survive without me, you silly little whore.'

'Fifty quid and you will leave me alone?' she asked again.

He stopped laughing. 'Yeah, I said fifty, didn't I?'

Randy stepped forward. 'This girl is my witness. Here, take the fifty quid and don't come back, Mehmet, 'cos I have now paid my debt. You don't own me now, so fuck off.'

He snatched the fifty-pound note and was about to slap her, but she dived behind the onlooker again.

Mehmet snarled and left.

***

Randy was so grateful, she unexpectedly hugged her saviour.

'Thank you so much. Oh my God, if you hadn't been there, he would have made me . . .' She shuddered. 'Well, anyway, you stopped him.'

Eden smiled. 'I didn't do anything. I just came out to have a walk. I couldn't sleep.'

'What's ya name?'

'Eden.'

'Mine's Miranda, but everyone calls me Randy. Mad, really, 'cos it's short for Miranda, but 'cos I was a, well, you know, a prossie, I kinda relate it to that.' She shivered. 'Shall we go back in? I'm cold. I wanna drink and a fag. I ain't had a drink all night.'

Eden looked down and fiddled with her pink top. 'I don't drink.'

Randy laughed. 'Not even hot chocolate?'

'Oh, sorry, I thought . . .'

'Yeah, I know what you thought. A prossie, a skank, an alcoholic. Well, no, I don't drink or take drugs anymore.'

Eden blushed bright red, so much so that she could feel her face burning. 'I'm so sorry. I just, well, I didn't, er . . .'

Randy laughed. 'Hey, it's all right, ya know. Christ, I have had people spit at me in the street. I know you didn't mean anything by what you said. Come on, Eden, let's have a nice cup of chocolate and a chat.'

Eden nodded and smiled. Despite the blood on Randy's face and the bruise on her nose that was blackening her eyes, it was that forlorn and empty expression that she recognised in herself. *Maybe we could become soul mates*, she thought.

Randy's room was much like her own. It was sparse but it did have a wardrobe, a small electric fire, a table with food and a kettle, and a long mirror on the wall.

'You make yaself comfy, Eden, and I'll boil us some milk in the kitchen.'

As Eden realised that she hadn't actually been in there, she asked if she could see it.

It was basic, but it did have an old electric cooker, although only three of the rings worked. There was also a fridge, but, for obvious reasons, no one left their food in there.

'Sad news about Kat, eh? She wasn't a good friend of mine. In fact, she was a bit of a cow, really, but she was still one of us. In a mad way, we kinda help each other.'

Eden wondered if Randy was trying to get information out of her. She'd promised Dela that she wouldn't say anything, so she kept her mouth shut. It then dawned on her that 'one of us' meant she was now part of something, not a congregation or anything to do with the Kingdom Hall, but a new community, an entirely different one. The survivors.

The milk boiled, and Randy quickly removed the saucepan and poured it into the two mugs that she'd brought along with her.

Once they were back in the little bedroom and sipping the delicious hot chocolate, Eden felt a sense of belonging. In that short time, she realised that although the girls were so different, they all had one thing in common: they were working their way up from being at rock bottom.

'I hope he doesn't come back. God, I hate him so much. You know he promised the world when I was just a kid, and in the beginning, he gave it to me. I thought he was me boyfriend, but he wasn't. He got me on the drugs, and then I had to pay for them.'

Eden was entering the world of the real men of Satan. 'That's terrible.'

'I didn't mind so much the younger men, but it was the oldies and the violent ones that did my head in.'

'What you must have gone through, Randy, I just can't imagine.'

Randy nursed her hot chocolate. 'It was the reason I ran away from home in the first place.'

Eden's eyes widened. She really wanted to know if her new friend had suffered like she had, and at the hands of her father too. 'Was it your dad?'

Randy stared off into space. 'It was the man I trusted the most. The man I loved the most literally turned into the man I hated the most – my stepdad. Worst of it was me mum was too frightened to be on her own. Although she believed me, she took his side, and so I had to run. That's when Mehmet found me.'

'My stepdad raped me, and no one believed me. No one. He beat me and beat me, and turned everyone against me, and then he threw me out with just a thin dress on my back.'

Randy looked up from her chocolate. 'What about your mum?'

'She died. He let her die,' Eden said, with spite in her voice.

Randy gasped. 'How?' she asked, knowing that they were both sharing their personal stories. It seemed that the more she learned about Eden, the closer they might become, and she liked the girl. There was something very calm and serene about her. Maybe that was what had startled Mehmet.

'She was giving birth to my sister, and she had a home birth. Within our faith this is the normal thing to do, but something went very wrong. I think my father . . . stepfather used scissors to help get the baby out, but my mother bled to death. He didn't call an ambulance because we . . . I mean, they don't believe in blood transfusions.'

'Fucking hell, that's horrendous, Eden. You poor thing. Well, I like to think that although in this house we all have our issues, no one is better than anyone else in here. We're family. Dela's like a father to us. She's a big ol' lesbo. Ya know, she's trying to get her baby back from foster care. So she does everything by the book. And there's—' Randy stopped when she heard a stone ping at her window.

'Oh, is that Mehmet?' asked Eden, nervously.

'Speak of the Devil. Nah, that's Sapphire Rose Petal Porsha. Or Saffy for short. She's always forgetting her key.'

'Lovely name,' said an intrigued Eden.

'Yeah, her muvver was a West End showgirl.'

Eden smiled, not getting the connection. But eager to meet the girl with the exotic name, she followed Randy down to the main entrance.

Sapphire almost fell through the door. 'Thank fuck you were in, Randy! I thought I was a gonna.'

Randy pulled her friend the rest of the way in and closed the door, making sure it was locked.

'That fucking Mehmet chased me up the road. I swear, if I wasn't so out of it, I would've bricked the bastard. What's the matter with the Turkish prick? I don't fucking work for him.'

'He doesn't own me anymore. I paid him off. So I guess he's after you now, Saffy.'

Eden was mesmerised by Sapphire. She was tall with a long, slim neck and a short hairstyle that really suited her angular features. She was dark-skinned, possibly of Arab descent, with puffy lips and almond slanted eyes, like those of a cat. Eden jumped when the woman looked her way.

'And you are?' she said now, with her hands on her hips and exhibiting an exaggerated jaw action, as she chewed on her gum.

'Oh, er . . . Me? I'm Eden. I'm in the room upstairs at the end.'

'Ol' fella bashed you up, did he?'

Eden touched her cheek and shook her head. 'No, not exactly.'

Sapphire nodded. 'Okay, babe.' She looked back at Randy. 'So I heard Kat topped herself. Is that right?'

Randy looked to the floor. 'Yeah, we couldn't have stopped her.'

'Really? We were all supposed to look out for her. Taking it in turns, if need be. So how'd she do it?'

Randy deliberately avoided eye contact. 'Saff, she took an overdose. She saved up a load of tablets and did it. It was during the day.'

'I'd better not find out any fucking different, 'cos I swear I'll swing for someone.'

Eden could hear her own heart beating, but before she had time to think, the words fell out of her mouth. 'She took my tablets – morphine. I didn't know she was suicidal. I didn't know. I mean, I never knew her. I'm so, so sorry.' She suddenly felt clammy and sick as Sapphire's face changed. Her chin protruded, and her eyes became dark with fury.

Eden stepped back. 'I am sorry. I really didn't know.'

But her apologies meant nothing to Sapphire because she was close to Kat.

A bony hand grabbed Eden around the throat and squeezed.

Eden, however, didn't struggle. She just allowed her eyes to meet those of Sapphire's, and she held her gaze. In the background, though, she could hear Randy screaming for Sapphire to let go.

It was as if she'd just had a shot of morphine herself. The room began to darken around the edges, and a soft, warm feeling enveloped her. But she remained perfectly still, just staring until Randy began ripping at Sapphire's hand to stop her from committing murder.

Sapphire let go. But she continued to stare, her eyes angry; they also showed confusion.

'For fuck's sake, what is the matter with you, Saffy?'

Sapphire turned and instantly backhanded Randy, knocking her against the staircase. It didn't take much, since Randy was so skinny.

'You nasty bitch, Saffy. It wasn't fucking Eden's fault, ya know. If you were such a good friend to Kat then why did you fuck off for three days, eh? 'Cos you thought more of getting uptown to sell your skanky arse than keeping an eye on Kat, that's why.'

Sapphire's eyes were blinking with fury, yet every word that Randy spouted was correct. But too livid to care, Sapphire was on the point of clawing at Randy's hair when the sound of Dela's voice stopped her in her tracks.

'You fucking dare touch her, Saffy, and believe me, love, I'll turn you inside out. Now then, it's no one's fault that Kat died, except her own. She wanted out of this hellhole of a life, and that'll be the fucking end of it.'

Randy and Sapphire bowed their heads in shame and quietly sloped off to their rooms.

Eden was now feeling tired, but once she lay on her bed, her ears began to ring. The excitement was slowly leaving her body as she drifted off into a nightmare-filled sleep.

Chapter Twenty-One

Bernie parked his car across the road from Gina's house. He sat with one eye on the newspaper checking the horse racing, and the other watching out for Jordan. He'd not said much more to Mitchell about Jordan being the likely money belt thief because he wanted to find out for himself. If it was him, then the situation could be more serious than Mitchell had envisaged it to be. A whisper from HMP Maidstone certainly had Bernie very concerned.

Just as Bernie was about to doze off, he saw Gina's front door open. Out sauntered Sonny, followed by Jordan. They were both wearing jackets and had their hands in their pockets. Bernie grabbed his binoculars and zoomed in to Jordan. When Jordan took his hand out, holding a packet of cigarettes, Bernie could see clearly the lad's claw mark. 'So it *was* you. You little bastard,' he mumbled under his breath.

As he sat for a while thinking about his next move, he spotted a tall dark-haired, olive-skinned man, with a small suitcase next to him on the doorstep, knock at Gina's door. She appeared with her hair neatly piled up and wearing the shortest of skirts – more like a wide belt. She looked up and down the street before flinging her arms around the visitor and dragging him inside. Bernie shook his head. 'No shame, then.'

As he was about to pull away, he noticed the man turn around to pick up his suitcase, and for a moment, a silent gasp stuck in Bernie's throat. He stared with his eyes on stalks. Where had he seen this man before? With his thumbs tapping the steering wheel, he cast his mind back to his prison days. Suddenly, the penny dropped. The man had been inside for eighteen years. He knew the bloke – knew him well, back in the day. But it wasn't the fact that the bloke had turned up at Gina's door that had just sparked a moment of interest – and surprise. It was his obvious likeness to Jordan. At one time a huge muscly guy, he was slimmer now and Jordan's double.

Bernie wanted to go and knock at the door, but what would he say? It was none of his business. The one and only issue that was his concern was the rumour from the nick.

Dexter Michael Hanks, one of the Hanks brothers from Essex, was not the only brother to serve a long lump inside. They were all in and out over the years, but no one dared fight any of them because they would sure as hell pack together like wild animals.

The pieces were slowly falling into place. Dexter was younger than Donald, and back then, young Dexter looked up to him. They had shared a few business deals, but Dexter's manor was mainly in Essex while Donald did his business in Kent. Bernie recalled that Mitchell was on the scene around the same time as Dexter. However, Dexter was subsequently done for shooting a geezer outside his local pub and was sentenced to life, being granted parole after eighteen years.

Bernie rubbed his forehead and took a few deep breaths. The news from the nick was that Donald had taken umbrage to Mitchell's fortune, and he wanted a nest egg for when he came out of prison. Something was going to go down, so Bernie would continue to play detective. He liked Mitchell, but not only that, he was on a good earner, which he needed for his own retirement. But if the Essex lot were gonna move in on their business, then there would be a war, and it just might turn nasty.

***

Jordan and Sonny sat opposite their grandfather. Sonny hated the whole set-up: the queuing, the sweaty gym smell, and the embarrassing searches. He didn't want this life at all, and the more he visited his grandfather, the more he worried about what Jordan was dragging him into.

Donald was dressed in the grey Nike tracksuit that Jordan had acquired from one of the travellers who was pushing a load of stolen gear. Donald looked happier and fresher than the last visit they'd had with him. He was clean-shaven and bright-eyed.

'Cor, that bastard did you a right fucking good 'un,' he said, as he ruffled Jordan's hair.

'Cunt,' Jordan replied, with his eyes narrowed.

'I know, my boy, but listen, you will get your own back, believe me. Now then, tell me about the set-up. I wanna know who's running the show. How many faces does Mitch have working with him? Did you recognise any?'

Jordan gave him his conceited narrow-eyed smile. 'Bernie, Maxi, Jensen, Nobby, and fucking pretty boy George.'

Donald jolted in shock and frowned deeply. 'Nah, surely not? You mean to tell me that George is flogging drugs?'

Jordan shook his head. 'No. But he's flogging water at a fiver a go.'

Donald shook his head in disbelief. 'Seriously? Punters pay a fucking fiver for a bottle of water?'

'No, it's the bottle itself. It's a fancy contraption with a flip lid and a straw attached and it has the Swan name on it. I dunno. Anyway, they have these birds running around selling the ecstasy. Everyone's doing it.'

'So, really, there's just Mitchell, Maxi, Bernie, and Jensen, then, running it. 'Cos Nobby is as much fucking use as an arsehole with taste buds.' Donald laughed.

'Yeah, I didn't see anyone else, but then, there were thousands of people there.'

Donald was nodding his head, now getting excited. 'Yep, that's what I like to hear. The more silly fuckers at these gigs, the more money we'll make. When's the next rave?'

'Saturday night in West Kingsdown near Brands Hatch.'

'Good. Dexter will be staying at your mother's for a few weeks. He's just got outta the nick and needs a place to stay, so you two be nice, or you will get a bollocking from me.'

'So what do me and Sonny do now, then?'

Looking from left to right to see if anyone was earwigging, he leaned in and whispered, 'Between me, Dexter, and his brothers, including the ones inside with me, we will be setting up a right lucrative business. We need you to get as much info on Mitch's raves as you can. We want dates and times, and we wanna know the pills the kids are popping. You, my boys, are gonna be our eyes and ears. Dexter will be organising the firm and the muscle, and you will be part of a new empire. And when I get out of here, Dexter and his firm will be working for me.'

Jordan was now grinning from ear to ear.

'Fuck Mitchell Swan! You and Sonny will have what you were rightfully entitled to, and . . .' – he looked about again – 'if that little rat of a brother of yours tries to stand in your way, then all I can say is he'll get what he deserves, eh?'

Jordan nodded, but Sonny felt uncomfortable.

'He is still our bruvver.'

Jordan elbowed him in the ribs. 'He ain't *my* fucking bruvver. He's the creep that put our grandpops inside.'

Donald nodded. 'Yep, fucking 'ell. Imagine where we would be now if I wasn't stuck in this stinking jail, with me bones crumbling, listening to grown men crying night after fucking night.' He stopped himself from going into a full-on whinge. 'You're right, though, Sonny. And, Jordan, don't make the aim of this business to be about getting your own back on George. You stay focused on how we're gonna make us a fucking fortune. It won't be long, boys, and I'll be out.' He rubbed his hands together.

As the visit ended, the inmates made their way back to the door at the far end of the visiting room. Jordan noticed a couple of younger men who were patting their grandfather on the back and looking back at him smiling and respectfully nodding. He instantly felt as if he was a face. After all, his grandfather was the well-known gangster Donald Brennan.

Sonny shuffled along behind his brother, past the screws, and through the main gate. He may have been daydreaming, but he did catch their sniggers. 'Those two will be in here within the year.'

Sonny shot a daring look in their direction, but it didn't faze them; they laughed even more.

Jordan, however, was marching on with a cocky stride. His shoulders were back, and his chest was out. He was looking forward to meeting this Dexter bloke that his grandfather had gone on about. He revelled in the idea of being part of a firm, and one day, he would be running it himself. There was no way he wanted to pay taxes to the government. He wanted to have men kissing his boots and running around earning money to line his pockets like his grandfather had done. He wanted the name, the money, and the birds. Once his grandfather was out, he'd be reclaiming turf and re-establishing his firm. It surely wouldn't be long before he could take over from him. Besides, his grandfather wouldn't be alive for ever.

***

Bernie sat in his lounge waiting for his pal Ryder from HMP Maidstone to call him. With a cigarette in one hand and a large brandy in the other, he got up and paced the floor, trying to work out what the hell Dexter was up to. The second his phone rang, he placed the glass on the table and answered it.

'Bernie, it's me, Ryder. Those two grandsons of Donald's were up here on a visit.'

'And?'

'Come on, Bernie. What's in it for me?'

'I'll pop a monkey into your ol' lady's handbag.'

'Make it a grand 'cos what I know will be worth it to you, sunshine.'

'Go on, then.'

'Donald thinks he's in with the Hanks brothers. He's walking around the jail like a fucking peacock, giving it large. They are planning on taking over the drug scene in Kent. The Kent raves are gonna be ambushed. They are just collecting info at the moment, but watch yaself, Bernie, and tell Maxi and Mitchell to take precautions 'cos they are gonna go in hard. Dexter has a grudge against Mitchell. Serving eighteen years has made him an angry man.'

'Cheers, Ryder, er . . . Tell me, did Dexter ever have any dealings with Donald's daughter?'

Bernie could hear the chuckle down the phone.

'He's been fucking that bitch since she was fifteen. But Donald doesn't know about that, although how he doesn't is a mystery, mate, 'cos Dexter don't give a shit what he says and who he says it to. I fucking hate the geezer, and I ain't keen on Donald either. To be frank, Bernie, I'm surprised Donald ain't been killed. I know you were gonna have him done in. He ain't liked in here at all. There's a lot of the old school that liked his wife more than they liked him.'

'Cheers, Ryder. Call me in a few days, and I'll drop that little bit o' poke around for ya missus.'

***

As Jordan and Sonny reached the corner of their street, Jordan stopped. 'I wanna word with you, Sonny.'

Sonny was expecting some verbals since he'd stuck up for George.

'Me and you, Sonny, have had to practically drag ourselves up. Not that I'm disrespecting our mum, but we didn't get help from our dad, and you saw George. He had his fancy clothes and a whole fucking gym with the Swan name on everything. He wouldn't be living like that if he hadn't grassed on our grandfarver, who, all those years before, was there for us. Our fucking dad wasn't, that's for sure.'

Sonny looked up through his lashes. 'Blood is thicker than water, Jordan.'

Jordan snatched Sonny by the collar and pulled him a centimetre from his nose. 'No! It fucking ain't, Sonny. George *ain't* our bruvver. Fuck me, he doesn't even look like us.'

'So!' hissed Sonny, as he snatched his brother's arm and shook himself free. 'Don't fucking grab me again, Jordan.'

Jordan looked away. 'Yeah, sorry.' He didn't want to fight with Sonny. He was his best buddy. He'd always been by his side. He knew, though, that there were many times when Sonny didn't want to be.

They could smell the shepherd's pie before they'd even stepped inside. It was the dish their mother cooked them on special occasions, except at Christmas. She would always cook a turkey then.

Walking straight into the dining room, Jordan stopped dead. The table was laid with a linen tablecloth and the best cutlery; usually this kind of event happened only at Christmas. Even the best crystal wine glasses, which he'd chored from a shop in Orpington, were on the table. But sitting there in a pinstriped suit at the head of the table was a tall and lean dark-haired man.

Sonny, who stood behind Jordan, stared at the stranger; he knew that a bloke called Dexter would be staying with them, but he never expected him to have made himself so at home.

'All right, lads? How was your grandfather?' he said, with a deep voice for a slim man.

Sonny was still staring when Jordan answered. 'He's all right. He said you'd be staying here for a bit.'

Gina then appeared from the kitchen, her face glowing from the steam coming off the shepherd's pie. 'More than a bit, boys. Dex may be moving in for good.'

Jordan snarled, curling his lip like a dog. 'In your bedroom, Muvver?'

'Oi, oi, there's no need to get personal with ya mother. Show some respect, lad.'

Gina glared and nodded for her sons to take a seat. 'See, I told ya, Dex, that my Jordan is a cheeky one. Like you were, no doubt, in your younger days.' She laughed. 'Not that you're old, Dex. I didn't mean . . .'

'I was a fucker in my day, Gina. *But* I was respectful to me ma. We all were, or we got a right wallop around the earhole from me dad.' He glared at Jordan, who took the chair opposite.

'Well, this is nice, eh? So how was me dad?'

Jordan didn't answer his mother; he was still watching Dexter.

'He said that you, Dexter, wanted us to help you out. But I'm not sure what that looks like as yet. Maybe you can tell us exactly what you want us to do and exactly what our cut in it is,' chirped up Sonny.

'I see. So you, Jordan, are the muscle, and your brother Sonny has the brains.'

Jordan snapped out of his attempt at a threatening look and glanced at Sonny before he replied to Dexter. 'No, he's just a kid. I am the one with the business brain. Ain't I, Muvver?'

'Aw, er . . . Yeah, Jordan,' she replied, as she scooped a large slice of the pie and placed it onto Dexter's plate.

Jordan was aware how his mother was serving this stranger first.

'Just like me dear ol' mum, she never saw any failings in us lads. She still thought we were law-abiding businessmen, the day she died. I tell ya though, Gina, you do have a pair of handsome boys. That's no mistake.'

Sonny and Jordan both looked shocked as they watched their mother blush. Sonny wondered if his mother and Dexter were sharing a private joke.

Offended, Jordan grumbled, 'I don't take after me farver. He's a long lanky piece of piss.'

Dexter laughed and wiped the corners of his mouth with the linen serviette. 'Yep, Jordan, Mitchell *is* a lanky piece of piss. But' – he raised his voice – 'don't underestimate that man. He may be a quiet fella, but inside that fucking head of his is a cunning brain. I was inside Portsmouth Prison with the bastard.'

He turned his head to the side and lifted his hair to reveal a jagged scar. 'He took me own knife from me and cut me. So don't underestimate him.'

Jordan pondered for a few seconds. He couldn't imagine his father ever being violent. 'I ain't scared of him,' he said, as if to affirm his strength.

Dexter raised his brow. 'Cor, boy, you are so much like me. But when we go all in to take over his business, you be warned. He is a vicious cunt.'

Jordan pointed to his own fresh pink scar. 'I ain't afraid of the fat bastard who did this either,' he said, trying to act hard.

Sonny noticed the way the man's mouth tightened, and his eyes flicked to Jordan, who was wearing the same expression. It was as if Dexter was an older version of his brother, with the hairline, the cowlick, the thick eyebrows, and the olive skin. His mind now working overtime, he found himself comparing every little feature. They were identical. And then he looked at his mother; she seemed to be in a dreamworld all of her own making as she stared at both Jordan and Dexter.

Feeling brave, but not courageous enough to ask outright, he decided to question Dexter.

'So why were you fighting with my dad?'

Dexter looked away from Sonny and smiled at Gina. ''Cos he took something that was supposed to belong to me.'

'What was that, then?'

'Stop it with the nose ache,' said Gina, feeling uncomfortable.

Once they had finished their tea, Sonny followed Jordan upstairs. When his brother stopped on the landing and stared at himself in the long mirror for a few minutes before going to his bedroom, Sonny wondered if Jordan had the same thoughts as he did.

Chapter Twenty-Two

A week later

Randy thought her black eyes from the punch on the nose had healed nicely. Slapping on foundation and eyeliner and brushing her thin dark hair, sweeping it up into a ponytail, she then put on her baggy jeans, with a piece of flowery material tied as a belt, and her red T-shirt.

She heard the knock and opened the door. When she saw her friend, she chuckled. 'Blimey, Eden, look at you! Make-up really suits ya. With that little bit of mascara and bright-pink lipstick, I tell ya, the boys will all be after you, missy.'

'You don't think the top is too . . . you know, er . . . ?'

Randy laughed. 'Slutty? Nah. It's a crop top. Well, it is now that I cut the bottom off it. But it really suits ya figure. You'll have blokes' eyes popping out of their heads.'

Eden lowered her gaze. 'I'm not after a boyfriend. I just want to learn to live without having to be told what to do, what to wear, or what to say, every five minutes.'

Randy thought about what Eden had just said. No one had cared about her at all. 'Must have been all right having rules, though, surely?'

'I guess you think you're safe and protected by the congregation because they're your family. But now I'm facing the unknown, and, Randy, honestly, it really is the unknown for me. I like the freedom, but I'm terrified too.'

Randy couldn't understand those comments at all, but she liked Eden and decided to help the girl. She would start by taking her to the rave. She hoped that Big Bernie would give her another job, if, of course, she still had one now.

Eden watched Randy grab her keys and a tiny teddy that was almost worn down to the canvas. It was so dinky that it fitted into her hand.

'Are you taking that with you?'

Randy laughed. 'This is Pooh Bear. My mum gave him to me when I was three years old. I keep it to bring me luck, although I do sometimes wonder if it ever will. Come to think of it, I didn't have it with me at the last rave when that bloke nicked me bum belt. Let's hope I have better luck tonight.'

***

Eden jumped out of the cab on the edge of the field and gawped in wonder. The lights, the music, and the people – there were thousands of them. She'd never seen anything like it in her life. She'd heard about festivals from the girls at school but never imagined that she would be standing among the biggest satanic party she could envisage. The elders, like Gabriel, had referred to music festivals as Satan's work.

Eden was amazed by the young people dancing and smiling. They weren't dressed in black cloaks and chanting; they were all just dancing in their own way.

Suddenly, Randy grabbed Eden's arm. 'Come on. I've spotted Bernie.'

Eden allowed Randy to hold her arm as they weaved their way through the crowd to the big man leaning against a truck.

'Bernie, this is me mate Eden. She lives at the hostel. Any chance she could do some running for ya? She's sound, honestly.'

Eden was shaking so much, she thought the man could see how nervous she was. But as she watched him look her over, as though she was at a cattle market, her anxiety evaporated when he smiled. 'You ain't done this before, have ya?'

Eden shook her head. 'No, but Randy told me how it works, and I think I could manage it.'

Bernie was surprised by how well-spoken the girl was compared to Miranda.

'All right, I'll give you a go, but if you fuck up, then it's game over.'

'She'll be cool, Bernie,' said Randy, eagerly.

Bernie pulled the two girls away from the truck. 'I don't want anyone earwigging.' He nodded in the direction of the vehicle.

Eden glanced back and saw a young guy setting up a stand using orange crates by a white Transit. He was loading them with bright-coloured bottles with 'Swan' emblazoned along the side.

'Right, Eden, here's your belt and your hat. A word of advice: let them approach you. Keep a packet of pills in ya bra and a few in the belt, in case any fucker tries it on, like last week.' He glared at Miranda. 'Then they won't get away with all the tablets, will they? And, also, when you've got a monkey, you hand it over to me. Got it?'

Eden was nodding, taking it all in, although she knew she would have to ask Randy what 'a monkey' meant.

'Go and grab a bottle from George, 'cos it's gonna be a hot night.'

Randy was grinning from ear to ear as she dragged Eden over to the white van. 'See, I knew he would let ya. Just watch me for a while, and you'll soon get the hang of it.'

George stood up straight when he saw two girls looking at the bottles. 'A fiver each, ladies.'

Randy looked back at Bernie. 'Oh, he said, we could just take one each.'

George looked over to see Bernie nod. 'Okay, yeah, sure.' He picked up a pink bottle and handed it to Eden, but as she gingerly took it, their eyes met.

George had a sense of déjà vu. 'Uh, I think I know you. Have we . . .?'

Eden had the same feeling, and then her mind went back to the one time in her life when a perfect stranger offered her food and a drink. He was so young then, and his eyes were so kind and filled with empathy. How could she forget him? His face was embedded in her memory. It was what made her believe that other people outside the congregation were kind. But that evening, she'd suffered a beating for taking the offering.

As he held one end of the bottle, she gripped the other, and for a moment, she didn't want him to let go. She wanted to go back to when she was little and he was young too. They stared at each other. Although no words were exchanged, Eden felt her heart pump furiously.

'You gave me—'

'A burger . . . and a hot chocolate?'

She laughed nervously. 'Yes, you remember, then?'

'I'm afraid I can't forget that day, but I wish I could.' His eyes filled up, and he let go of the bottle.

It was awkward because that was not the response she had expected. She had hoped for something almost romantically magical – about two kids meeting and then fate bringing them back together. But she could see from the boy's face that he was seeing this very differently.

As soon as George saw her cheeks glow pink, he realised what he'd said. 'Sorry, that came out all wrong. I didn't mean it like that.' He smiled softly. 'It was the day my nan was murdered.' As soon as he said it, he was stunned because he'd never been able to talk about it up to now.

Almost tenderly, Eden put her arm out and touched his arm. 'I am so sorry.'

George realised he was acting emotional in front of a stranger; except she wasn't. He felt the warmth of her hand and wanted more.

'Come on, Eden. We've got work to do,' said Randy, tugging at her friend's top.

'Girls, when you've finished your water, come back, and I'll top up your bottles.'

Eden blushed again and nodded. 'Thanks, I will, er, George, isn't it?' She'd recalled his grandmother mentioning his name when she had screamed at Gabriel.

George frowned. 'You remembered my name as well?'

She nodded again as she was being pulled away and into the crowd.

***

Nobby jumped down from the van, red-faced. 'Fucking hell, George, how many bottles are back there?'

George was still staring off into the crowd.

'Georgie boy, stop eyeing up the birds. How many bottles have you got back there?'

'Another thousand. Her name's Eden. Nice name, eh?' said George.

Nobby flicked George's ear. 'Get the bottles unpacked and ready. And that probably ain't her real name, you dickhead.'

'What?'

'Those girls are drug runners, son. You don't think they will tell you their names, do ya?'

'Where do they get the drugs from, Nobby?' he asked, as he looked over in Bernie's direction.

'Never you mind. You're not selling drugs, lad, you're selling water, so mind this.' He tapped the side of his nose.

George wasn't surprised, though; he assumed Bernie and Maxi were up to less than legal dealings. Not that it bothered him. He had grown up around a few villains, and he wasn't the type of person to judge. That was for the courts. He wanted to be an above-board businessman when he was old enough.

Nobby unloaded the next box. This time it contained bright-orange bottles. He shook his head and laughed. 'They really do like this shit, don't they?'

In response, George smiled, with his blue eyes shining innocently.

***

On the edge of the field concealed by an old dumped car stood a man with hate in his heart and revenge on his mind. Using a pair of binoculars, he zoomed in on George and was instantly eaten up with jealousy. The fit-looking young man was handing out bottles, but it was the pretty-looking blonde girl who really captured his attention the most. She was wearing jeans that demonstrated her womanly figure and a crop top revealing her midriff. He swallowed hard as his heart beat so fast. He wanted her, and he would have her, even if it meant he would destroy everyone who stood in his way. As he removed the binoculars to glance around the field, he spotted Mitchell, who was dressed in a casual tan leather jacket and jeans. He was engaged in conversation with a huge man. Peering into the binoculars again, he focused on Mitchell. Every inch of his body was boiling as jealousy whipped him up into a ball of fury. He wanted to go marching across that field and stab the man right through the heart, but, instead, he growled under his breath before he stormed away, mumbling, 'I will get you where it hurts most, Mitchell Swan.'

***

As the hours ticked by, George was hoping that Eden would return to top up her water. He'd decided to ask her if her real name was Eden. The bottles had almost sold out, and the vast water butts were now in use to refill the bottles for a pound a go. Once there was a quiet moment, George looked around to see if he could spot the girl. But, instead, he caught sight of Sonny. His level of excitement went up through the roof, and he ran towards his younger brother, not realising that Sonny had already spotted him and was trying to avoid him.

'Sonny, wait up!' George called, but to no avail, as he was drowned out by the music.

Sonny stopped running, believing that George had given up, but, instantly, a hand was on his shoulder.

'Sonny, I thought it was you,' said George, out of breath. 'Didn't you hear me calling? How are ya? Is Jordan with you? I didn't know you liked this kinda stuff.'

Sonny was stunned. He wasn't supposed to see George. His orders were to count the runners. He was to see who was managing the rave, and if it was Bernie, Maxi, or Jensen who were on security. He was told to make damn sure that no one saw him. He had his hooded sweatshirt on and was wearing sunglasses, but clearly George had recognised him, and now he was overexcited to talk.

'Fucking hell, George, do you ever stop to draw breath?'

George felt a little deflated. 'Sorry, just pleased to see ya, that's all, Sonny. I just thought after the meeting at the gym, when you touched me hand, I . . . I guess I was wrong, eh?' He hoped Sonny would tell him that he wasn't wrong and that he wanted to be more of a brother than a stranger.

Sonny didn't really know what to say because George was asking so many questions, and all he wanted to do was to get away.

'I just came to see what all this rave music is about, but, George, it really ain't my thing.' He tapped George in the chest. 'I'll be seeing ya, mate.'

George was flummoxed. 'Hang on. This ain't my thing, either. Look, why don't you join me over by my stand. I've been selling water bottles at a fiver a go. Not bad, eh?'

Sonny was feeling guiltier by the minute, but he knew that if he did the off now, it would look mightily suspicious. So he agreed to join George, to see his set-up. However, the second they were by the van, Eden arrived. She looked hot and nervous, but her smile was broad.

'Eden, this is my brother, Sonny.'

Eden stopped smiling and tilted her head. She remembered the lad and knew who Jordan was, but she had no idea they were *all* brothers.

'Hello, Eden. How are you? I didn't know you were friends with George.'

George was gobsmacked. 'You know Eden?'

Sonny shrugged his shoulders. 'Well, kinda. We're sort of neighbours.' He turned to Eden. 'Jordan tried chatting you up, didn't he?'

Eden blushed. 'Well, he asked me out.'

George felt his heart drop. 'And did you——?'

'Oh, no, no,' she said, hastily.

Out of the corner of his eye, Sonny could see Bernie approaching. 'Nice business, George. Take care, Bro. I'll see you later,' said Sonny, as he patted George's shoulder and nodded at Eden.

'Yeah, see ya, Sonny,' he said, as his brother made a swift exit. George was still processing how they all knew each other.

'So you know Jordan and Sonny, then, Eden?'

'No, not really at all. I didn't even know Sonny's name. I only knew Jordan's because he introduced himself.'

George was staring at her eyes. They were such an unusual blue colour, but it was more than that. They appeared so childlike. It was the same look that he'd seen eight years ago.

'I wonder why they call the bottles "Swan"?' she asked, holding one and staring at the logo.

A proud feeling came over him. 'I designed the bottles, and that's my name, George Swan.'

Eden looked up wistfully. Sadness clouded her face. 'My mum used to call me her little cygnet.'

'Baby swan?'

'Yes. She died a few years ago now.'

Unsure what to do, George simply did what came naturally. He pulled her close and wrapped his arms around her. 'I'm sorry. It must have been tough.'

They held each other a little longer than a friendly hug would warrant until Mitchell came up behind them.

'George, if you've sold up, I want you to get off home. Do you understand?' His tone was deadly serious, and he seemed slightly out of breath.

Eden instantly let go of George and turned to face the man with the severe tone to his voice.

'Dad, this is Eden.'

George watched as his father's eyes widened and his face lost its colour.

Slowly, Mitchell stared at the girl. He had to blink twice. *Was he seeing things?*

'Nice to meet you, George's dad. I must get back to work or Bernie will wonder where I've got to.'

'Eden, I hope I will see you at the next rave,' called out George, who was gutted that she was off again.

She laughed and nodded before skipping her way through the crowd.

'Dad, are you okay? You look tired.'

Mitchell was still in a trance, having seen a girl who was so much like someone he once knew, and that name – it had been special to him and her.

'Yeah, er, sorry. Listen, George, get off home. We may have a spot of bother tonight, so the men are leaving, and I don't want you here alone.'

George screwed up his nose. 'What kinda bother, Dad?'

'George, just do as you're told, Son, all right? Get packed up and back home.'

Nobby appeared from inside the back of the van. 'I think I'm fucking deaf, with all that bleedin' bang-bang-boom-boom. All the bottles are sold now, George.'

'Nobby, pack up and make sure George gets home. There could be a few unpleasant visitors.'

Nobby nodded.

'Dad, what about that girl, Eden? I know she's a drug runner, but she's nice, Dad. Will she be all right?'

'How do you know she's a runner? And how do you know about all that stuff?' He shot a glare across at Nobby.

'Dad, for fuck's sake, I ain't stupid. I know what's going on. You have the toughest villains in the neighbourhood using the gym, but they don't even work out on a treadmill, and you think I don't see that stuff? Anyway, it's not my beeswax.'

'Okay, well, yeah, Bernie's pulling the runners off the field, so don't you worry about her. I haven't got time to chat. Just get going, will ya?'

***

Eden was thrilled that Bernie was going to pay her thirty pounds. The work was so easy. The ravers were coming up to her and handing her money in exchange for the pills. It was that simple. So no one bickered, no one questioned the price – they just paid and sauntered away. She'd handed the belt back to Bernie and thanked him.

He replied, 'You, little kitten, have done very well. I'll tell Miranda where the next rave will be. You passed your probation.'

'Oh, thank you so much,' she said, as she took the money.

'Where is Miranda, by the way? She ain't brought back the contents of the belt for some time now.'

Eden shrugged her shoulders. 'I saw her a while back, but the minute I find her, I will tell her to return the belt.'

'Yeah, no worries.'

***

Sonny walked away with the information that Dexter had asked for, but he'd done so with a heavy heart. He had really felt like giving his gentle blue-eyed brother a hug and actually having a proper conversation with his dad. But he was now going back with the news that could piss Jordan right off. Jordan had banged on about Eden for weeks. He knew his brother had wanted her for himself. But he was also very aware that if he knew George had an interest, then Jordan would go ballistic, and then he'd have even more reason to detest George. So he was between a rock and a hard place with this one. He would have to tell his brother because if Jordan discovered what he knew, then Jordan would start on him. Something else made him feel very uncomfortable with the situation. He suspected this was going to turn into an all-out war, and he didn't want to be a part of it.

However, as he followed some of the early leavers along the country lane, he spotted his dad in his Audi. Bernie and the other big men were in the car behind, and trailing in the van were an older bald man and George. His heartbeat slowed down; he knew they would be safe now. He hoped that Eden had also got away.

Because in the short time he'd got to know Dexter and the man's firm, he realised that they were a nasty bunch of men who had no morals, no consciences, and no brake pedals. All week, Dexter had occupied their living room, with Gina supplying drinks and food to the men in his firm.

Jordan had been revelling in the talks of violence, the scams, the torture, and weapons used. He'd joined in telling his stories of brutality, and the bullshit of how he had fought tooth and nail with Big Bernie until Bernie had tried to knife him and had only managed to slice his face. Jordan had lied about the fights he'd had up at the travellers' site, and he'd also lied about the big robberies he'd undertaken.

He himself was dragged into the stories every time Jordan said, 'Didn't I, Sonny?' as if he needed the backup. The men had laughed and patted Jordan on the back. But other than to offer support to his brother with a nod or a shake of the head, he had just sat on the arm of the sofa, with nothing to say.

For a while now, Sonny had felt uneasy with the way Jordan walked with a cocky swagger and how he talked with no respect for the women or the elderly.

But the only time he had shown his disdain publicly, was when his mother had brought in a tray of sandwiches and Dexter had put his hands up her skirt and pinched her so hard that she'd squealed. Then he'd slapped her backside and laughed. 'Sandwiches on a platter and pussy on a plate.'

'Leave off, Dexter. That's me muvver you're talking about,' he'd said, as he jumped up from the arm of the sofa.

Then Dexter had stopped laughing. 'You wanna show a bit more respect, boy! I'm the man in this house now. Didn't you see the rock on your ol' lady's finger and the new coat on her back. The cupboards are full to the fucking brim with food, so you, Sonny Swan, keep your trap closed,' he yelled.

Sonny had shut up and left the room, but he had heard the conversation through the thin walls.

'Your bruvver needs to be pulled into line if I'm to have you and him on the firm. Do you hear me, Jordan?'

'Dex, listen. Sonny will do anything I tell him. You just leave him to me.'

Chapter Twenty-Three

The rave was still in full swing. Everyone was dancing, sweating, and in a trance. Eden tried to dance to the music herself, but she found it hard and wondered if the pills were responsible for the ravers' constant movements. She scanned the immediate surroundings but couldn't see Randy, and an uneasy feeling came over her. Then she saw a familiar face. It was Jordan. He was with another man, but they didn't seem dressed for a rave at all. Jordan was wearing smart jeans and a leather jacket. Then she noticed the scar down his right cheek, which was red and distinctive.

Before she had a chance to attract his attention or even call his name, a hand gripped her arm so tightly that she winced and turned to see who it was. She gasped and her eyes bulged wide in terror. Gabriel. So petrified that he would drag her back to hell, she fought to break free from his clutches. But, aggressively, he almost yanked her arm out of its socket, making her scream out in pain. The people around weren't listening; they were dancing. She tried so hard to shake him off her, but his strength was so immense, his hands dug deeper into her arm. She knew that unless she could get Jordan's attention, he would haul her back to that house – to where all the horrors and the abuse had begun.

In a desperate attempt to stop him, she dropped to the ground, pulling him down, but he wrenched at her arm even harder.

A voice called out, 'Oi, what are you doing? Let her go.'

But Gabriel shot the raver a defiant glare. 'She's too young to be here. She's my daughter,' he screeched at the lad in orange baggy trousers and glow-in-the-dark paint patterned on his face.

The brave young man nodded as if to say 'okay' and danced his way back into the crowd.

Eden spotted Jordan again. He was walking towards her, but he hadn't noticed her.

'Jordan!' she screamed at the top of her lungs. 'Jordan!'

But Gabriel slapped his hand over her mouth. 'Shut up, you slut!'

Tears filled her eyes as the terror filled her mind.

But then, finally, Jordan saw her. He glared until he realised it was her. On full throttle, he tore his way through the crowd and yelled, 'Fucking let her go or I'll fucking stab ya, you nonce!'

Gabriel continued dragging Eden away from the crowd, not paying any notice, until Jordan grabbed him by the hair and bent him backwards. 'I *said*, let her go.'

Gabriel was fuming, but he did let go and faced Jordan. 'She's my daughter, and she's coming home with me.'

Jordan reached out for Eden's hands. Instantly, she grabbed him.

'Oh no, she ain't! She's coming home with me. If you have to force her, mate, then you're obviously going against her will.'

Gabriel looked from Jordan to Eden. 'You must come back to Jehovah and his organisation. Don't let the Devil get his teeth into you.'

Eden saw through his pathetic attempt at trying to drag her back. 'No, *you* are the Devil, Gabriel.'

Raging, Gabriel's face glowed red and his eyes darkened even more. 'You are the daughter of Satan. Go and fornicate with Satan's men, you whore.'

Jordan didn't hold back. He balled his fist and punched Gabriel on the nose, knocking the man backwards until he fell on his backside.

Then, to Eden's horror, Jordan pulled out a chain from inside his long deep pocket and used it like a whip as he smashed it around Gabriel's face. 'No, Jordan. Leave him.'

Gabriel tried to grab the chain but missed, and as Jordan pulled it back to whip him again, Eden grabbed it, but it hurt, and she screamed, 'Stop, please!'

Jordan lowered his weapon and Gabriel scrambled to his feet and ran for his life.

'Who the fuck was *that?*'

Eden was gasping to catch her breath.

'My . . . er . . . stepdad.'

'Shit! Why were you trying to get away from him? I thought he was just a paedo or a pimp.'

'He *is*, Jordan. He *is* a paedo.'

Winding the chain up, he slid it into his pocket. 'You've changed a lot, Eden. The last time I saw you, you looked like fucking Laura Ingalls Wilder off *Little House on the Prairie*.' He chuckled. 'I used to watch it as a kid.'

Eden had no idea what he was talking about because her family had never had a TV set.

'A lot *has* changed lately.' She wanted to ask what had happened to his face, but she decided he would tell her if he wanted to.

Jordan looked her over. 'Yep, you ain't kidding, are ya?'

Conscious of how she looked in her crop top, Eden covered her middle with her hands and changed the subject. 'Oh, I didn't know you had another brother, George. He was here a minute ago selling bottles of water. You've just missed him. Your dad said he had to go home.'

Jordan stared at her, totally miffed. 'You know George and Mitchell?'

Eden shrugged. 'Not very well. I was formally introduced to George tonight. But I didn't know who Mitchell was until he told me his name a few minutes ago.'

Jordan looked Eden up and down. 'What are you actually doing here, Eden? You're not on acid or ecstasy. I can see this ain't your thing. Christ, not so long ago, you were carrying Bible pamphlets.'

She tapped the side of her nose and giggled. 'Just earning some money.'

He grabbed her wrist and yanked her close to him. 'For Mitchell? Are you selling drugs for that wanker?'

Eden stiffened; she hadn't expected Jordan to turn so angry.

But as quick as his temper rose, it was short-lived. Immediately, he let go of her wrist and hugged her instead. 'I'm sorry, darling. It's just you are far, far too lovely to be working for that monster.'

'Isn't Mitchell your father too?'

'Biologically, yeah. But he's dead to me. I won't call him Dad. He's fucking evil.'

Eden thought back to the stern expression on the man's face when he demanded that George go home. And she wondered if Jordan was right when he said his father – this Mitchell – was evil.

'So George, Mitchell, and the others have all gone home then, have they?'

Eden nodded. 'Yeah, Bernie paid me, and they left, and now I can't find my friend Randy,' she said, not realising that she was saying too much. Scanning the field again, she felt anxious that her friend was nowhere in sight, which meant she had no way of getting home. Randy knew what to do. They had shared a cab to the field, and Randy had said not to worry about getting home because she would sort out something for them. But she couldn't find her, and now she felt uneasy. Jordan had saved her from Gabriel, but if he was hiding somewhere, then he could nab her if she made her own way home. Not only did she not know where to start, she didn't even know where she was. As for being streetwise, she was well aware that she was anything but.

Blocking her view was a tall slim man and beside him were two bigger built men. They looked so out of place. They were older and dressed in smarter clothes.

Jordan turned to see who Eden was staring at.

'All right, Dex? Mitchell, Bernie, and George have gone. They must have got wind that we were coming, although I don't know how.'

Dexter's eyes darkened as he glared at Jordan. 'Someone's fucking snitched. It'd better not 'ave been you, boy.'

'What? Don't be stupid. I want this as much as you. I have a personal grudge against Mitchell, remember?'

Dexter gritted his teeth and felt the scar behind his ear. 'Not as much as me. Right, well, no use in hanging about. This is bollocks! Where's Sonny, 'cos if it wasn't you who gave them the tip-off, I bet it was your brother. And he looked a bit sheepish when I saw him last. I bet he's a fucking turncoat.'

Dexter gobbed on the grass. 'I knew it. I knew you and that kid brother of yours would go running to daddy.'

With an evil snarl, he turned to each man on either side of him. 'If you see the little bastard, bring him to me. I want a word.' He glared back at Jordan and pointed a gnarly finger. 'If I find out that either you or that gutless fanny of a brother of yours warned Mitchell, then, believe me, I'll gut you like a fucking fish.'

Jordan wasn't going to be chastised like a kid, not in front of Eden.

'Fuck off, Dexter. I ain't a grass, so back off with your threats.'

For a second, Dexter just stared with a raised eyebrow. 'Cocky fucker. All right, well, there ain't no point in us staying.' He looked at Eden and grinned. 'I see you have some pussy to please.'

Eden knew he was being rude, but she didn't know what he meant. She took a step back and partially hid behind Jordan.

'Don't you disrespect her!' scolded Jordan.

Dexter held up his hands. 'All right. For fuck's sake, it was just a joke. You'd better jump in with me if you're bringing ya bird.'

Jordan nodded and grabbed Eden's hand. 'You can come back with me, in case that paedo's still out there.'

Eden was shocked. She didn't think that Jordan meant it when he told Gabriel that she was going home with him. She panicked. 'No, Jordan. Wait. I need to find Randy. We're going back to the hostel together. She got me the job, and she'll worry about me.'

Jordan let go of her hand. 'Eden, she has probably found herself a fella or taken some of the pills and got off her face.' He pointed to a van parked between some bushes.

Although the windows were almost blackened out, Eden could still see chinks of light coming from inside the vehicle.

'She's probably inside that gypsy van servicing someone for extra dosh.'

'No, she's not like that.'

Jordan threw his head back and laughed. 'Fuck me, Eden, you are so naive. All the runners at a rave or club make extra money. What do you think goes on inside that van? Look at it. The fucking thing is rocking.'

Eden felt a little out of her depth. Everything was so alien to her. She knew Randy had sold herself because Mehmet was her pimp. Her heart sank. Her friend had promised her that she would see her home safely. She glanced once more at the van and noticed two men queuing.

'Jordan, do you think you could ask Dexter if he could drop me off near Orpington High Street? I know you don't live too far from there.'

'I'll look out for you, darling, I promise.'

No one had ever spoken to her like that before. And no one had looked at her with such longing, not even Chloe's brother, Mark.

'But you don't even know me,' she whispered.

'I threw flea darts because I wanted to get to know you, but you never reacted. I stuck my tongue out because I wanted you to do it back, and then I hugged you because I wanted you to hug me back.'

Eden blushed and giggled. 'I was so young when you threw the flea darts.'

'Yeah, see, I have always secretly fancied you.'

No one had ever been so sweet to her. He'd defended her against her aunt and protected her against her stepfather. So why was she hesitant to go with him? She pushed her instincts aside and allowed him to guide her through the crowd to Dexter's car. She looked over her shoulder for Randy, but she was nowhere to be seen.

Chapter Twenty-Four

The drive to Jordan's house was spent with Jordan's arm around Eden's shoulders, with him whispering gentle sweet nothings in her ear. Eden would have savoured every compliment but Dexter's cigarette smoke was suffocating her. He was mumbling under his breath as he drove all the way erratically from West Kingsdown to St Mary Cray.

'Would you be able to drop me off in the High Street, please?' she asked, in her sweetest and most polite voice. But, instantly, she regretted it when she saw the man's mean dark eyes glare with contempt at her in the rear-view mirror.

'Jordan, I ain't in the fucking mood to be a taxi driver. When you get in, you call a cab for her,' he said, totally dismissing Eden.

Jordan leaned into Eden. 'It's best that I get you home safe and sound. I'll call a cab from my house. We can have a coffee and get warmed up. What d'ya say, treacle lips?'

Nodding silently, Eden was so thrown by all the evening's events. And she hadn't realised just how the temperature had dropped; still, it was two o'clock in the morning. Her brain wanted to process everything, from meeting George again, to being dragged away by Gabriel, and now worrying about Randy. Life outside the community was so different, so fast-paced, and – she dared to think – even quite exciting. It was such a contrast from her blinkered perspective on life. She was used to the *same minded* people, the *same* ideas and beliefs, and the *same* book to read – the Bible. Something in that thought shot an arrow of guilt right through her. She would never be accepted into The New World Order; she would never be chosen to live in God's kingdom. Not now. Yet feeling the warmth of Jordan's body and the safety of his arm, the thought slipped away from her veil of shame.

As they passed her old home, she looked at the bleakness of it. The trees and bushes were all overgrown, the weeds were at least three feet high, and the gate needed repainting. The street lamp certainly didn't cast a kind light on the garden. There was nothing in that place that would ever pull her back – only the memory of her dear mother.

Dexter stopped outside Jordan's house and sparked up another cigarette. Eden was only too pleased to get out. She felt her nostrils on fire and her throat burning from the smoke.

She followed Jordan to his front door and then had the wobbles. 'I can walk home from here.'

'No way. You, my girl, can stay, and I'll call a cab. It's dark, it's cold, and it's dangerous out here.'

Aware that to walk to her hostel in Orpington, she would have to pass Gabriel's house, she accepted his offer to wait for a cab.

***

Sonny remained at the rave and hid behind the dense bushes. He would have walked to a phone box and called for a cab. But he wanted to make sure that his brother, Dexter, and Dexter's men were well away from the rave before he even attempted to undo their sick and twisted wrongdoing. He glared in the distance at the van and clocked the two lads, who were roughly eighteen years old, hanging around outside, obviously waiting their turn.

Then he saw the light from the back of the gypsy van as one of Dexter's firm, a massive monster of a man, came out. Sonny's heart went out to the poor girl who was obviously trapped inside. He wished he'd tried to stop both his brother and Dexter dragging her into that van. He couldn't because he was too far away, and Dexter's men and his own brother had grabbed and bundled her before he could even shout 'Stop!' But they had long gone, and so it was Dexter's younger brother, Gary, who had sly eyes, rotten teeth, and a tattoo, which covered half his face, who was now the main threat. He was guarding the van and collecting the money. But then Sonny clocked him leaving as soon as the large man got out. He watched as they made their way to the car, which was parked near the entrance to the rave.

It truly sickened him, and after this, if he managed to get away in one piece, he would leave the Cray for good. Dexter was a nasty piece of shit, and yet his mother seemed to want him around. It was obvious why: the likeness between Dexter and Jordan was uncanny, and it was so apparent that Dexter was Jordan's father. Sonny felt more and more detached from them as each day went on. The malarkey Jordan and he had got up to had been all fun and games when they had been younger. The boyish pranks seemed amusing at the time, but this wasn't a game anymore. He was afraid of Dexter and of his men because they weren't small fry. They were dangerous psychotic gangsters who wouldn't care that he was Gina's son or Jordan's brother. They would beat him to death if he even thought of going against them. Dexter had hissed in his ear that he would break his arms and legs if he so much as smiled at his father.

He saw Gary drive off, and then he ran towards the van, looking around him as he approached it. He just managed to make it before one of the younger lads, who had been queueing, discovered sufficient courage to go inside.

Grabbing the lad by the back of his sweat-stained shirt, he pulled him back. 'Get the fuck away from the van, ya pervert!'

The other lad, playing the hard man, punched Sonny in the back. 'Piss off. We've paid, so you can't push in.'

Sonny turned to face the bloke who'd slyly punched him in the back. He shook his head and pulled his fist back, landing a punch clean in the middle of the guy's face. The attacker's nose exploded, and blood shot in all directions.

'Fuck off, or I'll knuckle-dust ya fucking ribs next,' yelled Sonny, who wasn't bothered by too yuppy-looking kids. He could fight because he and Jordan had often had fights – not with each other but with the travellers up at the site for money. It was a pastime, if nothing else.

Both lads looked at the substantial menacing contraptions on Sonny's hand and decided it was best to run rather than fight. They weren't fighters, that was for sure. They had just left grammar school and thought they could pay for a shag to finish off their night.

The lads scarpered pretty quickly. The injured guy, blinded by the sheer force of the punch, ran aimlessly across the field with his soppy friend behind him.

Not knowing what he would find, Sonny carefully opened the door and peered inside. It was lit up with battery lights. A mattress with a quilt was covering the floor, and squirming around on the mattress completely starkers was a very petite young girl.

The second she saw Sonny, she shook and tried to curl into a ball.

'Hey, hey, listen. I'm not gonna touch ya. I'll stop anyone coming in. Get dressed, and I will get you out of here,' said Sonny, as he kept one eye on the door. 'What's your name?'

The girl was whimpering and struggling to get her clothes on.

Sonny kneeled down beside her. He snatched the red T-shirt from beside the mattress and helped her get it over her bruised and battered face. He found her jeans inside out and turned them the right way. 'Here,' he said, holding them in front of her. She had managed to put her knickers on, but Sonny could see the blood and mess up her back. He wanted to cry for her, but he had to get her away, before anyone else laid claim to her and tried to ruck him for the goods.

He could see that with every effort to get dressed she winced in pain.

'It's Randy, well, Miranda,' she replied, in a nervous whisper.

'Here, put your trainers on, Randy. Me name's Sonny. Please hurry up before anyone else comes in.'

The sheer thought of another man entering the van had Randy rushing to get her trainers on her feet. She scanned the floor of the van. 'Oh no! Not again. Someone has taken my bum belt.'

'Don't worry about a bum belt. Let's just get out of here.'

He grabbed her hand. 'Don't let go of me, Randy,' he said, as he kicked open the door, hopped down, and then began to meander through the crowd.

Once they had reached the far side of the field, Sonny stopped and allowed Randy to catch her breath. That was when he saw the marks on her face. 'Bastards. Fucking scummy bastards.'

Randy had to sit down. She was still wobbly from the drugs, and now the pain was really kicking in. 'Why me? Why did this happen to me?' she cried, as she ran her shaky fingers over the lumps and bumps on her face.

Sonny sat down beside her and gently put his arm around her shoulders. ''Cos the men who did that to you are the dregs of the earth.'

'Do you know them?' she asked, hoping he didn't.

'Yeah, I know Jordan very well. Dexter not so much.' He sighed, exhausted. 'But I'm not like them, Randy. I promise you that.'

The crowd was beginning to disperse. It was late and cold. Sonny could see her searching for someone. 'Who are you looking for?'

'Oh, my friend, but she must have gone home already. And Bernie, a big man. He—'

'I know Bernie. I saw him leave a while ago. Let's get you to the village. There's a phone box, and we can call a cab for you, unless you need the hospital?'

Randy shook her head. 'I just want to get back to the hostel. Away from here, from . . .' She choked on her words and was silent for a second as she tried to stop herself from crying. 'I just want to feel safe. I can lick my wounds there.'

Assuming the coast was clear, Sonny walked with Randy towards the village. He placed his hoodie around her shoulders and held her hand in case she wobbled and fell down. It turned his stomach every time he caught a glimpse of her swollen eyelid. To think that a grown man had done that to her. She was tiny like a doll, and now she was broken.

The phone box was in working order, much to their relief. Knowing the cab number off by heart, Sonny asked for her address and ordered a cab to pick them up as soon as possible.

'So you live in Orpington, then? I live in St Mary Cray. We can jump in together, if ya don't mind. I'll drop you off first, of course.'

Randy noticed his face now they were standing under the street lamp by the phone box. He was handsome in a rugged way, with thick dark hair that fell in different directions. His eyes were hazel brown and huge. She could see he was young, but he had a maturity about him. What she liked more than anything, though, was the fact that he'd saved her and hadn't attempted to touch her himself, except for placing a comforting arm around her shoulders.

A car slowed down enough for Sonny to realise that it was Dexter driving. His heart went in his mouth as the vehicle suddenly did a fast U-turn.

'Randy, get in the phone box and stay there for the cab, okay? Whatever happens in the next minute or so, *don't* come out.'

Randy did as she was told and stared through the murky glass pane.

The car screeched to a stop, and a tall man, with his dark hair pulled so far back he resembled Count Dracula, jumped out. Instantly, she recognised him. As much as she wanted to run to Sonny's rescue, she found she couldn't move an inch, too paralysed with fear. She watched him push Sonny so hard that he fell onto the pavement smashing his head on the concrete bollard directly behind him that separated the shops from the road.

Randy heard the bang and felt her stomach contents rise. She so desperately wanted to help Sonny, but she knew she would be like a paper bag in the wind. Gripped by terror, she could only pray that he would leave Sonny alone. *No,* she thought, *please don't drag me away again.* She'd wet herself when he and a younger guy had pinned her down and poured pills down her throat. No wonder Sonny had pushed her out of sight to stop the man from recognising her.

'I fucking knew it was you who grassed. You're Mitchell's boy all right. You're just like your brother George an' all. He was a grass. He got your grandfather locked away, and now there's you. Running to daddy, are ya? Telling him all about my business, are ya? Well, are ya?' His voice was filled with temper, and as he yelled, his lips tightened and his teeth clenched like a snarling Dobermann's.

Still trembling, Randy watched Sonny clamber to his feet. She was surprised because the sound as he'd hit his head would have had most grown men incapacitated. She clocked him slide his hands into the back pocket of his trousers and pull out a metal object. As soon as he put his fists up, Randy could see it was a knuckleduster.

'You might beat me, Dexter, but I won't go down without a good fight, you fucking perverted, skanky cunt!'

Randy saw the surprised look on the man's face as Sonny jumped into the air and smashed the man on the nose.

Dexter's eyes widened in shock. His nose splattered, but he was unperturbed. Feeling the instant flow of blood, he looked at his hand and laughed. His car was just behind him with the door wide open. In a flash, he spun around and grabbed something from down the side of the seat. He was so quick that Sonny didn't have a chance to run before Dexter was almost in his face and wielding an axe.

Randy's heart was beating so fast that she felt as though she would wet herself again at any minute. She'd seen many a fight and been in a few herself, but a mad axeman was the stuff of horror films. Petrified, she turned and grabbed the phone, and with trembling hands, she dialled 999. She turned back around to see what was happening. Sonny was on the pavement and gripping his shoulder while his T-shirt turned claret. She screamed as he smashed the axe against the phone box. Fortunately, it didn't break the cloudy window but instead just bounced off the metal frame.

Holding the axe in the air ready to swing again at Sonny, Dexter bellowed, 'If you grass, I will make sure your mother never speaks again. I'll cut her tongue out of her fat fucking mouth! Got me!'

Sonny was white and slumped, still on the ground, trying to stop the blood as it seeped through his fingers.

The commotion had awoken the neighbours and the people living in the flats above the shops. They shouted down that they had called the police and that was when the man jumped back into his car and roared off into the night.

Randy sat with Sonny until an ambulance arrived. Fortunately, the cab appeared at almost the same time. The paramedics wanted to help her, but all she wanted was to get home. She held his hand until the very last minute that the stretcher was carried into the ambulance.

'Shall I let your mum know? What's your address?'

She could barely hear his faint voice as he managed to whisper, 'No, no, I never want to go back there again.'

She waited until they closed the door, knowing that Sonny was in the best hands now.

Sirens were sounding from all directions, with police cars and more paramedics arriving almost at once. But Randy didn't want to get caught up in it, and so before the police could even take her name, she slid into the back seat of the cab and urged the driver to get going. Looking back, she saw the neighbours giving statements. She just hoped that the young lad who had saved her life would not die. His injuries seemed pretty bad, if his face, which was grey from the blood loss, was anything to go by. *But look on the bright side*, she thought. *I've made a true friend. He's probably been the only boy in my life who has shown he cares for me.*

***

Dexter raced through the backstreets before the police had even taken a description of him or his vehicle. Craftily, he had thought to stick on fake plates before going to the rave. He couldn't afford to go back inside. One reckless move, and he would be serving the rest of his life sentence.

Chapter Twenty-Five

Inside Jordan's home, it was warm and smelled of fried onions. Jordan had guided Eden to the first room on the left – the living room. It was clean, tidy, and homely. A chunky three-piece suite dominated the room. To the left of the stone-clad fireplace was a sideboard, and to the right a bookshelf, which displayed ornaments and DVDs. On top of the cabinet was a large TV set and underneath was a DVD player.

'Take a seat, babe,' he said, as he pointed to the sofa. 'I'll make us a cup of coffee. How about that?'

Eden had been anxious because she had really wanted him to call her a cab. They chatted for a while before she said sweetly, in a voice that wouldn't insult his hospitality, 'Jordan, what about the cab?'

'Why don't you stay the night? . . . On the sofa, of course.'

'What? Oh no, sorry, Jordan. I must get home,' she said, in a panic.

'Yeah, of course.'

Eden listened while he dialled a cab firm from the phone in the hallway. She heard him mention his address and then he finished the call with, 'Thank you, mate. See you in half an hour.'

Eden hoped it would be sooner; she was still concerned about Randy.

Jordan returned shortly with two mugs of coffee and placed them on the coffee table. 'Two sugars, yeah?'

'How did you guess?'

He winked. 'I reckon you're a lot like me. Except, of course, you're so much prettier.'

Before he even had a chance to sit next to her, a shrill voice called from upstairs. 'Dex, babe, is that you?'

Jordan huffed loudly. 'No, Muvver, it's me.'

He rolled his eyes when he heard his mother bustling down the stairs.

As she stood in the doorway, Eden felt her face flush. Jordan's mother was wearing a skimpy red satin baby-doll nightdress. It just about covered her private parts.

'Oh, hello.' She stared at Eden. 'Ain't you the girl that me mate across the road took to the hospital?'

Eden nodded. 'Yes, it was me.'

Gina looked at Jordan and then back at Eden. 'Well, you'll do better with my boy than ya last fella, that's for sure. He did you over good and proper, eh?'

Eden didn't know how to answer, so she just bit her lip and nodded.

'Muvver, er . . . leave us, will ya?'

Gina suddenly felt awkward. 'Sorry, Son. Yeah, sure. Where's Dexter and Sonny?'

'I dunno where Sonny is but Dexter's got the hump. He drove off somewhere.'

'Aw, for fuck's sake!' said Gina, before she stomped back up the stairs.

'Drink that coffee, babe. It'll warm you up, and the cab will be here soon,' Jordan said, as he rubbed her knee.

As soon as Eden put the mug to her lips, she noticed that the coffee wasn't at all hot. She assumed Jordan had cooled it sufficiently so that she could gulp it down before the cab arrived. It was a tasty drink, with cream and probably a heaped teaspoon of sugar. 'It's lovely, Jordan. Thank you.'

She watched him closely; his eyes lit up and a beaming smile spread across his face. She hadn't really noticed how handsome Jordan actually was until now. In fact, she hadn't thought him good looking at all before tonight.

In between mouthfuls of the warm drink, she smiled coyly.

As he moved in closer, she noticed his teeth seemed so vividly white – and those very dark brown eyes captivated her attention.

Her heart was beating so fast, and a very hot sensation came over her. She wondered if this was what it was like to really fancy someone. As her body became detached from her mind, the room began to move. It wasn't a frightening feeling but a soft, warm, and dreamy sensation.

As his lips pressed hard against hers, she didn't fight him off. She allowed him to kiss her. She tried to kiss him back, but her mouth was numb, and her lips wouldn't move. Every muscle in her body started to feel limp and so relaxed that she knew then she'd been drugged. Yet, strangely, she wasn't afraid because the feeling of floating was calming. Any thoughts about getting home and the concerns for Randy simply faded away.

When he carried her upstairs, she was still unafraid.

He closed the door behind them, using his foot, before he carefully laid her on the bed. She didn't protest because she couldn't. She was falling into something deep, quiet, calming, and unreal.

***

The distant sound of a radio brought Eden out of her deep sleep. Her eyes flickered around the room, and right away, they stared up at the ceiling. She didn't recognise where she was. She could feel a warm body beside her, and as she ran her hands down her front, she quickly established that she was naked.

It took a few minutes before she grasped what had happened. Feeling sick with fear, she slowly turned on her side, swung her legs around, and pushed herself off the bed. At first, her legs felt unsteady, but she drew in a deep breath and then searched the room for her clothes. She found her underwear and jeans, and as quiet as a mouse, she pulled them on, all the while staring at Jordan. He was face down on the pillow, not moving. She then scrambled around the dirty floor, searching for her top and trainers. One trainer was on his side of the bed and the other at the foot of the bed. Her top was on his cabinet. Carefully, she crept around to his side and snatched it. Slowly and quietly, she turned the bedroom doorknob praying that it wouldn't creak.

Bingo! She was out of the bedroom and down the stairs before Jordan had even noticed she'd gone. However, as soon as she passed the living room door, she heard Jordan's mother's voice. It stopped her in her tracks.

'Hello, darling, want a bit o' breakfast?' she asked, now more modestly dressed in a long red satin dressing gown.

'Oh no, I must get going. Sorry, er . . . but thank you.'

There was a pause before Jordan's mother spoke. Eden noticed that she was staring at her in a peculiar fashion as if she had just seen a ghost.

'Okay, suit yaself. Oh, by the way, this must be yours? I take it, it doesn't belong to Jordan?'

Eden waited for a second while Jordan's mother retrieved something from behind the living room door.

It was a money belt; the zip was open, and a small teddy was partially visible.

Eden's eyes widened, and her legs felt like jelly. 'Yes, yes, sorry, er . . . Thank you,' she replied nervously, as she took the belt from Jordan's mother and ran to the front door. In a flash, she was out of the house and running along the street. Gripping the belt, she tried to recall the evening's events. She remembered Jordan taking his long leather jacket off and dropping it beside the sofa behind the living room door. So she guessed his mother had retrieved it from there. But why would he have Randy's belt in the first place?

Beginning to feel very sick, she eventually had to stop to catch her breath before throwing up. Her body shook all over. She was in shock. Clutching the belt, she slid to her knees and began to cry. She sobbed like she had never wept before. The world she had known was cruel but was the outside – the freedom – any better than the life she had experienced before? She had never given Jordan permission to have sex with her. But she knew he had: she was sore and bruised down below.

How was she going to survive? She was cast out of her community, and yet she was too weak for the life outside. Slowly, she removed the teddy and held it in her hand. The poor girl had held on to this tiny stuffed toy, and it wasn't for luck, surely not. Eden guessed it was for hope. Randy had hoped that her mother would come and find her and love her, like she was supposed to.

As for herself, no one could hurt her anymore. She had reached the pits of pain and now felt something she'd never dared feel before: it was revenge – a terrible sin.

After getting to her feet, she marched on ahead until she reached Gabriel's house. She would have been quaking in her boots, but not this morning. She didn't care anymore. As she approached the gate, she heard a sweet, sickly voice. It was the same one that had grated on her for years. The voice that told tales, that laughed at her. It was her spiteful, nasty sister. She was standing there by the gate, and, of course, she would be. It was Sunday. Her family would be going to the Kingdom Hall.

Beatrice was in a beautiful dress, and her hair was up in a bow. She pointed to Eden and laughed. 'No one likes you. You are the sister of Satan. You are not allowed to talk to me because you are very bad.'

Eden would have walked by and ignored her, but not today. Today, she was not going to put up with any more taunts, even from her little sister. With an almighty shove, Eden pushed Beatrice in the chest. The young girl flew backwards into the three-foot-tall nettles. Eden smiled. Her prissy sister was screaming and struggling with the weeds as she scrambled to her feet. The rash on Beatrice's face was instant, which gave Eden at least a tiny flicker of accomplished revenge.

She marched on and didn't look back, even when she heard Gabriel bellowing after her. All she could do was stick her two fingers up, a small gesture of retaliation. It was as if she sensed that he wouldn't chase after her. Even if he had, she would have given him a fight.

Gripping the belt, she stormed along the main road, through Carlton Parade, past the duck pond, and along the High Street. Every wrongdoing, every slap, every beating, and every cruel word, was stirring up a violent storm inside her. Revenge was choking the kindness right out of her.

She should have felt a pang of guilt for pushing her sister into the nettles, but she didn't: not the tiniest bit. She smiled as she visualised her sister's alarmed expression.

By the time she reached the hostel, she was fuming. She wasn't sorry for herself but for Randy. And her first call was to go to her friend's door. If she wasn't in, then Jordan had done something to her. Why else and how else would he have her belt?

Her key, along with her thirty pounds, was still in the back pocket of her jeans. She opened the main door and could hear voices upstairs on the landing by her room. Running up the stairs, she found Dela leaning on the door frame to Randy's room and Sapphire inside.

'What's happened?' asked Eden, trying to look past Dela.

Dela pulled her back. 'She's been fucking beaten, that's what. Where were you, Eden? I thought you two were supposed to look out for each other?'

Eden felt gutted. 'How bad is she?'

Dela didn't answer but stepped aside for Eden to see for herself.

A gasp left Eden's mouth as she stared at Randy's battered face. One eye was completely closed, her cheeks were black and blue, and above her lip there was a nasty bite mark.

Sapphire shot Eden a look. 'I swear if I find out that this had anything to do with you, Eden, I will murder you with me bare hands.' She looked down at the money belt in Eden's hand. 'Is that hers?'

Eden nodded.

'Are you gonna tell us, Eden, how Randy got beaten the fuck out of, taken to a shagging van, forced to take pills, and was then sold time and time again?'

Eden threw her hands to her mouth as the tears filled her eyes and tumbled down her cheeks. It was shocking. Randy was lying on her side, shaking, with a sick bucket on the floor and Sapphire beside her, wiping her face with a wet cloth.

The room was quiet as Eden absorbed the words that left Sapphire's mouth. This moment was worse than the threats of Armageddon. That congregation was so close, it would never have happened to one of them. It was girls outside The Truth who this happened to, but it wasn't fair. Another spear of anger stabbed Eden.

'She didn't know,' whispered Randy, in a faint, weak voice.

But Sapphire wasn't having it. She glared back at Eden. 'So why does she have your belt? I am assuming it *is* yours?' Not waiting for an answer, Sapphire rose to her feet. 'I don't give a fuck *what* that poor kid says, Eden. You should've stayed together. What was it, eh?' She stepped closer, almost in Eden's face. 'Fucked off with a fella, did ya?'

Eden shook her head. 'No, I waited, but . . .'

Sapphire curled her lip, and with a quick swipe, she caught Eden around the face with her long talons. 'Well, then, you didn't wait long enough, did ya, you stuck-up bitch.'

The instant sting and the cruel expression on Sapphire's face sent Eden into an unpredicted frenzy. She dropped the belt, grabbed the girl's hair, bent her backwards, and punched her in the face.

Sapphire tried to fight Eden off, but Eden was glaring like a caged lion as she bent Sapphire so far back that she fell to the floor.

Out of breath, through rage, Eden yelled, 'I waited, and I waited. I was looking for her, I never just left. I thought she had gone without me.'

Everyone stared in surprise at Eden's anger.

Eden sighed and tried to rein in her temper by lowering her voice. 'Jordan Swan, my old neighbour, was going to give me a lift back to the Cray and then call me a cab. He gave me a drink, and I had no idea he'd drugged it. I woke up naked in his bed. I didn't know until I was leaving his house that he had Randy's belt in his possession.'

Sapphire's eyes glared antagonistically. 'Oh yeah? *Really?*'

Eden replied with a bitter tone, 'Don't you dare ever suggest I'm a liar, Saffy, and don't ever touch me again. I have been beaten and beaten until I couldn't sit down.' The suppressed anger that she had held down for so long had now risen to its peak. 'You have no idea what I've been through. I wasn't attacked by my boyfriend. I was attacked and raped by my *stepfather*, and now by Jordan Swan as well.' She stopped and took deep breaths, still staring at Sapphire, in case she retaliated. 'So don't call me stuck-up and don't blame me.' She glanced at Randy. 'I am so sorry, Randy. If I'd known, I would've stopped them. I would've helped.' The tears rolled down her cheeks as the sobs stuck in her throat.

Randy held her hand up. 'It wasn't your fault, Eden. How could you have known.'

'Did you say Jordan?' asked Dela.

Eden spun around. 'Yes, Dela. Jordan Swan.'

'I hate that prick. He's a nasty piece of work. He has hurt other girls, you know. He lives in St Mary Cray.'

Eden nodded. 'Yeah, that's him. He has a brother called George as well.'

Dela frowned. 'I only know he has one brother, but he calls half the gypsy site "bruv".'

Sapphire felt the lump under her eye and glared at Eden. 'Don't ever larrup me again, Eden.'

Dela laughed. 'Or what, Saffy? Come on, she's just kicked your arse, and you rightly deserved it. Eden's been through enough herself.'

Sapphire still wasn't buying it but she looked away before Dela pushed it too far. No one in the hostel would ever stand a chance with Dela. One punch thrown by her and it was game over.

'We should call the police then,' said Eden, now resigned to the inevitable.

'No point,' replied Sapphire, with her hands on her hips. She pointed to the belt. 'That will have drug residue on it, and how does Randy explain selling drugs at a rave? And not only that but she's also known to the Ol' Bill for soliciting. They won't take much notice of her. So, clever fucking clogs, what's your next plan, eh? You think it's easy, don't you? We are at the bottom of the shitpile, in case you haven't realised. No one believes us. We all have a past and it sounds like you do too. So unless you wanna spend hours down the station, then just shut up and give Randy some painkillers, if you have any, 'cos, Eden, you're fucking good at giving them out as well, ain't ya?'

Dela instantly launched herself off the door frame, grabbed Sapphire by her arms, and threw her out of the room, where she almost toppled over the banister.

'I told you, we will not have another word on Kathleen's death. Now, fuck off, Saffy! You're nuffin but a shit-stirrer.'

Eden left the room and went to her own because Sapphire was right. She did still have painkillers. She had paracetamol that Kathleen had given her. When she returned, Sapphire had left, and Dela was sitting on a rickety chair stroking Randy's head.

'I am so sorry, Randy.'

Randy tried to sit up. 'I was saved by some young lad. He knew the guys that did this to me. I am sure he said the name "Jordan". But there was an older bloke who helped this Jordan. I think his name is Dexter. They drugged me and locked me in that van, but then this young guy rescued me, er . . . Sonny. That's his name. He nearly got killed, 'cos that Dexter geezer pulled out an axe and almost cut his arm off.'

'*Sonny?* Did you say Sonny?' asked Eden, now puzzled.

Randy nodded. 'Why? Do you know him?'

'Yes. He's Jordan's brother. So, he saved you and got hurt in the process, did he? Where is he now?'

'The ambulance took him to the hospital. Why?'

'I just wanted to know that he's okay, I guess.'

***

Eden left Randy in Dela's care and returned to her own room. After locking the door behind her, she stripped off and stepped into the shower. The water dribbled out but there was enough to wash off the copious amounts of soap that she had lathered into every inch of her skin. She wanted to remove the feeling of humiliation, deceit, and disgust. She was angry with Jordan, Gabriel, the whole idea of The Truth, and herself. Now a fully-fledged member of the outside world, after being part of a congregation that had fed her lies and had given her a false sense of security, the realisation was a shock to her system.

Slipping into a tracksuit she'd bought from the charity shop, she lay on her bed and tried to get her thoughts in order. This was no way to live. She needed a real job and to get as far away from Orpington as she could. She would take Randy with her. They could rent a flat, work as secretaries or receptionists. Her thoughts became daydreams until a gentle tap drew her back to reality. She spun her legs around and sat up straighter until she swooned. The drugs Jordan had put in the coffee were still making her feel woozy.

The second she opened the door, she jumped back in surprise.

Dressed in black baggy jeans and a white shirt, with his face glowing, stood George. Behind him was Dela.

'This bloke, 'ere, says his name is George. Do you know him, Eden?'

Eden nodded. 'Yeah, it's okay.'

Dela nodded and left them to it.

'I hope you don't mind, Eden, only I left the rave, and I didn't see you again. Bernie said that Miranda lived here. He was gonna come himself and find out what had happened to her. She's got something that belongs to him, and I'm not silly. I can guess. So, anyway, I came to ask where you lived as well.'

Eden tilted her head to the side. 'Why?'

Now feeling awkward, George looked down as his cheeks flushed red. 'I dunno, really. I thought, well, I just wanted to make sure you got home okay and—'

'Come in,' she replied, in a flat tone.

'Eden, are you okay? You seem, oh, I dunno, different, sad even.'

She chuckled sarcastically. 'George, I don't know you. In fact, I don't really know anyone. I would love to be able to trust you. Perhaps we could have even been friends. In my nonsensical brain, I would also love to believe in magic and fairies, but I'm afraid I have been slapped in the face with the harsh, cold reality of life.'

'But you were so happy last night, and now you even look different. What happened, Eden?'

She stared at his eyes and his dewy complexion and then her mind went back to Jordan. To his olive skin, and his dark eyes sucking her in, lying to her, deceiving her. *Was George the same?* she wondered. *After all, they were brothers.* A nervous feeling crept over her.

'George, I'm sorry. Could you leave? I don't feel too good. Please don't come back. I don't know you, and I don't want to.'

'Why? What have I done? What's happened?'

'Nothing. Please, leave me alone. Tell Bernie that if he lets me know what Randy, I mean Miranda, owes, I will find a way to get the money back to him, but not today.'

George stood with his hands limp by his side and a hint of sadness in his eyes. 'You must tell me what happened, Eden. Bernie was more concerned about Miranda than about what she owed him.'

Eden opened the door and waited there for George to leave. 'Please, George. Just go.'

Dela was on the landing hovering, in case there was any trouble. Men or lads were not allowed in the hostel at all. All the same, she thought George looked like a kind gentleman, not a scallywag.

'Hang on, are you Jordan Swan's brother?'

Eden sighed. 'Dela, leave it, will you please.'

Dela shook her head. 'No, Eden. He should fucking know what his rapist brother did.'

George's eyes nearly popped out of his head. 'What!' he shrieked.

'Nothing. Just go home, George. Stay away. I don't want you or any of your family knocking here again. Please!'

'Wait!' George turned to Dela. 'Did Jordan rape Miranda? Is that why she left the rave? Please, *someone*, tell me.'

Dela knew then that she'd said too much and looked at Eden to reply.

'No, George, your brother raped *me*. He drugged and raped me. He also drugged Randy and sold her to have sex in a van at the rave. She's black and blue.'

George threw his hands to his mouth as he slumped down on his haunches. The blood drained from his face and tears filled his eyes. 'My God. My brother did *that* to you?'

Eden looked down at George and nodded.

Dela pulled George up onto his feet. 'Your brother is evil, George.'

Dela and Eden could both see that George was shocked to his core. His face was pale, and his eyes seemed almost dead.

'You had no idea, did ya, mate?' said Dela.

Silently, George shook his head. 'I don't live with them. It's a long story, but I was pushed out. My mother turned her back on me, and so did my brothers. I was lucky my dad supported me. To be frank, I am ashamed of Jordan, and I really don't want to know him, not after this. He's nothing like me, I can assure you of that.'

'You were lucky that you had a dad, because after my mum died, I was left with . . . my stepfather. He was basically a torturous bully with a holy name, a high standing in the community, but a very black heart.'

George wanted to hold Eden to give her comfort, but as he reached out, she backed away. 'Please don't touch me. I have had enough. You'd best just go, George. No offence to you. You're probably a lovely guy, but I am done with the Swan family. It's a shame, though, that the name brought me pleasure as a child.'

George politely nodded and walked away.

Dela put her arm around Eden. 'I think he is a genuine geezer, 'cos I know Jordan, and he is a bastard. But that George ain't nuffin like him. Still, babe, you probably need to rest and get over your ordeal. I'm gonna check on Randy again. I'll make her a nice cup of tea, bless her heart.'

'I think I'll go to the church in a bit.'

Dela nodded and walked away.

Eden closed the door behind Dela and put her hands to her face and sobbed hot tears of anger. Once she'd stopped crying, she lay on the bed in a foetal position, but something by the wall on the floor caught her eye. It looked like a letter. She hurried over, picked it up, and looked at the handwritten envelope. It must have been posted and pushed against the wall when she opened her door. Removing the folded paper from inside, she read the words.

I am your father, and you need to come back.

Your sister needs you.

Jehovah will forgive you, if you repent.

I will never give up. I know your every move, Eden.

'Aaaarrrghhh! You bastard! You evil bastard!' she yelled, as she ripped the paper into a thousand pieces.

With her nostrils flared, she paced the floor. This life was no life. There was no happiness, nothing to look forward to. There was no one she could love and who would love her. She had merely been used and abused time and time again. Gripping her hair, she wanted to rip it out. But nothing was going to calm her down or dampen her anger. She would never be able to live this life without always looking over her shoulder or being in fear of every man who looked her way. Everything she had believed in was a lie. Suddenly, she had to get out of the room, breathe in some air, before she would go insane. After tying the laces of her trainers, she jumped to her feet. She didn't even lock the door behind her. After all, there were no valuables inside to steal. She had nothing, she had no one, and so she had nothing to lose.

Orpington was remarkably quiet for a Sunday. The Kingdom Hall would be emptying now. Would the community really shun her, like they said? The sisters and brothers who had known her since she was a baby? Surely not? She marched on ahead, her mind spiralling out of control. Trying as hard as she could to rid the feeling of hate, she couldn't recall any happiness, apart from the precious time she had spent with her mother.

As she approached the Kingdom Hall, she slowed down and stared at the practically empty car park. She was too late: they had already left. Perhaps Gabriel had finished a few minutes earlier. She knew he would be the last one to go, so there wouldn't be anyone around to stop him, if he wanted to hurt her.

Across the road, she noticed two teenagers and it wasn't until Eden blinked twice that she recognised them – Chloe and Caleb. Her heart skipped a beat. She realised that she had missed them so much. It was the familiar feeling – a sense of comfort. She crossed the road and waved as they walked towards her.

'Chloe!' she called out, wondering if perhaps Chloe hadn't recognised her. After all, she herself was wearing a tracksuit and trainers, so very different from her usual clothes. However, Chloe looked past Eden as if she wasn't there.

'Chloe!' she called out again, but there was still no response.

Stunned, Eden ran up to her friend and grabbed her arm. 'Hey, Chloe, it's me.'

With that, Chloe shrank back and wouldn't even look Eden in the eyes.

It was Caleb who removed Eden's hand from Chloe's arm. 'Go away, Eden. We cannot ever speak with you. You are dead to us.'

'But you can't say that! No, you don't understand. I never left the congregation. I was—'

'Stop!' said Caleb, as he placed his arm around Chloe's shoulders and guided her away, leaving Eden feeling bereft.

'Please, Chloe. You are my oldest and dearest friend,' she called after her. 'Please, please, Chloe. I have no one, no one.'

'Go away, Eden,' said Caleb, turning to her. 'You are not to talk to anyone from the congregation. You are cast out, disfellowshipped.'

Tears pricked her eyes as she watched her friends hurry away as if she had some dreadful disease. Then, across the road, she saw Gabriel. He was staring at her. His glare turned into a sadistic grin as he waved at her as though he was acknowledging an old friend.

'Jump in, Eden. I will give you a lift!' he called out, in such a polite and normal tone.

Eden felt sick. It wasn't with fear this time but with rage. She wanted to run over and smash his ugly face against the bonnet of his car. But she couldn't move because her legs were rigid. He said no more, got into his car, and pulled out of the car park. Just for a moment, Eden assumed that he was going to try to drag her into his motor, but he didn't. Then she spotted men on the flat roof of the Kingdom Hall. So, that's why he was behaving so out of character, she concluded.

There had been talk of a new roof for the building for some time. The large flat roof had been leaking for two years, and the pitched part of the hall needed new slate tiles. She watched the men climb down, taking with them their tools. She also noticed that they had a key to the place and were storing their equipment inside.

Something urged her to go inside herself. Perhaps it was the feeling of familiarity again, a meaning of belonging or of comfort. Or maybe it was a sense of closure. Her heart felt as though it was beating outside her chest as she approached the car park and watched. The workmen were too busy to notice her as she slipped inside the hall.

But someone else noticed.

Chapter Twenty-Six

George was fuming as he drove back to the gym. Jordan was his flesh and blood, and yet he was so far removed from his brother's disgusting behaviour and from everything he believed in. He would have to break the news about Eden and the events surrounding her to his father because these would bound to come out anyway, and if his inkling about the rave promoter being his father was correct, then he may well be pulled in by the police for questioning. The details that Dela and Eden had given him were probably only half the story. The full picture was most likely a whole lot worse.

His Ford Fiesta was his pride and joy, and he had only been driving for two weeks. By rights, he should have driven with more care and attention, but the news had knocked him sideways, and all he could think of doing was to put his foot down and head back to the gym.

He ran through the main fitness room and up the stairs to the office. His father was sitting behind the desk, and Bernie along with Maxi and Nobby were seated opposite.

Mitchell looked up and clocked the flustered look on his son's face.

'All right, boy? Did you manage to find this Eden girl and Randy?'

George looked first at Bernie and then back to his father. 'It's Jordan. He, well . . . he, er . . .'

'Speak up, Son. You normally have a lot to say.'

George looked nervously at Bernie and Maxi.

Bernie got the hint. 'Sorry. Did you want to have a private word, Georgie boy?'

Shyly, George nodded.

'Hang on, George. We're like family here. Unless you wanna tell me you're gay, or something of a personal nature, speak freely.'

'Right. Well, Jordan attacked Miranda. He gave her drugs and sold her to let men use her. You know what I mean.'

Bernie jumped up from his chair. He stretched his fingers and pulled his shoulders back. 'The fucking little cunt. So let's get this right. He sold one of my little runners for sex, did he?'

George nodded. 'Not just one runner, Bernie. It was two of them. He took that Eden home and drugged her as well.' He turned to his father. 'And, Dad, he raped her.'

With his eyes glazing over, Mitchell sank deeper into his chair. 'My eldest son is a fucking rapist, right?'

The room fell silent as everyone absorbed those brutal words.

'He needs seeing to, Mitch. I said he was a wrong 'un. But there's something else you should know. I don't think he *is* your son.'

Mitchell snorted in disapproval. 'Bernie, Jordan may or may not be. But I have no idea who *my* own father was so Jordan may take after him. But it doesn't change the fact that he is a rapist, and I could've possibly spawned a monster like that.'

'George, tell me about this girl Eden. Why are you so interested in her?'

George blushed, as he often did when he was embarrassed. 'I don't know what it is. It's hard to explain. But I met her the day Nan was killed. She was in the High Street, with her mum and dad, I think. Nan said they were Bible-bashers—'

'What?' interrupted Mitchell, as he slowly inclined his head.

'Yeah, her dad was talking about Bible stuff, and Nan shouted at him for throwing my burger and hot chocolate, which I'd given to Eden, in the bin.'

Bernie attempted to dismiss their conversation, but Mitchell hushed him up. 'George, what else do you know about her?'

George shrugged his shoulders. 'Only that her mum died, and she lives in the hostel. She is not like other girls, Dad. She's so different.'

'What was her mother's name?'

'I dunno, Dad. Dad, why are you asking me all these questions?'

Nobby stood up and walked around the desk. ''Cos, George, your dad's first love was a girl called Claire. He told me a long time ago that if they had got married, they would've called their first girl Eden. They were both Jehovah's Witnesses at the time.'

'Leave it, Nobby,' said Mitchell.

'The boy should know, just in case. What if Georgie boy really likes her? I mean, you know, *really* likes her?'

George's eyes flicked from Nobby back to his father, who looked as white as a sheet.

'Bloody hell, Mitch. Just 'cos you liked the name Eden don't mean nuffin. Christ, you don't seriously think she's your *daughter*, do you?' exclaimed Bernie.

Mitchell hung his head in sorrow. 'If she is, then the woman I loved is dead, and the girl I never knew I had has just been raped by my son.'

Nobby patted Mitchell's back. 'I have a picture of Claire, the one you had when you were inside.' He opened the bottom drawer and pulled out the photo. It was the very one that Mitchell had stared at every night in his cell.

'Here, George, this is Claire. Does Eden look like her?'

George stared and tears welled up in his eyes. 'Bloody hell. It's like looking at her, Dad.'

Mitchell took the photo and stared at it before placing it back in the drawer. 'You're right, Son. Of course! She was the girl at the rave, wasn't she?'

George nodded. 'Yes, she's the one I introduced you to, but you were preoccupied.' A gasp left George's mouth. 'Oh my God, Dad. She said that her mother called her a baby swan.'

'Baby swan? Are you sure about that or did she say cygnet?'

'Yeah, that's it. She said her mother used to call her, her little cygnet.'

Mitchell put his hands over his mouth and suddenly choked back a tear.

'Oh, fuck,' he said. 'Oh my God, why didn't she tell me? I would have married her right away.'

Bernie looked hard at his friend. 'So is she yours, Mitch?'

'Oh, Christ, I dunno. Maybe I'm still living in the past. Claire said that one day we would have little cygnets of our own. But the thing is, she was always fascinated by my surname. She thought it was a name to be proud of. It's crazy. I mean, she married someone else, so why would she still call her little girl a cygnet?'

But Bernie's main concern now was with what had happened to Miranda. 'Is Miranda in a bad way?'

George shrugged his shoulders again. 'I couldn't tell you anything about her. I never got to see her, if that's what you mean, but, fucking hell, I should bleedin' well think so, after what those bastards put her through.'

Bernie cracked his knuckles. 'I have a soft spot for that kid. I know I gave her a hard time, but she's one of life's cruel aftermaths. But know this: if you don't sort out Jordan, I fucking well will. And, Mitch, there is a queue of men behind me. He's gone too far this time.'

Mitchell wasn't going to defend Jordan's corner because there was simply nothing to defend.

'If I do find out that Eden *is* my daughter, *I* will kill Jordan myself with my bare hands.'

'No, Dad, if she's my sister, *I'll* kill him.'

Maxi, who had remained quiet throughout the entire conversation, spoke up. 'Ya know they say that separated siblings are attracted to each other.'

'Shut up, Maxi. That thought makes me sick.' George coughed and exaggerated a gag.

Maxi waved his hands. 'No, I didn't mean you would wanna, you know. I meant it's like a mirror image, so they can be drawn to each other. You said you didn't know what it was about Eden that attracted her to you. You just said she is different from other girls you know. Do you think it's like a sibling bond you might have?'

Bernie rolled his eyes. 'Don't go all Sigmund Freud on us.'

Maxi laughed. 'I watched a fascinating programme about it, that's all.'

'Right, I need to find out if this kid is mine, and you, Bernie, will want to see that your little runner is okay. So what are we waiting for, lads? Let's go.'

***

Mitchell decided to take only George with him in the car. He wanted to talk to his son alone.

'How are you doing, Son?'

'I feel sick to me stomach. If it's true what we've discussed, and I do believe it is, then Jordan needs to be dealt with or locked up.'

'Sorry, what I said came out wrong. I meant how do you feel about the possibility that Eden could be your sister?'

'I feel equally bad because I know in my heart she's led a terrible life. I saw it in her eyes that day years ago when I gave her the food and drink, and this morning, she just looked resigned.' He stared ahead in silence, merely thinking for a few minutes. 'How are you going to explain that you could be her father?'

'I have no idea, but I want to make sure that she is okay. If she is Claire's daughter, I still want to look out for her. I loved Claire, you see. I'm hoping, though, that she is not, and Claire is out there somewhere alive and happy with her own little cygnets.' He laughed as he finished the sentence, to hide the real pain.

George tried to recall everything that Eden had said, in the hope that she was his sister.

'Dad! There's something she said about her stepfather. She said: "He was a bully with a holy name and a very black heart."'

Mitchell felt his whole body turn cold and his skin prick with goosebumps. A holy name – *Gabriel*. The one man he'd hated all his life. He shook his head, removing all the snippets of possibilities. Now, he simply needed to know the truth.

They reached the hostel, with Bernie directly behind them. Mitchell looked up at the building and felt uneasy. A million thoughts ran through his head. He was only too aware of the ways of Jehovah's Witnesses, and he knew that if the girl was living here in this shithole of a place, then she would have been disfellowshipped – an outcast. Every member of the congregation, every person she knew and could call family, would shun her. He cleared the lump in his throat.

George pressed the intercom and banged on the door. It was Dela who appeared. 'George, you're back, then?' She looked over his shoulder to see two big men, much older, approaching the front door.

'I need to talk to Eden and Miranda,' said George.

He noticed Dela's eyes widen.

'Please, let us see them. We ain't here to harm—'

Bernie decided to take over. 'I'm Bernie. Tell me, love, is Miranda all right? I've heard that someone attacked her at the rave. I swear, babe, I'm not here to collect any money or anything like that. I just wanna know that she's okay. 'Ere.' He pulled out some cash from his back pocket. 'Give her some money. Tell her that Big Bernie's downstairs, if she wants to tell me who the fuck it was who hurt her. 'Cos I'll pay *them* a fucking visit.'

Dela knew then that the big man was not going to hurt Randy at all. And as much as Dela was like the bodyguard in the hostel, she could see that these men were no small-time chancers. Bernie's deep commanding voice told her he was a straight-up kind of geezer.

'And Eden?' enquired Mitchell.

Dela shook her head. 'She's gone to some church or other. I *am* worried about her. She ain't from my kind of life, and know this: Jordan Swan drugged her. And to be quite honest with you, I think she's acting too normal. I mean he *drugged* and *raped* her. Most girls would be traumatised, but she's not.'

Unexpectedly, Randy appeared from behind Dela. Her tiny frame was covered in faded pyjamas three sizes too big for her. Her eye was still closed and swollen, and her cheeks and lips were puffed up from the bite marks.

The men gasped, but Bernie didn't hold back. In a state of shock, he pulled Miranda close and hugged her. 'Fucking hell,' he yelled.

Randy didn't fight him off her; she allowed his huge meaty arms to comfort her.

'Bastards! Fucking bastards! They won't get away with this, Miranda. I can assure you of that, girl. Right, first things first, get some clothes on. You're coming home with me.'

Dela put her hand up. 'Oh no, mate, she ain't.'

Randy pulled away from Bernie and turned to face Dela. 'He ain't like that, Dela. Honestly, he ain't.'

Bernie was offended. 'Oh, for fuck's sake, I'm old enough to be her fucking grandfarver. I wouldn't touch her. I feel guilty, and I hate feeling bad. I've got a nice home so she can stay there and get better. She needs a few steak pies to fatten her up. And if anyone tries to get to her, then they'll have to get through me first.'

Dela nodded as if she had the right to make decisions on behalf of Randy.

Mitchell was still reeling from seeing Miranda's facial wounds. He felt ill. He couldn't comprehend why Jordan would have let this happen to a harmless waif of a girl.

George glanced across at him as they returned to their car. 'Perhaps we should wait for her to come back, eh, Dad?'

But Mitchell just stared into nowhere – in silent contemplation.

Chapter Twenty-Seven

Eden hid in the small room until she heard the workmen's van start up. Then she entered the main hall again. She'd never been entirely alone inside the Kingdom Hall before. She saw that the rows of chairs were arranged in neat lines with a gap down the centre to enable easy access for the congregation to come and go. At the far end, there was the platform for the speakers. Behind that hung the heavy mustard velvet drapes and on either side were large vases filled with dried flowers.

Everywhere there was wood, from the uneven water-stained parquet flooring blocks to the panelled walls that covered most of the original windows. The building hadn't always been known as the Kingdom Hall. It had once been a community centre. She thought for a split second that she would feel some comfort from being here, but there was nothing but cold silence and the familiar smell of damp. The panels hid more than the original windows. They disguised the actual state of the outer walls, which had leaked over many years from neglect. She wondered if repairing the roof was too little, too late. Still, what did it matter to her now? She thought the room actually personified Gabriel quite well, and all that was wrong with him; for whereas he was all smiles and smart on the outside, there was a lot of evil lurking within.

She noticed that the workmen had left all of their equipment behind the door, from the rolls of modified bitumen to the roofing torches and the propane gas cylinders. She had taken one last look at the platform and decided that there was nothing to be gained from being inside the hall, so she made her way to the entrance. Her foot kicked something that slid across the floor, making a clanging, echoey sound. For a moment, she was unnerved by it, but, quickly, she bent down to retrieve the object. It was a particularly nasty tool. Known as a roofing hammer, it had a massive spike on one end and a flat head on the other. She turned it around in her hand and felt the grip of the handle. She imagined using it if anyone ever tried to hurt her again.

The thought was too sinful, so she opted to return the implement to the corner where all the tools were kept. Her eyes again caught sight of the torch and the gas bottle. Out of curiosity, she picked up the torch and clicked the switch, but nothing happened. The gas bottle was turned off. She flicked the lever to 'on' and tried again. This time, she could hear the hiss of the gas, but there was no flame until she pressed the second button. At first, the flame was orange and dancing, like the flames from an open log fire. Then, as she held down the trigger, the flame turned blue and vicious. Shocked, she gasped and released the trigger.

The blue flame changed back to the gentle orange flame, until she turned the gas lever back to the 'off' position. After placing the torch back down, her eyes were drawn to the roofing hammer, and although stealing was a sin, she fathomed that in any case she wasn't going to be part of God's New Order, not ever. Clasping the tool in her hand, she decided to leave and never look back. This part of her life was over. Period.

She was jolted from her thoughts when she heard the key turn in the lock of the entrance doors. It had to be Gabriel or one of the workmen because who else would have the keys? Although her Aunt Rachael had them, she never came here alone. There was nowhere to run to and nowhere to hide. Her heart was in her mouth, and fear covered her body like a black veil.

The door opened and there dressed in a dark-blue suit stood Gabriel – the very Devil himself. He stared expressionless at her, closed the door behind him, and then silently regarded her with his menacing narrow dark eyes.

'I saw you sneak your way in here, Eden.'

She could hear her own heart beating through the fast pulse in her temple. She kept her hands behind her back, hiding the roofing hammer, while trying to calm the riot in her mind.

'You belong to me, Eden.'

She stared unwaveringly.

'I raised you. I protected your mother from the wicked outside world, and I saved her dignity in the congregation. I married her so no one would know that she was pregnant by another – a son of Satan.'

As he stepped closer, she was hit by the overpowering, sickly smell of his aftershave.

His voice changed and became merciless. 'She was repentant in the end, Eden. But only because she begged me to get help, but *I* knew what was best for her. They would've given her a blood transfusion, you see, and that would've made her impure. So I told her to ask for Jehovah's forgiveness for her sins. You have to understand, Eden. I know what Jehovah wants. I know what's best for the community. That's why *I* am an elder. Surely, you can see that?'

He chuckled. 'Ahh, dear, it's such a shame that you are not like your mother. You see, she died sacrificially. I watched the life leave her body as the last drop of blood fell to the floor.'

The vision of her mother begging him to get help consumed her mind. She could visualise him smiling with his twisted lips as she left this world. That thought instantly saddened her. But it also made her angry.

'She, Eden, will live in God's Paradise and you, Eden, you can too. But you must be repentant.' His tormenting grin twisted into attempting that familiar smile of his. 'If you come home with me and be grateful to me for all that I did for your whore of a mother and you, then Jehovah will see that you are good and welcome you back into The New World Order.'

The word 'whore' swirled around her head, stirring something new – an entirely different feeling – something she'd only partially experienced that day she'd hit him with the chair. Now she felt such anger: a rage that had started at the bottom of her stomach was now unravelling like a giant viper that had been poked awake from its slumber.

She raised her chin defiantly and shot him a crucifying glare.

'Oh, so you dare challenge me, Eden, with your slutty confidence?' he said, as his dark eyes flashed and his nostrils flared. 'You will do as you are told, young lady!'

A small grin that began at the corners of her mouth now spread into a fully-fledged smile.

As he lunged forward to grab her arm, she turned to run. But she wasn't fast enough. He managed to grab her from behind and slap his hand over her mouth. To his astonishment, she didn't struggle. However, before he realised why, it was too late.

With every ounce of strength, fuelled with every hate-filled muscle, she swung the spiked end of the roofing hammer over her shoulder and directly into his forehead. The feeling as the hammer embedded itself into his head was such a relief, but the sound was horrific, and the suction noise as she removed it was sickening. Right away, she believed she'd murdered him because he sounded like a sack of potatoes when he hit the ground.

But his moans and groans plucked her from her state of stillness. As she turned around, she saw him trying to get to his feet while clutching his head. Stepping back, she glared at the man who had made her whole existence a nightmare. She realised then that she'd wanted to kill him. She still wanted to kill him. Then came the rage: the monster inside her was unleashed.

'You bastard!' she screamed, at the top of her voice. 'You let my mother die. You wanted her dead so that you could have me. I heard you every night torturing my mother. You heartless son of a fucking bitch. My sweet, sweet mother.' Tears fell like waterfalls down her cheeks as she screamed and cried. Then with both hands gripping the weapon, she swung it forcefully into his palm that he'd held up to protect himself.

He cried out in pain and rocked while holding his hand that now had a hole right through it.

Again, she lifted the hammer. 'Who is my real father? Tell me!'

'Please, Eden, stop!' he begged, knowing he was facing a totally deranged young woman. Her eyes were red, her teeth were clenched, and her mouth was foaming and spitting out foul words. Who was this girl? It couldn't be Eden because she was the epitome of subservience. She was the shy one with her head down, always trying to please.

'Who is my father?' she yelled again, as she grabbed one of the propane bottles and a torch and dragged the equipment over to him. She pulled the trigger and then watched as he held his breath and sighed when he saw that nothing had happened.

'Who is my real father?' she yelled, yet again.

He stared in disbelief when she clicked the trigger that lit the gas, and, like a child, he let out a high-pitched scream. She aimed the blue flame at the chair to his right, and instantly the material on it ignited.

Gabriel was now terrified. His eyes were stinging and blurred, his head was pounding like nothing on earth, and his hand was bleeding profusely. He only had his jelly legs to stand up on and one functioning hand. But he could see Eden was in control. She had the torch and the power to burn him alive. Dread crept its way through every part of his being as he watched Eden with that disturbed look on her face waving the torch and setting the chairs alight.

He tried to back away before the torch caught his suit. He could see the devastation that a split second's contact with the power of the flame could create.

'WHO IS MY FATHER?' she cried out. But Gabriel was too terrified to speak. His complete focus was on not becoming a human torch.

The chairs were on fire, the wood panelling was ablaze, and with no fire retardant covering the walls, the flames danced up and licked the ceiling. The intense smoke was choking him, but still, he could hear her screaming for him to name her father. He tried so desperately to speak, but whether it was the bang on the head or the shock, he couldn't get the words out. He tried so hard. But the smoke was getting thicker, he was coughing and coughing, and yet there she was, still screaming like a woman possessed.

'Mitchell!' he finally managed to say, hoping that by giving up the name, she would help him to safety.

She held the flame close to his feet. 'Mitchell who?' she demanded, before she too started to cough, for the room was filling up fast with dense smoke. The walls were orange with dancing flames, and Gabriel's screams were drowned out by the hissing and spitting of the rampant fire as it destroyed the heavy velvet curtains.

'Mitchell *who?*' she screamed, as she coughed and choked.

But Gabriel was still trying to gasp for breath. His sight was fading, and his thoughts were dull. He could barely breathe, but he wanted to hold on and escape alive. He didn't want to die – not now, not knowing whether Jehovah would forgive him for what he'd done. Or maybe this was the day of Armageddon – the day all non-believers faced, and the burning flames symbolised God's judgement. But he wasn't a non-believer. He had preached The Truth. Surely, Jehovah would see fit to welcome him into his Earthly Paradise when the time came? 'Forgive me, Jehovah. I repent!'

***

Instead of waiting for Eden, Mitchell suggested that they take a quick drive over to the Kingdom Hall. It was the building that all the Jehovah's Witnesses from around Orpington and the Crays attended. As soon as they turned into the road, they saw the smoke billowing from the roof of the building.

Without driving into the car park, Mitchell stopped dead in the road, leaped from his car, and tore towards the burning building like a bat out of hell. Without thinking, he pulled open the main door. His rash actions caused a backdraught of air inside the hall to suck the raw flames along the ceiling and through the doorway before finding their way back inside. Fortunately for Mitchell, he was behind the door. If he had been in front of it, he would have been burned alive.

The thick grey smoke blocked his vision. He used his hands to clear the smoke from his face, but he couldn't see anything until he heard coughing and spluttering. As he entered the hall, some of the smoke partially cleared, and there, lying on the floor, was Eden, with the roofing torch in her hand. Behind her was a man.

It wasn't until the smoke briefly cleared again that he recognised the man as Gabriel. He was choking and coughing and holding his arm out, begging to be rescued. But Mitchell only had one thing on his mind, and that was to get the girl out of there alive. Pulling his T-shirt over his nose and mouth, he dropped down on his hands and knees and crawled to her. Just as he managed to grab her ankle, he spotted the propane bottle. Frantically, he tugged the girl towards him. In a quick movement, he scooped her up, rose to his feet, and hurried out.

Red-faced and panicking, George hadn't been quick enough to stop his father from rushing in, but now he could breathe with relief. Not only was his father safe, but so was

Eden. She was coughing and semi-conscious, but she was alive.

'Run, George, run!' yelled Mitchell, as he tore across the car park towards the bushes on the other side of his car. They managed to clear the area before the blast. Covering both his children, Mitchell watched as the Kingdom Hall literally exploded. He could hear fire engines in the distance but knew he didn't have time to wait.

The Audi was untouched by the explosion. George opened the back door and gently laid Eden across the rear seats. Then he hopped into the front, just managing to shut the door as his father drove away, heading towards the hospital.

George opened the windows, leaned over, and passed Eden one of his bottles of water.

She was coughing and moaning, but it was clear to both George and Mitchell what she was mumbling. 'What is my father's last name? Tell me.'

George then climbed into the back and tried to get Eden to sit up. 'Eden, drink this. Come on, open your eyes.'

After a few good lungfuls of air, Eden opened her eyes, sucked on the plastic straw, and drank the cold water, allowing some to trickle over her dry sore lips. 'George,' she managed to say, in an extremely croaky voice.

'Eden, are you hurt? Are you burned? Do you feel okay? What can I do? Are you okay?'

'Christ, George, let her answer.'

'I'm okay, George. What are you doing here?' She wiped her black smoke-stained eyes and glared back at the towering blaze, which could be seen a mile away. 'Did he get out alive?'

'Who?' asked George, now puzzled.

'If you mean, Gabriel, he is probably dead by now.'

Those words had Eden sitting up straight. 'You know him?'

Mitchell stared ahead as tears pricked his eyes. 'Let's talk about it when you're feeling better. First, let's get you to the hospital, eh?'

'No, please, if you take me there, they will arrest me for burning down the Kingdom Hall, and Gabriel, I mean.'

Mitchell could hear the stress and tiredness in her voice. 'Don't worry anymore, Eden. I can take you to my house and get you cleaned up, and George and I can keep an eye on you so you don't need to see a doctor. But smoke inhalation is a killer.'

Having gone through so much in the last twenty-four hours, Eden fell asleep in seconds. She woke up once she felt the car come to a stop. Slowly, she opened her sore eyes and blinked a few times before she could adjust to her surroundings. Allowing George's father to carry her, she felt strangely comfortable. They entered a plush apartment block that was surrounded by beautiful gardens. The second floor only had two main doors opposite each other. Once they were inside, the apartment appeared huge, as though she had stepped into a Tardis. The spacious lounge had floor-to-ceiling windows that overlooked a park. The carpet was beige, and the chunky sofas were made of thick light-brown corduroy material. The television was enormous, and the open-plan kitchen appeared to house every conceivable cooking device. She gazed around in wonderment since she'd never been inside a home so bright, clean, and luxurious. It was going to be such a downer when the time came for her to return to her own pad.

She couldn't remember George's father's name; it had been such a brief introduction. In fact, she wasn't sure if she had ever known what it was.

'There now, George. See if you've got a nice tracky for Eden and then go and run the bath for her.'

Eden stared at George's father. Although he appeared to have a serious face, she could feel the warmth behind those cold eyes.

'Thank you so much for saving me. Can I ask how you know Gabriel?'

George stood there, waiting for his father to answer.

'George, go and run Eden a bath and find her some suitable clothes will you, Son?'

Reluctantly, George nodded and left the room.

Mitchell sat on a large padded pouffe opposite Eden, who had chosen to sit on one of the sofas. He stared for a moment and then bit his lip.

Eden sat herself up straight. She could see the tears in his eyes were beginning to well up. Something was going on. Then she remembered Jordan telling her that Mitchell, his father, was an evil bastard – *Mitchell!*

She could feel her throat tightening and a lump lodged itself there. Was he? Could he be? He obviously knew Gabriel.

'Eden, was your mother called Claire?' He held his breath, almost fearfully.

She nodded, but the sob stuck in her throat and wouldn't allow her to speak. A tear tumbled down her cheek.

'I think that you might be my little——'

'Cygnet!' she blurted out, finishing his sentence, hoping he was going to say that.

He stared for a moment, desperate to hold her, but what did *she* think? Was she angry? Could she forgive him?

But it was George who had been listening in on the conversation from the hallway who ran to her. 'Oh my God! You're my *sister*, then!'

He threw himself on the sofa, practically squashing her. 'Fucking hell, Eden. If only I had known. I would've given anything to have been in your life.'

Mitchell watched his two children clinging to each other as if their lives depended on it. He could see she wasn't cross; she was desperate to be loved.

'She's ours, Dad. She's all ours.'

Wiping her eyes, she gently pulled away and looked at Mitchell. 'Did you know about me?'

'No, darling, because if I'd known I would never ever have left you anywhere near that evil bastard Gabriel. I loved your mother so much, Eden. She was the love of my life. Please, tell me, how did she die?'

Eden sniffed back the tears. 'She died having my sister. And she died because *he* left her to die. He wouldn't save her, even though she begged him to.'

Mitchell had to walk away for a moment to allow the tears to fall down and the pain to leave his face. He had his back to her as he stared out of the window.

Guessing the answer but needing to ask the question, he said, 'Was Gabriel cruel to you?'

'Oh my God, he was beyond cruel to me *and* to my mum.' She coughed again and wiped her stinging eyes.

As he turned around, she was on her feet, her head tilted to the side, just like her mother. Stepping forward, he held out his arms and instantly she fell into them. He kissed the top of her head. 'You're safe now, baby swan.'

'I wish my mum had told me sooner. I would have tried to find you.'

'We can't change the past, Eden, but we can make a good future for ourselves. When you are well, I will tell you about your mother and me, but now I think you should take a bath and get that shit out of your eyes while I make you a nice hot chocolate. Don't lock the bathroom door in case you faint or whatever.'

Eden suddenly had a flashback to Gabriel and the cold bath. She looked at her father — her real father — but he wasn't looking at her like Gabriel had done.

'George, did you find Eden some clothes?'

George laughed. 'Yeah, I've got me new Nike tracksuits.' He held up two of them, both with the labels on. 'I reckon the light-blue one will suit you. It's proper soft inside an' all. I wear these ones just to doss around in.'

Eden suddenly felt a part of something more than the congregation.

'There are warm towels, shampoo, soap, everything, really. But like Dad said. Shut the door but don't lock it, and sing so we know that you're okay in there.'

***

The bath experience was how it should be. Hot water, bubbles, pretty smells, and warm towels. She scrubbed away the smoke stains, the dirt, and the feeling of hate. She sang funny nursery rhymes, and then, in her sweetest voice, like her mother's, she sang the Scott Fitzgerald and Yvonne Keeley song 'If I Had Words'.

Pouring the hot milk into the chocolate, Mitchell felt his heart melt. It had once been Claire's favourite song. If only he had fought for her. He had loved her more than life itself.

He recalled standing under the large oak tree in the middle of the woods in Poverest Park as though it was yesterday. The rain had let up, and the air was warm. He had waited for Claire. It was a Sunday, and she was able to escape for an hour or so after the talk at the Kingdom Hall. It was their only chance ever to be alone. He was nineteen then, and she was seventeen – his secret sweetheart. He smiled to himself as he pictured her pretty smile and her round baby eyes that were full of hopes and dreams. With the tartan picnic rug under his arm, he tried to listen for any sound that would tell him she was skipping her way through the trees. He remembered looking at his watch. It was late. Where was she?

Then he saw her, dressed in a forget-me-not-blue summer dress, her long fair hair hanging straight on either side of her face. The colour of her eyes matched her dress, and her lips were like pink rosebuds. So innocent, so angelic – so perfect.

Out of breath, she'd glanced behind her. 'Oh, Mitch, I am so sorry. I had to stay behind. Gabe wanted to talk to me. He suspects something is going on, you know.'

Mitchell, a good two feet taller than Claire, gently stroked her cheeks. 'He can't know anything, unless he followed you.'

She quickly replied, 'Oh, he didn't follow me.' Her eyes rested on the rolled-up blanket and her cheeks reddened.

'I didn't want your pretty dress to get ruined.'

'Oh, okay.'

He rolled the blanket out and placed it on the ground. 'I've missed you all week.'

'I've missed you too, Mitch. I wish . . .'

Holding her hand, he gently pulled her to the ground beside him and placed his arm around her shoulders.

'I can't, Claire. I just can't go back. My life is so different now. I don't know if I even believe in God anymore.'

Claire gasped. 'Oh, Mitch, please don't say that. I want us to be *together* in God's heavenly kingdom.'

He gave her a sad smile. She was so brainwashed that no matter what he said to her now, he could never convince her of an alternative life for them both.

Gazing into her eyes, he wondered if those glassy pools full of aspiration were for him or for her faith. Either way, it sucked him in, and all he wanted was to kiss her lips and hold her tight.

She blushed again as he leaned forward. Cupping the back of her head, he pulled her close. She didn't stop him; she allowed his lips to brush hers and his tongue to search inside her mouth.

He felt her body relax as he kissed her again and again. The sweet smell of her skin shot waves of desire through his mind. He wanted her. More than anything, he wanted to feel every part of her. She didn't stop him. She allowed his fingers to tenderly stroke her skin. Slowly, he unzipped her dress and pulled it down, revealing her shoulders so pure and untouched by the sun. As he kissed her neck, she reacted by unzipping his jeans. He paused, pulled back, and looked at her face. She nodded.

It was the first time for both of them, and it would be the last. They were so caught up in the passion that neither of them stopped for breath until it was over. As if a wave of guilt took over her mind and soul, she suddenly looked up at the sky and cried, 'Oh, Mitch, what have I done? It's a sin. How could I have . . . It's Satan's work. Oh, I should have stopped myself. I should have resisted. Oh, no . . . I will never be in God's Earthly Paradise.' She jumped to her feet while struggling to zip up her dress.

That was when he saw the absolute terror in her eyes. Those round pretty eyes, awash with fear, and he felt so helpless. He had done this to her. He had filled her head with dread.

'I'm sorry, Claire. I am truly sorry, but I love . . . I love you.'

She shot him a look while desperately trying to slip her feet back into her shoes. 'But it was wrong. Aw, Mitch, we are not married. I will never be in God's New Order. I have committed the cherished sin. I should have stopped myself.'

In a nanosecond, she sprinted out of his reach.

He tried to catch her up. She ran through the woods, crying, but he tripped awkwardly on a tree root and tumbled. His damaged hip was now burning in pain. As soon as he got himself up, she was gone, with only a few strands of her hair remaining, hanging from a branch. He felt a hot tear ready to tumble as he removed the golden lock of hair.

***

Stirring the hot chocolate, he realised back then that he should have been more manly. He should have stormed into that Kingdom Hall and claimed her, but he feared the place. And he feared Gabriel, who was older and a bully. He reached down and massaged his hip; he always did when he thought of Gabriel and the day he'd kicked him so hard that his hip had snapped, which would forever cause him pain.

Still, there was now one consolation. He had seen Gabriel begging for his life. He himself was the only person who could have saved him, but he was glad, almost excited, that he had let him die and probably in the most abhorrent way possible.

Chapter Twenty-Eight

Gina wiped the last of the dishes and looked across to the dining room where Dexter was snoozing in what used to be her father's chair. His nose looked sore, and she could see blue shadows under his eyes where the bruises were coming out. He had said that he'd got into a scuffle and was caught by a lucky punch, but she didn't like the way he demanded that she kept her nose out of his business. She glanced at the ring on her finger and wondered why he had chosen that particular style. It was large and garish, and perhaps, a few years back, she could have loved it, but not now. She wanted to be seen as a classy woman with poise and taste. She sighed to herself and lit up a cigarette.

Jordan still hadn't left his shit pit, and she wondered where Sonny had got to. Assuming that he was up at the travellers' site with one of his or Jordan's pals, she gave no more thought to it. Jordan's new girlfriend seemed very lovely, and after all the years of raising boys, she thought it would be a change to have a girl around the house. She was pretty in a wholesome way, very much like someone she had once met. She shuddered when a memory flashed through her mind. That girl was pretty in a natural way too.

In fact, she was very much like Jordan's current girlfriend, with long blonde hair and big blue eyes and not the tiniest smidgeon of make-up on her face. She took a long pull on her cigarette and tried to rid herself of the memory, but it kept popping up, time and time again.

As much as she had liked Dexter at the time, she had been head over heels in love with Mitchell, and if she was true to herself, she still was. But no matter what she did, she knew in her heart that he would always love that blonde girl in the plain clothes and the flat sandals. She wished that she'd never stooped so low. She took another drag and flicked the ash before letting out a long sigh as well as a plume of smoke.

She could still see the girl's face almost dissolve in pure heartache. She had never in her life witnessed someone so hurt before.

***

It was eighteen years ago. Mitchell was training at the Cray Boxing Club, and, as usual, there were a few girls hanging around. A couple of the gypsy boys liked to work out, and with the place drawing in bad boys, it had its attractions. Mitchell, though, wasn't bad; he was handsome, fit, strong, and carried an air of mystery about him. Every Sunday, he would be there with his skin covered in sweat as he pummelled the punchbags. The shy blonde girl would come over but she'd only stay for a few minutes. Bang on 2 p.m., she would arrive to watch Mitchell working out, and they would talk before she would scurry away like a church mouse and leave a wide smile on his otherwise deadpan face.

The look in his eyes when Mitchell greeted the blonde girl made Gina green with envy, and she wanted more than anything to have him look at her that way.

That next Sunday neither Mitchell nor the girl showed up, and Gina felt gutted. However, the following Sunday when he arrived, he seemed angry. Hardly acknowledging the other lads, he laid into the punchbag like a Trojan. Watching him, she became bored so she decided to buy a load of booze. Her father had given her enough money to do whatever she wanted.

Her mates joined in with the idea because simply watching the boys box wasn't much fun. So they helped Gina to carry the bottles of vodka, cans of beer, and her portable JVC music system over to the club.

The car park area outside the club was empty. Gina played some Bob Marley, and eventually, some of the lads came out and joined in with the fun. They swigged the booze and danced, smoked, and paired up with the girls.

Mitchell came out and looked about. Gina guessed he was looking for the blonde girl. Acting quickly, she gave a beer to one of the gypsy boys to pass on to him. She half-expected him not to drink it, but, surprisingly, he did, and then he leaned against the wall, no doubt still looking around for the shy girl, she suspected.

Gina watched him crumple the beer can once he'd finished with it and aim it into the litter bin. Pulling another can from the plastic ring, she handed it to him. 'There you go, Mitch.'

He looked at her and smiled, but it was a sad smile. Nevertheless, he accepted the can and drank it fast. In between 'nonsense chat', he'd consumed four cans. His cheeks were glowing, he laughed at her silly jokes, and he even persuaded Nobby to let them continue to play music when he had come out to moan. As soon as a slow song came on, she took the can from his hand and popped it onto the wall. 'Come on, Mitch. Dance with me.'

He didn't know how to dance; he'd never tried it in his life, but he was merry and up for anything now. Gina was stone-cold sober when she spotted the blonde girl hurrying towards them. Immediately, she turned Mitchell around so that he couldn't see her. Still swaying with him to the music, she leaned in close. With her arms tightly around him, she kissed his neck while staring straight at the girl.

The blonde girl froze for a moment, like a rabbit caught in the headlights. It was evident that she was stunned by what she saw.

Gina watched her blindly run from the car park, almost getting run over by a motorbike.

***

Taking the last drag of her cigarette, Gina stubbed it out and sighed again. She wondered what had happened to the shy girl in the end.

***

She remembered her coming back to the club a few weeks later; she looked different – pale and sickly. Gina was hungry for Mitchell and wasn't going to let a pathetic kid have him. She had spotted her approaching the club. He was sparring at the time and so he wasn't looking at the door. In a panic, she hurried outside and stood in front of the girl.

'What are you here for?'

'I need to speak with Mitch.' Her meek voice lacked confidence.

Gina stood with her hands on her hips. '*My* Mitch, you mean. You can give me the message, and I'll pass it on.'

The girl inclined her head, tears filled her eyes, and her white face was now speckled with pink. 'Oh, I didn't realise that he was seeing . . .' She ran her hands over her stomach and a tear fell from her face.

Gina had an inkling what the message was, but she was going to fight for what she wanted.

'Yeah, he's my boyfriend. And you are?' She expected the girl to say that she was his girlfriend.

With trembling hands, the girl wiped her tears and simply said, 'No one,' and walked away.

For fear of the girl returning or getting a message to Mitchell, Gina made plans to ensure he would be hers. She knew he was a moral-minded man and the type to stand up to his responsibilities. A few more late Sunday afternoons and some evening car park parties with copious amounts of booze, and she had Mitchell just where she wanted him – in the back of a gypsy's van.

Dexter was locked away the very next day and a couple of the gypsy boys, whom she shagged on a regular basis, backed off once it was rumoured that she was expecting Mitchell Swan's baby. As much as Mitchell was no gangster or even a wannabe gangster, he was still a vicious fighter and earned his respect from boxing.

***

Had it all been worth it? she mused now. Then the blonde girl's face came back to her. One day she would rid herself of the mental picture of that girl's desolate expression. It had haunted her for far too long.

Sonny was ready to leave the hospital. He felt tired, and a bit sick but his injuries turned out to be less life-threatening than even he imagined. He had suffered a broken collarbone and a deep gash that needed a couple of stitches. But other than that, he was okay to be discharged. He wanted to call home to let his mother know that he was okay, but she would ask a hundred and one questions, and with her reckless mouth, she would ask Dexter if it was true that he'd been responsible for nearly killing her son, and then there would be serious trouble. When Dexter had said that he would cut his mother's tongue out, Sonny had believed him. The man was a total psychopath. He would certainly have no qualms about taking out his anger on his mother after attacking him — just a sixteen-year-old — with an axe. So he was seriously capable of anything. And if he could wipe out the son of his fiancée, then killing Mitchell and George to take over the drug business at the raves was clearly a foregone conclusion.

Taking the medicine bag from the nurse, he climbed down from the bed and slipped his feet into his trainers.

'Are you sure you don't want to speak to the police?' asked the attractive petite nurse.

'No, I don't remember anything,' he replied, flatly.

'Okay, Sonny. Take care now.'

Sonny nodded to the nurse who had been kind enough to allow him to wear a T-shirt that belonged to one of the male nurses. He felt clean at least. Making his way to the main entrance, he hoped that Dexter or one of his brothers wasn't there waiting for him. The police obviously hadn't pulled him in over the incident. And, in any case, Dexter was smart; he wouldn't have driven a car with his own number plates on it.

The fresh air and smell of newly cut grass hit him. It was a vast improvement on the reek of hospital disinfectant. Sitting on the grass verge, Sonny thought over everything. Jordan's quick decision to work with Dexter and even side with him was clearly upsetting their own brotherly relationship. There was a time when Jordan would have stuck up for him. But not now. All Jordan wanted was to be in the firm. He saw himself as a gangster, a villain, but all the while, though, he was simply a thug.

For a moment, he felt lost. He didn't belong anywhere. His mother was clearly besotted with Dexter, and so was Jordan. Mitchell hadn't been in his life for years, and he didn't know George all that well, although he wished he did now. It was apparent that Jordan *was* Dexter's son, unless, of course, he needed glasses. George was clearly Mitchell's son, and so, as everyone used to say, he, Sonny, was a mini Jordan. He shuddered at the thought that Dexter was also his father. He detested him, and even more so, now that the man had tried to axe him to death for suspecting that he had grassed. He hadn't, but there was nothing to stop him from doing so now. After all, he didn't owe Dexter a thing.

Lying back on the grass, he allowed the sun to warm his face as he tried to unravel the mess in his life. His Nanny Sylvia had been a good person, and yet he had let himself be brainwashed into believing that his grandfather hadn't been responsible for her death – of course he had – and that Jordan hadn't raped that young girl from Orpington – of course he had. And Jordan had ruthlessly beaten and sold Randy to a bunch of men who did the most despicable things. He didn't see himself like them – not deep down – but he wasn't like George either, with his honest work ethic and enthusiasm. He didn't belong anywhere, but he could at least put something right. With that thought in mind, he rose to his feet and walked towards Chislehurst – to the man who might just listen to him.

***

Sonny was sweating buckets by the time he reached the large house with the Georgian windows and beamed frontage. This time, he decided to knock at the front door, unlike last time, when Jordan had made him creep around the back.

It wasn't long before Bernie came to the door. His sheer stature compelled Sonny to step back.

'What the fucking hell are *you* doing 'ere?'

Sonny was exhausted. It had taken all his strength to walk this distance and he was in so much pain. 'Please, Bernie, please, I just . . .'

Bernie could see the lad's arm was in a sling, and blood was seeping through the cream bandages up by his shoulder. His face was turning grey, and he was about to faint. In a flash, he managed to stop the young lad from hitting the deck.

'All right, son, let's get you inside. This is all I fucking need. I feel like I'm running a military hospital.'

Bernie helped him into an armchair. 'Don't move, mate. I'll get you a drink.'

Randy was asleep on the sofa but she flicked her eyes open when she heard Bernie's deep gruff voice.

'Sonny, what are you doing here?' she asked, as she sat up and pushed the blanket off her.

It was a lot for Sonny to take in. He was at Bernie's; and now, so was Randy.

''Ere, Sonny, drink this,' said Bernie, as he handed him a tall glass.

He was grateful for the ice-cold water and as soon as he'd finished the drink, he began to feel human again.

'Bernie, it was Sonny who rescued me from that van. A bloke tried to kill him with an axe. He was a big ugly bloke.'

Bernie stared at Sonny's shoulder. 'I take it, the axe was blunt? Who was it, Sonny?'

'Dexter. I had to come here, Bernie. I can't be a part of their scams. They are going to take over the raves. They are strong-handed, Bernie, with fucking machetes and guns. They want to run the drugs. They are gonna kill me anyway. So let me tell ya, the next rave, they are turning up mob-handed, and they plan to take out your runners and use their own. But their shit pills they'll be punting are lethal. They're cut with everything from baking soda to rat poison. They are already having you and Maxi followed to source your supplier, 'cos they plan to petrol bomb your set-up, or home, or whatever.'

Bernie stood rhythmically, nodding away. 'Well, fuck me, there's a turn-up.' He laughed. 'So Dexter and his motley crew really ain't playing, then. We left the rave early because we thought there might be a bit of trouble and we didn't wanna be there when the Ol' Bill arrived. But something must be telling him that he stands a good chance of taking over. I suppose a significant number of years inside has taught him how to blow smoke up people's arses. Greasing the palms of the right people will get you places, but Dexter, as far as I know, ain't got a suitcase full of dough.' He let out another chuckle. 'And Dexter hasn't got the brains or the balls, not when it comes to crossing your farver.'

Sonny frowned. 'My farver?'

'Don't look so surprised, Sonny. I tell you, your ol' man will kick Dexter's arse all day long. I've seen Mitch clear a fucking dining table in the nick. He smashed the living shit out of Dexter, his wanker of a bruvver, *and* another wannabe hardman. So Dexter is definitely working with someone higher up the food chain.'

'My Grandad Donald. He told us to do as Dexter said, on the last visit.'

'I can't see that, Sonny. Your old man ain't well-liked. Dexter would have to be working for someone with money to front the drugs.'

'Yeah, it couldn't have been me grandad 'cos his house got repossessed, and he doesn't have a pot to piss in.'

Bernie scratched his bald head. 'Hang on, Sonny, lad. Your grandad's house was sold. My pal told me it had a "for sale" sign in the garden. Surely, your muvver would've known?'

Sonny shook his head. 'Me mum only goes to the places she needs to go to, like the pub and the shops. If me grandad said his house was repossessed, she would've believed him. She believes every word he says.'

'Fuck me, so your grandfarver is the man fronting the dosh for the drugs. He may not be liked, but these poxy younger villains have no moral compass. They're driven by greed and money. So, a wad of cash in the right hands will allow people to see beyond the fact that the man's a cunt.'

Bernie realised then that he had misread the message from Ryder. He had assumed that Donald had got in with Dexter before Dexter's release and was brown-nosing the man, but it all made sense now. Donald was getting Dexter and his brothers onside to get the business up and running before his own release. He had cashed in everything he owned and was gonna make sure that he took over everything that Mitchell had accomplished. He had always known Donald to be a vindictive, jealous man, but now he was old, he needed a young firm to back him. Dexter and his brothers were the scum of the earth but they were easily bought.

Sonny gingerly got up from the armchair and handed Bernie back the glass. 'Cheers, Bernie, for the drink.' He looked at Randy, who seemed markedly better. 'You take care, Randy.'

Randy smiled in acknowledgement but felt her heart ache as Sonny walked back towards the hallway.

'You're a good 'un, Sonny. Pity about Jordan.'

Sonny stopped and whirled around to face Randy.

'Yeah, he raped me mate Eden last night. I know now he's your brother, but I wish someone would kill him.'

'He raped *Eden*?' asked Sonny, totally stunned.

Randy nodded, with a sad expression on her face. 'I take it you know her, then? Well, yep, he drugged her as well – the fucking coward.'

Unable to look Randy in the eyes for the disgusting acts of his brother, Sonny turned to leave.

'Where are you gonna go, Sonny?' asked Bernie.

'I have to go and say sorry to someone. It's been a long time coming. Er . . . Bernie, would you mind if I pinched one of your roses?'

Baffled, Bernie nodded. 'Yeah, sure, but listen, you can stay here for a bit. I'll do us a nice roast beef, and you can rest that wound of yours.'

Sonny smiled, thanked Bernie for his kindness and understanding, and sauntered down the garden path, picking a beautiful red rosebud along the way.

When Bernie returned to the lounge, he noticed that Miranda was wiping her eyes.

'Do you think that his mother will protect him? Wouldn't she kick that Dexter bloke out? I mean, look what he's done to Sonny, the bastard.'

Bernie bit his bottom lip and then sighed. 'Women like Gina go through life believing that the world is always greener on the other side. I've known her since she was born. And I've never known her to consider anyone other than herself. She won't choose her son over Dexter, if that's who she's happy with.'

'Like *my* mum, then,' Randy said, sadly.

Bernie looked at Miranda, and his heart sank. She was so frail and battered that he just wanted to fix her. Perhaps it was his way of paying back for all the wrongdoing he had done in his life. 'Right, let's get that joint in the oven, and those spuds peeled,' he said, as he headed back to the kitchen. He would wait until the girl was asleep again before he made the calls. He wanted to spare her from hearing the plan.

***

Jordan sat up, stretched his arms, farted, and got up from his stinking bed. It suddenly hit him that Eden wasn't by his side. He glanced at the clock. It was half past four in the afternoon. He wished he hadn't snorted that cocaine that had kept him up all night because now he had practically lost a day. And where the hell was Eden?

He scrambled around and pulled on the same jeans and top he had worn at the rave. Slipping his bare feet into his trainers, he hurtled down the stairs, hoping that Eden was sitting in the living room and making conversation with his mother. But he soon realised that she had scarpered.

His mother was nursing a coffee and leaning against the kitchen door frame, staring at Dexter. He followed her eyeline and was surprised to find Dexter's face bruised, with dried blood surrounding his nose.

'Muvver, where's Eden?'

Gina looked at her son. His hair was dishevelled, his skin was greasy, and she could smell his BO from where she stood. 'She's gone. Oh, and I gave her the money belt she left in the living room.'

The blood drained from Jordan's face as he instantly realised the implications of what his mother had done. 'You did *what,* you fucking interfering stupid mare? Going through my pockets, were you? That wasn't *her* fucking belt! Oh my God!' he screamed, as he grabbed his hair in panic.

'I didn't go through your pockets. The belt was hanging out of it. It was only a bleeding bum belt for fuck's sake. What's the flaming matter with you?' she shouted back, in retaliation.

'Oi, what's all the fucking racket?' said Dexter, as he pushed himself up from the armchair and rubbed his cheeks. 'Well? What's going on?'

'She!' – yelled Jordan, rudely pointing to his mother – 'has just gone and given Eden, the bird I brought home last night, that skanky runner's fucking bum belt.'

Jordan could see the cogs turning before Dexter fully grasped the facts.

He looked at Gina. His eyes were wild with fury and his top lip quivered in rage. 'You did *what*? Are you trying to get me locked up again?' He lunged forward and grabbed Gina by the throat and pushed her hard against the wall. 'Well, are ya? I mean, look at you, dressed in those smart jeans and long shirt. Out to impress Mitchell, are ya? I bet you wanna go running back to him now. What is it, Gina? I'm not up to your expectations? Is that it?'

Gina didn't answer. She looked at her son, expecting him to pull Dexter off her, but he was pacing the floor and still pulling at his hair, ignoring the fact that Dexter was choking the life out of her. Finally, Dexter let her go. She instantly clutched her neck and coughed, gasping for breath before she fled the room. Running for her life, she headed for the front door, but Dexter obviously hadn't finished with her. He managed to drag her back by the tail of her shirt. 'Don't you go anywhere, you fucking divvy bitch.'

It was only at that point that Jordan appeared. 'Leave off, Dexter. She didn't mean anything by it.'

Gina felt at least she had some backup, albeit a tad too late.

'You keep your nose out of it, Jordan. She's *my* missus and *my* fucking business.'

Glancing a look at her son, she hoped for support. However, she soon grasped that he wasn't going to stand up for her. He was standing there looking awkward, like a limp lettuce, with his hands hanging by his side.

'Do something useful. Get in the kitchen and make me a coffee! I have an issue now to take care of. And it's all because you stuck your fucking great beak in where it didn't belong. If the filth come knocking, then it's down to you,' he spat, as he poked her hard at the side of her nose, digging his dirty fingernails into her skin.

She was too afraid to argue. Instead, she barged past Jordan, forcefully pushing him against the wall as she stormed into the kitchen.

It was true. She *had* wanted to change the way she presented herself. She had read in a magazine that less make-up was now classed as flattering. The style was out with the bright pinks and reds and in with new muted tones. Women her age were covering themselves up, and she wanted to do the same. She felt cleaner, and of course she fancied Mitchell. Who wouldn't? He was handsome and toned. He had all his own teeth, and none were black or chipped, unlike Dexter's. With his fag and beer breath slobbering all over her, he was hardly a turn-on. She turned the kettle on and pulled a cup from the cupboard, added a spoonful of coffee, and four sugars.

While Dexter and Jordan were talking in the hallway, she heard Sonny's name mentioned. The kettle boiled, and she made the mug of coffee. 'Where *is* Sonny?' she shouted out.

Dexter appeared, still wearing his manic face. 'I said, mind your own fucking business!'

Holding the mug, she glared at Dexter. 'My son *is* my business. I heard you mention his name, so do you know where he is?' She looked down at the steaming coffee and wanted nothing more than to throw it at Dexter's spiteful face.

Dexter laughed. 'Don't even think about it,' he said, as he snatched the mug from her hand. 'Your grass of a son is probably hiding somewhere, possibly at Mitchell's place.

We had a plan to earn decent money, and your little shit of a son grassed to your ex about the plan. He's a turncoat.'

Gina's eyes scowled at him. 'And you know that for sure, do you?'

'Are you questioning me, Gina? 'Cos you'd better not be. How else did Mitchell know we were going to show up? Someone told him because he and his firm fucked off before we got there. Your boy had one job, and that was to go in and feed back to us who was there, but it's obvious he did more than that. He fucking well grassed us up.'

The expression on Dexter's face drove Gina to think the worst. 'You ain't gonna hurt him, are ya?'

Dexter laughed again. 'Who's to say I ain't already given him a taste of what happens when you fuck over me or mine?'

Gina felt her skin prickle. 'What have you done? He's a fucking kid. He's only sixteen years old. Where is he?' she screamed, as she launched herself at him, her arms swinging in a frenzy.

The punch was fast, and she didn't have time to block it. He caught her on her cheek, and now she saw stars. He slapped her hard across the face, and she fell against the wall before sliding to her knees. He then threw the rest of the coffee over her.

It was then that Jordan pulled Dexter away. 'Leave off, Dexter! What's the matter with you? And where is Sonny?'

Dexter took a few deep breaths as he glared with hate at Gina, who was now crumpled on the floor. 'Get off me, Jordan. You lot are a fucking bunch of idiots. Go and find that Eden bird and get that money belt back. And when you find her, warn her that if she so much as breathes a word, then I will skin her alive.'

Jordan stepped back. 'I asked you where Sonny is?'

Yet again, Dexter laughed. 'Fuck off, Jordan, with your evil-eyed stare, you silly prick. I thought me and you could have this manor wrapped up in time for Christmas. But look at you, worried about your little brother instead of the consequences that belt being in the wrong hands may have. We'll have that big bastard Bernie blowing the fucking door down, or, worse, the filth arresting us for all manner of shit. Now, shut the fuck up about your brother! We need to get that belt back.'

'I ain't worried about me bruvver. I just wondered where he was, that's all. I mean, if you gave him a taste, then I am sure he'll have learned his lesson.'

Gina felt her face. Only a tiny fraction of the coffee had caught the tip of her chin – most had covered her shirt, and the rest had soaked into her clothes – but her cheek still hurt from the punch. Slowly, she got to her feet and silently left the room to take a bath. Jordan and Dexter ignored her as they sat down to talk about what was to be done.

When Gina went into the bathroom, she saw her chin was only very slightly blistered. It looked as though she had just suffered from mild sunburn. She didn't put any make-up on, only some cream. She didn't blow-dry her hair either; she left it to dry on its own and then decided to wear a plain cream velour tracksuit that she used if she was doing the housework.

Within the hour, Dexter had his firm sitting around the dining room table. They made plans to take down Mitchell's firm, starting with bringing his gym to its knees. Dexter had made it clear that he wanted Mitchell's head on a plate, and he wanted his two brothers to hold him down while he kicked the living shit out of the man.

She sat at the top of the staircase and watched as Jordan with his cocky walk left the house and slammed the front door behind him. He was always so heavy-handed. Leaning against the wall, she only half-listened to the men plan and scheme because the rest of her mind was set on feeling sorry for herself. Half the conversation was about some girl in a caravan. It appeared they had drugged and sold her for sex. And, she learned, Jordan had also been involved. He'd earned a few quid out of it. But she switched off at that point, hoping that they were exaggerating. Because if she believed their prattling then she would have to admit to herself that she truly had raised an animal.

Then she heard those words: 'Ol' Donald thinks he's gonna get his lion's share when he gets out. The silly ol' codger,' said Gary, Dexter's brother.

Gina hated Gary with his ratty features and gnarly teeth. She felt the hairs on the back of her neck stand on end. How dare they talk about her dad that way. She strained hard to hear more of their conversation.

'All right, Gary, you just keep ya mouth shut, right? I want that old cunt to believe that we're working for him. He's sent out a nice lump of cash, and I want it in my pocket, well, our pockets, by this afternoon. With no hiccups. I want a smooth transaction, got it? And then we can fuck him off.'

Gina gritted her teeth. It sickened her to hear that they were making plans to go against her own dad – and while Dexter was living in her house as well. 'The cheeky bastard,' she mumbled under her breath. Anger ripped through her, and she fought to stop herself from flying down the stairs and smashing Dexter and his weasel-looking brother across the mouth. But as she got up from the step, the wooden staircase made an almighty creaking sound, and before she could run out of sight, Dexter was there at the foot of the stairs. She held her breath, but he said nothing –

only pointing threateningly before returning to the dining room. She knew this wouldn't end well.

She wished she'd never said he could stay at her house. He was nothing more than a quick shag all those years ago, but now it was a whole different story. He was carrying hate and fury around as if these were his sole reasons for existing. She'd seen a glimpse of his anger and jealousy, and it reminded her of her father years ago. Still, she didn't hate her father, but right now, she hated Dexter.

Creeping into her bedroom, she quietly lifted the phone receiver and dialled the prison. She would leave a message for her father to call her urgently. Keeping her voice low, she hoped that Dexter wouldn't hear her. The prison reception staff took a few details and agreed to pass on the message. She glanced at the bedside clock. It was flashing five o'clock. In another hour, her father would ring. When he called, it was always bang on six o'clock. She needed to hover around the phone to make sure that she answered it before Dexter.

Lying on the bed, she went over the past and exhaled an enormous sigh of guilt and hate. If Dexter walked into the room and even tried to stop her speaking with her father, she would claw his eyes out. But then when she looked at her nails and noticed they were bitten down to the quick, she knew that wouldn't be an option. She'd always had long painted fingernails. and her hair regularly bleached. Her roots were long and very dark now, but she didn't care. She wanted to achieve a more natural look anyway. She glanced at the clock; it was now five past six. She sat upright, now puzzled. Perhaps there was a queue for the phone. Watching the minutes tick away, she willed the phone to ring, but it didn't. There was a lot she wanted to talk to her dad about — mainly the double-cross that Dexter had up his sleeve — but she also wanted to find out about this money he was supposed to be sending out. She thought her father was skint. She picked up the receiver and listened for the dialling tone. It was dead. She might have bloody well known. Dexter had cut the line to the upstairs phone. Bastard!

Chapter Twenty-Nine

Donald tried one more time, but the phone was dead. 'Fucking silly prat,' he said to himself, assuming Gina hadn't paid the bill. But the second he hung the phone up, a voice he recognised whispered in his ear, 'Malcolm wants a word with you.'

Donald turned around to see Ryder, Big Bernie's long-time friend. 'Oh yeah, and what's Malcolm want, and why did he send one of his minions to relay a message?' replied Donald, acting hard.

Ryder stood with an erect posture and a mocking smirk on his face. 'You really do think that you're invincible, don't ya, eh? Well, let me inform you, Mr Billy Big Bollocks Brennan, that you ain't well-liked in 'ere. In fact, most of the lads wanna see you dead, mate.'

Donald felt uneasy. He glanced to the right of Ryder to see a young but big lad. But, worryingly, standing to the left of him was another inmate caked in tattoos and with an evil scar down his face. It was Sherman Lancaster, the nutter on the wing, whom they called Bomber for short.

Donald knew he couldn't appear as though he was shitting hot bricks.

Donald gestured to Ryder to move out of his way.

However, Ryder stood steadfast with his arms crossed over his chest and his chin tilted up, daring Donald.

Believing that he had some kudos in the nick, Donald sighed. 'You can fucking tell Malcolm I'll be along in a minute.'

'No, Donald, you won't. He wants to see you now. He has a message from his older brother. I think you know the man and I think you know him well.'

Donald knew Malcolm. He was ten years younger than himself and one of Bernie's sidekicks. But he had never asked much about Malcolm, let alone whom he was related to. Still, something in the way Ryder smirked told Donald that it was someone who held a grudge. That meant it could be one of many people. He wasn't dumb enough to believe that he was a popular man; he never had been because of the way he'd treated people in his previous line of business. A spear of resentment struck him. He had been feared and respected years ago, so now he was older, he believed that the younger inmates were taking liberties. He glanced at Bomber. 'See the likes of you standing there with ya cocksure front? A couple of years back, I would have smashed that smirk clean off your fucking boat race.'

Bomber moved in to clump Donald, but Ryder pulled him back. 'Easy, Tiger.' He then nodded for Donald to walk ahead. They were going to have a meeting in Malcolm's cell.

Malcolm was serving a twenty-five-year recommended sentence for the murder of two men. One was a magistrate. He let the rapist off who raped his wife. The other was the rapist himself.

Feeling his legs turning to jelly, Donald was still determined not to lose face. He marched along the landing hoping that one of Dexter's brothers, Otis, or Little Dickie as he was known, who wasn't little at all, would spot him and get to him before he took a beating. He attempted to run his tongue around his gums, trying to wet the inside of his mouth. His tongue, however, was glued to the roof.

Suddenly, he was taken aback by how quiet it was on the landing. There was no one around, no one hanging by, at the doors of their cells, no one downstairs playing snooker; it felt odd and eerie. He faltered, not wanting to go any further.

But Bomber shoved him hard in the back. 'Move on, prick,' he whispered in Donald's ear.

As Donald reached the last cell at the end of the wing, the cell door opposite opened and there being held up by two men was Otis. Donald was poleaxed; he gasped at the state of him. Otis's head was slumped forward, and he was obviously unconscious. His grey tracksuit was now a two-toned burgundy. There was so much blood, it turned Donald's stomach.

A million thoughts ran through Donald's head, but the main one was what the hell — was it all over?

Ryder stopped outside Malcolm's cell and grinned from one side to the other. With a flick of his head, he indicated that Donald should go inside.

Donald still maintained a confident expression, although, really, he was bricking it.

Inside, Malcolm was sitting on a chair with a table in front of him. He had a single cell, and so he had room for a few home comforts, like the bookshelf and the cabinet with his canteen goodies on it.

'Take a seat, Donald,' he said, in a firm but polite manner.

Donald felt tense, but he continued to try and act unperturbed. 'So, what's this all about, Malcolm? I mean, as far as I'm aware, me and you have no unrest. If I'm being honest, I don't even really know you.'

Malcolm was in his fifties but he had the toned physique of someone much younger on account that he trained every day, even when he was sick. After losing the fight with

Mitchell many moons ago, he vowed he would never lose another one. Yet he had granted Mitchell the respect that the younger man had earned that day, and from that point onwards, he, Big Bernie Blackstone, and Mitchell became friends.

'No, we personally have never had any beef, I grant ya that. But, ya see, I am a man that tends to fight me own battles, so I rarely get involved in other people's business. Yet, Donald, it has come to my attention that you have upset two of me pals, Bernie Blackstone and Mitchell Swan. I've heard that you are working with that deadbeat Dexter Hanks and his wanky gang to take over the rave scene in Kent.'

Donald searched Malcolm's eyes for a clue as to what was going to happen next, but Malcolm merely smiled sadistically. 'You know why I'm inside, don't ya?'

'Are you asking me or telling me?' replied Donald, in his cockiest tone.

Malcolm smashed his fist down hard on the table.

The noise echoed around the cell, and Donald flinched. He realised then that he looked a fool, jumping like that. But what unnerved him more was the sudden noise outside the door. It was as if the silence had ended. Inmates were talking, shouting, chatting, and making the usual prison noises. Donald accepted that it was to drown out whatever sounds would emanate from Malcolm's cell.

'I'm in here for killing the scum that raped my wife. You see men that hurt woman, whether it be bashing them, talking down to them, or sexually assaulting them, I take personal offence to.'

'So what's that got to do with me?' asked Donald, still in a confident tone, knowing that if he was going down, he would at least go down like a man.

'I have been informed by a reliable source that your firm – and by that, I mean that wanker Dexter and your vile, nasty fucking grandson, Jordan – have taken right serious liberties.'

Donald felt the sweat now trickle down his back, and he hoped it wasn't showing through his light-grey prison-issue tracksuit. 'Jordan?'

Malcolm's face tightened. 'Yes, Jordan! I know you were told to warn him about his behaviour, after he took liberties with that young Orpington girl, but it seems to me, and the rest of us in here, that it landed on deaf ears. We all know you were behind the Kent rave takeover. That's what you let everyone believe, but, ya see, Donald, a real face would learn to shut his mouth.'

'You've lost me.'

Malcolm nodded to the man standing behind Donald.

Before Donald could spin around to see what was happening, Bomber grasped his arms, pulled them behind his back, and wrapped something around them.

Donald struggled to get his arms free. 'What the fuck's going on?'

Malcolm laughed. 'Your grandson Jordan, Dexter, and Dexter's brother took a tiny fucking bit of a kid and drugged her, and *then* they sold her over and over to any Tom, Dick, or Harry. That girl worked for Bernie and Mitchell as a runner. She was just trying to earn a few quid.'

Donald's eyes widened in shock. 'What? No way! My Jordan wouldn't do that! I never told them to do anything like that. I'd never hurt a woman. I mean . . .'

'You wouldn't hurt a woman? No? Well, I bet you never knew that my older brother is Shay the Brick and he tells me differently. He loved your missus, ya know. Your Jordan is gonna be taught a very valuable lesson so that he doesn't turn out like you.'

Donald's eyes widened as he gritted his back teeth. He'd always been jealous of Shay. It was Shay who had attracted the birds with his looks. Donald wanted to be the man who had the pick of the young girls, not Shay.

Inwardly, he seethed. 'Your brother was a grass!'

'My brother helped take the scum off the streets, meaning you,' spat Malcolm, as he nodded to Bomber again.

'Come on. This is ridiculous. What are you going to do?' asked Donald, his voice on the point of hysteria, as he struggled to break free. But the more he fought, the more Bomber tightened the rope.

In one quick movement, Bomber grabbed Donald and threw him to the floor, face down. Then he stood over him, grabbed his arms, and bounced him along until his head was in the doorway.

Donald sussed what was going to happen, but as he let out a scream of terror, the thick metal door was slammed against his head. The sound of the impact was gruesome and unforgettable, and the echo turned many grown men's stomachs. Blood shot from his nose and ears, but he was out of it.

Bomber untied the rope and Malcolm pushed Donald outside the cell. While the screws were kept busy, Bomber dragged Donald's lifeless body to the end of the landing where Otis's body had already been dumped. If any con was questioned, they would say that both Otis and Donald had a grudge against each other, and it had got nasty.

***

By 10 p.m., Sonny was feeling cold. The summer was coming to an end, and the nights were drawing in. He rose to his feet and brushed the dried grass off his jeans and looked down at his grandmother Sylvia's grave for one last time. He shook his head in shame. No one had cared for the grave. The neglect was so much more apparent compared to the travellers' burial plots. They had colossal, monumental tributes and endless amounts of flowers in pots and vases. Surrounding them, the lawn was mowed and some even had little defining fences.

His mother never visited his grandmother's grave. Yet, she only lived in the next street to St Mary Cray Cemetery. Obviously, his grandfather couldn't because he was inside. Even so, Sonny guessed that he wouldn't have, even if he hadn't been in the nick. And of course, he himself had never visited the grave, not since the funeral. He felt guilty because he probably walked past it with Jordan at least twice a week to go up to the travellers' site at the top of Star Lane.

But one person had been visiting the grave. It was made clear from the dried bunch of roses that were laid against the headstone. The note inside was protected by a plastic bag.

Sonny removed the card and read the words.

I still miss you every day, Nan, and forever. Your George.

The red rose that Sonny had just laid on her gravestone was beginning to wilt in the sun. And a petal fell like a teardrop.

A voice from over the wall dragged Sonny from his peace and quiet.

'There you are. I've been up at the site looking for you. What the fuck are you doing 'ere?' Jordan shouted.

Sonny glared and shook his head. 'Minding me own business, Jordan.'

Thick-skinned, Jordan didn't take the hint. His mind was on other issues. 'Listen, Sonny, come 'ere. I need your 'elp.'

Sonny stared at his brother, wondering if he'd noticed his arm in a sling, or the blood, or the fact that he hadn't been home since last night. The half-light seemed to cast a monstrous shadow over Jordan's face. For a moment, Sonny wondered if he was actually seeing his brother for who he actually was – a demon.

'Sonny, hurry up. Come on, I need you to do something for me.'

'You have no remorse, do ya, Jordan?' said Sonny, with an air of menace in his voice.

'You what? Stop talking shit, Sonny. And come 'ere, will ya. I told ya, I need your 'elp. I've got to get a poxy bum belt back before the gavvers nick me.'

'Bum belt?'

'Yeah, I need to get it off that Eden bird, before she goes to the filth and that silly bimbo tells the Ol' Bill she got it from our house. 'Cos it will put me in the frame . . . er . . . for a load of ol' nonsense. Come on, Sonny, help us, will ya? I could end up in prison for this one.'

'Might be the best place for you, Jordan – prison.'

Jordan's mouth dried as he realised that his brother was acting very strange. Usually, they would join forces, and Sonny would be up for whatever the plan was. But now, there was something icy and even sensible in Sonny's tone.

'Sonny, what's the matter with you?'

Taking slow, deliberate strides towards the wall, Sonny kept shaking his head, all the while holding a tight begrudging grin. 'You're bad, Jordan.'

Jordan laughed. 'Yeah, I know, but everyone loves a bad boy. And now, Bruv, I need you to do something.'

'No, Jordan, I mean you're fucking sick-in-the-head bad.'

Jordan looked around him, making sure no one was around. 'Sonny, stop it, mate. You're acting like a divvy. Cor, did Dexter give your head a good whack? 'Cos you're talking shit.'

Sonny stopped just before the wall. 'You raped Eden.' He paused, waiting for a reaction.

Jordan's brows snapped together. 'Shut the fuck up, Sonny. You don't know what you're on about. Who told you that pile of crap?'

Sonny sighed heavily. 'Randy, the other girl you abused. The runner who you and Dexter drugged and threw in that shagging van.' Just those spoken words made Sonny's heartbeat increase and his breathing quicken.

But Jordan was astounded, and it showed by his very troubled expression. 'How do you know this stuff? Who told you . . . ?' He looked nervously around him. 'Who knows, Sonny?'

'So it's true, then?'

'Well, no . . . I mean, Sonny, who knows about the runner and the van?' The beads of sweat on Jordan's forehead glistened in the moonlight. 'For fuck's sake, Sonny, it ain't a game. I could go down for kidnapping and a load of other stuff. You'd best tell me how you know!'

'I saw you, Jordan. I watched you and Dexter, and his psycho bruvver, Gary. I saw what you all did.'

Jordan let out a premature sigh of relief. 'Thank fuck for that. I was sweating. I thought someone else had seen something and had come after you, Bruv, assuming you were involved. It's always been you and me. And you know I'd never let anything happen to you. I mean, I would smash their heads in.'

Sonny wanted to laugh. All his life, he had looked up to Jordan. He believed his big brother would protect him; after all, Jordan was always saying 'If anyone touches you, Sonny, I'll smash their heads in.' Looking back, though, they had all been empty threats. He himself had taken a few beatings, mainly from the travellers. But although he had won more fights than he'd lost, he never recollected Jordan jumping in and saving him. In fact, it was the other way around. He had fought two older gypsies when they were on Jordan's back and punching him in the face. He'd managed to get them off his brother and given them both a good larruping.

'This ain't team Swan anymore, Jordan. You sicken me, mate. You are a wrong 'un, and even if I get murdered for saving that girl, I don't care, Jordan. I don't care a bit. You, Donald, and Dexter are rotten to the core.' He paused to calm his temper and slow his words down before they became inaudible. 'You're fucking savage, Jordan. You're an embarrassment, and I want nuffin to do with you ever again. And watch ya back, big bruvver, because there's a line of people who will want to run a knife right through it.'

For the first time in Jordan's life, he was stumped. He felt every sense of his brother's hate for him through the cold way he delivered those words. But it angered Jordan. *How dare Sonny talk to him like that. He was the one calling the shots, not Sonny, not Sonny the baby.*

'Don't fucking ever talk to me like . . .' He stopped when he saw his brother turn his back and begin to walk across the graveyard. 'I said, don't you ever talk to me like that, and don't walk off when I'm talking . . . Oi, Sonny!'

Sonny was sick to his stomach. He detested everything that Jordan stood for. But he was also walking away from the only brother he'd ever known.

'Oi, you fucking little cunt!' bellowed Jordan, as he leaped over the wall and began chasing after his brother.

Calling him the word he detested the most riled up Sonny. And as he felt his brother approaching, he ran and took an extra-long stride just before Jordan had the chance to grab him. Earlier that day, he had watched a grave being dug by an excavator, but even though the machine had broken down, the grave was still four feet deep.

It was dark now, and unlucky for Jordan, whose only aim was to stop his brother from running off, he didn't see the hole, and he fell awkwardly into it.

Sonny stopped and spun around to see his brother struggling to get up and attempt to get out of the hole. Still fuming with Jordan, he retraced his steps and swiftly kicked him in the face hard enough to floor him. Jordan, with a look of thunder, was now on his back scrambling again to get to his feet. But Sonny hated that look on Jordan's face. It was a look he had feared on and off, but not today. He kicked him again and again until Jordan had his hands up covering his face and screaming for him to stop. But he couldn't. He was raging, and with the final kick to Jordan's chin, his brother hit the ground and didn't move. Jordan was dazed and Sonny was out of breath.

The mound of clay that had been dug from the hole contained a few nasty jagged rocks, and in his temper, Sonny managed to pull out a large one. He held it in both hands and lifted it above his head.

Jordan moved and opened his eyes. 'No, Sonny. Please, you're my bruvver. Don't do this.' His voice sounded pleading and pathetic.

Sonny gripped the rock tightly, but the frightened eyes looking back at him compelled him to throw the rock to the side of the grave and walk away. But his brother's feeble attempt at begging hadn't changed the fact that he still despised him. He just didn't have the courage to finish him off. Perhaps he hadn't detested him as much as he thought he had. Not paying any attention to his brother climbing out of the grave, Sonny rubbed his shoulder. Holding the rock above his head had triggered a sharp pain in his fresh wound that made him feel sick. Exhausted and suffering in agony now, he didn't hear Jordan until it was too late. The smash to the back of his head was like having his head forced underwater. His legs instantly gave way, and he flopped to his knees and fell face down onto a prettily arranged grave.

The way his brother fell so suddenly gave Jordan the impression that he had killed him. His first thought was to run and take the rock with him. It was darker, now clouds had covered the moon, and as he anxiously looked around, he felt a sense of relief that no one was about. Concealing the rock inside his jacket, he ran down Star Lane and past the Mary Rose Inn, crossed over the road, and threw the rock into the river. As soon as his deed was done, he stopped and gasped for air; then, lighting up a cigarette, he managed to slow down his racing heart rate.

In fear of being caught, Jordan made his way back home by carefully walking close to the fences and hedges away from the street lamps. However, the moment he reached his house, it hit him. He hadn't murdered a stranger: it was Sonny, his little brother, his best buddy. Trembling all over, he struggled to get the key in the lock. Then, he heard sirens. He couldn't discern the difference between an ambulance and a cop car, but he knew the sound was coming from the next street. He felt his stomach in his mouth. They were there for Sonny, and soon, a copper would come knocking – perhaps for him. He couldn't spend a night in a cell, let alone a lifetime. He rationalised his thoughts. Surely, *he* couldn't get nicked for killing Sonny, could he? No one saw him, and the rock with his brother's blood on it was now being washed in the River Cray. He had to get cleaned up though and throw his dirty clothes in the washing machine.

As he opened the door, he saw his mother in the hallway kneeling down and taping up the phone wires. He guessed that Dexter had ripped the phone from the wall. Just as he was about to pass her, she looked up, her eyes red against her pale face. For a moment, she appeared to glance straight through him, but then she blinked. 'What's all that blood on your face?' she asked, but her voice sounded different – cold and flat.

He wiped his cheek and checked his fingers. 'Oh, nuffin. Me mate was preparing a chicken for his ol' dear's dinner. The blood must've shot over me when he cut its head off. Where's Dexter?'

She turned away and shrugged her shoulders, before hooking the phone back on the wall where it belonged. 'I have to go to Maidstone tomorrow, to the prison, to identify your grandfarver's body.'

Jordan was on the first tread of the stairs when he processed those words. '*What?*'

'Your grandfarver was murdered this afternoon. Dexter had pulled the phone out at the wall, so the prison governor couldn't get through. So they sent the police to tell me.'

He watched his mother turn back to fix the phone cable. It all seemed surreal. His breathing became fast and laboured. He was now in a real panic, but he had to get in the bath and also wash his clothes. He shut and locked the bathroom door and then turned the taps on. Peeling off his clothes, he stepped into the scorching water and turned the cold water tap on, on full blast. Once he had sat down and the water temperature was just right, he leaned forward to grab the shower gel. It belonged to Sonny. He dropped the container in the water and felt vomit rising. He found it hard to visualise Sonny face down on that grave. It had been too dark to see the amount of blood on him. He turned his attention to cleaning himself up. However, once he'd lathered up the soap and began washing himself, he could see spots of pink in among the foam and knew then that his brother's blood must have splattered onto his neck and across his face. Taking deep breaths, he held down the vomit until he couldn't anymore. He shot out of the bath and expelled his stomach contents down the toilet. He heaved a few times until his head was thumping. A tear slid down his cheek, and another dreaded feeling coiled around his stomach at one terrifying thought – prison.

Once Jordan was dressed, he hurried into the kitchen, threw the soiled clothes into the washing machine, and stared blindly at the dials. 'Muvver, how do I use this?'

There was silence.

'Muvver, where are you? How do I use this fucking machine?'

Chapter Thirty

Gina lay on her bed and blew the cigarette smoke up to the ceiling. She pondered over whether she should call the police now or tomorrow, or when would be the most appropriate time. She'd never been in this predicament before. But she couldn't leave the body there; it would start stinking. The biggest surprise to her was how calm she actually felt. Since being a child, she'd been quite the drama queen, and deep down she knew it too. Now, though, when she should have been running around like a cat with its tail on fire, she was remarkably composed.

All those years she had visited her father in prison, she'd looked forward to the day he would be home. But in a split second, that dream had been snatched away from her. She went over the policeman's words; he was sorry, and everything, but she wondered if the jumped-up shit of a copper was getting some kind of kick out of relaying the graphic details. Nevertheless, the description of how her father had died would haunt her forever. Apparently, his skull had been completely cracked in half, and his brain had turned into mush. She was sure that that wasn't a medical term – merely the officer's version of events.

Now, she would never get to sit opposite him in his usual chair in the dining room by the fire, where, on occasions, they would talk to each other for hours at a time. She'd never have the chance to ask the question that she desperately wanted the answer to – why did you kill my mum?

'We believe it was a prison fight,' the copper had said flippantly, 'but we don't have all the details to charge anyone as yet.'

She'd wanted to finish his sentence by saying, 'and we probably never will.' She knew how it worked. The prison authorities didn't want to take the time or spend the money to delve too deeply. After all, her father was a murderer, as far as they were concerned. Still, they didn't have to mention any names; she knew who was most likely behind it.

She peered down at the body just to check he was actually dead and not faking it. He was staring straight up at her, with that grotesque grin on his distorted face. His eyes were wide, just as they were when she plunged the knife right into his stomach and up into his rib cage. She had intended on cutting him in half.

She smiled to herself as she recalled the last few moments of his life. The horror on his face – that image of him when he realised what she'd done – she would take to her grave.

But he'd bloody well asked for it. Stupidly, he'd assumed the police outside were for him not for her. So, like a coward, he'd hidden in the bedroom. However, before she had run down to answer the door, he'd demanded she tell them he didn't live with her and that she hadn't seen him.

She was getting sick of his demands. She could have put up with his moods and even the odd slap. Yet, being bullied in her own home was a step too far. He'd choked her and nearly poured the hot coffee all over her, which had been bad enough, but then, when she'd heard a snippet of conversation about a girl in a van, it had made her blood run cold. She'd hoped she'd heard it all wrong.

Nevertheless, it was all getting out of hand and she wanted him to leave. Her home wasn't hers anymore. It had been overrun with his family and his mates. She had become merely the cook, the cleaner, and his regular shag.

Her hopes of Jordan and Sonny having a father figure around to instil some discipline had had the opposite effect. Not so much for Sonny, but Jordan was worse than ever, as far as she was concerned.

Once the police had left, she felt as if she'd been turned inside out. From the conversations she'd overheard between Dexter and his brother, she assumed they were involved. Her feelings of dislike for Dexter had now turned to disgust. It was time to right some wrongs. After a brief trip to the kitchen where she'd taken the sharpest knife in the drawer, she headed upstairs to where he was hiding.

He'd looked over her shoulder. 'Did you get rid of them?'

She'd nodded and studied his self-assured expression as he raised his chin and curled his lip.

'Well, woman, what did they say?'

With the knife behind her back, she stepped closer, her nostrils flaring and her blood boiling, but she managed to keep her tone even. 'They told me my farver's been murdered.'

Dexter's eyes pierced hers. 'But did they say anything about me?' His tone was urgent.

Had he not heard her? 'No, they came to tell me about my farver.'

'Fuck, I thought—'

'They had come because you drugged a girl and let men rape her. Is that what you expected them to say? Is that true?'

'Er . . . what are you on about, you silly tart?'

'The girl in the van, that *you* and *my* son drugged and fucked.'

'You wanna watch ya mouth, Gina. You can't go around spouting that kinda bollocks, and it was your son, not me.'

Feeling the red mist descending, his threatening words only fuelled her temper and spurred her on to end it all.

'You're not even bothered about me dad, are ya?'

'What? Yeah, but you need to keep your mouth shut, Gina.'

So from his sheer lack of concern about her father's murder, she'd had no second thoughts. Without hesitation, she'd rammed the knife into his stomach. He was only wearing his strides, and so the six-inch blade had gone through the bare skin and muscle as though she'd been carving a joint of pork. She hadn't been prepared to listen to his pathetic attempt of compassion because he had none. She had always known that.

Thinking about it now, she wondered if any of the men around her had compassion or empathy or even understanding.

But she'd been surprised he hadn't fought back. Although he'd clutched the knife with both hands, she'd lifted him up in the air. She'd astounded herself by her strength. The sound he'd made was minimal; in fact, it reminded her of when she'd given birth to George.

Although it had been painful, she hadn't had the strength to let out a deep guttural scream then. Perhaps it had been the same for Dexter.

She'd relished watching him slide down the wall beside the bed. That would be another image she would take to her grave.

Her thoughts were interrupted by her sodding son shouting from downstairs.

***

Jordan's urgent voice irritated her. In these last couple of weeks, he was proving to be the nasty piece of work everyone said he was. She took another drag of her cigarette and considered the last few years. As much as she would laugh at Jordan's naughty antics and foul language – and she had – for many years now – she was aware that perhaps she wasn't the best parent. Her mind drifted to George. He was a good lad; she could tell just by his aura. His warm, friendly disposition was so unlike Jordan's cold eyes and vindictive sneer. Then there was Sonny. She noted how he'd stuck up for her against Dexter, but Jordan hadn't. His lack of loyalty saddened her the most. He hadn't stopped Dexter from hurting her. An unexpected tear trickled down the side of her face. She sat up and sighed.

'Muvver, how does this fucking washing machine work? Answer me, will ya!' bellowed Jordan.

After stubbing her cigarette out on Dexter's forehead, she left the bedroom. She took her time going to the kitchen.

Upset by her son's snarl, her temper began to rise again. 'Stop shouting, Jordan. Did you not hear me, when I said that your grandfarver has been murdered?'

'I heard, Muvver. It's sad. Can we talk about it once I get this washing machine on?'

With her hands on her hips and her head tilted to the side she said, 'What dirty secret are you trying to wash away, Jordan?'

He turned to face his mother, and for a moment he didn't recognise her. 'What are you on about, you cranky bitch?'

'So why are you so flaming well desperate to get those clothes washed, then?'

'They've got chicken blood all over them. Like I said, me mate cut a chicken's head off and—'

'You're a liar, Jordan. You've never in your entire life washed your own clothes. You just leave them on the floor for muggins 'ere to pick them up after you and to do all the washing. Even Sonny puts his clothes in the laundry bin. And where is Sonny?'

Gina noticed how her eldest son's face seemed to go very pale.

'Where is he, Jordan? Where's my Sonny?' Her tone was now accusing.

'I dunno.' He looked back at the washing machine. 'How do I turn this on?'

She pushed him out of her way and almost ripped the washing machine door off its hinges before pulling the soiled clothes out. She held up the T-shirt and saw a few drops of what looked like blood.

'What evidence are you attempting to destroy? Tell me!' she yelled.

He jumped. 'Nuffin. I wanna wear that top and jeans tomorrow, that's all.'

Gina flung the top on the floor, left the kitchen, and stormed off to her bedroom. She had to get away from her son before she did something she'd regret.

As she sat on her bed with another cigarette on the go, she thought about her dear mum. She would lay a bunch of flowers before she called the police. It would be her way of saying she was sorry. She pondered over the idea of serving a long time inside; she would, that much she was sure of. Would they let her go to her father's funeral? She took a deep drag on her cigarette.

***

Sonny was surprised to see the same kind nurse who had given him a T-shirt the last time he was in A & E.

She wiped the blood from his pale face and sighed. 'You should really speak to the police, Sonny. It's evident to anyone that you're not safe. If you were my little brother, I'd keep you indoors.'

Sonny smiled. 'I'm okay, really. I just need a few stitches and something for my headache.'

She was an astute and sweet-looking nurse, with her white cap perched in front of her ginger hair, which was pulled up in a bun. She had freckles that seemed so even they looked almost like a work of art. And her green eyes were round and dewy.

'It wasn't a few stitches though, sweetheart, it was fifteen. And the headache is because most likely your brain is still swollen from the injury. Are you sure you never saw your attacker?'

'No, it was dark.'

'Well, all I can say is you are a very unlucky young man, Sonny Swan.'

She wiped the last of the blood from around his ears. 'There you go. Handsome as ever.'

He blushed slightly. 'I am lucky really, not unlucky. If someone hadn't spotted me then I would have most likely died. Do you know who it was who called for an ambulance?'

'Er . . . yes. The policeman said it was an elderly lady who was searching for her cat. Apparently, she has dementia and often wanders to the graveyard to see if she can find him. She alerted a woman in a nearby house.'

'Do you know the old lady's name?'

'Actually, I do remember. It was Brenda Garnet. My mum's called Brenda, you see.'

Sonny smiled to himself. He liked ol' Brenda, and he knew she often wandered off. He'd found her himself a couple of times roaming the streets in her nightie. He had merely steered her back, helped her into her bed, and closed the door behind her. Perhaps she had unwittingly returned the favour.

'The doctor will be here in a minute or so. He's looking at your X-ray results, but you're staying in tonight. We want to be assured that there is no more damage to your brain.' She half-expected him to want to leave the hospital as soon as possible, but, surprisingly, he nodded and closed his eyes.

It was less than a minute later when the consultant arrived. He glanced at Sonny and assumed he was asleep. 'Nurse Atkins, how is he?'

Sonny listened intently.

'He is in good spirits, considering, and he is happy to stay in under observation.'

'That's good. I don't want him anxious or upset. The blow to the head has fractured his skull, so I should imagine that whoever caused this injury, had, to all intents and purposes, tried to kill him. Let's hope the police apprehend this dangerous attacker soon, before he strikes again.'

Sonny felt his heart sink. He knew his brother had wanted to hurt him for running off. But now, listening to the doctor, he realised that his own flesh and blood had indeed tried to murder him. And if that was the case, then Jordan's level of integrity was lower than he had comprehended. Now he was convinced that Jordan was a psychopath or a sociopath – he wasn't sure which. As the doctor's words became distant and inaudible, Sonny fell into a deep sleep.

Chapter Thirty-One

Eden woke up in the spare room of her father's apartment feeling as if the last twenty-four hours had all been a dream. She listened for any sound that would suggest someone was up and about. There was silence. A twinge of excitement shot through her. Mitchell Swan was her father, and George was her brother. She had a real family now. Not like the brothers and sisters from the congregation who had led her to believe that they were one big like-minded family who would protect and love her – liars.

She surmised that Mitchell was usually a more laid-back person. But the present circumstances had pushed him to an angry place. Even though he'd been in another room, she'd still heard him attempting to quell the rage in his voice. He'd called Bernie and another man whose name she didn't recognise. From the gist of the conversations, she concluded that they were going to give Dexter and his firm a burial service. The graphic torturous words that Mitchell hissed down the phone didn't sound like empty threats.

She'd instantly warmed to Mitchell, but she knew underneath his calm exterior there lay a perilous man.

Listening again, she heard nothing but a few birds tweeting outside. She decided to climb into the tracksuit that George had given her and wander into the kitchen area and get some water. She crept quietly because she was still more or less a stranger in Mitchell's home, although he had said it was now her new home, if she wanted it to be. Of course, she did. It was stunning, and she would have the chance to be close to her real father and her brother George. An unexpected cold shiver ran through her when she thought of Jordan as her brother and how he'd sexually assaulted her.

'Morning, Eden,' came the deep voice from the sofa.

Eden nearly jumped out of her skin.

'Oh, morning, er . . .'

'You can call me Mitch if it feels awkward to call me Dad.'

She blushed and tilted her head down. 'I like Dad.'

Mitchell lowered the newspaper; he didn't want her to see the headlines. The Kingdom Hall had burned to the ground with a man believed to be Gabriel Cordell now dead.

'Me too. We can go to the hostel and collect your belongings if you are still happy to move in with us?'

She felt that emotional lump in her throat preventing her from speaking.

'Or, if it's too much too soon, I'll rent a flat nearby so you can have your own space.'

'Dad, you don't have to buy me the world. I am a simple girl, really. I don't want material things. I just need a family. I want to hear you talk about my mum when she was young. I want to know that she was happy once upon a time.' She paused and sniffed away the tears.

Mitchell rose from the sofa and walked over to her. He lifted her chin, as if she were five years old, and ruffled her hair. It was at that moment she felt like a father's daughter should. He was so unlike Gabriel.

'I'm gonna do us all a well-deserved fry up. Shout your brother. All the excitement must have left him shattered.' He glanced at his watch. It was eight o'clock and so unlike George to be in bed. A cold feeling shot through him, and he hurried past Eden. Instead of tapping on his door, he pulled it open, only to see George's bed made and the room empty.

'What's wrong? What's happened?' asked Eden, stunned by a look of panic on her father's face.

'Nothing for you to worry about, darling.'

She watched him whizz past her and snatch his keys from the side table.

'Dad, please tell me where you are going?'

'I am going to find George. I bet the stupid little sod thinks he can take Jordan on, but he has no idea that Dexter will be there.'

'I want to go as well.'

Mitchell shook his head firmly. 'No way, absolutely not. There is going to be one enormous fucking fight, and I want you safe. I've heard that Jordan is dangerous. Apparently, he fights with weapons, and if Sonny is there defending Jordan, then George won't stand a chance. Even if he did manage to come out on top, Dexter would finish him off, and so this, my sweetheart, will get very messy.'

He pulled on his jacket from the coat stand, but Eden was adamant. 'No, you don't understand. I *need* to go.'

Mitchell turned to see her forcing her feet into her trainers. 'Why? Eden, you've had a bad ordeal, love. You need to rest, and I need to concentrate on getting George out of there alive, if, of course, that's where he's gone – back to Gina's place.'

'Dad, I have been told what to do literally every second of my life. I *want* to come. Don't stop me because you will be just like them, if you do.'

'Come on, then! But please don't say I'm like the congregation, 'cos you have no idea.'

Eden felt as if she had thrown him an insult dart. 'I'm sorry.'

Mitchell marched on ahead. 'We need to go, then, but stay in the car. I don't understand, though, why you want to come.'

She hurried behind him. 'I want it all to end. I know what Jordan did to me, but it's over. I'm safe, and if I can stop this, I will.'

He held the car door open and slammed it shut once she was inside.

As soon as he drove out on to the road, he glanced at her and said, 'This won't go away, Eden. As much as you believe it will, well, it won't. I've heard all about Jordan's antics. People keep me informed because he's my son and yet I do nothing about it because he doesn't see me as a father unless it's to hand out money.'

Eden looked down. 'Do you see me that way? I mean, after you for money?'

'What!' he screeched. 'No, I don't, not at all, Eden. Christ, I'm just happy that I have you in my life, unlike your beautiful mother.'

***

The loud bang on the front door made Jordan instantly believe it was the police. They always banged hard. His room was at the back of the house, but his mother's bedroom was at the front, so he wondered why the racket hadn't disturbed her. The heavy pounding started again, causing him to jump. With wet palms wringing with sweat and with a racing heart, he scrambled from his bed, still fully clothed, and hurried to Sonny's room, which was also at the front. Slowly, he peeked from behind the curtain. At first, he didn't recognise who it was until the young man looked up. An instant feeling of relief relaxed his muscles before curiosity took over.

'What the fuck do *you* want?' he mumbled, under his breath. A mad notion shot through his brain. Perhaps he could get George on his side and con him out of a few quid to make his great escape. He wanted out of the Crays anyway. After running his sweaty palms through his unruly hair, he ran down the stairs and pulled the front door open to give his brother the biggest fake smile, but he had a rude awakening.

'You bastard, Jordan!' yelled George, as he lurched forwards and grabbed his brother by his T-shirt, forcing him back inside the hallway. Angrily, he rammed him against the wall, knocking the wind out of him. 'You raped Eden, you fucking bastard!'

Jordan was so shocked that he didn't have time to collect his thoughts, let alone stop George from attacking him in that manner. What surprised him more than anything, though, was the strength behind his younger brother. However, arrogance drove him to believe that George couldn't be a match for him.

'Get the fuck off me, you wanker!' yelled Jordan, as he put his hands up between George's arms, grabbed his throat, and began to squeeze, intent on choking George to death.

Unable to breathe, George raised his knee between Jordan's legs with such force, it compelled Jordan to double over and instantly release his hold.

George let rip a flurry of punches to the side of Jordan's head, while screaming, 'Take that! And that! You dirty bastard!'

Grabbing a handful of Jordan's hair to lift his head up for one final blow, George assumed he would knock his brother clean out. However, he was shocked when Jordan seized his hand and bit into it.

Having already felt the force behind George's punches, something inside Jordan truly snapped; nothing and no one was going to hold him back. He knew that the only way to beat his brother was to fight dirty, and he was good at that. His teeth were sharp, and at times, he would like to leave a reminder of what he was capable of in a fight.

Brutally, he sank his teeth deeper into the side of George's hand. He wouldn't let go. Biting down hard, he shook his head like a wild dog tearing into the flesh. No matter how much George clawed at his face to stop him, he was raging and wasn't letting go. Savagely ripping into George's hand until he succeeded, he finished by cruelly spitting out the chunk of bloody flesh. *Now you won't box again*, he thought, pleased with himself.

George clutched his wounded hand. The pain was like hell on earth. A moment of relief came when Jordan left the hallway and headed for the living room. He naturally assumed that his brother had had enough, but, in a flash, Jordan came tearing back out wielding a poker. George knew then he couldn't fight against a metal weapon, but as he turned and reached the front doorstep, Jordan grabbed his hair, dragged him back inside, and kicked the door shut.

'You ain't going anywhere, you little prick! You wanna fight, then fucking fight!'

Instinctively, George held up his good hand to stop Jordan from caving his head in. The instant the poker made contact with his knuckle, he knew what damage it could do if Jordan smashed him in the head with it.

Again and again, Jordan viciously pounded George with the fire iron to his legs, his arms, and his ribs. 'Take that!' he yelled. In between each relentless blow, he roared, 'You weedy . . . little . . . cunt!'

George slumped to the floor. All he could do was to hold his arms up to try to protect his head, but Jordan caught him twice, battering his ear and cheek. Then through blurred vision, he could make out his mother flying down the stairs. The buzzing sound in his ears prevented him from hearing her voice clearly, but she was shouting something, and he hoped it was for Jordan to stop. He realised she was behind Jordan, trying to pull him away. But his hopes of being saved were dashed when Jordan spun around, and, whether he meant to or not, struck their mother with the poker, knocking her over. He was mortified that his brother had actually hit their mother in her face. He assumed that Jordan would instantly stop in shock. But it was clear that Jordan was totally unfazed.

Terrified, George watched as Jordan came at him again, lifting the poker way above his head. Viciously, he smashed it down again and again on his shoulder and his hands – anywhere, in fact, where the poker would land. All he could hear from Jordan was 'You fucking bastard, cunt, wanker!' in between each attack, as if he was being whipped as some kind of punishment. Seconds later, he passed out.

When he came round, he immediately thought he was lucky to still be alive. The buzzing sound in his ears and the relentless blows had stopped as quickly as they'd started. Then he saw why. Standing above him were both of his brothers. He'd always known that Sonny and Jordan were close. He was the outsider; the one he believed they hated. But as he blinked to focus, he witnessed the look of horror on Jordan's face.

Jordan dropped the poker and leaned breathless against the wall. His face turned a greyish colour, and his brows snapped together.

When George heard what Sonny had to say, he understood why Jordan appeared stunned.

'So you're trying to kill us *all*, are ya, Jordan? You thought you'd mullered me, left me on that grave, thinking I was dead. You didn't even call an ambulance. You're a wrong 'un, like everyone says you are.'

Gina staggered to her feet, feeling the lump that was slowly building along her cheek, where her eldest son had struck her. She caught sight of her Sonny's arm in a sling and his bloodstained T-shirt. But then she saw the back of Sonny's head where it had been shaved and an enormous wound stitched like a patchwork quilt. Her stomach turned over. However, when she focused on the state that Jordan had made of her middle boy, she felt incensed. Poor George. He'd been the innocent one, the one she'd mercilessly neglected. And now her eldest son had added insult to injury. Guilt flushed through her veils and vibrated every inch of her body, but it was the anger that she was struggling to hold back. She had to know what her violent son had indeed done. So she listened as Sonny stood toe to toe with Jordan.

'Every fucking thing you do, Jordan, you think it's okay, so go on, Jordan, tell our mum how you drugged that tiny bird Randy. You're a disgusting, vile bastard! Tell her how you sold her to lowlifes like yourself for sex.'

Jordan was shaking his head, but his eyes remained glued to Sonny's.

'Don't fucking deny it,' hissed Sonny.

Jordan was silent, his lip curling as he continued to gape.

'And, big bruvver, tell, our mum how you tried to kill me.' His voice was stern but worryingly calm.

That was when Gina saw the glint of metal in Sonny's hand. A knife. It was her kitchen knife. So he must have come in by the back door and through the kitchen.

'Noooo, you've got it all wrong,' said Jordan, still numb from seeing his brother, who he'd genuinely believed was dead.

'Oh no, I'm done with you, Jordan. You tried to murder me with a rock. Me! Your own fucking bruvver. And now look what you've done!' He flicked his head to George.

Sonny was glaring with eyes like a madman. 'Look, Jordan!' he screamed. 'Look at our bruvver! He is still our bruvver, our George, you bastard!'

Now that the realisation had kicked in that Sonny was no ghost, Jordan clawed back his senses. Instantly, he returned to that place of rage. He pushed Sonny away and leaned down, quickly picking up the poker, and then pointing it at him. 'Get the fuck away from me. You and that weedy wanker boy there are well suited to each other. You're both grasses.'

With narrowed eyes, Jordan spitefully prodded Sonny in the chest hard enough to push him back. 'Get out of my way. I'm gonna finish that lying wanker off.'

'Stop it, Jordan! Just stop it! You're the only liar in this house, along with that crazed man Dexter.'

Sonny glanced in his mother's direction. 'Where is he an' all, Mum? 'Cos he tried to cut me arm off with an axe.

And you're like him, Jordan, ain't you? The pair of you are nuffin but ruthless rapists.'

George was finding it hard to breathe. His ribs were broken, his head hurt like hell, and he couldn't move his left arm. He guessed Jordan had broken it. He sensed that Sonny had more guts than he did because his little brother was utterly undeterred by Jordan. But their mother had to know the full extent of Jordan's evil ways. Taking a deep painful breath, he yelled, 'Eden's your sister, Jordan. She's *our* fucking sister, and you raped her,' he cried, as blood bubbled from his nose and mouth.

'*What?*' gasped Gina, holding her hand to her bruised face. 'Who?'

George tried to get to his feet, but he could hardly stand. '*Eden.* She's our *sister!*'

Jordan's breath was laboured as he tightened his fist around the poker. 'Shut your mouth!' he said, as he swung the fire iron at George.

Before the poker could make contact, Sonny managed to grab it. Still, he could only use his good hand, which meant he automatically dropped the knife. He was so focused on stopping Jordan that he hadn't registered the blade clang as it hit the laminate flooring.

Jordan, who had been struggling to pull the poker clean from Sonny's grasp, spotted the knife on the floor. But now having control of the fire iron, he instinctively pushed Sonny aside and lunged down to snatch the weapon.

'Get back, Sonny, or I'll fucking cut ya.'

Retreating a yard or so, Sonny glared into his brother's incensed dark eyes.

'You have no feelings at all for anyone, do you, Jordan? You even made out to me that you actually liked Eden. But ya never did, did ya?'

Brandishing the knife, Jordan dared his brother to step closer. 'Fuck off, Sonny! Go on, get away. You know nuffin about me.'

But Sonny wasn't backing down. He stood there defiantly. 'I do, though, Jordan. I've been at your side every fucking day, and I've watched you turn into a sly, slimy predator. That's it, Jordan, you're a predator, a psycho, who, like a dangerous dog, needs putting down.'

Something in those words hit Jordan, and he glanced from George, who was a semi-conscious wreck, with blood dripping from his ear and his head, to his mother, who was visibly shaking. The left side of her face had ballooned. With no make-up or bright clothes on, she appeared an old woman. Her eyes seemed full of fear, or was it sadness or disappointment? He couldn't tell.

A sound from outside the house had Jordan assuming it was the police, ready to smash their way inside. That meant he couldn't escape past his mother or Sonny. But he was the one who held the knife, and no one would be stupid enough to argue with that.

'Move, Muvver!' he yelled, as he attempted to barge past her to get out through the back door, but without a knock, the front door almost imploded. Jordan turned to see what on earth had made that massive bang and found Mitchell kicking his way through until he was in the hallway.

The livid expression on Mitchell's face, as he looked at George in a crumpled heap, told Jordan the man would take no prisoners. In an attempt to knock his mother out of the way, he was stopped by Mitchell who dived on top of him, crushing him to the floor.

Grabbing a lump of hair from the back of Jordan's head, Mitchell lifted his head back and smashed it down hard, crushing Jordan's nose. 'Son or not, you're a monster. You hurt my George, and you hurt my girl. Your own fucking sister!'

Smash! Mitchell bashed Jordan's face against the floor again.

'Aaargghh! Stop, please!' Jordan begged, knowing that Mitchell had the strength to cave his head in.

Mitchell smashed him again, but the clanging as Jordan's head hit the floor was enough for him to climb off Jordan and wait for him to get to his feet so that he could really punch his face in.

But Jordan stayed down. He wasn't going to fight Mitchell; the man's brute strength was immense, and Jordan guessed that Mitchell could easily rag-doll him up and down the hall if he wanted to. But the anger was raising its head, and although Jordan didn't want to get hurt anymore, he wasn't going to be beaten by an old man, as he saw him.

***

Mitchell took a few deep breaths and tried to help George up off the floor, but he was a dead weight.

Sonny came to Mitchell's aid and slid his good arm under George to help carry him to Mitchell's car.

With the front door hanging off its hinges, Eden, who was sitting in the car, could see her father holding up her brother. The state of George's face sent a burst of rage through her. She guessed who was responsible, and instead of waiting, as she'd been instructed to do, she shot out of the car and ran to help George.

'Oh no! What happened?' she yelled, looking over her father's shoulder. When she glanced at the awkward expression on Sonny's face, she knew for sure it was Jordan who had done this.

'Get back in the car, Eden,' demanded her father.

But Eden wasn't listening: she wanted to front out Jordan. So like a whippet, she skirted around her father and ran past him.

While Jordan was getting to his feet, it was his mother who Eden noticed first. Despite the purple bruising and the lump on the side of the woman's face, she appeared very pasty. Yet her eyes bulged wide, full of disbelief.

'Dear God, you really are Mitchell's daughter. I thought the last time I saw you, you reminded me of someone,' said Gina, holding her hands to her mouth. 'I am so sorry. I wished if only—'

'You whore! You caused all of this!' spat Jordan, who was now firmly on his feet with the knife in his hand.

Eden didn't have a chance to move. Jordan pushed her up against the wall, holding the blade at her throat. His eyes were penetrating her, hating every fibre of her being. She could feel his hot breath on her face and the cold blade against her neck.

'You should have died at birth. You're no sister of mine.'

***

Mitchell left George and Sonny by the car and frantically tore back to the hallway. He stopped in his tracks when he saw Jordan holding Eden at knifepoint.

'Leave her alone. You've done enough harm to her.'

Now having the upper hand, Jordan shot a grin at Mitchell. 'Horrible ain't it, Mitchell, having the person you love taken away? A bit like when you and George had me grandfarver taken away.' He huffed. 'He's dead now, murdered in jail. I suppose that was your doing an' all!'

Mitchell looked at Gina and noticed her swollen cheek, and something else. It was an expression he'd never seen before – deep compassion.

Not knowing what to do, Mitchell remained quiet, hoping that Jordan would get everything off his chest and let his daughter go. He couldn't lose her, not now that he'd just met her. He saw the pain in her eyes, and the fear. She looked so much like her mother, the last time he'd seen her.

But Gina also recognised that desolate look. It was the day she'd told Claire that Mitchell was her boyfriend.

'Let her go, Jordan,' she said. 'Mitchell and George didn't lock your grandfarver up. He did that all by himself. He killed your grandmuvver.'

Jordan cast his mother an evil glance. 'Shut up, you liar. You're all liars.'

'Yes, Jordan, you're right. I am a liar. I have told some horrible lies, but not this time. I didn't want to admit that my farver was a wife beater, a bully, and, dare I say it, a rapist. I know he raped me mum. She once told me that, but I loved my dad so much I ignored her. That's the truth of it, Jordan.'

'Shut up. You're a slag, Muvver, so you can keep out of it.'

'Yeah, Jordan, I am that as well and ashamed of myself. But it wasn't Mitchell or little George who got your grandfarver locked up. It was the factual evidence that did that. I wished I hadn't been so selfish at the time and not pushed George away.' Looking at Mitchell, she smiled. 'Still, he was brought up good and proper – not a fucking sick demon like you, Jordan. But what could I have expected? Your farver was a demon an' all.'

Jordan shuffled from foot to foot, still holding the knife at Eden's throat. 'What are you on about? That wanker there's me farver.'

Gina shyly looked at Mitchell. 'No,' she snivelled. 'No, Jordan, Mitch was the man that I wanted to be your farver. The truth is, Dexter is, well, he was.'

'What the fuck do you mean, you stupid cow?' yelled Jordan, who was now unsteady from the bashing that Mitchell had given him.

'I was my farver's daughter, Jordan. I looked up to that man, and I lived as he did. I cared for no one but meself. I never thought about other people's feelings.' She turned to Mitchell. 'I lied to you, Mitch. I was jealous, you see. I knew that girl of yours was pregnant. She came to the boxing club. She had something to tell you, but I sent her away. And I still can't get the image of her face out of my head.'

Mitchell would have gone ballistic, but he was more intent on saving his girl. So, instead, he swallowed down the anger and watched his ex-wife step closer to Jordan.

'Give me the knife, Jordan, or, believe me, you'll go to prison like your grandfarver for a long time, and I know you, Son. You wouldn't last five minutes inside. You've created enemies, boy – a lot of them. We both know it. And they will come after you, so let her go.'

'Get away from me, Muvver. You're no one to me now. Dexter!' he yelled. 'Where's Dexter?'

Gina pointed upstairs.

'Why is he up there and not down here?' quizzed Jordan, trying to fathom out what the hell was going on.

'He's dead, Jordan. Your farver, the scumbag, is dead. Now, give me the knife and let that poor girl go. Can't you see, Son? She's an innocent in all of this.'

Glaring at Eden, Jordan had to ask himself why he hated her so much right now. Perhaps she represented purity, and by violating her, he represented the epitome of vulgarity.

Jordan felt waves of sickness wash over him as his head began to pound like a bongo drum. He gazed around him, slightly dazed. His eyes rested for a moment on Sonny in the doorway.

His brother was staring with tears rolling down his cheeks. 'Please, Jordan, give Mum the knife. Don't hurt Eden. She's our sister.'

'No, she ain't our sister, Sonny. She's George's sister, not ours. Didn't you know? Our dad is Dexter. Not that prick there, Mitchell.'

Sonny's eyes cast down to the floor as a real sense of deep sadness crept through him. He'd always secretly felt proud that he was Mitchell's son. Even though he wasn't in his life and never had been, he'd known that Mitchell was a good person, and so was George. And he detested Dexter.

He glanced at his mother, hoping she would deny it, but she was staring at Eden in a trance. He looked back at Jordan. It was then he saw that there could be no mistaking that Jordan was Dexter's son. So, he reasoned, if Jordan was, then because everyone said he was Jordan's mini-me, he had to be Dexter's son too.

***

Eden took a deep breath and relaxed her shoulders, accepting her fate was in Jordan's hands. 'Jordan, I may not be your sister, but before you gave me those pills, I did like you. You were kind to me. Remember when you stuck up for me against my aunt? And at the rave, you even saved me from—'

'Shut up, or I'll cut ya throat.'

'No, you won't, Jordan, because you are better than that.'

'I said, shut up. You know nuffin.'

'Give me the knife, Jordan, now, or when the police get here and see this, you will be arrested and chucked in the nick. Now stop being an idiot and give me the fucking knife,' said Gina, desperate to prevent another murder.

Jordan knew he was fading; he was struggling even to hold himself upright. He leaned with one hand on the wall and the other with the blade against Eden's neck.

Gina stepped even closer but clocked that Jordan hadn't responded. He was staring into Eden's eyes in a trance. She assumed Jordan was losing consciousness, so she lunged forward, grabbing his arm away from Eden.

The second he realised that his mother had managed to get him away, a surge of adrenaline livened him up. Still gripping the knife, he held it above his head and tried to push his mother away, but she ran into him with her head pinning him to the wall and snatched the knife from his grasp. Before anyone could intervene, she plunged the knife into her son's chest and then jumped backwards, gasping for breath.

Jordan stood with his head tilted down, just staring at the knife embedded in him. He looked up and into his mother's eyes, almost imploring her to tell him why she had done this. He couldn't speak, but he knew she understood what he was asking.

Mitchell immediately ripped his T-shirt off and helped Jordan to a sitting position where he applied pressure. 'Call an ambulance, someone!'

Sonny rushed to the phone to find it was dead. He tore up the stairs hoping for a miracle – that the one in his mother's room was working. As he leaned across his mother's bed to pick up the phone, he saw Dexter lying there at a funny angle with the ugliest twisted expression on his face. Jordan looked so much like him, and in that second, he knew that Jordan was bound to grow up to be just like Dexter, and perhaps worse. He hesitated before lifting the receiver – in the hope that now the phone wouldn't work after all. He picked up the receiver. Relief flooded his face. It was dead – just like Dexter.

By the time he returned downstairs, Jordan had taken his last breath.

Sonny stared at the mess. He had never seen so much blood. It was pooling around his brother's body. His mother was slumped on the floor, and Mitchell was holding Jordan in his arms. He could see Eden outside the front door; she was throwing up and gasping for air.

'Why, Mum?' he asked, calmly.

She peered up at him. 'I brought that boy into the world, but I raised a monster, so I had to be the one to take him out.' She sighed heavily and got to her feet, her hands covered in blood. She looked at them and turned them over. 'I never did put these hands to good use.'

Horrified at his mother's sadistic comment, he couldn't get any words out in response.

'Jordan wanted to kill you both, his own flesh and blood, and one day, who knows what he would have done. I have done some bad shit in my life, Sonny. I just wanted to put something right. And, my baby boy, I will grieve forever over Jordan, but you and George will now be safe.'

Chapter Thirty-Two

10 months later

Mitchell pulled the 'sold' sign down and then got back into his Audi and headed up the long drive to the new house. Eden and George were behind, in his Ford Fiesta, both excited to get inside. Diane arrived last with Nobby, but Mitchell waited until they were all together before he opened the front door.

They had all seen the photos, but only he had been inside. It was perfect for his family, mostly since his mother wanted to move back to the area and to be a big part of her grandchildren's lives. The coast was great in the summer if she had visitors, but cold and miserable on her own in the winter. But she had Nobby, who was happy to be her companion.

The house was a five-bedroom affair with an office-cum-art room for Eden. George shared the office at the gym with his father for his new venture. As they wandered from room to room, it was apparent to everyone that Mitchell had been in the house many times before they had. The removals men had moved in the furniture the previous day, but it was the special touches that evoked particular interest. The upstairs bedrooms were fittingly decorated, in subtle colours, suitable for his mother, his daughter, and his sons. Beautiful floral pictures hung on the wall of his mother's room, and the bed was draped in chintzy furnishings. Eden's room was sleeker, with a huge mirror and wall-to-wall wardrobes. It was a dead giveaway when they entered what would be George's room. He had a huge canvas print of an Aston Martin, his all-time favourite car, that one day he vowed he would own.

Mitchell watched his family and smiled, enjoying their pleasure. But as his eyes focused on the door at the end of the landing, his smile dissipated.

'Dad, whose is that room?' asked George.

'That's Sonny's bedroom, when and *if* we ever find him.'

George looked to the floor, feeling embarrassed. It went without saying that his father would have room for Sonny in his life.

Diane put her arm around her son's waist. 'You will find him, Mitchell, when he *wants* to be found.'

Mitchell nodded while feeling the letter in his pocket that he'd received from the prison.

After careful consideration of the circumstances, Gina was sentenced to twelve years for the manslaughter of Dexter and Jordan. She took it with dignity. Of course, Mitchell had to attend because he was a witness, but he didn't throw her under the bus. She wanted the truth to be told and pleaded with him not to say that she killed Jordan in self-defence, which could have resulted in a non-custodial sentence. She wanted to serve the time inside that the court believed she deserved.

But that morning, Mitchell had received a letter from her. She was hoping that he had heard from Sonny. Every other week she wrote asking the same thing. He sent her money, and Eden bought her decent clothes to wear inside, for which she was very grateful. He visited her once a month just to make sure she was okay and to update her on any news about Sonny, which, sadly, amounted to nothing much apart from a few calls to say he had been sighted in Orpington.

Sonny had disappeared the second the police had arrested Gina. Mitchell and Eden were so busy getting George to the hospital that they hadn't seen Sonny slip away. And Gina had been so desperate to talk to him. She'd wanted to apologise and also she needed to tell him the truth about his father. Sonny had only heard the fact that he was Dexter's.

After Gina was sentenced, the council reclaimed the house; a new family were living there now.

Social Services had no interest in Sonny, and neither had the police. But he was still reported to them as a missing person.

Although Mitchell had employed a private investigator, no one could find Sonny. It seemed he'd vanished into thin air. Determined not to give up, he searched everywhere himself and asked practically everyone in the Crays if anyone had seen him, but with no luck at all.

However, today, he had received a call at the gym that someone thought they may have seen Sonny coming out of Horton Tower looking a bit untidy. Wanting to have the move all sorted and off his mind, he would still do what it took, though, to find him. But he didn't want to get anyone's hopes up, not after they had been dashed so many times before. And another issue that bothered him was that all of this could be a set-up.

The raves had been running smoothly with no wannabe promoters or drug dealers trying to take over. Gary Hanks had disappeared off the scene, but still, Mitchell didn't want to act cocksure that everything was kosher.

Nonetheless, now the family were all settled in, he drove over to St Mary Cray and parked at the bottom of the tower block. He gazed up and sighed as he counted the fourteen-storey building with four flats on each level. It meant that Sonny could be in any one of fifty-six flats. *And,* he thought, *who was to say that what he'd been told about Sonny's whereabouts wasn't a load of rubbish or the sighting was a case of mistaken identity?*

Mitchell sat in the car for an hour listening to old tunes, before he finally decided to go and knock on a few doors. He followed an older lady inside the entrance and climbed the stairs to the first floor. He was about to knock at the first flat on the left when from inside he heard a woman screeching at her husband that she wasn't his fucking skivvy.

Deciding instead to knock at the flat opposite, he was beaten to it when a woman opened the door holding a baby while puffing on a cigarette. With dead eyes, she looked him up and down, and then, assuming the smartly dressed man was a debt collector, she said, 'So how much does he owe ya?'

He shook his head. 'Sorry, wrong door.'

The door slammed shut behind him, and so he decided that perhaps he would come back tomorrow with cash in his back pocket to bribe a few people for information.

Gripped by sadness and almost a sense of nostalgia, he drove from the tower block along the main road to the old boxing club. He stopped the car and stared at the rickety old building and the brick wall that he had sat on so many times in his youth. The building had become derelict. He had sold it to a property development firm years ago, but it was evident that the company had suffered money issues because the place was still empty. Even the old signage remained above the door.

He got out of the car and wandered along the concrete path to the side of the building. The tall metal bins were still there. He smiled when he recalled driving the getaway van and throwing the holdalls over the wall and directly into the containers. *Good ol' Nobby*, he thought. He smiled again thinking of how he'd grown from a boy to a man in that club – under Nobby's wing. The scurrying of rodents stopped him from taking his trip down memory lane. He sighed, thinking how it was a shame that the building was infested with rats and not in a fit state to have young lads sparring in the ring. He considered the idea of repurchasing the hall, if the property investors ever wanted to sell it.

He removed part of a metal fence, there to deter trespassers, and squeezed in. As he wandered around the back, he noticed all the tarmac was cracked and grass was growing through it. He had trained outside in this square when it was too hot inside. The pale-blue paint on the back door was peeling, but he noticed that it wasn't even locked – the huge padlock was missing. He looked around him and decided to have one last look at the old place.

As he opened the door, the dark interior lit up. The boxing ring had been removed, although the ropes were still hanging from the ceiling. The familiar smells of sweat and wood polish were replaced with a damp odour. As he scanned the room, his eyes drifted to a pile of blankets in the corner. He assumed an old vagrant had taken up residence, or squatters had moved in. Still, it wasn't his problem; he didn't own the place anymore. As he turned to leave, he heard a cough and spun around.

A lad whose hair was long and greasy and swept across his face appeared from under the blankets. He coughed again.

Mitchell could hear the rasp in the young man's throat, so he stepped closer. 'Hey, mate.'

But as the wind blew the door wide open, a spear of light lit up the teenager's face.

'Sonny? Is that *you*?' he asked, completely blown away.

Sonny's eyes were red raw sore from a dreadful cold. He coughed and coughed, unable to answer.

But Mitchell didn't need to ask again. He bent down and could see who it was. Pulling back what he initially thought were blankets but which were actually old coats, he saw the state of the boy. His jeans and sweatshirt looked rotten, and his trainers had holes in them.

'Jesus, is that really *you*, Sonny?'

Sonny moved his long fringe out of his eyes. 'Hello. Sorry . . . Mitchell. I wasn't doing anything wrong. I was only sleeping here.' He put his hands over his mouth and coughed until his eyes bulged and his face turned blue.

Seeing that Sonny was so sick, he bent down. 'You're coming with me, boy.' As he scooped him up to carry him to the car, he was pushed to tears when he felt how light the lad was.

Sonny was too weak to protest.

Carrying his son proudly out of the old gym, he couldn't wait to get him home.

'I've been searching for you for ten months. Why did you leave? Where have you been, Son?' he asked, although with so much emotion, he knew his voice was barely audible.

The bright light outside gave an even clearer perspective on how sick Sonny was. His skin was grey, brown rings circled his red eyes, and he had a huge sore on his top lip.

'Christ, Son, what happened to you? Why? I mean, look at you.' He set down Sonny to open the car door.

'Where was I to go? I read in the paper that Mum got twelve years. They took the house back . . . And finding out that I'm not your son, I'm Dexter's, I knew, then, I had no one.'

'No, no!' He grabbed the back of Sonny's head and pulled him close. 'You *are* my son. Jordan wasn't. He *was* Dexter's kid. Everyone knew that, I guess, except me. But Dexter was in prison when you were conceived.'

'Seriously?' asked Sonny, his voice a mere whisper.

'My mother, your Nanny Diane, admitted to me that you looked like my father. He was dark-haired, like you.'

Realising that Sonny was too sick to stand up, he helped him into the car, turned the heating up to full blast, and tore away.

Sonny's head gently fell to rest against the door as the warm air filled the car and sent him into a comfortable sleep.

Mitchell felt awash with emotions – sadness for his youngest son, who had been living like one of the rats inside the old gym, but happiness, now that he had found him. As he pulled up in the drive to his new home, he noticed that Bernie's car was already there. He smiled to himself. His oldest friend was indeed a nosey bugger.

Sonny opened his eyes the second the engine was turned off. 'Oh, where am I?'

Mitchell patted Sonny's knee. 'You are home, Son, where you are supposed to be.'

Sonny stared at the beautiful double-fronted house with the sweeping drive and thought for a split second that he was dreaming.

'Let's go in. They are all inside, so get ready for the shrieks because they have no idea that I've found you.'

Sonny turned to his father. 'Really? Do they really want me to be part of the family?'

Mitchell frowned. 'Of course, Sonny. You are family. You're my son.'

Mitchell got out of the car. He walked around to Sonny's side, opened the door, and helped him out. His son was still weak but he could stand.

Eden must have seen Sonny from the lounge window because Mitchell could hear her scream from the drive. The front door flew open, and George and Eden came rushing out, eager to assist.

'Oh, Sonny!' squealed Eden, as she tried to hug him and kiss his dirty cheeks.

She turned to her father. 'He is all ours, Dad, eh?'

Mitchell looked at George, who was beaming, and laughed. 'Yep, kids, Sonny is all ours.'

Once they managed to get through the front door, Randy appeared. 'Fucking state of you, Sonny. It's good to see you again, though.'

'Miranda, I told ya. Stop the fucking swearing.'

'All right, bossy boots.' She turned to face Mitchell. 'We cooked you a casserole for ya new house, Mitch, but I see you've got a better present, eh?' She smiled at Sonny before hugging him. 'I'm glad you're home, Sonny. Really, I am. You saved my life once upon a time.'

***

It was Diane's turn to greet her grandson, but the excitement was a little too much. Sonny had to sit down. She hurried and retrieved a blanket and some tablets along with a mug of hot chocolate. Diane knew that Sonny would be starving, and it ripped her heart in half. But once he'd regained some energy, after he had wolfed down a bowl of casserole, she saw the colour begin to return to his cheeks.

Bernie dropped Nobby off at the club before he drove Miranda home. She had work in the morning. He'd secured a job for her in the bookies, and she loved it, being in charge. He had offered to lease the flat above the betting shop, but she much preferred the idea of someone looking out for her even though he was strict. Yet it was what she'd been missing in her life. And even though her mother never did come for her, she didn't long for her anymore: she had Big Bernie.

***

Once Sonny had the energy to move around, George and Eden took him upstairs to show him his bedroom. As they opened the door, Sonny's eyes widened, and he gazed in wonderment. The room was a typical teenager's room. From the bed to the wardrobes, everything was colour-matched in red and black. The stereo system and TV were on the cabinet. But it was the picture on the wall that cemented the idea that his dad truly had been searching for him. It showed a flash car and its number plate – SONNY1.

Eden filled the bath and George presented his little brother with tracksuits. ''Ere, Sonny, these are so comfortable, I uh . . .' He blushed and showed the label that read 'Swan'. 'These are samples of a new range that I'm trying to get off the ground, and I would value your honest opinion.'

Sonny felt the soft material and stared at the logo – SWAN. 'Pukka, Georgie.'

George reddened again. 'Glad you like them. Now leave the bathroom door unlocked and sing so we know you're all right.'

Sonny looked at George as though he must be mad. 'George, I'll be okay. I survived for ten months on me own.'

Eden raised her eyebrows. 'Barely, Sonny. Anyway, you'll never be alone now, and' – she chuckled – 'I bet you didn't bank on having a sister, did you?'

It was Sonny's turn to blush.

***

After a good hour, Sonny descended the stairs, looking relaxed and clean. He'd tied his hair in a ponytail, using one of Eden's hair bobbles. The tracksuit fitted like a glove, and he had used half the bottle of aftershave that was in his room. He was still tired and unwell, but he was warm, full of decent food, and – more than anything – he felt loved.

George, Eden, and Diane left the lounge so that Mitchell could talk to Sonny alone. They could see that the excitement was overwhelming.

'Come and sit down, Sonny. Are you okay, Son?'

Sonny smiled. 'Yeah, of course.' He sighed. 'I do worry about me mum, though. I don't suppose . . . No, sorry, of course you wouldn't have heard from her.'

'That's what I want to talk to you about. I speak to your mum every couple of weeks. I visit her once a month, just to make sure that she has everything she needs. Eden sends her clothes, and we have been keeping her updated on the progress of trying to find you. All she asked was that I would never give up.'

Sonny's eyes filled with fat tears. 'I really miss her.'

'I have a stack of hopeful visiting orders. She sends them every week addressed to you, for the day that we would eventually find you.'

He nodded. 'Is she okay, though, Dad? I mean, really okay?'

'Yeah, she's found something in her life that brings her peace.'

'What's that, then?'

'God, Sonny. She's found God.'

Other books by Kerry Barnes

Ruthless

Ruby's Palace

Raw Justice

***

Cruel Secrets

Wicked Lies

Ugly Truth

Raising a Gangster

***

The Hunted

The Rules

The Choice

***

Deceit

Voice of Reason

Printed in Great Britain
by Amazon